STORM

OF

EMPIRE

STORM
OF
EMPIRE

by

Paul D. Batteiger

13/30

Storm of Empire is a work of fiction. Names, characters, places, and events are fictitious or are used fictitiously.

Copyright © 2017 by Paul D Batteiger

All rights reserved.

First Print Edition: 2017

Printed in the United States

For my Readers: without whom, nothing.

Chapter One

STAR OF OMENS

The star arched over the city, its tail like a curtain of colorless fire that glowed even in the daylight. Karana looked up at it from the narrow window of the archive and wondered what it really was. She had never seen one so large, seeming so close she felt she could touch it. They called bearded stars omens of evil in the histories, but she knew they were more often said to portend momentous events – things that might change the course of empires.

A pall of smoke fell across the sky above her and she flinched away as a cloud billowed down the street and filled the plaza below, obscuring the crowds all moving toward the harbor. The archives were too far from the walls to hear the ongoing assault, but the smoke of the fires of thousands of barbarians blew across the city, bringing the smells of burning wood and flesh. Perhaps the star spoke truly, and these were the last days of the city of Ilion.

She turned away from the window and felt another surge of dizziness, caught at the parapet to hold herself steady. For days now she had been caught by the sudden spells of vertigo and weakness. She told herself there was nothing to it but weariness. She had worked day and night for a week now, sleeping little and eating less. They all did what they could, those who remained.

She turned back to her work and drew fragile scrolls from their slots on the walls and placed them as carefully as she could on the rolls of untreated rawhide – they had run out of vellum and real leather days ago – and then rolled them up. The layers would help to protect the old parchments from crumbling when they were moved. Once rolled, she packed them in crates, pushing them down snugly. She already had three boxes ready to be nailed shut and carted off. The wagon was late.

It was hot in here, high summer outside and barely a breath of wind. She drew the veil off her hair and fanned herself for a moment, unobserved, but she quickly covered her head when she heard footsteps. She just had time to arrange the silk over her braids when Marius came in. He was the assistant Master, and while she did not like him as well as she had liked old Master Sabos, she got along with him well enough. He was a thin man just reaching middle age, and he was as tired as the rest of them, the few that were left.

"Three waiting?" he said, looking at the crates. He sighed. "I don't know if they are coming back."

"They'll come back," she said, wanting to believe it. "We have to get as many of the scrolls aboard ships as we can."

"They said the harbor was chaos, last trip," he said. "People are desperate to escape."

"The Almanni have been only been laying siege for ten days," she said. "Without ships to blockade the harbor I don't see how they will expect to take the city."

"If we had legions of old guarding the walls, I would not worry much either," Marius said, sitting down. The fingers of his left hand were knotted up, and he could not straighten them, but he pushed things around well enough with his fixed fist it was hard to notice. "But the soldiers we have are not the best, and they are fewer than makes me comfortable."

Karana did not argue with him. Second-guessing military matters was his special interest, not hers. She preferred histories of people, not armies. It made her nervous to hear him say it, though. Behind all the assurances that the barbarians could not possibly take the city was the crawling fear that perhaps they could. After all, why else were they laboring so hard to preserve the library?

"I am beginning to wonder if we should not go as well. We have packed a great deal." He took out a cloth and wiped at his sweaty neck, then fanned himself with it. The upper floors were stifling this time of year, especially during the day. "If we put as much as we can in the cellars, it should be safe enough."

"Do you think so?" Karana did not believe it. In her mind she saw the archive in flames, books and scrolls curling in the heat. The thought turned her stomach and made her feel sick in her heart. She took more scrolls down from the shelves and then stole a look at him. She saw the way he did not look at her, and she smelled more smoke and she knew he was afraid. He wanted to just run away, and perhaps that would be the wise thing to do.

There was a silence, and then she turned away from him, began to lay the scrolls out, her small hands with their intricate henna stains moving carefully on the aged documents. These were lists of kings from her homeland, Sydon, far across the sea to the south. The home she had never seen. "Well, and you may go if you wish. I am not going to prevent it."

He was silent for a moment. "They say the Autarch has already left the city. He fled in the night with wagons of gold and took ship for Orneas – or even for Archelion." He shifted. "I would say when the rats desert, it is time to swim."

She snorted a little at that. Marius could be very funny when he wanted. "You and I both know that would be the story no matter what the truth is." Autarch Desius – the Emperor's vice-regent in Othria – was not a popular man in a good season. It was said to be his ill-treatment of the barbarian auxiliaries that had brought down the horde upon them, and so just now he was the closest villain to hand.

Karana heard him stand up, and she turned to face him, wondering how hard he would push her. Now she saw how afraid he was. "I think the city will fall," he said. "I am going to load a last wagon, and then I am going down to the harbor to get on a ship. You should come with me. If the savages get inside the city. . ." He didn't finish the thought, but then he didn't have to.

Voices came from outside in the street. Calls and cries, shouts, the sounds of mules and barking dogs. She heard distant drums, the barbarians calling their men to war. Obstinate, she folded her arms and bit the inside of her lip. "I'm not going yet," she said.

"Consider it, please," he said. "I will call you when I am ready to go."

She felt dizzy again, put her hands back on the table and leaned on it, trying to hide the way the room swam around her. Marius looked at her, concerned. "Are you all right?"

"I'm tired," she said. She closed her eyes, and that helped a little. "I am very tired."

"You should eat something," he said. He came a step closer, then turned away. "I'll call you, and we'll go."

She turned away and went to the window, leaned on the stone and took slow breaths, trying not to be sick. Her head hurt now, a slow pounding. The smell of the smoke was oppressive. She waited until he left, and then she wanted to sit down but she stayed for a moment, looked up at the sky and saw the tail of the star shimmering through the smoke. She felt as if the whole city was simply taking itself apart around her. The familiar sounds of the bazaar were gone, the smells of the bread baking two streets over beside the park were vanished, leaving the smell of war behind.

She looked west, down the wide avenue, and from here she could just see the waters of the sea between the tall towers there in the old city, the domes of the ancient temples. The horizon was dark, and she felt a slight breath of wind. Rain coming in, probably after dark. It would be a welcome thing, to cool the streets and rooftops, and clouds to cover up the cursed glow of the star. Three days now it had lit the sky. It could not go soon enough to suit her.

Karana wished for wind, closed her eyes and breathed in, imagining the cool air on her face, heavy with coming rain. She breathed out, and the air stirred, washing away the smoke, blowing through the window and rustling the papers, rolling the scrolls over against one another. Glad of the breeze, she breathed in, and the wind shifted, blew the other way, ruffling her veil and her cotton robe. She opened her eyes, wondering, and she breathed out, slow and even, and the wind stirred again, as if in answer. She gripped the stone parapet hard, feeling the heat of the day radiating out onto her skin.

She looked to the sea, feeling the wind die away. She wondered if she were asleep, and dreaming. There, on the horizon, darkness waited, and she saw just a small white flicker of storm.

☙

Arthras spat the smell of pitch into the dirt and looked up at the walls. From the hills above the city they had not looked like much of a barrier, snaking around the cramped streets like a long worm, but up close they were tall enough. He was not even that close, stuck here making ammunition for the catapults. There was a mass of men chipping rocks into rough balls to make them fly better, and then they were carted over to Arthras and the other thralls. They dropped them in tubs of hot pitch, then pulled them out and rolled them in the piles of dry straw until they were covered. They piled them up on cowhides and then they were dragged off to feed the stone throwers.

It was stinking, sweaty, ugly work that made his hands black and sticky, and there was no glory in it at all. He heard the drums beat to muster the men for an assault on the walls, but he was trapped here, not to be given a chance to fight. He stood for a moment and glared at the stone fortifications, seeming to float on a cloud of smoke, and then he looked up to the star – the bearded star that filled the sky.

King Usiric's red banner hung slack over his cluster of men, and Arthras wished he could march in there and rub tar in the bastard's face. They'd had victory over an army in the north, chased them here, to the gates of the empire itself, but only a fool would pit this army against a city. They were not just warriors; their whole people was encamped in those tents – women and children and old men. They could not go back to their homelands – there was no harvest – so they came to war.

But there were good lands close enough. They had turned away from attacking Helicon in the north, and instead come to the seat of the Autarch himself. Arthras wanted revenge on that treacherous bastard as much as anyone, but now the army had been idle for ten days, sitting and staring at the walls, building useless nonsense like catapults. They needed to storm the gates with rams and ladders and ropes. Yet they sat while children went hungry and the fat cowards inside the walls packed away their gold and food and sailed away with it. From the heights the stream of ships leaving the city was easy enough to see.

Something hit him in the back of the knee and knocked him down; he came up fast and faced the hulking shape of Thros, his commander, and his tormentor. Thros carried a heavy axe in his hands, and though he had a maimed leg that slowed him down and made him limp, he was strong as a bull. Athras' hands itched to draw his long knife and spill the giant's guts.

"Get to work," Thros grunted. "The battle starts soon, they need fireballs." He brought his axe up and scraped it at his hairy cheek. His beard was patchy from old burns, and it made his face even uglier. Athras ground his teeth and turned back to his pile of stones and his barrel of pitch. He promised himself he would kill Thros another day. He was a thrall, and so while he might not be a slave, he was still less than a free man like Thros. The giant was denied the front line by his wounds, and so he took it out on anyone in reach.

The drums pounded again, and then the horns, signaling for the attack to begin. Arthras reached for another stone and felt a stabbing pain behind his eyes, grunted and winced. Another headache. This was the third one in as many days. He grimaced and put the back of his hand against his forehead, keeping his tar-smeared fingers away from his face.

"Get working," Thros growled, lifting his axe threateningly. Arthras knew the big man would be more than happy to crease his skull with the haft if he stalled any longer. He picked up the stone. It was heavy, the size of a human head, and he looked at the bigger man, feeling anger boil in him along with the pain.

Thros saw the look on his face and stepped in close, slammed the haft of the axe into Arthras' ribs and knocked him down, pain exploding in his side. He wheezed, the pain lancing through him, and then the pain in his head bloomed like a sunrise and he clenched his eyes shut, hands digging into the mud.

He looked up and saw Thros there, looking as tall as a tower, and drawing one foot back to kick. Arthras saw it all very clearly, and everything seemed to slow. The pain in his head and the pain in his chest twisted together, and he dug his fingers down into the earth, and he felt something tremble. A small tremor, and then it grew. He felt it through his hands like a pulse, and then in his chest, grinding through the pain in his ribs.

Then the earth shuddered, and Thros staggered away, off-balance, and fell against a pile of rocks. Arthras got to his feet and reeled to him, fell on him with his knife out, and he pressed it across Thros' ugly face, digging the dark iron edge in against his skin. He thought of killing him – just cutting his throat and leaving the corpse behind. But there were men looking, and there was no honor to be won from killing a man with a crippled foot. There would be a blood price for such a killing, and perhaps exile.

Instead he got up, and then he reversed the long knife and smashed the heavy pommel into Thros' knee – the good one – and heard bone crack. Thros cried out in pain and glared at him murderously. The pain in his side was intense, and he gritted his teeth. "I owed you that," he growled. "And no more." He turned and spat on the pitch and turned toward the walls of Ilion, watched as the war-banners marched toward the gates. He bent down and picked up Thros' fallen axe, hefted it in his hands.

The horns blared and then fires kindled along the lines of the army as the catapults ignited their missiles. Each one went up in a sudden glimmer of flame until they all burned, like fallen stars. The drums called and he heard the cries to loose. Ten, twenty, then thirty balls of fire launched into the hazy sky, trailing dark smoke as they hurtled forward to smash against the stone walls. Some of them did not reach it, bounded along the ground and then cracked against the stone, but he saw two of them shoot clean over, and he smiled. That would rouse the defenders.

Arthras firmed his grip on the axe. There was an energy seeming to buzz in his joints and his bones, and he looked at his hands, saw they were not shaking, but steady. He felt hot, and angry. He was not going to stay here meekly rolling pitch and straw while the city was taken, he was going to fight. He left the onlookers behind and stalked toward the city. There was pain in his chest, and the earth seemed to thrum and shudder under his feet.

☙

Karana woke with a start, seeing the light was dimming. She sat up, feeling stiff and thick-headed, her neck sore from lying bent down on the table. She had drooled on herself and she wiped at it with the corner of her sleeve. There was a breeze, and she heard a distant mumble of thunder, like a giant stirring in the sky over the sea. It was not yet evening, but the light had turned strange, seeming to come from nowhere. The sun was hidden, and clouds were creeping in to cover the shimmering light of the star.

She got up, listening for voices, for sounds, and she heard nothing. Her sandals made small sounds on the floor as she left the room and passed through two more filled with half-packed books, seeing no one. The incoming breeze rustled the papers, and she paused to pull the shutters closed and latch them in place. It smelled like rain.

The great hall on the ground floor was empty, the silence almost unbearable. She stopped on the stairs, then coughed and called out. "Lenscar? Destos? Marius?" Her voice sounded small in the big room, and it made the silence seem louder.

They were all gone. She had fallen asleep, and they all fled. Marius had said he would come back, but he had not, or could not. She went to one of the high, glassed windows and looked out into the plaza, saw it was almost empty, save for an old woman who looked lost, and a few dogs robbing a tattered vendor's stall.

Thunder growled again and, as if in answer, she heard the drums of the barbarians. The sound was more intense this time, was it closer? She felt fear in her throat like a heavy lump she could not swallow past. She turned and went back up the stairs, then up to the topmost level and ran to the windows that faced the gates of the city. The light was not good, and she could not see very well, but she saw enough.

There was fire, in the dark, and light glowed from behind the walls, illuminating them with a red gleam like phosphor. She saw points of light that arced and fell – arrows, or something else – and she heard beneath the wind the oceanic sound of thousands of men, all moving as one. She breathed in and the wind reached through and almost whipped the veil from her hair, and she grabbed it and held it tightly. Ilion's doom was coming, and it was coming now.

Chapter Two

Gates of Empire

Arthras held his side with one hand and carried the stolen axe in the other as he jogged forward. He heard the battle drums call for the charge, and he was swept up in a great forward rush. All around him were other men of his people, or of related tribes. They wore their hair in braids and their faces were dark with soot and paint. They surged forward with spears and shields and swords in a glittering, deadly wave, shouting as one, and he joined his voice with theirs. He felt as if he were part of one great animal, huge and hungry. The power of the Almanni released at last.

They entered the shadows of the gates, and arrows began to sheet from the walls of the city, rattling down like hard rain that struck shields and armor and men. Arthras had neither armor nor shield, so he hunched down, tried to shelter behind the shields of the men around him as they held them up to block out the missiles. Men screamed and fell wounded or dying, but the wave came on. Balls of fire hammered against the walls, and Arthras wondered if they would stop firing when the lines met the stone.

Closer now, those men with bows bent them and fired upwards. He did not see how they could hit anything, for down here there was no sign of the enemy, only unflinching stone. He was being swept in toward the gate itself, and men around him rushed forward with ladders and tried to fling ropes with iron hooks up against the towers. They could not throw them high enough, and the ladders went up but he saw they were far too short. They did not even reach halfway up.

Now they were close against the walls, and the defenders began to hurl stones down at them. He heard the terrible sound of them as they struck shields or crushed in helmets. He felt a sudden fear, realizing there was nothing he could do to avoid being hit – it was simple chance. He closed his eyes for a moment and offered up a prayer to Bora, that she might protect him.

Then the army was hammering at the wooden gates, axes and swords beating against the iron-hard wood. He was caught in the press and had to fight for enough space to move and breathe. He cried out, not sure if he was angry or afraid, pushing to try and get free of the mass of men. Shields and spear-hafts battered at him, rattling against each other and hammering on the gate. Stones fell and crushed men to the ground, and Arthras realized how helpless they all were.

There was a crushing wave in the mass of men, and more warriors appeared, carrying the body of a great tree. The end was cut to a point and armored with iron plates nailed into the wood. The branches had been cut off long and stripped of bark to leave handholds. They dragged it forward until the iron tip dug against the gates, and then they started to swing it.

It seemed to take a very long time, drawing back a distance that didn't seem far enough to matter, and then they swung it in and it crashed against the wood with a sound that echoed off the towers and made the seemingly impregnable gates shudder under the force of it. More men rushed in to help, and Arthras tried to get closer and join, but in the press he was held back, fighting against a mass of sweaty, bloodied men. The ram swung back, and then forward again. There were too many men hanging on it, holding up their shields to protect themselves, and the second blow was not as powerful.

The men on the ram began to chant, getting a rhythm going, driving the terrible weapon forward to strike again, and again. Arthras could not believe anything could withstand such punishment. The whole mass of them became a single, heaving force, pushing the ram against the gate again, and again, until he almost boiled with frustration to see it remain unbroken.

Something splashed down from above, heavy and stinking, and at first he thought it was water, then he smelled it and knew it for rendered oil. Men cursed and fought to wipe it from their faces, their hands slipping on the wooden grips of the ram. Some of the men suddenly turned and tried to fight their way clear of the ram, and Arthras didn't understand why until he saw torches drop from the walls above.

There was a moment when his mind cleared, and then fire burst alive and spread like a mantle across the men, igniting shields and arms and faces. The ram itself blazed with fire and the warriors dropped it, thrashing as they beat at the flames that clung to them. More oil came down and exploded into fire, covering the ground in a lake of flame and immolating men whole. They staggered like shadows, wrapped in light as they were devoured. He saw them fall.

Arthras was thrust aside as men tried to flee, but they were trapped by the press of men still dashing themselves against the walls. Arrows scythed down, and he fell, pinned under a man who writhed with an arrow through his neck. The ground was covered in dead men, the air thick with choking smoke. Arthras shoved the man off him and cried out as pain lanced through his head. He had lost his axe, and he had nothing to fight with. He looked at the smoke-blackened gates and bared his teeth, feeling a heat boil inside him. He looked at his hands, and he saw his skin turn black.

ঃ

The pounding was distant, but steady, and Karana wondered what it was. It sounded like some terrible force beating against the walls, or the gates. She imagined it must be a ram, but in her mind she pictured a giant as were said to exist in the far north, striking down at the stone with a great axe or a hammer. She felt another wave of dizziness and clung to the windowsill until it passed. The wind coiled around her, cool but humid and heavy with rain, like a portent.

Tentatively, she breathed in, closing her eyes, feeling the air flow around her, waiting for it to answer her as it had, and there was nothing. She let her breath out in a long huff, almost glad. Of all the people who might seek the blessings of the gods, she was least among them. Karana was not even sure she believed in the gods. The Church of Attis was everywhere, the sign of the great warrior with his thunderbolt uplifted, frowning on all other gods. In her homeland they had gods far older than he. Vasa was the mother of the sea, and it was she who wrought storms with her sons thunder and lightning, and her daughters the wind and rain.

She heard a noise downstairs, and she turned and hurried down, hoping it was Marius. She passed the stacks of books and felt her heart heavy in her chest. If all of these documents were left behind, they would be destroyed. If the archive did not burn, then ten thousand barbarians would use them all to wipe their backsides. She was afraid, and she wanted to escape, but she did not want to leave. There was too much here, and she had spent too much time here to give it up easily. She had lived here in the archives for almost five years, making her own small place, and now it seemed it would all be destroyed. It made her feel empty and afraid.

Downstairs, the great hall was dark as the light failed, and there was no one to light the lanterns. She saw the side doors were open, wind coming through, and there were people coming in, but she was close before she saw they were men she did not know. They looked rough, and dirty, and they had a gleam in their eyes she did not like.

One of them saw her, reached out and caught her sleeve. "You! Show us where you hide the gold!"

For a moment she was speechless, not even sure what to say in answer. She tried to remember and think if there was some money in the archives she had forgotten, but then he twisted her arm and it hurt and she cried out, and she realized these men were not supposed to be here at all. "Let go of me!" she said, and she wrenched at him, but he did not loosen his grip.

"The gold, where is the gold, we know you have money hidden in here!" He shook her. "Where is it?"

He was angry, and now she could smell wine on him. There were two more of them, and they were coming closer. She pulled again, but he was too strong. He was still talking, but she could not make it out; it was as if he were speaking gibberish. He yanked her arm painfully and she screamed and a flare of lightning turned the world white for a flickering instant just before a thunderclap all but deafened them all. The man's grip loosened and she ripped her arm free, almost fell down from the effort.

The others began angrily slapping scrolls and books from the shelves, and Karana lost her temper. The man grabbed for her again, and this time she shoved him back as hard as she could, shocked when he flew back more than ten paces and bounced off the door frame, his head striking with an ugly sound. The force sent Karana staggering back and she fetched against the balustrade of the stairs, stared at the man as he groaned and rolled over, the other two stopping their vandalism to stare at her. She felt a heart-speeding terror mixed in with her anger, and she saw their faces uncertain and confused in the flash of lightning.

"Out," she growled, and then she raised her voice and shouted with a terrible rage. "*Get out!*" She shook with the force of it, and something seemed to flare inside her like a trail of fire up her spine, and then the wind shifted with a sudden and terrible roaring. Rather than gust in through the door it reversed itself and blew out through the open doors. The men were picked up bodily and hurled backward, sucked in toward the doors, only to slam against the stout wood as the wind yanked them shut.

The wind shattered the windows and sent glass scattering into the night, and then the doors gave way and ripped off their hinges and hurtled out into the street along with the intruders. Karana clutched at the railing as the wind coursed around her, bringing up a gyre of loose papers and books that scattered across the room and billowed outward into the growing storm.

She sagged down to the floor, staring, unable to believe what she had seen, what she had felt. Her heart was pounding, and she found her veil was gone, leaving her hair uncovered. She felt a jolt of irrational embarrassment and then she focused on the scattering papers and hurried after them. Alone in the dark, she got down and crawled on the floor, catching scraps of parchment and vellum, trying to save them from blowing away.

☙

Arthras thought he was burning alive. He was on his knees in the black, bloody earth, and he watched his skin turn black and screamed. He was filled with a terrible heat that grew and grew and then seemed to radiate from his skin. His tunic smoldered and smoked and then caught fire. Panicked, he tore it off and threw it away, found his breeches were on fire. He leaped up and tried to run, fell against the ram and tripped over the broken handles.

Then he realized he felt no pain, and he lay for a moment and looked at his black hands and down at his arms and his chest. He gripped one of the branches that had served as a handle for the ram and saw the wood smoke and burn under his touch. He did not understand what was happening. His heart was beating hard and fast, but he did not hurt, he was not burning. The pain in his ribs was gone – there was no pain at all. He pulled himself up, stood there as his boots incinerated from his feet and left him naked and smoking, black as a figure etched on an urn.

He looked around himself, saw the army was falling back, shouting and dragging wounded men with them. The attack had failed. He saw warriors pointing at him, staring and saying things he could not hear. He looked at the gates, then up at the walls, still untouched and arrogant above him. He snarled, baring his teeth. He knew his face must be black, and he wondered how he looked.

Something hit him in the chest and he grunted, looked and saw a broken arrow on the ground. He rubbed the place where it had struck him and felt no wound, nothing at all. Another one hit him in the mouth and he flinched as he felt it glance off his tooth. Anger grew inside, and he felt again that tremor in the earth, like the one that had made Thros stumble. Arthras spat out a piece of broken metal and then he began to smile.

This was the power of the gods. He had prayed to Bora, the war-goddess, and she had answered him. He did not know why he was given this power, but he knew it was meant to be used. He bent down and put his hands on the earth while arrows fell all around him. Not knowing what he should do, or say, he only closed his eyes and called the earth to shake.

A ripple passed through the ground, and it was as if he *felt* the earth and the rocks beneath as they coiled and gathered, and then convulsed. The ground seemed to leap, and Arthras dug his fingers into the soil and held on. The walls shook, and he saw them wave like walls made of leather or cloth, while mortar fractured and spat out from between the stones. The arch above the gate buckled, and cracks raced across the stones. The wooden gate bulged and twisted, and bolts shot out of the wood like arrows.

The sound was incredible – a deep-voiced roar like thunder that never ended. Arthras clung to the ground as he felt the vibrations pass through him, thrumming up his arms, down his back, through his skull. The gate buckled, and then the heavy wood snapped and tore as the arch collapsed. Once the cascade began, it spread, and he looked up as the gate towers twisted, slumped, and then disintegrated under the unending quaking of the ground beneath them. A wave of broken stone swept down and dashed Arthras aside, turned him over and ground him between heavy stones.

The shaking began to subside, tremors diminishing, echoing themselves again and again, and Arthras realized he was not dead. He shoved at the rocks and they moved as if they were made of straw. Broken rock melted to his skin, and when he burst free he was half-sheathed in a layer of molten rock covered by the dark, cooled surface. It cracked when he moved, and the red glow showed through. Still there was no pain, and he grunted as he scraped the stuff from his skin.

He stood in the towering column of dust arisen from the broken gate, and then he looked back and saw the army there, men all dashed to the ground by the tremors, staring at him as he climbed from the ruin. He stood there for a moment, and then he thrust his fists to the sky and howled a war cry. "*Take the city!*" he screamed, and a thousand voices rose up to join him.

೦ಸ

Karana was on the floor, hands full of papers, when she felt the earth shudder. It began as a low roar, and she thought it was more thunder, but then she felt the floor under her ripple, as if it were the surface of the sea, and she looked up to see the whole building shuddering, heard the joints and beams of the structure creak and crack as though it were about to fall in on top of her. She tried to get up but she could not, lay clinging to the floor as if that would do any good. Two more windows broke and glass fell to the floor and shattered, echoes by thunder from above.

It stopped, and she realized it had not gone on very long, or so long as it seemed. She staggered to her feet, wondering. She had felt the earth shake years ago in Evanos, where such things were common, but not here. She had been years in Ilion and never felt it, but now the earth shook as if under the tread of a giant.

Another roar came, distant but sharper, and she turned and ran for the stairs again. Up, up so she could get to a vantage point and see what was happening. The windows were broken, shutters ripped loose by the wind, manuscripts scattered on the floor. She climbed up until she could see east, toward the walls. The sky was darkening, clouds moving low and rain beginning to scatter down, but she saw the walls, and she saw the great broken gap at the center where the gate had been, and she felt a knot of terror in her chest like a stone.

What should she do? If she stayed here she would be killed, but was there any place safe to go? She wondered if there were still ships to be had in the harbor. If there was any way out of the city at all. She could not defend the archive. Or could she? She closed her hands into fists, remembering the strength that had hurled a man across the room like a doll, the way the wind had answered her. What was this power? What could she do with it?

Looking at the broken walls, she saw lights begin to move in the dark, and she knew the barbarian army was flooding in, torches in hand to burn and plunder. How could she do anything against so many? There would be thousands of them, tens of thousands.

Perhaps, perhaps she could at least prevent the city from burning. She looked up to the dark, roiling sky, flickers here and there as the lightning walked in the clouds, and she reached out her hands. She reached with her thoughts, with her will, into the sky, and she *pulled.*

For a moment, she felt foolish, a girl alone in a library wishing for rain, believing she could control the very storm itself, but then rain fell all at once like the stroke of a thousand swords, and she flinched back from the sudden downpour, felt it blown in on the winds to spatter her face. She felt the ends of her braids coming loose, tapping her neck.

She hurried back down, thinking to herself of the way to the harbor. Rain would perhaps keep the invaders from burning the city. What else could she do? Even if she were blessed by the gods, surely she had by now exhausted their favor. Why would they give such power to someone like her? Perhaps she was only going mad, or she was dreaming and would soon awake with her head pillowed on her arms, sore from sleeping at the table.

She almost ran into Marius as he staggered through the doors, soaking wet and wiping rain from his face. He caught her shoulders. "Karana! I can't believe you're still here."

"What are you doing?" she said. It was hard for her to bring her thoughts back to the moment. Thunder echoed overhead and she seemed to feel it, in her bones. She felt dizzy again, gripped Marius' arms. "I thought you left."

"I brought a cart," he said. "Help me load what crates we can manage, and we'll go. I have a man with a small boat – he will take us, but he won't wait very long."

"The Almanni have breached the gates," she said. "I saw it from the window. We don't have time to take anything." She felt her eyes burning, thinking of all the books and words lost to savagery. "We don't have time." She chewed her lips, trying to decide. She wanted to stay, wanted to find a way to protect the archive, but she did not believe she could. Instead she had to decide if she could live with abandoning what she so loved.

There was shouting in the streets, out in the rain. Karana would not have believed there were people still in the city left to flee, but there were. Marius went to look, and she followed him, gathering up the many small braids of her hair and holding them, feeling for the pin she used to keep them in place. She felt naked with her hair uncovered. The wind was less now, and the rain had begun to fade.

She stepped out under the sky, and the light was strange. The clouds were higher, their underbellies flickering with light as the lightning stalked here and there. There was almost no wind, and the light was greenish and pale, seeming to outline everything clearly yet to have no source. Karana knew it was the light of the star, filtering down through the clouds. She had hoped for a greater storm, and perhaps she could make it so. The thought made her belly feel tight and shivery. What was happening to her?

There were people running through the streets, frantic, wide-eyed. They had trusted in the strength of Ilion's walls, and now that strength had failed them. Their robes and tunics flapped as they ran, clutching whatever of their possessions they had managed to grab before they fled.

More shouts, and she felt the earth shudder underfoot again. She looked across the plaza, toward the gates, and she saw men running, but they did not look like city people. They wore armor and carried spears and swords. She saw the strange light glint on helms and shield-rims, saw their pale skin and pale hair. Almanni. She had never seen so many in one place.

Marius caught her arm. "Come quickly! The cart, we can still get away."

The oncoming horde of warriors moved like the sea, crashing against the houses and buildings, flowing in through doors, knocking over whatever it came upon. She saw fleeing people cut down and speared to death in the street, heard screams that made the flesh crawl on her arms and neck.

Then the crowd parted, and something else stepped through. It was shaped like a man, but was all black, as if the light could not touch him. Smoke rose from his skin, and every step made the earth boom and shudder at his coming, his footprints black and burning in his wake.

Chapter Three

City of Fire

Arthras led the charge through the shattered gate, climbing over the heaps of broken stones as a wave of his fellow warriors swelled behind him. Rain slashed down in a torrent, and he heard it hiss and boil off his skin. He felt like a giant, or a god himself, impervious to harm or death. When a large stone blocked his way, he set his hands against it, saw the stone melt and run under his fingers, and then he shoved it aside and it tumbled out of the way as if it were made of straw. He laughed, looked back at the men coming behind him. They were not too close, and so he could not see the fear on their faces that he was certain he would see.

He walked like a titan out of old tales through the ruins of the gate and then into the streets of the city. The roar of the men behind him rose as they let their fury free to vent upon their enemies. They had lost so much, now they were a nomad people, with nothing to return to. Now they would take what they wanted.

Soldiers poured in from the side streets, rushing to try and stem the attack. Shields gleamed in the storm light, rain pouring over the steel bosses. They blocked the street, forming a line two deep, then four. Spears jutted out from behind the wall of lapping shields, green sparks on every tip. The wind coiled and buffeted along the street, snapping shutters against walls and whirling trash up in spirals.

Arthras laughed, glancing back at the men in his wake. He wanted them to see this. He moved faster, jogging ahead toward the enemy, every footfall making the earth shake under him, as though he were as tall as the clouds. What a feat, to attack a battle line naked, without so much as a buckler. He clenched his fists and charged into the center of them.

The wall of spearpoints came closer, and closer, and he felt his skin crawl with fear, but he didn't stop. When the first spear lunged at him he flinched, but it struck his skin and glanced off, drew back with the tip glowing red from the heat, and then he smashed through them, splintering the hafts like twigs, and he struck the shield wall like a thunderbolt. He shoved through them, then balled his fist and punched a shield and saw it split in half.

The soldiers battered at him with their shields, drew swords and cut at him. The steel would not scratch his flesh, and where they struck the rock melted to him, their blows showering sparks on the ground. A shield rammed against him and he staggered, then he gripped the edge and dragged it down. With his fist, Arthras hit the soldier in the helm and the metal caved in under his blow. Blood poured out and the body pitched backward.

In a rage he hammered at them with his fists, smashing them back, knocking them down to the earth where he trod on them and his feet burned their armor and their flesh. Behind him came the warriors of his people, howling for blood, and before they even reached the line, the defenders broke and ran, vanishing into the rain, leaving their shields behind in a shameful scatter. Arthras kicked them out of his way and kept going, feet hissing as he stepped in the water running down the street. He would not stop; he would break anyone who tried to bar his way.

The army spread out behind him, smashing in doors, beginning to loot whatever they could find. Mostly what they wanted was food, and they hunted for it relentlessly. They had been camped outside the city for ten days, after a month-long march, and there had never been enough food. Within the border there were ripe fields of grain, but what could they do with it? An army carried no sickles, and could not stop to mill wheat and make flour. No, they wanted meat and cheese and bread already baked, and wherever they found it cries went up.

People ran from the houses, and the men mostly ignored them. Some of them chased fleeing women, some caught them and threw them down and searched them for whatever they might carry. Arthras laughed, glad to see the arrogant people of this city run and scream. They should pay for their crimes against his people; they should suffer as the Almanni had suffered. The men swept around him, like a tide, and they went ahead of him, breaking windows and doors. They did not come too close to him, though, and he walked alone, like a god himself.

But he had never been in a city like this, and it stunned him. So many buildings, so tall and clean and all of stone, not like the houses his people made of split beams and thatch with earth piled up around the walls. There was glass in the windows, which he had heard of but never seen. The streets were paved with stone and were flat and smooth. He could not decide if he wanted to stay in a place like this, or if he wanted to tear it down. It was beautiful, but so strange.

He wanted to stop and gawk at it all, but he could not, he had to keep going. He was leading the charge, taking the city. Bora had chosen him as her instrument of justice. He could not stop.

Thunder called overhead, and he laughed as the rain sizzled on his skin. The storm was waning now, and he could see more clearly. The light was greenish and strange, and by it he saw he had come to a wide plaza, hemmed in by tall, ornate buildings. It was lined by pillars that held up nothing but statues, and the paving stones were white and wide. Lightning flickered overhead, and he saw something move ahead. He saw an old man, and beside him was a dark-skinned girl.

☙

Karana watched him come on, the earth shaking with his footfalls, and terror twisted in her throat. What was he? Was this a monster out of ancient times, or was he like her, touched for an unknown reason with the power of gods? She looked at her hands, caught in agony of indecision. Marius pulled at her, but she shrugged him off, not really noticing how easy it was. She was stronger, now. So much stronger. Why?

The Almanni spread across the plaza, wrecking anything they touched, breaking down doors and smashing windows, rushing into buildings with axes in hand. She pictured them inside the archive, ripping down the shelves, trampling her manuscripts underfoot, and she could not stand the thought.

Marius caught her arm again. "We have to run! Now!"

"Then go," she said. "I will not." She pulled free of his grip and stepped closer to the enemy, and she raised her hands. She did not know what power was inside her, or why, but she called on it now, called on it answer her. She felt the wind stir and coil, seeming to gather overhead, pulling scraps of parchment up into the sky. Marius said something, but she could not hear it over the sudden roar of the air. She held her hands there for a breath, willing power into the wind, and then she brought her hands down and outwards, toward the incoming enemy.

The wind suddenly became a shriek, and she staggered as the barest edge of the power buffeted her. The air came down, and it screamed as it washed across the plaza, carrying bits of refuse and dirt along the front of it, so to the eye it looked like a wave in the air, almost invisible. It smashed into the front ranks of the barbarians like an unseen hammer, and the first of them were lifted off their feet and hurled backward, while the rest were simply driven back, tumbling along the stones like child's toys. They crashed into walls and into one another, swords and spears scattering with the wind like deadly rain. The wind tore through windows and sucked tiles off rooftops, whirled them up into the sky and then let them fall to shatter in the tumult.

Karana stared, almost unable to believe the force of it. Her ears popped, as they did before heavy rain, and she *felt* the masses of air and clouds above shifting, roiling in reaction to what she had done. It was like feeling shards of pottery move inside her head, grinding against one another. Lightning flared sudden and violent, and she looked on the only man not swept away by her wind. The black one, the one who left flaming footprints in his wake.

There were gouges in the stone before him, from where the wind had driven him back, but it had not lifted him, nor moved him far. His red hair, caught in messy, thick braids, whipped around his head, and he was close enough she could see the look on his face, and he was angry. She saw there were patches of what looked like black stone clinging to him, light showing through when they cracked as he moved. For a moment she wondered if he was even human, but then she realized what he must be: another one like her. He was someone gifted with sudden power, and he was turning it to his purpose, even as she was.

She felt moved, wondering if he was as afraid as she was, if he wondered or if he knew what was happening to them. There was a kinship between them, this man and she. They were alike, and in that moment, Karana wondered if there were others. There must be. Something had changed in the world, and now some walked with the power of gods.

For that moment, she wanted to speak to him, to tell him they were alike, and she put out her hand. He did not slow, but came toward her, and then he lifted both hands and brought them smashing down to the earth. His fists struck the ground, and the earth cried out.

The first peal of it was like thunder, but so much deeper it was like thunder below, in the chambers of the earth where no light dwelled. Then the smooth stones of the plaza split apart and the crack raced toward her even as the shockwave lifted her into the air and slammed her against the wall of the archive. Pain flared in her skull, and she slumped to the ground even as cracks raced across the walls of the buildings. She saw the records library across the street cave in, the front collapsing in a cloud of dust that billowed upward, and then she heard stone breaking and looked up to see the side of the archive falling on her.

She had no time to think; she thrust up her hands and cried out, and the winds answered her. There was a crack of thunder and then air rushed in on her and then upwards in a sudden column, and it lifted her off her feet and hurled her toward the falling rubble. A cascade of broken stone and tattered papers avalanched down on her, and then the wind struck it and blasted it apart and she shot through the center, untouched, tumbling end over end as she rose higher. For a moment she felt exhilaration, as she rose higher, spinning, free of the earth.

Then she fell, screamed once and then tumbled and hit the ground on her hands and knees, startled to be unhurt. She felt light and strong, and she stood up. All around her was the ruin of the archive walls, and a look back showed her the great old building was gutted, the inner rooms exposed to the rain and wind, papers falling and fluttering everywhere. Even as she looked, the roof slumped and collapsed, and her heart with it. She covered her mouth and turned away. Years of her life, her home, all gone in a moment. She felt the earth shake beneath her, the footsteps of a giant.

☙

Arthras closed in on her, kicking chunks of stone aside as he came closer. She was small, and she was too dark to be a Carinthian. Why would she defend the city? And where did her power come from? He was not the only one blessed by the gods today, it seemed.

She covered her eyes when he came close, looking away from the building, and he wondered what it had been. There were scraps of parchment everywhere, but that meant nothing to him. Arthras could not read in any language. He stood over her, and he raised his fist, but then he found he didn't want to hit her, didn't want to kill her, even if he could. She was not fighting him, was not even looking at him.

"Who are you?" he said, wondering if she spoke his tongue. "Where did your power come from?"

She looked up at him, and he saw sorrow and anger in her eyes, and he wondered who she had lost to be filled with grief. She did not say anything, so he grunted and touched his chest. "I am Arthras, blessed by Bora, goddess of the moon. Who are you? Speak."

She stood, slowly, never taking her eyes from him. "Turn away, and get out of the city," she said, her voice low and angry. "Take your savage horde with you." Her speech was stilted and accented, but he understood her.

"You are not one to give me commands," he said. "Mine is the strength of gods, and if I will it the earth will shake until the city is destroyed. Do not oppose me."

She shook water from her face, as the rain was growing heavier again, hissing where it touched him. Her dark hair was wound up in a twist of many small braids, now coming loose. They looked like snakes in the bad light. "I have given my warning," she said. "I will not give it again."

Arthras felt angry, and the earth shuddered in answer. "As the gods will it," he said, and he raised his fist.

⊗

Close to him, Karana felt the heat radiating from him, as if he were a piece of red-hot iron. The rain vanished into steam the moment it touched him, and it made a constant haze around him. His eyes glowed like embers, and the melted stone dripped down his hide, dull red with cracks of yellow when he moved. He raised his hand, fingers closing into a fist, and she called on the wind as hard as she could, pulling with that inner will she could barely describe. Over a wide front, she had not possessed the strength to move him, but now she focused on only him, and the air turned to sudden fog, a finger of it reaching down and enclosing him, before it twisted like a rag and the wind blasted him off his feet.

The edge of the blow slapped Karana down among the rubble again, but Arthras was hurled across the plaza to smash into the old counting house, shattering two pillars and then demolishing the front entrance in a collapse of marble and a great cloud of dust. Thunder roared overhead, and lightning lanced back and forth within the clouds. She could feel the effects of her power, changing the course of the storm, forcing it to adapt around her like ripples in a pond. She wondered what those ripples might do, if she were not careful, and yet she did not yet know how to be careful.

She staggered up, her robes wet and sticking to her, feeling cold, the wind slicing through them. Her hair was wild like a fistful of serpents, and she looked at the place where she had hurled him, wondering if she had hurt him, wondering if she could. The whole thing was madness, everything like a moment from a legend. It would be a legend, she realized. People would tell stories about this battle, no matter what came of it.

The wall of the counting house disintegrated under a terrific blow, the sound of it echoing and making her flinch. Something moved there, and then Arthras emerged into the light again, and he did not any longer look like a man. The broken stone had melted to him, covering him entirely in black, smoking armor that dripped with molten rock like the blood of the underworld.

He staggered free of the rubble, clawed at his face until he could get the stuff out of his eyes, and then she saw them blazing like coals. He roared and stomped his foot down hard, sending a shock through the ground that fractured the paving stones and knocked her off her feet again. More of the archive fell in on itself and for the first time, Karana felt a real anger boil up inside her. It was a good thing to feel, because it drowned out the sorrow, and the fear. Anger was clean, and bright, and it brought her to her feet as he came for her. He looked bigger now, like a true giant, covered over with armor of blackened stone, pieces of it breaking off as he moved.

Karana felt trapped. Her winds could hurl him away, but she could not hurt him, not before, and surely not now. Rain could not harm him either, and that left only one power of the storm to call upon, and she felt terror inside when she contemplated it. Could she do it? Could she survive it?

He bore down on her like a beast from a nightmare, and she felt the heat coming from him. She closed her eyes, and she called on the lightning. It flashed and blazed overhead, crowning the sky with light. The thunder intensified, until it was a constant roar.

He reached her, and his great hand closed on her, burning her clothes as he drove her back, smashed her into the wall so it broke and fell in on them both. He rammed her down into the ruin and she felt the heat on her skin. There was pain, and she felt his other hand closing on her neck. When she fought him, his armor cracked under her hands and molten stone poured out and burned her. She screamed, spitting out dust and gravel, and then she called, and the sky answered.

There was a sound like the crack of a whip, and then a flash so bright that it almost blinded her, even through her eyelids. For a moment she felt weightless, as if she were floating, feeling nothing, and then trails of fire lashed through her body and she screamed again as the thunder stroke blasted so loudly it was not like a sound, but like something too big to be heard, blanking out everything.

She came to herself, feeling rain on her face and pain in her skin. She rolled over and spat out stones, coughed and gagged at the agony scrawled into her. The rain was pouring down, and it was hard to see. She got up, reeling with dizziness, and she heard him groan.

He lay on the stones, still moving, half the stone armor blasted off his body. He smoked and hissed in the rain, moving slowly, groggy and stunned. She had hurt him, and the rush of exultation she felt at that made her feel revolted at herself. When she looked at herself, her robes were burned and tattered, and blue traceries of lightning flickered across her skin like ghosts.

"I have given my warning!" she shouted. She held up her hands and the sky bellowed and flashed and roared. Lightning walked across rooftops and shattered pillars and statues. It arced across her skin and between her hands, and then a bolt thin as a thread snaked down, touched the ground between her and Arthras, and then it swelled and became a river of light that flashed and cried out in a voice like the end of the world. She felt the force of it hurl her back, felt herself strike something that crumbled under the impact, and then she was rolling, tumbling, and she saw nothing but bright-slashed after images in her eyes. And then she knew nothing else.

Chapter Four

Seas By Night

K arana woke slowly, feeling a gentle rocking motion and feeling stiff and heavy with aches. She opened her eyes and saw gray light and a small space, roofed over with a sheet of canvas or sailcloth that rippled slowly in an unseen breeze. She heard the groan of wood and the lap of waves and knew she was at sea.

Memory came to her slowly, in pieces, but she did not remember how she came to be here, and then she heard voices and knew she was not alone. She sat up, grunting and pulling the tattered blanket closer around herself. The air was chilly, and she was still damp, her hair feeling limp and cool, her braids slowly stiffening as they dried.

A flap of the canvas drew back and Marius pushed through, letting in a bit of fresh air and more light. She saw a heavy gray sky, clouds low and rippled, and she heard gulls calling. He smiled when he saw she was awake, but he looked tired, and there was a watchfulness in his gaze, something careful and searching. He sat down, moving slowly, as he was not a young man. "You are awake," he said.

She nodded. "You brought me to the ship." It wasn't really a question, as that much was obvious. "Thank you."

"I'm glad you were all right," he said. "You were senseless, and you were. . . on fire."

"I was -" She pulled her hands under the blanket and felt the skin of her arms, there were parts that felt strange, as though she could not feel with all of her skin, and she suddenly pushed to her knees and turned shyly away from Marius, opened the blanket and looked at herself.

What remained of her robe was burned and tattered, and she swallowed when she realized how close to naked she was under the blanket. She pulled the fabric apart and looked down at her arms and body, saw the shocking trails of scars on her flesh in the shape of lightning strokes, coiled and branched. They were paler than her own dark skin, and when she touched them they did not hurt, but only felt rather numb. She shivered.

"Are you. . . is it bad? I did not. . . examine you too closely." He sounded embarrassed. He had not wanted to intrude on her privacy, or perhaps he had not dared.

"I think I will. . . will live," she said. She folded the blanket over herself again, turned back to face him and sat down, wondering if those same scars were all over her body. She touched her face but did not feel them there. She remembered how the scars came to be and looked at Marius. "You saw."

He hesitated for a moment, then nodded, pulling on his short beard. He looked away, then back at her. "How did you do those things? What. . . what -" He seemed at a loss, no less than she was.

"I don't know," she said. "It came very suddenly, just after we spoke yesterday – was it yesterday? I noticed the winds shifted as I breathed, and then they answered my command. I have been feeling dizzy for a week now, strange feelings." She trailed off. How could anyone explain this? "It just all happened."

"The power of the gods," he said. "You flung thunderbolts like Attis himself."

She winced. "I have never really believed in gods," she said. "I read myths, I study folklore and stories." She looked at him. "Tell me you do not believe that."

"Attis was a real man," he said. "We know that."

"He didn't hurl thunderbolts from his hands," she said.

Marius arched one brow. "Perhaps he did."

She shook her head. "And was slain by a demon of fire? Don't look for simple explanations, not for this."

He grimaced, then looked away. "Sorry."

"You might say it does not really matter where this power came from," she said. "But actually I think that matters a great deal."

"Do you still have it?" he said. "Or was it burned out?"

She closed her eyes, feeling the wind moving above and around the ship. She could even feel the rough size and shape of it, feel the single sail luffing in the breeze as it shifted. "I still have it. I can feel the air, feel how disrupted it is by what I did to it. Every command was like throwing rocks into a pond, creating ripples."

"And who was the other one?" he said, and she flinched inwardly, remembering the burning eyes.

"He said his name was. . . Arthras," she said, remembering.

"A barbarian name," Marius said.

"Yes, there was a king of the Almanni called that, some sixty years ago." She gathered her braids together, stroked them. She wondered why they were not burned. "But this was not him. This was a young man, new to his power."

"How do you know that?" Marius said. "Perhaps he is some demigod of theirs."

"I do not believe in demigods, and neither should you," she said. "No, he had just gained his power, knew no more of it than I knew mine." She shook her head. "The Almanni camped outside the city for ten days, why would he have waited? No, no something changed." She grew quiet, and looked up, as if she could see through the canopy.

"What change would give you and he the powers of gods?" Marius said.

"The star," she said under her breath.

"What?"

"The star," she said, louder. "Think about what has changed, what is new. The city is the same, the empire the same. Nothing was different, but the star is different. It is a new thing, a strange thing. Bearded stars are said to foretell doom and danger. Perhaps this one has done something else."

Marius looked doubtful. "That would still leave the question of why it chose you," he said.

"Not only me," she said. "It chose one other, and I think it likely that we are not the only ones." She spread her hands. "There is nothing special about me, nothing grand or heroic. Nothing I can see." She sighed. "Who can say how many other unworthies are awakening to this day and finding themselves very different?"

"I would not call you unworthy," he said. "Unexpected."

"That would be the kindest thing I could say," she said. She leaned back against the hard wood of the hull, hearing the water moving just there, so close. "Very unexpected."

☙

Arthras stirred and found he could not move. It was dark and tight, and he could not move even his fingers. He tried to open his mouth and scream but nothing happened, and then he panicked and thrashed as hard as he could. There was a cracking sound, and suddenly he was moving. Stone fell away from him, and he tumbled down and landed in the street, surrounded by a perfect mold of his body made from hardened rock, now broken into pieces.

He coughed and staggered to his feet, shaking broken rock from his hair, brushing it off his shoulders. He looked at his hands, down at his body, and saw that he was normal again, not black and smoldering, but the same color his flesh had always been. He spat out gravel and pulled pieces of stone from his beard.

He remembered now. The girl, the girl who commanded the storms had flung thunderbolts at him. He remembered the flash, and then he must have been buried under rubble, and the heat of his body had melted the stone and when it cooled he was encased.

It was daylight, and the sky was covered only by a few tattered clouds. He looked up and there was the star, bright even by day, like a linen shroud pulled across the sky, flickering with strange colors, like it was moving. He shook his head, looking around him, seeing that he was still in the same open space in the city, the ground littered with broken stones and other detritus, pieces of paper scattered everywhere. He saw pages floating in a puddle, the ink on them streaming away.

It was quiet, and he saw no signs of anyone. To one side he saw a few corpses, heard the flies already buzzing, but the city sounded like a tomb. He would guess all the men who could be were drunk and sleeping it off.

Somewhere King Usiric was holding court with his spearthanes, or preparing to, he would give away gifts to reward those who had done him service in the battle, and no man had done more than Arthras. He did not intend to be left out.

He started walking, annoyed that he was naked. He was a hero, and he wanted to look like one. He remembered the girl from last night and wondered who she was. If she was the defender of the city, then she would still be here. No, if she were here, she would have driven the Almanni out with her power. Perhaps she was dead, or buried in a mound of rubble as he had been. He looked at the ruined building she had defended so fiercely and did not understand it.

He left the plaza for the narrower streets, and here he began to see some signs of life. There was a place on a corner with the door broken and several warriors slumped in the street outside. Broken jugs of wine told the story well enough. Arthras kept going, not wanting to bother with waking up drunks. He rounded a corner and found a knot of ten or so men gathered around a fountain. They were drinking from it, washing their faces, and poking at the carved spouts, trying to see how it worked.

They saw him coming and tapped one another, motioned towards him, and by the time he reached them they were all looking at him, amused smiles on their faces. They were sons of wealthier men, he could tell. They had fine cloaks and wore swords with gold on the hilts and scabbards. They had an arrogant look, and it angered him. It was a sweet anger, because he intended to do something about it and knew they could not stop him.

"Lost your clothes?" one of them said, and the others laughed, looking him over.

"They burned off," he said. He looked at the tall one – the one closest to his own size. "I'll take yours."

They were silent for a moment, and then they all laughed louder. They came closer, starting to close in on him, and one of them drew his long knife. "I think we'll take your hair instead, boy. You should be marked for losing your spear. A man should always keep his spear." They all laughed at that.

Arthras didn't flinch, he just reached out and caught the blade of the knife, and then he turned black and burning with an act of will. The heat drove them back, shocked, and he ripped the knife away from the man, squeezed it in his fist until the iron melted and ran between his fingers.

He closed his eyes for a moment, and he willed it away, and it went. His skin cooled, and the iron in his hand became like mud rather than oil. He dropped it red hot on the ground and looked at them while they stared. He picked up the knife man by his belt and threw him into the fountain, pleased by how light he felt, how easy it was. He turned to the tall one, and saw his formerly smug face was white as clay.

"Your clothes," he said, cracking his knuckles. "Give them to me."

☙

When Karana emerged onto the deck, she found the small ship was crowded with people, and it surprised her. She had thought everyone who was going to flee had probably already done so, but there were all manner of people crowded against the gunwales of the small ship. There was enough weight that she could see it was riding rather low in the water, wallowing a bit on the gentle waves.

People stared when she came out, her blanket wrapped tight around herself, as she had no other clothes than her burned and torn robes. They were at sea, and she could see the smudge of low land to the left. There was not much wind at all, and the single square sail was mostly slack.

At the sight of her a murmur passed through the refugees crowded into the ship, and they looked at her and muttered to each other, some of them pointing. Nervous, she stepped back and almost ran into Marius. "What did you tell them?" she whispered, half-accusing. Some of them were getting up, coming closer as best they could on the crowded deck.

"Nothing," he said. "But some of them saw, and I could not stop them from speaking."

She cursed inwardly, wished she could duck back inside her shelter, but just now that scrap of sail drawn across the prow to make a little hut seemed a wholly inadequate refuge. She tried to avoid making eye contact with anyone. "Where are we bound?"

"Orneas," Marius said, and she frowned. Orneas was the next large city south down the coast, but was not far enough from the invaders to really feel secure. It was also the seat of the Church of Attis, and she wondered what kind of reception she could expect there.

"Might be better to make for Calliste," she said. "Put the strait between us and the barbarians."

Marius shrugged. "Perhaps, but we have no food aboard, and little water. It will be hard enough making it to Orneas, especially in this calm. We will be parched after a few days at sea."

She put her foot up on the gunwale and stood as tall as she could, looking back the way they came, then all around. Her hope was that she would see another ship of some kind

– someone who might be able to offer them aid. Or surely there were places along the coast where they could put in for water. She was embarrassed by the fact that she could recite the lineages of kings who died five hundred years ago, but could not picture in her mind one useful thing about the land they were sailing past.

Hands plucked at her and she turned, startled, to find a young woman there, hollow-eyed and very pregnant. The girl drew away when she turned, and there was a kind of fear in her eyes Karana had never seen or wanted to see.

"Please," the girl said. "Please I am afraid for my child." She spread her hands over her belly. "She has been kicking inside me so much. I am afraid for her." Tears in her eyes, she caught Karana's hand. "Please won't you give her your blessing? I know you can help her. Please bless her for me?"

Karana was stunned, felt a lump in her throat, and then she saw all the others watching. Some of them hopeful, some angry. She swallowed and stepped down from the gunwale, took the girl's hands in both of hers. "Oh, child. I have no such powers." She groped for something to say. "But I will pray with you. Let us pray together." She drew the girl down and sat on the deck with her. "Surely if we implore Attis, he will take mercy on us."

The girl nodded, wiping tears from her eyes, and Karana saw others were bowing their heads, holding their hands up in supplication. She did not want to lead a prayer, but she felt she had to. She closed her eyes. "Great Attis, son of Acollan son of Ouranos. You who were born of gods but lived as a man. Help us in our need. Show mercy on us."

"Call on Vasa," the girl said. "She is the sea-mother. She can help us."

"I, well -" Karana looked around. Worship of the old gods was not forbidden, but many disliked it.

"You are her daughter, aren't you?" the girl said. Her eyes grew wider. "Or you... you are she?"

Karana got up, almost laughing at the suggestion that she could be a secret goddess. She was dirty and tired and dressed in rags. She backed away, but the girl's hands caught her blanket and pulled it down from her shoulder, exposing her lightning-scarred skin. Angry, she pulled it back up. "I am not a goddess," she said, trying not to sound angry. "I am not... not anyone."

"You have lightning marks on your skin. They say you called the thunderbolts of Attis down to smite the barbarians," the girl said, half in tears. "Please, help us!"

Karana turned back to Marius, but she saw on his face that he was not certain of where he stood. He had seen, he knew what she could do – even if he did not understand it, he believed. Others were nodding, talking to each other, pointing. Someone said, "I saw her," and someone else said, "She flew into the air."

She turned away and covered her ears. "Stop," she said. But they came closer, crowding her, touching her, and she flinched away, put her back against the rail. "*Stop!*"

A gust of wind suddenly tore across the ship, slapping spray into the faces of the passengers and making the sail snap and shudder. They all drew away from her, and Karana covered her mouth. She hadn't meant to do that, she hadn't meant to do anything. "I'm sorry. I'm sorry. Please. I'm not... I'm not..." She looked to Marius, but he looked almost as afraid of her as the rest of them did.

She looked over the rail at the smudge of land, wondered if she really could fly away. It would be easier to just go and not have to face these people. But then she would be leaving them here without water or food. And Marius had probably saved her life. She drew in a long breath and the wind stirred in answer.

Karana sighed, closed her eyes, and then made herself open them and look at these people. More than twenty of them shoulder to shoulder on this boat that was meant to hold a dozen. They looked afraid, even the ones who were trying to look angry looked afraid. She wondered how many times she would look into the face of someone else and see fear, now that she had been given this power.

"I am not divine, and if I am blessed, I don't know why, or how," she said. "I am like you." She looked from one face to the next, wishing for a flicker of understanding, but there was nothing to see. "I am like you." Her voice cracked and she looked down, shook her head. The sail billowed and sagged lazily, and all she could think was that if she did nothing, she could be aboard this ship for days with people going hungry and thirsty.

So she held up her hand, because it felt right to do so, and called on the air. She did it gently, as gently as she could. She knew she could wield the power like a sledgehammer, but now she wanted to use it for something besides destruction; she wanted to be careful, and keep control.

A breath of wind stirred across the bow of the ship, and then it backed around to the north and the sail billowed out, snapped taut, and she felt the ship lean and dig into the waves. Sailors rushed to the lines and hauled the sail in tight, getting the best from it as the ship began to move. She did not know if she could keep the wind going for days, or if perhaps it would begin to blow on its own and she could try to manage the direction of it. She had a long way to go, and a great deal to learn.

The passengers stared at her, but none of them spoke. She leaned back against the rail and closed her eyes, trying to study the flow and motion of the air, to learn how it worked and how she could control it. She did not want to look at anyone, or speak to them. They wanted answers, but she had none to give.

Chapter Five

Touch the Sky

In stolen clothes and armor, Arthras entered the palace of Ilion, angry and feeling ill-fitted. The tunic was too big for him, too broad across the shoulders, and he didn't like the smell of it. It was too clean, like something worn by a man who never got his hands dirty. He remembered mucking in the hot pitch and wished he had some to rub their faces in, all of them. He wore iron armor that felt light, and the belt was set with gold. There were jewels on the hilt of the sword, and he didn't like that either, but he hoped it made him look important. He felt foolish, and that made him even more angry.

The palace was ancient, ruins that were older than the city itself built on and over to make a confused jumble of arches and towers that Arthras could hardly make sense of. It was a mess, the floor scattered with broken pottery, shattered glass, scraps of clothes, and bits of food. He smelled wine and smoke and the whiff of a dead body. It seemed like the place had been rather thoroughly looted.

He stalked down the long hall and came to a dizzying bridge that extended out over the rocky cliff below, forming a single path that cut off the heart of the palace from the rest of it, and here he found guards. They were the king's men, with silver-gilt scale armor and crested helms; they bore tall spears and well-worn swords, and they looked at him dispassionately when he approached them.

"I am come to see the king," he said, looking them in the eye. He would kill them if he had to, to get past them, and he wanted them to see it in his face.

"The king is seeing no one save his own thanes and those he chooses," the leftmost guard said. "Turn and go."

"Those who have done deeds in the name of the king have a right to an audience," Arthras said. "I invoke that right."

The man almost laughed. "And what deed have you done?"

"I broke the gate of the city," Arthras said.

They laughed at him, and it seemed his vision narrowed with his rage. He stepped closer and one of them brought up the haft of his spear, to jab at him with the bronze back spike. Arthras caught the haft and snapped it easily, the wood feeling brittle in his hands. He flung the pieces away, and then the other one lowered his spear and stabbed. Arthras felt the point strike his scale armor under the arm, slip off and dig at his flesh, but it did not bite. He brought the edge of his hand down and broke the spearpoint off cleanly.

His anger almost got away with him, and he saw smoke begin to rise from his clothes, felt the heat creeping over him. He grabbed the astonished guard by the front of his scaled cuirass, the silver-gilded scales crumpling in his hand. He lifted the man off his feet and held him over the edge of the bridge, dangling him over the steep fall to the crashing waves and sharp rocks.

The other guard had his sword in hand, but stopped when he realized a strike could send his companion plunging to his death. Arthras felt the seams of the guard's armor popping loose and smiled, but it was not a warm smile.

"I broke the gate of the city, and I will break you as well, unless you take me to the king."

☙

Arthras had never seen such immense rooms, had not even imagined such a place really existed, but he tried not to show his amazement as the guards walked him through the halls of the palace. The floors were set with patterned stone, the walls all of marble and hung with rich curtains and tapestries. There had not been looting here, and there were pedestals with golden bowls, statues and delicately carved reliefs. He wanted to stop and admire some of them, but he could not.

The two guards were nervous, and more joined them as they proceeded. Arthras wondered if they would make the mistake of trying to stop him. He didn't want to have to kill them – it would begin feuds with their families, and incur the wrath of the king. He didn't want to start a war, he just wanted his due. He wanted to be acknowledged and honored as he should be.

He had an escort of six guards by the time they came to the great hall. He heard it before he saw it. Voices were raised, and there was laughter and shouting. He smelled food and felt hungry, then wondered why he was not moreso – he had not eaten in over a day, he should be starving.

The great hall of the palace was truly a grandiose place. It had high windows and a vaulted ceiling covered over with lapis and agate pieces worked into intricate designs. There were great braziers and lamps to light the room, and the walls were heavy with rich hangings that looked big enough to make tents from. The floor was scattered with fresh straw and flower petals, and the smoke of incense hung sweet-smelling in the afternoon air.

The long table was groaning with a feast, and there at the head sat the white-haired shape of King Usiric. He was not an old man, and he had massive arms and shoulders, but men said his eyesight was not good any longer, though he tried to hide it. At the table with him were more than thirty of his most trusted warriors and captains, all of them feasting and smoking and drinking as they laughed. Here was a pantheon of the great men of the Almanni – all the famed warriors and men of importance, and for a moment Arthras felt very poor and inconsequential.

Before the table there stood five women, and they all were naked, with their torn gowns pooled at their feet. The four younger ones looked ashamed and afraid, hugging themselves close and looking down at the floor, while the oldest of them stood defiant and glared back at the king. She was beautiful, with dusky skin and a fleshy body that Arthras could not help but look at twice. Her hair was a black mass caught up in an elaborate pile of braids and ornaments just beginning to come loose.

The king squinted at her and beckoned. "Come closer, woman. Let me see you."

Then some of the men at the table noticed Arthras and the chagrined-looking guards, and a ripple passed through as more of them turned to look at him. He felt himself start to wither under their arrogant, assured glares, but then he remembered what he was and stepped forward boldly, his head up.

"Who is this?" a man said, rising from the table. He was tall and had sharp, cruel features. His eyes were blue and cold as he looked Arthras up and down. "Guards, why do you bring some vagabond boy into the presence of the king?"

Arthras shoved the guard out of his way and stepped up to stand face to face with the taller man. "I am not a vagabond, and I have a right to audience with the king. Who are you to speak to me this way?"

The blonde man drew himself up stiffly. "I am Ethric Gold-Handed, boy, and if you beg my forgiveness now, I may let you keep your head."

Arthras felt a drop in his belly, as he knew Ethric was a famous swordsman, a warrior who had killed more than twenty men with his own hands. He took a breath and remembered his power and made himself stare right into the taller man's eyes. "I will not. I gave insult for insult, and if you wish a fight you shall have it, but I will not bow my face to the dirt from fear of you, old man."

Ethric stiffened and Arthras felt a rush in his belly, but then the king's voice cut through the sudden quiet. "Stand aside, Ethric. Show me this bold boy."

Arthras met Ethric's furious stare for another moment, and then the other man stepped slightly aside, and Arthras found himself facing the king himself. The naked girls gathered up their torn clothes and tried to cover themselves as the attention of the king turned away from them. Usiric looked immense, his heavy shoulders draped with his vast sable mantle, and the iron crown of his people on his head. His grey-white hair flowed long, and his beard was full and stained with wine. He squinted at Arthras. "Who are you, boy? You have dared much to come before me. Tell me why."

The men all fell silent, the king's companions waiting to hear what he would say, and he was pleased to have them listen. "I have come to take my place here, among all your greatest warriors, for I am greater than all of them."

There was muttering, and some laughter, but Usiric's face was serious. "Tell me what deeds you have done to earn such a place."

"I broke the gate of the city," he said. "It was my hand that opened the way, and because of me you sit here enthroned in luxury, instead of sleeping in a tent." He was quiet for a moment, considering. "I come for what is due me, as a hero among your warriors."

"The gate was broken by the shaking of the earth," the king said. "No man accomplished that. Not me, and not you." He made a small gesture, and Ethric shoved Arthras aside, sent him stumbling with the unexpected blow. He caught himself, and anger boiled in his stomach.

Ethric picked up a heavy golden goblet. "You don't deserve my sword, boy. So I will beat you with this – perhaps you will crawl away and survive, if you are favored." He came towards him, hefting the weapon in his hand.

Arthrus felt rage wash over him, and the heat consumed his body and smoke began to pour from his clothes. He caught the goblet in his hand as Ethric swung it, and the gold crumpled in his grip. He had a moment to savor the shock in the other man's eyes as he found his strength easily matched, and then Arthras shoved him away and he all but flew into the table, knocking over his chair and scattering other men he crashed into.

He took a deep breath, controlling himself, keeping the fire under control, but he reached down and stroked the powers of the earth and the room shuddered and shook, rattling the windows and the plates on the tabletop, and then the men looked at him, and he saw fear, sweeter than honey. He pointed at Ethric. "You. You can put your face in the dirt and ask me to forgive you, or we will fight." He crumpled the gold cup in his hand like a leaf and threw it on the floor where it rang and bounced. He met Ethric's gaze and held it. "Do you beg my forgiveness?"

Ethric glanced side to side, all the other men watching him, and Arthras knew he would not. Slowly, the blonde man straightened and then drew his sword. "Let us fight then, puppy."

Arthras looked at the sword at his side, put his hand on it, and then drew it out. It was heavy-hilted from the gold, and he didn't like how it sat in his hand. He didn't need it, and so he threw it on the floor and advanced to meet the other man.

Ethric looked uncertain, but then he drew off his cloak and threw it aside, closed on him with death in his eye. Arthrus did not slow, just walked right to him, and when the taller man drew back and struck with his blade, he tried not to flinch. The sword hit him on the shoulder, tore loose a handful of scales, and cut through the leather straps. Arthras did not even really feel it, save for a sensation like a birch rod laid across his shoulder.

In answer he grasped the sword blade and wrenched it from Ethric's hand, threw it away and heard it ring against a wall. Then he gripped the taller man by his shirt, lifted him up over his head, and hurled him a dozen paces so he landed on the feast table, smashing platters and spilling cups. Arthras closed on him, and the other men scattered out of his way. He caught Ethric by the leg and dragged him back.

The blonde man clawed at his face, and then he drew his hand back and screamed, his flesh burned.

Arthras raised his fist and Ethric cried out, and then the king stood and shouted out. "Enough!"

For a moment, everyone was still, and then Arthras looked down at his foe, seeing the terror on his face, and it was enough. He smashed his fist down into the table beside Ethric's head, splintering the wood with a sound that made everyone in the hall flinch. Then he let him go.

He breathed deep, getting control of himself, letting the heat built up inside him fade, and cool. He faced the king and inclined his head. "As you wish."

King Usiric leaned on the table. "It is. . . customary to reward a great warrior after a battle. What reward would you have, young bull?"

Arthras picked up a heavy golden cup, then tossed it aside. "I do not want gold or treasures, nor do I desire fine swords or gilded armor. They are useless to me. I want. . . I want to be accorded the respect I deserve, for what I have done." He glanced aside and saw the women still there, all of them looking at him as though he were a monster, all save the older woman, who met his glance evenly and did not turn aside, only gave a small incline of her head.

He pointed at her. "Who is that woman there? The fearless one."

Usiric seemed surprised. "That is Nicaea, the wife of Galbos, the Autarch. I was going to give her ladies in waiting to my men, and I commanded the harlot to dance for me, but she refused. I had not decided her fate."

"I will take her," Arthras said. He did not wait to ask, or to consider. He left the table, not looking back, and he took the proud woman by the arm. She was holding her torn dress together, and she said nothing to him. He looked her up and down, nodded. "Tell your girls to follow," he said, and then he pulled her after him, the younger ladies hurrying in their wake, and no one raised a single word to stop them.

༼

After nightfall Karana was able to let the breeze go and the wind kept going on its own. She could feel the disturbances she caused in the air with her power, and she tried to be gentle, because she did not know if she could summon a storm without meaning to. There was so much she didn't know, and she felt oppressed by her ignorance. She found her body was not tired, but her mind was, and so she retreated to her small shelter and managed a fitful sleep. She dreamed of nothing that reassured her, only pieces of the past few days caught in frustrating patterns of repetition.

With fair winds, it was just before nightfall the next day when they came in sight of Orneas. It was a bigger, younger city than Ilion, without the massive walls and ancient monuments, and it spread out along the rolling hills almost as far as she could see. The smell of smoke from so many cooking fires was sweet to smell, and so was the prospect of getting off the boat, despite that she had no real idea of where she would go, or what she would do.

The tallest point in the city was the grand temple of Attis, the white dome, gilt with gold, gleamed high on the hill that dominated the north end of the city. The lowest point was the harbor, and as they drew close, she saw the harbor was choked with ships in a bewildering profusion. She saw galleys from Sarda and Lyria almost rail to rail with lean merchant craft from Sydon and Atagia. Many of them were the heavy, square-rigged cogs used in the coastal waters around Othria, and as they drew closer she saw many of them were crammed full of refugees.

Somehow, she had not expected it to be this bad. She had known that for days people who could flee had been leaving Ilion, but she never really imagined where they were all going. It had not really occurred to her that all those people and their hastily-gathered possessions had to go somewhere.

Her ship was smaller than most, and so it threaded in among the larger craft with relative ease. Close to the docks, the crowding was worse, and they bumped into a few ships as they headed in. There was a great deal of cursing and waving of hands, and the people aboard more than one ship were using pikes or staves to shove other boats out of their way.

Somehow they waded through the confusion and scraped up against a stone jetty in a place between two larger ships that was too small for any other craft to make use of. Karana ignored the pointed looks of the other passengers, knowing they expected her to do something to help them all, but what could she do? Calling a wind in this mess would just make a worse mess.

The sailors flung ropes ashore and then the captain jumped overboard to argue with someone while the people dropped over the side and streamed away into the crowd. Karana watched them go and felt even more apprehensive: by nightfall a thousand people would have heard the stories about her. She looked for Marius, but did not see him. Had he already gone?

She thought hard about just staying here aboard the ship. There was no reason for her to stay in Orneas, and with her winds they could sail away and be in Archelion in a few days. No barbarian army would cross the Strait of Amytris to Calliste. It would be safer.

Then she saw two of the sailors coming towards her. They held heavy rope hooks and they looked at her with a mix of fear and determination. One of them gestured toward land. "Get out."

Karana felt an unpleasant weight in her belly. "Where is the captain?" she said, trying to keep her voice even.

The sailor held up the hook and jabbed it at the city. "Get out, witch."

They were not shouting, but there was a dangerous look on their faces, and it frightened her. She didn't want to fight them – she wanted then to not be afraid – and anything she did would only make that worse. Sick inside, she gathered her blanket around herself and climbed over the side of the ship. It was a bit of a drop, but she told herself not to be foolish and jumped.

The stone jetty felt incredibly hard and unyielding after two days at sea, and she staggered a little until her sea legs went away. Karana had spent her childhood on a number of ships, so she was used to the transition, though it had been years since she last sailed. She gave one last look up at the sailors watching her go, and then she turned away and headed into the crowds, glad of the sudden anonymity when the mass of people closed in around her.

The whole waterfront was crowded with people of every kind – young and old, exhausted men carrying bags of their belongings beside women with their children and infants. Some of them were stoic and implacable, while others cried or swore or shoved each other. The smell of so many desperate people was a close, heavy scent that put Karana's back up. She kept her head down and made her way through the mass, wondering why so many of them were just standing here, as if waiting for something.

She heard shouting and was jostled around, and then she came up against a barrier made of heaped bales of cloth and manned by armed guards. There was just one narrow way through, and she heard more shouting from that direction, pushed through the mass to see what was happening. Why were they walling the people off? Surely they had to know what was happening.

There was a small gap in the makeshift wall, and there were a half-dozen guards there blocking it. At least, she had to assume they were guards, as they were armed and arrogant and here quite blatantly. They were in the process of going through the bags of an elderly woman, dumping her possessions out in the street and sorting through them. As Karana watched, one of them took the woman and started searching through her clothes with groping hands, and she felt anger spark in her chest.

"Stop! Stop it!" She shoved through the crowd, her new strength letting her clear a path. The guard was reaching up under the woman's dress when she got to him, grabbed his arm, and dragged him away. He fought, but she was so much stronger now that she threw him on the ground without really meaning to, and the crowd surged back to give them room as the other guards came forward, brandishing clubs and spears.

The man fought to his feet and snarled at her, drew back a hand as if to strike. Karana's blanket was slipping off and she hastily drew it around her again. He glared at her and she glared back.

"What do you think you're doing, girl?" he spat, wiping at his mouth.

"What are you doing to these people?" She saw barrels behind the barricade, and suddenly she understood it. "You're *robbing* them?"

"No one asked them to come here," he said. "They want to come and stink up our city, they have to pay the tariff."

"Tariff?" Karana said, incredulous. "These people are escaping the fall of their city by the hands of barbarian invaders! You should be offering them comfort and help, not robbing them of what little they have!" She looked at the half-dozen armed men and wanted to spit. "This is absolutely *disgusting.*"

"Fine then, what have you got, girl?" The man came towards her, pulling a short bludgeon from his belt. "Let's see what gold you got hid under there."

Karana's anger rose higher, like boiling water about to spill, and she gave him a slit-eyed glare. "If you touch me, you will regret it."

He almost seemed unnerved for a moment, but he could not hesitate before his fellows and all the other refugees gathered around. He grabbed her arm and she shrugged him off, then he grabbed her hair and she cried out in complete outrage. She caught his wrist and squeezed down hard, and he yelled and hit her in the face with his leather-wrapped club.

The blow stunned her, and she felt her teeth click together and she waited for the pain, but there was just a stinging sensation, and she shook her head and turned to look at him, and then he looked afraid. He drew back to hit her again and she wrenched at his arm and felt something snap inside, and then he screamed and fell on the ground, holding his arm. She looked up and saw the crowd gathering behind her, as if she were leading them. They were shouting and pushing at the barricade, and some people threw things.

The guards started forward, spears held out with the points gleaming, and Karana felt a fear in her belly, and then she pushed it away and drew in her power. The wind boiled and swirled around her, gathering up her braids and whirling them around her face. The guards stopped, looking nervous, and then she pushed out with her hand, trying to keep the wind gust as focused as she could.

It bowled them all over, sent them skidding and rolling across the ground, and the sides of the sudden gale smashed the barricade open and sent bales of cloth and straw tumbling, knocking over other guards, scattering them. The backblast knocked the front ranks of the crowd to the ground, and Karana heard screams, someone called on Attis to save them.

Frightened or not, the crowd surged forward, tearing through the broken barrier and trampling the fallen guards underfoot. Some people managed to take their clubs and deliver vengeful blows as they passed, but no one could stop. Karana herself was swept up by the rush, clutched her blanket close as she was carried along. Someone lifted her up on their shoulders, and she yelped and hung on as she was borne over the heads of the crowd, away from the sea, into the unknown city.

Chapter Six

HANDS OF VENERATION

Karana did not know Orneas, so she could not even say where she was. The crowds of refugees spread out through the city and she let herself be carried along with them. The big man who picked her up eventually put her down, and she lost track of him. She fetched up in a plaza that had seen better days, surrounded by older buildings that seemed either empty or neglected. The people set up a kind of camp here, taking blankets and other scraps to make canopies to keep out the sun. She found a small corner and tucked herself away, knees drawn up to her chest.

She felt stormy inside, seeing over and over in her mind's eye the guardsmen scattering from her fury. She had struck before at the invaders in Ilion, but they had been far away, and they were barbarians, so it was easier. This was not the same. She was embarrassed by how quickly she had been roused to brute anger. With the power she had been give, she had to be more careful. It would be too easy for her to hurt someone, or kill them. Who was she to mete out judgments?

Some men came and climbed the old pillars, tied lines to them and hung tarps, and then she realized they were making a canopy over her head. She froze, not sure what to do, and then some women came and they laid out a blanket and put food on it and gave her wine, and she wanted to refuse, but she did not want to be cruel to them. They looked at her with hope in their faces, and she wondered if they simply wanted her to protect them, or if they thought she was a goddess. It was not a question she could ask, after all.

So she drank a little and ate a little, and she smiled and thanked them profusely. They smiled and seemed happy, but they did not say much to her. The blanket slipped off her shoulder and they saw her tattered clothes, and one of them, an older woman, became terribly annoyed.

"What is this?" she said, pulling at the torn and seared fabric. "You cannot wear this."

"It's all right," Karana said, suddenly embarrassed. "I don't mind."

"You cannot stay like this," the woman said, adamant, and then she stormed off into the crowd and Karana was not sure what to think. She watched the people set up a temporary shelter here, in this rather bleak place. She wondered if more guards would come to try and drive them out, and while she knew she could prevent that, she did not see an end to that conflict and it was disheartening. Mostly, it wounded her inside that men would be so callous to others who needed them. She had never thought of herself as very worldly, but that degree of avarice had never occurred to her.

The older woman came back carrying a pile of cloth, and she dumped it all out and sorted some of it into dresses and some into simple bolts of cloth. She hung up makeshift curtains to give them privacy, barking orders to the younger women, and then she made Karana stand up and started to fit her. There didn't seem like a good way to protest, though Karana felt her face go hot with embarrassment as the woman stripped off her blanket and her torn robes and started to dress her all over. Karana looked at herself and saw the scars trailed across her skin, looked away. The other woman said nothing of them at all.

The woman seemed very determined as she draped her with a dress, cut it and resewed a seam to let it out, needle in her teeth and muttering under her breath. Then she affixed another bolt of cloth over Karana's shoulder and wrapped and pinned it so it hung artfully. This seemed to make her happy, and she nodded. "There," she said. "Better, much better. Not good enough for a goddess, but better."

"I am not a goddess," Karana said, more forcefully than she had meant to. She bit her tongue. "I am not."

"My advice is when people say you are a goddess, you do not argue," the woman said. She began rolling up her cloth again, and Karana took a small swatch of silk and wrapped it over her hair, around her braids to cover them. Just that made her feel very much better. She sat down, and the older woman nodded to her and left her alone. She was glad, for the moment, to be alone.

ଓଃ

The refugee camp grew through the day, into the evening. Karana imagined this was not the only one in the city, and she worried that she could not protect the others, but no one came to trouble them. She heard voices singing and talking, and she lay back and dozed for a while, feeling almost comfortable.

When she woke up there were small things left just inside her small shelter. There were some coins, and flowers, and some sweet-smelling oil in a tiny stoppered bottle. She wondered at them for a while, and then she felt ashamed when she realized they were offerings. Small children peered through the curtains at her, ran away if she seemed to see them. She felt alone, but she understood then that every person in the camp knew who she was and that she was here. It made her feel a great deal less safe.

The day faded into night, and there were some fires and candles, but Karana found herself in the dark very much wishing she had something to read. Now the rush of the escape and the voyage was fading, she was beginning to wonder what she would do with herself. There were several libraries here in Orneas, and the archive of the Archpriest himself. Perhaps she could find work.

The thought made her scoff at herself. A city had fallen, thousands of people were homeless and displaced, and she thought of finding a job. She had been given this power, what was she to do with it? Perhaps she should go and seek an audience with the Archpriest himself. He might tell her what she should do, give her guidance. She desperately wanted some kind of guidance, someone to tell her what she should do.

Voices came and went in the dark, and then she saw a light coming closer, a lantern carried in someone's hand. It came closer, and she heard a voice say, "Is this the storm girl?" and she almost laughed. All of this and she was called the storm girl. She stood up, wondering if this was another pack of guards thinking they could drag her away to prison or simply come to kill her. She closed her eyes, resolved to fight no more than she must, and to be careful.

Then there was someone outside the curtain, and she heard a low voice. "Hello? Is someone there? We are seeking the storm girl."

Karana took a breath and pulled the curtain back, braced for an attack, but instead she saw three young boys who looked no more than thirteen, and they stepped back when they saw her, startled. She looked them over. "Who are you? Why do you seek me?" She wondered if they meant to ask her to bless them, or to make offerings. She hoped they did not expect her to heal anyone of illness or wounds.

The three of them bowed their heads, and she felt sick at the sight of it. "Please, don't bow. Tell me who you are."

"We were sent by our lady to find you. She heard of you, and wants to meet you," one of them said, barely daring to peek at her. "Are you the one who calls the winds?"

Karana had a hundred things she could have said, but she only nodded. "Yes."

"Then please come with us to meet our lady, Thessala. She would meet you," the boy said.

"Why does she want to meet me?" Karana said, not wanting to go.

"Because. . . because she says she would meet another who has been touched by the gods." The boy looked at her, then quickly away again.

Karana felt her heart speed, and then she found herself nodding. "Very well," she said. "Yes. Take me to her."

ଔ

She kept her head down as they left, hoping no one would notice she was going, but people saw, and some of them called out or stood and looked after her. It made her feel as if she were abandoning them. What if the guards came to chase them out or worse while she was gone? She resolved to return as quickly as she could, then hurried to keep up with her small guides. Like all young boys, they moved with an unstudied quickness she had a hard time matching.

The city was dark, and the part of it they were in seemed run down and rather empty. Above them she could see glimpses of the better part up on the hill, the towers lit and white-sided in the moonlight. Down here the streets were narrow and wound around among abandoned houses and fountains that did not flow. The people she did see huddled behind doorways and window curtains, peering out as she passed.

The place they led her to was old, she could tell that by the way it was built. It had a long central courtyard lined with crumbling pillars, and there was a narrow pool in the center filled with dirty rain water, rather than clean water from the broken fountain. She saw people here, in the windows and looking out from the doorways. She saw a lot of children, and people who moved with difficulty or leaned on crutches. By the time she saw the sign of the albatross, she knew what this place was.

"This is a House of Uraria," she said, and one of the boys nodded. Uraria was the mythical Tenth Paladin, the only woman accounted among Attis' champions, who had been blinded and given her life over to caring for the sick and the maimed. The best such places were refuges where the sick and hurt could find aid; the worst were almost prisons for the malformed and the mad. She hoped this was not one of those. The veneration of Uraria was not sanctioned by the Church of Attis, and so the priests did nothing to help her houses.

The boys led her to the steps to the central building and motioned her to go on, and so she went up the shallow steps and into the shadows of the shrine. There were only two oil lamps burning dim in here, and ahead she saw the moonlight that shone down in the small garden she knew would be the heart of the sanctuary.

There was a terrible quiet in here, and she moved as softly as she could down the hall, past a row of small candles that were almost burned down, and then through the archway marked with an owl and into the silver light of the moon. After the dark of the interior, the moon seemed bright as day, and she squinted a little, seeing the small patches where herbs were grown, the little fountain that still poured a trickle of water into a pool, and the marble bench before it. At first she thought the white shape was a statue, but then it moved and she realized it was a person draped in a long white robe, a cowl over their head. The person faced the pool, their back to the door.

"You sent for me," Karana said, not knowing what else to say. "You are Thessala?"

"I am," the woman said, and her voice was rich and beautiful, darker and deeper than Karana expected. "I am glad you have come. I would have sought you myself, but I cannot leave the sanctuary just now." She shifted her head, and Karana saw a long, thick braid of black hair looped at her neck, like a serpent. "You are the girl they say called the winds, and the storm. You have been touched by the gods."

"I don't know what I have been touched by," Karana said. "I do not know what this power is, or where it comes from. I know it is real." She came a little closer. "The boys you sent. They said you had been touched as well."

Thessala laughed a little bit, a hard sound. "Yes, I have been touched. I have not left the sanctuary for a week now, nor allowed those who dwell here with me to look upon me. You were given a great power. My transformation has been somewhat different." She lifted her arm, held her hand out until the sleeve fell away and revealed her skin. At first Karana could not tell what she was seeing, thought perhaps the woman wore some other garment, but then she moved closer to see and realized the other woman's skin was covered with scales like finely-worked armor.

ය

"Oh," Karana said, coming to sit beside the other woman. "Oh what happened?" She took the scaled hand in hers, but Thessala pulled it away.

"My skin grew dry and parched, no matter how I drank or bathed, and I was hungry, so hungry all the time. I ate and ate, and it was not easy, because I need to preserve food for the others, the ones who need it." She tucked her cowl more closely around her face, turned her head slightly away. Karana looked at the scaled hand and tried to match it with the flowing, lovely voice.

"Was there pain?" Karana said, fascinated and yet somewhat horrified. She had thought what happened to her was a curse of a kind, but this was terrible.

"No," Thessala said. "No pain. But my skin peeled away, as it does when you burn in the sun? Like that. It simply fell away, layer after layer, and then this was underneath it." She held up her hand. "All over me. I am waiting for my hair to fall out, but it has not. I am taller now, and... and I am stronger. I am so strong."

"As am I," Karana said. "I threw a man across a room without meaning to, and when the guard hit me with his club I barely felt it."

"But you do not look different," Thessala said, her voice almost accusing. "You are still beautiful."

"Well," Karana was embarrassed. She had never thought of herself like that. "I have been marked, in my way." She glanced around, assuring herself she was alone, and then she stood up. Her face felt hot as she shrugged her dress off her shoulder and slipped it down. "Here."

"Attis' mercy," Thessala said, and Karana felt the light touch of her fingers on her scars, flinched a little. She shrugged the dress back up, settled it in place. Thessala was quiet. "Those marks appeared?"

"Not by themselves," Karana said. "I was in a... a battle, in Ilion. I summoned a lightning bolt, but my aim was not the best. I think I almost killed myself, but the power of it scarred me."

"I have seen scars like that before," Thessala said. "They are the marks left by lightning, on those fortunate enough to survive."

"You have seen them?" Karana was surprised, sat back down on the cool stone bench.

"I care for all manner of injured and sick people here. Those who are hurt for a time, and those who will always be ill or weak. It is the place I have chosen for myself. To care for and protect those who cannot care for themselves, or speak for themselves." Thessala moved her head under her cowl. "It is why I sent for you – because you have raised your hands to defend the weak."

"I... well, it was not quite that simple." Now she heard it said like that, Karana was embarrassed. She had not thought of it that way at all. "I just don't know what else I could have done."

"Tell me about the other one. They say you fought a giant in Ilion," Thessala said.

"A giant? How do these stories travel so quickly and so far?" Karana shook her head. "He was no giant. He was... just a boy, really. No older than I am, or younger. His power must have been new to him, as was mine to me. He could shake the earth, and he gave off a terrible heat. His skin was black as soot, and he melted earth and stone to his body, like armor. He was terribly strong, and the earth shook when he walked."

"He was a barbarian?" Thessala said.

"Yes, he was of the Almanni. His hair was red, and braided the way they do. I felt the ground shake and then the gate was destroyed, and he led the horde into the city. I saw them running and killing and robbing, and I... I tried to stop them. I didn't want to fight him, but he would not stop." She shook her head. "It was not much of a battle. The thunderbolt left me senseless. I don't know what happened to the boy." She rubbed her mouth. "Arthras. He said his name was Arthras."

Thessala was quiet. "I think you did a worthy thing," she said. "And at the docks, when you kept the guards from robbing the refugees."

Karana made a disgusted sound. "I could not believe they were doing that. This is the city of the Archpriest, how can he allow such cruelty?"

Now it was Thessala's turn to scoff. "The Archpriest is a foolish old man more concerned with silver and protocols than with people. The guards have tried to tear down this sanctuary many times. With all the refugees coming in, there will be trouble, and I would like your help to try and protect them.

"I... why would there be trouble?" Karana didn't really want to understand it, but what else could she say? "These people are escaping a barbarian invasion, and it could come here as well, sooner than you would like to think."

"What I think is that Ilion is four days away by swift travel. For an army, I think perhaps ten. If the Almanni come here, they will come soon, and the rulers of this city will try to force the refugees outside the walls before that happens." Thessala shifted, her face still hidden. "They will not want to share the stores of food with anyone."

"I cannot fight an army, or a city," Karana said. "I do not even know if I want to."

"You have been given a gift," Thessala said. "Not cursed, as I have been."

"Perhaps I am more cursed than it seems." Karana looked at her hands, the henna designs fading, scrawled over by her new scars. "I did not ask for this power, any more than you asked for what was done to you." She looked at the other woman, and then she reached over and drew down the white cowl so she could see Thessala's face.

It was strange, seeing the human features covered over with the fine layer of scales, how they caught the moonlight and flickered with little shimmers of color – pink and blue and green. Her hair was in a single heavy black braid, and her eyes were wide and yellow, with pupils black as broken obsidian slits. She blinked, and Karana saw a dark membrane slide across her eyes as her lids closed, then vanish when they opened. She also saw that she was terrified.

"You have been given strength," Karana said. "And splendid armor. You have been given power as well. You should use it as you see fit."

"I am not a warrior," Thessala said. "I never wished to be."

"Nor did I," Karana answered. "But we have been chosen, all the same. Sometimes, we must all become warriors."

Chapter Seven

LADY OF SHADOWS

Once out of the hall, Arthras let the woman go and looked at her. He did not know the palace, and he had no rooms or place to sleep of his own. He realized he had nowhere to go, so he simply gestured for her to lead, and she turned and led without a word. The other girls followed in their wake, uncertain as foals, and he paid them no attention. They did not interest him at all.

He followed Nicaea up a long flight of smooth steps, down a hallway thick with hangings, and then she opened a set of wide doors carved of a deep brown wood. He studied the designs on them as he went through. The wood was worked with figures of heroes and monsters locked in battle, and he had never seen anything so grand or so well-made, and here it was, a simple door inside this place. The opulence of the palace itself irritated him, and he tried to shrug it off.

Through the doors was a set of rooms, and he was momentarily taken off guard by the size of them. The outer room was high and dim, with a few lamps burning, others unlit or burned out. Blue gauze curtains billowed over the arch that led out to a balcony, and he heard the rush of the sea come dimly through them. To the right was another door, and ahead what looked like a bedchamber, the entryway draped with red. Just these rooms were finer than any place he had ever imagined a king might dwell in. There were colorful rugs on the floor, and censers hung on hooks and trailed threads of sweet smoke.

He snorted. "These are the chambers of the Autarch?"

The woman Nicaea looked at him, as if measuring him. "No. These are my chambers. Your king took my husband's rooms." She said the word "king" as if it were a curse, and he liked that. He glanced back at the other girls, and they scattered as if he were a wolf eyeing fowl. He turned back and looked at Nicaea. She held her torn dress closed over herself casually, as if she did not care to notice it. He had seen her standing naked in the great hall, and yet now he wanted to see her again.

"If you intend to take out your anger with my husband upon me, I believe you will be disappointed," she said coolly.

He laughed a little. "Is that what you imagine I want?"

"I know you hate Galbos, and I know why," she said.

"Do you?" he said. "You know he gathered us together and promised to help us fight our enemies?"

"Yes," she said. "He used you against the Borunai. He offered your king gold and titles to join with the auxiliary cohorts and drive them back across the Sethion River, and so you did."

"Gold, and titles?" Arthras snorted. "Perhaps he offered those to the king and his spear-thanes. To us he promised land. The Borunai had driven us from our best lands, and so when he promised us new ones within the border, where we would be protected, we were eager. He promised food as well, because the fields had been burned, and there would be no harvest this year. We faced a winter of hunger, and death. War is better than that."

She watched him. "It is."

"So we fought for him, and with the cohorts we turned the Borunai back. And then he broke every promise, and took the cohorts away, and left us with nothing. He sent no food, no supplies. Perhaps he thought we would starve." Arthras remembered the day when they realized they had been deceived, how the despair raced through every camp, and how it turned to wrath.

"He hoped you would starve," Nicaea said. "Then he would have eliminated two threats to the border with a single stroke. The emperor would have been pleased with that." She walked slowly to the balcony and parted the curtain, looked out into the night. "He did not expect you to invade."

"Then he was a fool," Arthras said. "What else was left to us?"

She smiled without humor. "The border forces were intended to hold you off if you tried. But your king bribed one of the commanders, and the other one was incompetent. You broke through the frontier and came to Ilion, and my husband had no forces left with which to stop you." She sighed. "When he left the city, he claimed he was going to get reinforcements. Even then I knew it was a lie. He is a coward."

"You do not care for him at all, then?" Arthras said.

This time she did laugh, and it was bitter. "I was married to him for political reasons. I spent as little time with him as possible. He left me here because if I am slain by savages then he will be free to choose a new wife." She let the curtain swing closed and looked at him. "As I said. You would be disappointed. Galbos would not care in the slightest, whatever you do to me."

Arthras licked his teeth. "I do not think anything about you is disappointing, lady."

Her brow arched. "Well. And why do you want me, then? If not for the base pleasure of taking from your enemy what was his?"

"You were not afraid," Arthras said. "You stood stripped before the king and his men, and you were not afraid." He came closer to her, and she did not step away. "And then you saw what I did, what I can do, and still you were not afraid." He looked at her. She was a kind of beauty he had never seen close up. Her skin was almost a bronze color, but soft, without tattoos or scars. She was tall, and she did not have to look up very far to meet his gaze. "I like that you are not afraid."

"What good would it do me to show fear?" she said. "Would it turn aside the wrath of your king to cower and grovel before him?"

"It might," he said.

"Perhaps I do not feel my life is worth my pride," she said.

He snorted, then nodded. "I understand that."

She gave him a long, measured look, and then she turned on her heel and walked into the bedchamber, and he followed her, liking the flash of her bare feet from under the hem of her dress. The room was smaller than it looked, the walls hung with red and gold, and the bed itself was bigger than any he had ever seen. The wooden posts were stout enough to serve as yoke-poles, carved in swirling, polished shapes.

He watched as she let her damaged dress fall to puddle at her feet. He had seen her naked in the hall, but here it was much more intimate, and it made his heart speed to see the soft, filtered daylight on her smooth skin. With complete dignity, she sat on the bed and put her hands up, began to pluck out pins and clasps and stack them on the table beside the bed. Her hair uncoiled and fell over her shoulders in black curls touched with lighter streaks. Unadorned and nude, she looked more like a woman to him – wilder, like the women of his people.

Neither of them said anything when he came to her, and then he pushed her down on the bed and kissed her neck, and her shoulders. His stolen clothes annoyed him and he stripped them off, pressed himself down on top of her, liking the feel of her soft skin. He let his hands roam over her body, and she did not protest. He kissed her and touched her, and then she kissed him in answer and she laughed softly. "Have you had a woman before?" she said, very soft.

He grunted, annoyed. "Yes," he said.

"I do not mean your caterwauling barbarian girls," she said. "I mean a woman."

"Be careful what you say," he growled, and she laughed again. She moved under him, rolled until she was on top, and he let her, unsure what she was doing.

"Be quiet," she said. "Let me show you the difference." She reached down, her hand on him, and he groaned as she stroked him. He arched up, and then she slid up and pressed against him, and then she slid down and took him in. He gasped; he'd never had a girl do it like this.

She braced her hands on his chest and rode up and down, panting, her heavy hair swinging over him, tickling his face. He groped at her flanks and groaned, pushed up against her. She swiveled her hips as she worked on him, bringing sensations more intense than he expected. He gasped and clutched at her, and she laughed again. He felt it, inside.

"Let me show you," she said. "Let me show you what I can do."

⊗

Arthras lay in the dark after, listening to her breathing. The sun was setting, filtering golden light through the curtains. He found he was not sweating, and he doubted he could sweat at all, now. He was not tired or out of breath. He turned his head to look at her, and she was propped against the head of the bed, watching him.

"How did it happen to you?" she said.

He did not pretend he didn't know what she meant. "Nothing happened. There was no moment when I knew. I just changed."

"Surely there was something," she said. "Something that made you different from the others."

He grunted. "My head hurt, for days. The pain came and went, but every time it was worse." He rubbed at his forehead, remembering. "The battle was begun. There were men at the gate, swinging the ram, and I wanted to join them. I wanted to fight." He didn't want to tell her how lowly his place had been before. "I went to the gate, and it was a disaster. There were arrows falling everywhere, and rocks dropping on us. The ladders were too short to reach the top, and no one could throw a grapple high enough to hook on the walls. It was almost dark, and I thought the king was a fool to wait so long."

"He probably didn't want to attack," she said.

"What?" He turned to look at her.

"You think your king does not know the ladders were too short? Or that his men had no way to breach the gates? He knew. He was laying siege to the city, but his captains wanted a fight, and the soldiers wanted a target for their rage. So he let them attack, but he knew it would fail, so he attacked close to dark, so they would have to break off before too many lives were thrown away." She shifted and stretched out her legs.

Arthras was silent for a moment; he had never thought of any of that. The king ordered an attack, and so there was an attack. He wondered if she were right. "They poured oil on us, and I just realized it was oil when they dropped torches and lit it. There was fire everywhere, and then I was so angry. I didn't feel pain, I felt the heat, and then. . ." He held his hands up and looked at them. "I saw my skin turn black, and then the heat came from me."

"And you made the earth shake?" she said.

"Yes. I commanded it, and it shook, and the gate collapsed. Great stones fell on me, but I could push them aside. I was strong, and when the arrows struck me they glanced off my skin. I saw them on the ground with their points turned red hot. Nothing could stop me. Nothing. I led the army into the city. I broke the soldiers that came against us, and that was the end."

"Except for the girl," Nicaea said quietly.

Arthras sat up. "What do you know of it?"

"I watched it, from that window there," she said, pointing to the curtains. "You can see the Scrivener's Plaza from there, and I saw all of it. It was far away, but after, one of the servants said it was a girl. A girl who wielded the wind and the lightning. They said she had killed you."

He snorted. "No, she just buried me in ruin, and the stone melted around me. I had to break loose when I woke up."

"Who was she?" she said.

"I don't know. I spoke to her. I told her to stand aside. I did not want to fight her. We are alike, she and I. But she would not listen to me. She was angry about all her papers scattered in the street." He scoffed again at the idea. "Papers."

"Did you kill her?" she said.

He shrugged. "I don't think so. I didn't see her corpse when I woke. She must have fled." He shook his head. "Though I don't know why she would. She could have destroyed the whole army."

"Perhaps she did not want to," Nicaea said.

"Why not? We invaded her city, we burned her papers and her books. She was angry about that." Arthras heaped the many pillows against the head of the bed and leaned back against them. It was very, very comfortable.

Nicaea laughed a little, turned and lay against him. "Not everyone is like you." She touched his hair, toying with the small braids over his ears. "I wonder where the power comes from."

"From the gods," Arthras said. "Bora has touched me, given me her strength to fight for my people." There was no doubt in his mind of that, or very little.

"Don't all your people venerate Thax?" she said. Her accent speaking his tongue was so smooth, he was surprised to hear her use the imperial name.

"He is named Tacis," he said. "And do not pretend you know anything of our beliefs."

"Teach me," she said, running her hand over his chest lightly. "I would know what you believe."

Arthras was irritated, but not for any reason he could name. "We revere Tacis, yes. He was the first king of the Almanni. He brought fire down from the mountain, and he taught us to forge iron and ride horses. His blood runs in all of our kings, even down to Usiric."

"But Usiric is an usurper, or so I thought," Nicaea said. "He was a thane of King Sauderic, and he took the crown after the king died in battle."

"Some say that," Arthras said, uncomfortable. "Sauderic died when I was only a boy. I don't remember him. And they said Usiric was his half-brother, gotten on a slavewoman by Sauderic's father. Many times the king's thanes bear blood kinship to him, whether acknowledged or not." He shrugged. "The blood runs true, or so the oracles say. When they crowned him he trod upon the sacred stone and it sang for him."

"And what sound would it make for you?" she said. He didn't answer, for he had been thinking the same thing, but it did not seem right to say so. She shifted and slid her leg over his. "Tell me of the goddess you follow."

"Bora is the goddess of war and of the wild. She pursues her prey and drags it down with her teeth, she slays men with her claws and drinks their blood. She is stronger than any man, and she puts them over her shoulders and breaks them in half. It is proper to sacrifice enemies slain in battle to her, so she may give favor to you." He was quiet for a moment, remembering long nights in the wilds. "When I was young, I had to hunt for my family, and I learned well to honor Bora."

"Where is your family?" she said softly, and he grunted.

"Dead," he said, not wanting to say more. He tugged on the three small braids over his left ear, and then he snorted. He would not wear them any longer; they marked a man who was a servant of others, and he would serve no man any longer. He got out of the bed, leaving Nicaea alone. "I want a knife," he said.

"Here," she said, and she reached for the small table beside the bed. To his surprise, part of it slid out, revealing a shallow space. She took a small knife from it and unsheathed it. "Will this do?"

He grunted again and sat on the bed. His hand found the three thin braids and held them out. "Cut these off."

"Very well," she said. "Why?"

"They mark a thrall," he said. "Each braid is a year of service, and each year one is cut off until you are free. If you perform a great deed one may be cut off sooner. I will wear them no more." He looked at her. "It is most proper for a woman to cut them."

She quirked her small smile at just one corner of her mouth. "I will, then."

He felt her take hold of his braids, and then the knife came close. He had a moment of fear, worrying that she would cut him, but then he remembered arrows glancing from his flesh and almost laughed. She could not hurt him if she tried, and if she tried, then he would have learned something useful.

He heard the brittle, dry sound of the edge sawing at his hair, and then again, and again. She cursed under her breath and tried again, and then she shook her head. "Your hair won't cut – it's like wire."

Arthras pulled a braid up and looked at it. It did not look any different, but if it could withstand the heat he generated, then it must be different. He took the knife from her hand, coiled the three braids around his fist, and set the knife. Nicaea leaned back to give him room, and then he cut hard, once, and severed the hair from his head.

He looked at the braids in his hand. "They should be burned, but I don't think they would." He looked at her, held them out. "Keep them for me."

She seemed amused. "I will." She took the knife and coiled the braids around it, put everything back in the hidden slide and pushed it closed. She looked at him. "Now you are a free man, what will you do?"

He didn't know how to answer that. This was the palace of the Autarch, and this was his woman. He should be satisfied, and yet he was not. Surely he had not been gifted with this power only to take one city?

"If you stay here, it will be a disaster," she said. "Do you understand that?"

"Tell me what you mean," he said.

"It is early summer. My husband will have gone to Orneas, to the south. There he will have time and money to raise a new army and return here. The walls will not stop them – you tore a hole in the walls. Even if they were rebuilt, you would be besieged in here, without enough food for all of you and all the people who still remain. There would be rioting before winter was out. It happens here more years than you would believe, even without an invasion." She lay back against the pillows. "You caught him off guard, but he'll come back with greater numbers and crush you."

"Not me," he said. "He can't defeat me."

"How many of your fellow Almanni will pay the price, then? You may be unconquerable, but the others are not." She watched him with narrowed eyes, careful and considering.

He looked at her. "You think we should go on then. Move south and attack Orneas." The city was only a name to him, a place so far from his homelands it meant nothing to him, like a dream.

"It is a greater city than this one," she said. "It is the seat of the Church of Attis, and the coffers of the Archpriest overflow with silver and gold. It is a much richer prize than Ilion."

"You want revenge on your husband," he said. "Should Almanni die for that?"

"They will die in any case," she said. "Better to die taking a great prize than defending a poor one. If you took Orneas you would control Othria, and from there you could negotiate directly with the emperor. You would have a position of power, not simply a stolen city and plundered food stores for the winter."

He looked hard at her. "You speak as if I lead my people. I don't."

"You will," she said. "Your king will not be able to let you lift yourself so high, so quickly. He will try to get rid of you, one way or another. When he does, you must kill him and become king in his place."

The idea of it stunned him. Arthras shook his head, got up from the bed and paced the cool stone floor. "I cannot be a king. I do not have the blood."

"You have the power of a god," Nicaea said. "That is all the mark of favor you need."

"I will not kill the king," he said. "No, his men would never follow me."

"Not all, but some would. You cannot simply be killed and gotten rid of. They will come to terms with that and decide they will follow you." The calm certainty in her tone both elated and frightened him. He knew she was probably right, and he was not sure whether he liked that or not. He remembered the thanes at their feast, the sneering face of Ethric Gold-Handed. *He* would not forgive. That he knew.

"Even if they did follow me, I am a hunter and a fighter. I am not a noble, or a thane. I don't know how to rule," he said. It galled him to admit it, but it was true.

Nicaea smiled slowly, a hard smile. "I do."

Chapter Eight

WARNING OF DANGER

Karana was so glad to have a bath, even a lukewarm one, that she almost fell asleep in the basin. Thessala's sanctuary was built in the ruin of an ancient baths, and some of the pools were still intact. The cisterns that gathered rainwater filled it easily, and a few rocks were heated in the fire and then dropped in to warm the water. It was still rather tepid, but welcome.

She gladly soaked herself in the water, wishing there was a room for steam, but she would take what she could get. It had been days since she felt clean. She soaked her braids and squeezed them out, then again. She didn't want to go to the time and trouble it would take to unwind them and brush them out, so she settled for washing the dirt and salt spray out of them. After, there was some unscented oil to rub into her skin and then a little bronze strigil to scrape off the excess. Carinthians liked to oil and scrape first, then loll for hours in hot water, but she had no patience for that.

There was no mirror in this room, just a lamp to see by, and when she climbed out she looked down at herself, taking time to turn and bend and try to see all of the scars she bore now. They looked like lightning, or like little rivers under her skin, darker than her brown flesh but not raised. When she pushed on them the skin around them changed color, but the scars remained, and it seemed they were slightly numb, as if they felt touch less keenly. That frightened her, because what if more scars marked her whenever she touched lightning? She could become numbed all over, unable to feel.

She took a length of thread and set to plucking out the small hairs of her body, as she had since she was a girl. Legs and armpits and between her legs. It was harder to pull the hairs out, and the thread broke many times. She was annoyed by the time she was done and could dress again. She would have to find other clothes, because the ones the old woman had found for her would need to be cleaned.

Out under the stars it was cool and pleasant, and she looked up at the thin, silvery clouds drifting across the sky. Tentative, she felt outward with the new inner sense she seemed to posses, felt the masses of air sliding slowly over the city. Warm air rose over the harbor, cooled, and drifted back down over the sea to be pushed inland again, making a gentle breeze. There was a pleasing smoothness to it all, like the surface of a fresh jar of honey.

She heard voices and wondered if there were always people up and about in this place, but then she heard raised voices, and her heart thumped in her chest. She thought of the other encampment of refugees and cursed herself. What if something happened to them while she was having a silly bath?

The voices grew louder, and a general commotion spread through the sanctuary. Karana hurried outside and into the courtyard, feet bare on the cracked, ancient paving stones. She saw people hurrying away from the entrance, and then she saw a pressed knot of armored men advancing toward her and she felt a sick swirl of fear and anger in her guts.

She stepped out into the center of the long court and waited, letting the others pass around her, getting away from the soldiers. There were a dozen of them at least, and she had an impression there might be more outside, waiting for trouble. They all carried spears and shields, and they looked nervous. When they saw her they drew up, slowed their steps.

"Captain!" Thessala's rich voice came from behind Karana and she almost sighed with relief. It was a tremendous weight lifted just to not be alone. She turned and saw the other woman emerge from inside, wrapped in her white robe with her face hooded. She walked with a slight limp on her left leg, which Karana had not noticed before.

"Captain, what is happening here?" Thessala's tone was mild, but there was danger in it. Karana knew these men did not understand how much danger.

She had a sense these two had met before, and the guard captain looked uncomfortable. He took off his helmet and tucked it under his arm. "Lady Thessala. I don't want trouble, but I am here to look for a newcomer to the city." He looked significantly at Karana. "A dark-skinned girl who assaulted some of my men today. I am also told she has claimed powers that the Archpriest has deemed heretical. I have been searching for her, and I was told she might be here."

Karana stepped forward before he could say anything else. "I am she," she said, her heart going faster.

The man looked her up and down, seemed skeptical. "You assaulted my guards?"

"Your guards were robbing the refugees as they came into the port, taking what little they had left, and they attempted to assault me," she said. The anger at the injustice of it was still fresh, and it made her jaw tighten. "I defended myself."

He still looked as if he did not believe her. "It is unlawful to lay hands upon a city guardsman."

"To be fair, I did not touch most of them, only the man who touched me," she said.

"That is still a crime," he said, stepping closer.

"So a guard may assault and rob me, and that is legal, but if I defend myself that is a crime?" she said.

He nodded. "Indeed."

"Well, I don't agree with that," she said.

He gestured his men forward. "I am ordered to arrest you," he said.

Thassala stepped forward, and Karana laid a hand on her arm to still her. "No. If there is a fight, your people will be in danger."

Thessala glanced around at the sanctuary, seeing anxious faces peering out at them. She sighed angrily, but she nodded. "You are right."

"I will come back, but until then, you must be here to protect these people," Karana said.

Thessala nodded, and Karana saw the glint of her eyes from inside her hood. She wondered what these men would say if they got a look at her face. Their mental definition of heresy might be considerably expanded.

Karana stepped away from her and the guards grabbed her by the arms and dragged her off her feet. It was so sudden and unnecessary that she was too stunned for a moment to react, but then she got her feet back under her and wrenched free of them. They grabbed for her again, and she shoved one of them hard enough to send him off his feet and he knocked over two others. The rest of the guards jumped back, pointing their spears at her, and she held up her hands.

"Enough," she said, keeping her voice calm. "Captain, I will go with you, but I will not be handled like that."

The captain swallowed and looked at her, then at the three men picking themselves up, and he swallowed again, visibly. "You are under arrest. You have to be chained."

Karana sighed and held out her arms. "Very well."

Another guard came forward, and he shackled her wrists while she held still, and then the captain gestured and the soldiers formed up around her. She held her head up as she walked with them, though deep inside she was completely and shiveringly afraid.

☙

They walked her through the city, and she found the weight of the shackles was less bothersome than the way they clinked as she moved. It was a constant reminder that she was chained. The soldiers walked close around her, crowding her, but also hiding her from anyone who looked, and she found that a small mercy, as she felt an irrational shame at being seen like this.

She didn't know the city, but they led her continuously uphill, and she noted that the soldiers grew winded while she did not. Ahead of them loomed a massive edifice studded with high towers and clean white walls. It looked as if a half-dozen smaller palaces had been haphazardly stacked on top of one another. She saw the forked sign of Attis on the banners and blinked. "Is this the Citadel of the Archpriest?"

They were closer, passing other guards, underneath a vast arch. Karana craned her neck to look up at it. "This is the Arch of Thesian, built to commemorate his victory at Cerasia," she said. "I've always wanted to see the bas reliefs."

"Quiet, you," one of the soldiers grunted, giving her a shove. Karana bounced off the man in front of her, almost tripped, and then she lost some of her temper. She twisted her arms and yanked hard on the iron shackles, and the metal gave under her hands like clay. The links snapped and she was free, and she turned to face the man who had pushed her. He almost ran into her, and she grabbed him by the shoulders of his armor and lifted him off his feet, thrilling at how easy it was.

"I *said* I would not be handled like that," she said, her voice raised, and the others jumped back from her. She let the man drop and he collapsed, scuttled away while the rest of them pointed their spears at her. She turned to face the captain, who looked at her as if she were something terrifying, and the wind picked up and gusted around them, billowing her head wrap so she had to grab at it. "Captain, enough of this nonsense. Where are you taking me?"

He looked side to side, at his men, and then he put his hand on his sword. "You are under arrest. I'm taking you to a cell."

"I'm being imprisoned without a hearing? I am entitled to a hearing before a magistrate." Karana knew her law only fairly well. The fact that she was not a citizen of Orneas told against her, but she resolved not to be docile about it. "Or do you not wish me to see a magistrate because your men's behavior is indefensible?"

He scowled at her. "You are arrested for heresy. You are not entitled to a hearing. A legate will interrogate you when it is your turn. Until then you will be confined."

Karana grew angry. They had never intended to play fair with her at all. She gripped the shackles that still hung on her wrists and wrenched them off, the metal making little squeaks as it bent and then snapped. She threw the twisted metal on the ground in front of her. "I doubt that very much. I have been reasonable about this, but I will not languish in a cell on anyone's whim." She was getting angry, and she felt the wind stirring around her. Clouds grew and thickened above, blotting out the stars.

The captain looked nervous, and his men edged away from her, muttering to themselves. He tried to put on a brave front, drew his sword and held it at his side. "Stop it. Whatever you are doing, stop!"

Karana almost laughed. "I'm not doing anything, yet." She could not help calling down a little wind, and it pushed at the men and scattered dead leaves in the courtyard. "Now if you say the Archpriest accuses me of heresy, then take me to him, and I will discuss it – with him." She reached into the sky with her mind, found a thread and plucked it. The gathering clouds flickered, and a low rumble of thunder passed overhead, distant yet unmistakable. The guards stared at her, and the captain wavered.

"Don't make me force the issue," she said. "I truly don't want to do that."

He sighed. "I can't take you to the Archpriest. I will pass you along to someone else." He sheathed his sword and gave his belt a hard tug. "I won't take any more responsibility for this matter."

Karana let out a long breath and nodded. "Very wise, Captain. Very wise."

☙

Karana had never expected to see the Citadel, at least not from the inside. She was handed over by the guard captain to anther pair of guards, who seemed not to know what to do with her, but handed her off to an official, who looked bewildered and contemptuous, until the guards whispered fiercely to him, and then he looked at her as though she were a serpent. She was growing tired of this.

At last the official summoned another one, who led her onward through rooms so opulent she could barely believe them. The carvings on the pillars and balustrades were so elaborate they seemed impossible, and the rugs were so ornate and richly-colored she hesitated to step on them, felt them soft under her bare feet. She began to feel poorly dressed and rude, especially when accompanied by an official who wore enough gold and jewels crusted on his collar and coat to make for a dazzling array of glinting light whenever he moved. Everyone she passed, even the servants, had a sort of slouching, well-fed look.

They progressed down a hall so tall she could barely see the roof in the dim light. She didn't know how late it was, possibly close to midnight. The whole edifice began to make her feel small and powerless, which was no doubt an intended effect. The official led her to a door and turned to stop her. "When you approach His Eminence, you will bow six times, and then, as a commoner, you will kneel and press your face to the floor. He will give you -"

She brushed past him and shoved the heavy doors open, stepped through into a hall that was taller than it was long.

A single strip of woven rug led from the entrance to the foot of a three-stepped dais on which stood a bronze throne adorned with lions and roofed over with a marble portico carved in the likeness of an oncoming storm. On the throne was an old man in a long, red robe embroidered with gold, and on his head was the golden skullcap of the priesthood. He looked up when she entered, startled.

There were at least twenty guards lining the sides of the room, and they all tensed as she strode purposefully down the length of the room and stopped before the throne. She felt a bit dizzy with her own daring, but she was not going to rub her face in the dirt for anyone. The Archpriest watched her with an uncertain but measuring eye as she came to the foot of the dais and bowed with what she felt was appropriate respect.

He arched a brow. "It is customary for a common-born seeker of an audience to show proper respect for my office, upon being received."

"Allow me to delay that until I have determined how much respect is due," she said, and she heard the guards grunt and gasp in consternation. She glanced at them, and she wondered how well these silver-gilt men would fare against barbarians. She doubted the post of personal guard to the Archpriest offered frequent hardships or tests of fighting skill.

"You tread upon the frontiers of blasphemy," he said, his voice cold.

"Do you allow your guards to rob and assault refugees who come to the city seeking shelter from war and privation?" she said, as though he had not spoken. Her heart was racing, and part of her could not believe she was daring to accuse the Archpriest in his very own stronghold. Yet she was angry, more angry, she realized, than she had expected.

He frowned. "That is not the issue at hand."

"But it is, it is the very heart of the matter. For am I not accused of using force against your guards when they were intent on that very activity?" She forced herself to slow her speech. She felt the winds about the Citadel growing restless as she grew angrier.

"You are accused of using witchcraft to arrogate for yourself powers only to be wielded by the Divine Attis himself," he said. "A far more serious matter than simple assault."

"One thing at a time, Eminence," she said.

He narrowed his eyes, then actually smiled a little. "Well, I suppose that is fair. You are a proud girl, aren't you?"

"Not usually, no. I am simply at the end of my patience. I came to your city as a refugee, having escaped from the fall of Ilion, and rather than help, I find the men in your employ stealing from the people who came here for safety. When I objected to this, I was threatened, and I defended myself. All I have done since I came here is keep to myself as best I can. And now you send men in the middle of the night to chain me and cast me into a cell?" She caught her breath. "Yes, I am angry." A rumble of thunder came from outside, and the Archpriest glanced up uneasily.

There was a silence, while he studied her. "You were at Ilion?" he said.

She nodded. "Yes."

"They say you did battle with a giant and called down a storm to defeat him," he said, sounding as if it were absurd. She supposed it sounded that way.

"He was not a giant," she said. "But otherwise, that is near to the truth."

He held her gaze, as if waiting for her to laugh, but she simply stared back at him. "I have no desire for trouble, Eminence," she said. "And I am not a priest or a ruler, but if I were, I would be far more concerned with the army of Almanni who could be here very soon, than with someone such as me."

He narrowed his eyes at her. "Do you deny that you practice witchcraft?"

"I do deny that. I am a scribe, not a witch," she said.

"Then, if you swear to abjure such things, and abstain from violence while in my city, I will forgive your transgressions and set you free," he said.

"I was free when I came here," she said. "And I leave free. I came as a courtesy, Eminence. I wish no trouble. Give me none, and I will return none." She bowed again. "Good evening." She turned deliberately and gave him her back, hearing more gasps, and she walked straight-backed out of the hall. Perhaps she was foolish to hope she could deter further trouble. But escalation would only lead to terrible consequences. She would not be responsible for starting down that road.

☙

Thessala could not sleep, found herself pacing the quiet halls of her sanctuary, moving carefully on her lame left foot. Broken many years ago, it had never healed properly, and it seemed even the touch of the divine power had done nothing to repair it. She went to her private herb garden and sat beside the fountain, always calmed by the sound of the water. The starlight was bright to her, brighter than it used to be, and under the glow of the star, it was like day, or a full moon. She found now that she was able to see in almost complete darkness. It simply always seemed to be dusk to her.

The weather was as restless as she was, the wind shifting about from point to point, and clouds coming in to tatter across the clear sky. She wondered if Karana was responsible for it. She cursed herself a hundred ways for letting the girl go alone – she did not know how brutal the Archpriest's guards could be. Perhaps she was powerful enough to protect herself, but she was not wary.

But she knew Karana had been right. They could not both go, and leave the sanctuary unprotected, and if they had fought the guards here, the violence could have spread, become unmanageable. She had too many people here who depended on her.

By the starlight she slid the loose sleeve back from her hand and arm, held them up and looked at them. She turned her hand one way, then the other. She watched the way the scales shifted as she moved. It was still strange to her to think of it as her skin. She had been covered for a week now, keeping her closest helpers from seeing her face. They all suspected something was wrong, but none of them pressed her. Thessala had held this place together by her own will for almost five years, and they all respected her for it.

Thunder rumbled, and she thought of Karana again, hoping she was all right. Hoping her coming did not mean the end of her peace here. In this place Thessala had found a kind of absolution, she did not want to lose it. She already worked hard to fend off the robbers who wanted to fleece her charges, the guards and officials who wanted to take the building and the land. She had cajoled, and shamed, and stalled, and browbeat to have her way.

Now it seemed like everything was ending. The star had changed things. Its coming was the herald of dooms. She left her garden and went out into the courtyard, looked up at it. Half the sky was dark and scattered with stars, the rest covered by the shining tail of the omen star. The head of it was small, no more than a spark, but the wake it left seemed to cover half the firmament, and in the upper reaches of the sky, the clouds flamed with strange colors.

She heard thunder again, and then she heard the tramp of many feet. She turned and looked to the entrance, and there she saw another gathering of shields. Armed men crowded between the pillars of the arch with armor and swords and torches, and she felt a rush in her belly and a sour taste at the back of her throat. She came down the shallow steps, walked down the length of the court as the men began to fan out. There were a lot of them; twenty or thirty strong.

One at the head started giving directions, gesturing. "Spread out, go through the whole place. We're to clean out this rat's nest."

So this was it. They got Karana out, and now they came for her as well while they were divided. She went to meet them. "Stop!" Thessala said, knowing her voice had great resonance when she raised it. "Stop this! By what orders do you -"

The lead man moved very fast. Before she even realized it he had his sword in hand and flashing for her neck. She felt a slight blow, like the sting of a reed, and his sword made a sound like a hammer on a tree trunk. He staggered back, dropping his bent sword and shaking his hand, and Thessala felt something let go in her guts, a terrible mixture of fear and anger.

She stared at him while he stared at her, and the others hesitated, unbelieving. Slowly, she reached up and cast back her hood, unpinned her cloak and shrugged it off, leaving her in just her dress, arms and head bared for all to see. She saw the fear in their faces, their eyes widening and lips drawing back from their teeth.

"Very well," she said. "Have it your way." There was an anger in her like she had never felt before, almost uncontrollable, and she lifted her hands and closed her fists and clenched them until the knuckles cracked like neck bones.

Chapter Nine

Broken in Pieces

Karana made her way out of the palace, unescorted and trying to remember how she came here. It was late and there were few lamps, far too few to illuminate such large spaces. Her heart was pounding and she breathed evenly, trying to get control of herself. Part of her was horrified that she had spoken to the Archpriest as she had, part of her was elated. She felt the winds outside shifting and swirling restlessly with her mood and she tried to calm them as well. It did not help that she wanted to fling her arms wide and call the storm in. She wanted to feel her power breathe all over her, to enhance this dizzy sensation of freedom.

Yet there was a kind of fear in that sensation, like a yawning abyss. If she could truly do whatever she wanted, then what constraints were there upon her? It was brought home to her very strongly that while many people called themselves free, so many of them had few choices in their lives, free or not. There were always limits upon what people could do, and now many of those limits were gone, and she felt as if she had stepped off a great precipice.

She walked down a long colonnade and looked out over the city, seeing the clouds gathering over the harbor, and above that, the blaze of the star, turning the clouds into fiery outlines, dancing with strange colors. Was it really the cause of all this? Because of Arthras, Ilion had fallen, and because of that she was here, at odds with the Archpriest himself. She shook her head, unable to fit her mind around all the strange variables and changes. There had to be more of them, more people like Arthras and Thessala and herself. They could be anywhere, anyone, given powers she could not begin to imagine. If that was the case, then the entire order of the world was about to be overturned.

Lost in thought, she left the halls and stepped out into the open, started down a wide stair. She only looked up when she realized there were men gathered at the foot. She blinked, her steps slowing, and then she heard footsteps rushing behind her.

She didn't have time to turn all the way before a spearhead flashed in the light and rammed into her side. She felt a sharp pain and was knocked off her feet, sent rolling down the steps out of control. The men at the bottom rushed up, swords flashing, and then they started hammering at her, blades striking her head, her arms, her legs. The blows felt sharp and they stung, and her panicked mind imagined she felt blood. Surely they were killing her. She screamed, struggled to get away.

A hand grabbed for her head and snagged on her scarf, tore it loose, and then that same hand, or another, caught in her hair and pulled her head back. She saw the blade of a sword pass her face, felt the cold touch like a thin line on her skin, and then it dragged across her throat quick and hard, making her gag.

They dropped her, and she choked, clawed at her neck with shaking hands, and found her skin whole and uncut. Someone kicked her, hard, in the side, and she grunted. She was certain pain would soon consume her whole body, and she tensed against it. Another sword stabbed into her and she felt her clothes rip – the only clothes she had – and that was what made her become suddenly angry.

She got to her feet, and looking down she saw her clothes were torn, but there was no blood on her anywhere. The pain she had imagined seemed to melt away, and she realized they had not cut her, not even once. She looked at the ring of men, all of them breathing hard and pale under their helmets, and she saw their faces draw down in terror, and then the wind began to rise.

ఌ

Thessala gritted her teeth as the guard captain drew a long knife from his side and came at her. She was shaking but furious, and she realized she did not know what to do. She was no warrior; she had never struck anyone in her life, in earnest or in play. She knew nothing of blades or armor or shields. In fact she had never deliberately harmed anyone with her hands. She watched the man as he came closer, saw how afraid he was, and then he lunged in, grabbed her shoulder, and slammed the knife into her belly.

She felt it more than she had felt the sword blow, but it was still like being poked with a broom handle. She grunted a little and bent forward when he struck, but it was more from a mental flinching than any real sensation.

They were eye to eye, his wide and shocked behind his helmet, and Thessala grabbed him by the front of his armor, felt her fingers punch through his tunic and the mail under it, the metal like knitted wool under her hands. He gasped and clutched at her, and she lifted him easily off his feet and threw him away. She meant to toss him back among his men, but instead he sailed over their heads, bounced off an old column, and crashed down to the cracked paving stones with a cry.

The other men brought their spears up, the points shaking like reeds in the wind, and they clustered together with their shields held edge to edge, the rims clattering as they knocked together. They started to come towards her, but they were slow, and they crept to one side as each man hid as much as he could behind his neighbor's bulwark.

Thessala knew they would not give way – they would have to be taught a lesson, and she wanted to teach it. She felt a burning down in her guts, and it was a restless anger like she had never known in her life. It built and built, and she was afraid she would burst into fire if she did not give vent to it. She looked to the sides and saw faces there, her charges, her wards all watching from the shadows, shocked to see her as she was now.

The guards came closer, gathering to rush her, and she brought up her hands, looked at her right one as she closed it slowly into a fist, clenching it tight until it shook. She looked at the men and tasted bile in her throat, and then she went to meet them.

A sound came from her throat, and she did not realize it was her until she opened her mouth and it came out like the scream of a lioness. They stopped, cringing back, but then she came close and the guards lunged in, stabbing with their spears. They struck her arms and her chest and she felt the points dig against her scales and then refuse to pierce her skin. She caught the first shield she could reach and dragged it down, cocked her hand back, and slammed her fist into the man's helm.

To her shock, the iron crumpled under her blow like paper, and blood splashed out of the visor. His head snapped to one side with a hideous sound, and he flew back ten paces and landed in a splatter of red that looked black in the starlight. Thessala stepped back, stunned, and then the men rushed in and battered at her with their shields until she snarled and struck at them with her fists. The shields split and splintered under her blows, and the guards fell back, crying out, clutching dangling, broken arms. She caught one man and lifted him over her head, threw him into two others.

They ran for the entrance, and she came after them, kicking the ones who did not run fast enough. They turned at bay and rushed her again, spears hammering at her, and she swatted them away and then crashed into their line, bowling them over, shoving them back so they hit one another or bounced off the walls. Her arms ached to hit harder, and it was hard to rein herself in. Her hands shook as she knocked them down, scattered them when she could have killed them. She drove them back through the entrance, and then screamed after them as they ran from her. In a fit of wrath she turned and smashed her fist into the ancient pillar that marked the entryway, and the marble shattered under her blow and the whole thing spilled down to crash into the street, splintering the ancient flagstones.

�

Wind lashed down past the towers and walls, moaning through the stonework, and then it dashed across the steps and sent the guards staggering. Karana felt her braids come loose and coil and snap around her face like ropes, and then thunder cracked overhead. She felt a rage in her like she had never known, and she knew without doubt that she could call down the wind and the lightning and desolate the entire Citadel if she wanted. It was a dizzying moment of power.

Part of her shied away from it, and she clenched her fists, controlling herself, trying to hold in the energy that seemed to struggle to get free. Lightning stroked keen overhead, lighting the courtyard in a blazing blue fire. She saw green sparks spray from the iron peaks of gates and fences, and the guards flinched from the thunderclap that followed.

She seized the nearest man and gripped him by his tunic, hoisted him off his feet, though she had to lean back to do it. She wrenched the sword from his hand and put the edge against his neck under the rim of his helm. "Remember this, the next time you think to raise your hands to me!" She pulled the sword away and then let the man drop to tumble down the stairs. She threw the sword after him, the steel ringing on the marble.

The wind was growing, and she knew she had to get control of it. The other guards hunkered against the unpredictable gusts, gripping their shields, which threatened to become sails in the swelling gale. Karana closed her eyes and held up a hand, closed it slowly as she gathered the power in around her. The air felt heavy and humid as she pulled it in, and then she let it loose, and it lashed outward in a wave.

The guards were blown off their feet, reeling away to roll down the steps or roll over the balustrade and drop to the stone below. The wave ripped up planters and statues and flung them like leaves, and then the force of it struck the walls of the courtyard and she heard the terrible sound of dozens of windows being blown apart in a single moment.

She staggered at the shock of the blow, stunned at her own power. It was one thing to imagine she could tear the Citadel apart, another to realize it was true. Then she realized the air she had driven out was rushing back in, and she could not just stop it – she had to direct it. The gale coursed around her, thunder cracked, and then she was lifted up. She only had a moment to realize what was happening, and try to control it, and then she was airborne, hurled upward by the invisible force of the air itself.

For a moment she saw the whole of it – the Citadel spread out below her with all the intricacies of its many courtyards and towers and bridges and walls, and then she lost her balance and began to tumble over and over in the air, screaming as she realized she was actually flying, and that she had lost all control of her trajectory. She sailed over the walls, clawing at the air, panicked, and then she plummeted down and smashed through a tiled roof, falling through in a cascade of broken crockery.

༃

By the time Karana returned to the sanctuary, it was very late, and she was surprised to not be exhausted. Perhaps she was invulnerable to weariness now, as much as she was to swords. She still flinched when she thought of the spearpoints digging into her, and when she felt the places where wounds should be she found them tender and bruised, but the bruises faded with unnatural speed.

She saw the tumbled stone at the entrance, and her steps quickened. An old man with one leg stood guard at the entryway, a brass bell in his hands, but his eyes lit up when he saw her. "Lady," he said, smiling with his few teeth. "Lady!"

Karana smiled and went through, saw blood on the wall, and then a shape under a sheet, red staining the linen on one side. Others came and gathered around her, speaking softly, putting out their hands to touch her clothes. "Bless you," she said, mostly so they would step away. "Bless you."

They made way for Thessala, and she turned to see the other woman going bareheaded, no more concealing herself under a hood. Thessala wore her white robe, her long hair in the single thick braid draped around her shoulders like a snake. In the dim light of star and lantern, her eyes glittered like polished gold.

"What happened?" Karana said.

"The guards came to drive us out," Thessala said. "Once you were gone, I suppose they thought they were safe."

"You've been here for years," Karana said.

"Yes, and they have wanted to evict me for years," Thessala said, beckoning. "The Archpriest does not want actual homeless, needy people crowding his perfect city of faith. Every diseased child or deformed infant is a reminder that Attis is either not omnipotent, or not benevolent. Either one is unacceptable." She led Karana inside, into the shadows of the sanctuary. "I don't know what has driven them to act so rashly, but things are changing. I cannot even be certain that the orders came from the Archpriest, as there are many officials who could give such an order. But he would certainly not be displeased by it." She sighed. "I had to drive them off."

Karana looked a question back the way they came, and Thessala looked down at her hands. "I didn't mean to kill him," she said. "I hit him, and I do not know my own strength." She shook her head. "It was an accident." She stopped suddenly, reached out and caught Karana's dress, put her fingers through a hole. "What happened to you?"

"It was very interesting," Karana said. "I met with the Archpriest, and he as much as said he would leave me alone if I made no more trouble. Then, on my way out, I was attacked by at least a dozen men."

"That was the thunder I heard, then," Thessala said. "I wondered about it."

Karana leaned back against the wall and sighed, closing her eyes. "I didn't mean that. I get angry and it is hard to control. I tried not to let it get loose." She puffed breath through her cheeks. "But yes, I had to defend myself, and I. . . I flew away."

Thessala blinked. "You flew?"

Karana nodded. "Yes, or rather, I threw myself into the sky with wind and then fell." She laughed. "Maybe I can get better at that. Right now as a method of travel it leaves a great deal to be desired." She looked outside. "Do you suppose they will be back?"

Thessala nodded. "Yes. I. . . killed one of them, they will not let it pass. They will come and this time they will have more men."

They entered Thessala's little garden, and Karana was surprised by how soothing the sound of the fountain was. She sat down on the alabaster bench, the stone's coolness seeping through her clothes. "I don't know what to do. I don't know why they are doing any of this, so I don't know how to make them stop."

"They are afraid," Thessala said. "They know the barbarians may come here, and they are afraid they will lose the city."

"Then they should be preparing, gathering in those refugees who can help, organizing." Karana shook her head. "I have seen no sign of any preparations."

"Ah, but you see, they do not fear losing the city for their own sake, or for the sake of the people. They only fear losing their own power." Thessala sat down beside her. "You have been given power, and now they know it. I have been given power, and now they know it. They know it and they will panic, if they are not already panicked. Also, the Autarch is here, and that is surely causing infighting on a scale we cannot imagine."

"Here?" Karana was surprised. "I would expect him to go to the capital."

"And face the wrath of the emperor for losing Ilion? No, he will try to gather a new army here and march north to retake the city from the barbarians. The Archpriest will not want to help him." Thessala toyed with her braid.

"If he could drive the Almanni out, it would protect Orneas," Karana said.

"Oh I am certain he would like to defeat the barbarians," Thessala said. "But he will have no reason to wish to help his enemy, the Autarch. If he won a victory it would risk making a hero of him, and neither the Archpriest nor the emperor would like that. They will both wish to extend the Autarch's failure until he can be removed from power, and possibly blamed for all of it and executed."

Karana groaned and covered her eyes for a moment. "Politics." She felt a terrible frustration, and wished she could simply force the powers of the empire to behave themselves. It occurred to her that she probably could, but then she wondered how many other problems would spring up in the wake of every one she solved. Nothing was so simple as it appeared. She had read enough histories to know that, it was just strange to think of such things applied to the world around her. "I always think that men will be sensible."

"The only sense would be in assuming that men will always be foolish," Thessala said.

"If they are coming back, we should prepare, and plan. We have people to protect, and not just here. If they wanted to drive you out, then they may have moved on the refugee camps as well." Karana stood up, tugged at a rip in her dress and felt annoyed. They had to put holes in her only dress.

"I would have heard, if they had done that," Thessala said. "I think they came here at night because it is small and would make a good start. They will return at first light, if I had to guess, and they will strike the refugee camps at the same time. Well, not all at once. They don't have enough men for that."

"Well then, we need to prepare," Karana said. "Because I don't intend to let them do that. What do you think?"

Thessala nodded and looked at her. Karana liked seeing her face, seeing her show herself. She held up a scaled hand, and Karana clasped it. "Good," she said. "We had better get started. There's only a few hours until dawn."

Chapter Ten

Blood and Oaths

Arthras did not sleep well. His body was not tired, and he tossed and turned, feeling restless. At last he fell into a sort of dreamy half-state, and he saw the face of the storm girl again, her eyes dark and wide and determined. He saw the flash of lightning, so bright it blinded him, and then he sat up, found the sun was up. Nicaea slept beside him, the bed large enough that his restlessness had not awakened her, or perhaps she was used to it. He reached out to touch her, then drew his hand back. He wanted to be alone.

Naked, he went through the rooms, looking at everything. The tapestries and statues were so rich and beautiful, and yet so useless. A statue of gold did not feed hungry men, it did not make iron swords to fight with or buy horses. How much waste there was just in these chambers. He remembered the encampments last winter, the cries of hungry infants, the screams of horses when they were butchered for meat. All the while, as old men died of hunger and women starved until they no longer had milk for their children, this place had been here, with silk-draped women sleeping on soft beds and dwelling in this opulence. It made him angry.

He found a bath chamber, with a pool of water set in the tiled floor. He crouched down beside it and splashed water on his arms and his chest. He put his head under and came up with water running down his face. He slicked back his wet hair and started when he felt the place where the braids were not. He had taken that for himself, giving himself freedom. It did not seem real, and yet what man could deny him? He wiped his face and then pissed in the water. He wondered how it got in here, and how long it took to dry up.

He dried himself on a hanging and then went back to the bedchamber, found his clothes and donned them. He wore armor, but he did not need it, and the clothes did not fit very well. The tunic was too wide across his shoulders, and the pants were too short. He tucked them into his boots, so it didn't show as much. He looked around at the room, the sleeping woman on his bed, and wondered what he was to do now. The city was taken. Was Nicaea right? Would they be attacked again? He thought of Orneas to the south, an imaginary place. He did not know what it would look like. He had expected Ilion to be paved with gold, but it was just dirty and crowded. From a distance the towers were startling, and they looked unreal in the light of dawn, but up close the city was far from magical.

He went out into the hall and one of the slave girls came and bowed low to him. "My lord, one of your. . . companions comes with a message from your king."

He grunted. The king sending for him could mean more trouble, or it could mean they intended to treat him with respect. He was not worried for his safety, regardless. He nodded at the girl and she led him down the hall. At the top of the wide stair, there were three men who he did not know, but one of them wore a gilded helm, and so he could only be one of Usiric's companions. The man inclined his head, and Arthras did the same.

"The king would meet with you," the man said, and Arthras nodded, as though this were no more than he expected. The men turned and he followed them, though he could not keep from looking as they passed other hallways and turns, expecting an ambush. They could not harm him, he believed that, but they might not believe it. If they acted foolishly, he would make them pay. The only thing he could not decide was how far to go. Power was not something he was accustomed to.

They went down into the main body of the palace, into the grand hall where he had seen the king yesterday. There were more men here this time. He saw more than a hundred thanes, and many of them had a handful of warriors with them, so the hall was filled with several hundred men. They all watched as he came in, and he tried not to show how he tensed down in his guts. If they wanted to intimidate him, it would not work.

Usiric sat at the head of the hall on a heavy chair draped with furs and stolen silks. His sheathed sword lay across his thighs, and he stroked his beard. Atop the throne he looked wise and immense, his cloak draping over his wide shoulders. Arthras walked closer, then bowed, but as a companion would bow, not an indentured warrior.

"Rise, Arthras," Usiric said. "I cannot speak of who your father was. I did not know him."

"Ruras," Arthras said. "He was not a warrior – he bred horses."

"Mmm," Usiric said. "So you have no lineage?"

"I have lineage," Arthras said, angry. "I had a father, and a mother, both of them dead. I had a sister who died of fever last winter, and a woman I might have taken to wife, were I not kept in service for your war."

Usiric glared at him angrily. "You will not speak to your king in such a voice!"

"I came here yesterday, having done you a great service, and I was subjected to abuse and insults. I will speak how I wish, until I am given my due rewards. The generosity of King Usiric is shown to be no more than base greed and the hunger for glory you did not win." Arthras ground his fists, his hair standing up as he heard the assembled warriors growl and shift closer. He heard leather creaking, and the soft whisper of iron as blades were drawn.

Usiric stood. "You come into my hall and hurl abuse upon me! You come, a new-grown boy with no blood on his hands, and you claim the power of gods. You speak to your elders and betters without thought or care!" He pointed at the room. "Each of my thanes serves me because not only have they done great deeds of war, but they have proved loyal to me for many years. That is the measure of their high status, not just that they claim to be great fighters, but that they have proved it again and again." He sneered. "You will learn to temper your speech with respect for those older and wiser than you."

"Older you may be," Arthras said. "But wiser? You who led us into a treaty with the traitorous Autarch? You who caused us to spill our blood for the benefit of our enemies, and then stood by while they betrayed us?" He turned and looked at the crowd, seeing much anger, not all of it at him. "No man here can say he did not leave friends or kindred behind us thanks to your hunger for Carinthian gold. Now you would have us sit here and swill wine until the Autarch returns to attack us again!"

There were murmurs, and he saw some heads nod, and then, into the quiet, he heard a high, female scream trill down from the chambers above. He looked at Usiric, furious, and saw a knowing smile spread across the king's face. "The Autarch took much treasure with him, but I know he must have more. His wife will tell us where it is hidden, or she will die."

Arthras bolted for the door, the heat rising inside him. Two heavy men moved to block his way, but he hurled them aside as though they were toys and raced out into the hall. Back the way he came, he ran up the wide steps, down the long corridor, and then into the hallway outside Nicaea's rooms. He saw two men holding one of the slave girls, tearing at her clothes while she struggled and screamed. One man clapped his hand on her mouth while the other ripped her dress open, baring her breasts.

Arthras never slowed as he came for them, a growl building in his throat. They saw him, and one of them shoved the girl into the arms of the other one and grabbed for his sword. Arthras drew back his arm and punched the man full in the chest. He felt bones snap under his blow, and the man flew back a dozen paces with blood pouring from his mouth.

The other one shouted and flung the girl aside, drew his dagger with a quick flash, and lunged in to stab it into Arthras' neck. The blade struck hard and he felt it like the blow of a pointed stick. The blade bent almost double and stayed bent, and Arthras grabbed the man's arm and wrenched it until the bones snapped. He caught the sword from the man's belt and drew it as he fell, and then he turned and ran down the hall, following the sound of raised voices.

He hit the door to the bedchamber with his shoulder and splintered it, came into the room with fury boiling inside him. Two men turned and rushed to meet him, swords ready. They met him in a flurry of singing steel, and he shrugged off their blows and struck once, hard. In his hand, the sword sheared through the first man's armor under his arm and clove him to the spine. The sword snapped off in the wound, and he threw away the useless hilt.

Another blow fell on his skull, making him wince, and then he picked the man off his feet and dashed him against the wall, leaving him slumped and bleeding. Then he turned to face the last man, who held Nicaea pinned in front of him, his arm around her waist and his dagger at her neck. It was Ethric Gold-Handed.

Arthras took a long breath, controlling himself, the heat trying to take him over. "Will you hide behind her forever? Like a child behind its mother's skirts?" He growled, hands clenched. "You think you can escape me?"

"I will teach you a proper lesson in respect," Ethric said, baring his teeth. "But after I have from this whore what I want of her." He dug the dagger in and Nicaea grimaced. "I want to know where the Autarch hid the rest of his gold!"

Nicaea wriggled helplessly, and then she drew a long needle from her sleeve and stabbed it through Ethric's knife-arm. When he yelled and jerked the dagger away, she twisted out of his grip, and Arthrus lunged.

His skin turned black in the extremity of his anger, and smoke began to pour from his clothes. He caught Ethric by the throat and felt the skin sear under his fingers. Ethric screamed and stabbed his dagger in low, only for it to snap when it struck Arthras' belly. With a furious snarl, Arthras lifted him off his feet, took three steps to the balcony, and hurled him off.

Ethric screamed as he fell, twisting grotesquely through the air until he smashed down on the tiled roof below. Broken crockery slid down in a cascade, and the body lay there, wedged in the roof. Arthras blinked, realized that roof was so large it could be nothing but the great hall, directly below him. He bellowed, leaped the rail, and plummeted down after the dead man.

It was a very long fall, and he just had time to wonder the limits of his invulnerability, and whether this was a good idea, and then he hit hard beside the corpse and his weight smashed clean through. He crushed through the tile, and then he burst through into the air above the long table, crowded with men. He saw their faces, looking up as the roof disintegrated. Arthras saw them draw back as he fell and landed hard on the table, splitting the wood apart with the impact. Gold cups and plates and wine flew into the air as the table came apart.

Ethric's body slammed down on the floor not six paces away, blood splashing across the stone, and then Arthras pulled himself up, just as his clothes began to burn. Wreathed in fire, he hurled the fragments of the table out of his way and strode toward the place where King Usiric sat staring, his face waxy and pale.

The warriors got out of his way, and smoke poured from him as he crossed the hall. He gripped the iron-scaled cuirass he wore and ripped it off, threw it aside, where it lay dull red and smoking. Arthras shrugged off the burning remnants of his clothes, and then he brought his foot down and the earth shook.

It began as a small tremor, and then there was a sound, as of every joint in the structure of the great hall cracking. The cups and fallen platters on the floor began to rattle, and the men suddenly braced themselves as the floor shuddered under their feet. The first real shock brought dust and broken tiles clattering down from above. There was a sound of thunder clawing up from below, and then the whole room shook savagely, throwing men off their feet. The glass in the high windows splintered and the rods that held the tapestries broke loose and fell.

"I will not be trifled with!" Arthras roared, feeling as if his voice erupted from the deepest part of the earth. "You mock my family, you do not respect my war-prize? All those things you can do. But if you doubt my power, and send mortal men against me, then I will call down upon you the destruction I can forge!" He held up his hand, wondering how much destruction he could cause, if he chose. He did not know what limits there might be on him, and what he could do.

He held his hand out toward Usiric and clenched it into a fist, and then he struck the air, as if it were a wall, and then the ground convulsed. Men were hurled off their feet as the whole room shuddered and cracks raced over the walls. A great crack split the floor in front of him, and then it lanced through the marble, spewing chips of stone, until it reached Usiric and knocked over his throne, spilling the old man onto the floor. The king cried out, and his crown came off his head and rolled away across the floor with a thin sound.

"I will be no king," Arthras said. He paced steadily across the floor to where the crown lay, and he looked down at it. The gold was only a veneer over the iron band that had once been the crown of the Almanni. He bent and reached down, picked it up and held it in his smoking hand. The gold sizzled and ran like hot wax, pouring over his fingers. He held the crown until the gold was all melted away, and all that remained was the old iron, turning red in his grip.

"Warriors do not need a king. A king is a greedy old man who sits fat on a throne and calls on warriors to do what he cannot do. What kind of man calls on young men to die for him?" He paced closer to Usiric and stood over him. He waited for one of the thanes to rise up, to come and defend their king, but not a one of them spoke.

"So I would not be a king. I do not come from an ancient line, I do not descend from the line of Tacis. But I have been given power nevertheless. Bora has gifted me with this power, and I know what I shall do with it." He turned back to the watching warriors, and he held up the iron crown, now blazing red hot. "Will you sit here cowering and scraping for whatever the Carinthians left behind as they fled? I will not. What they abandoned is not enough payment for what I have lost. Nor enough for any of us. We have suffered too much and too long, and we fought and bled to stand here, and I say it is not enough! It is not enough for me, and I do not think it is enough for you."

He looked down at the king. "Look on the man who would have traded your blood for his gold, for his lands. I say no more! I will not wait here like a worm dug into the flesh of a dead city to wait for the Autarch to come and root us out. We have a victory, and do we call that our last one? I say no! I will go south, into Othria, into lands rich with plunder and food. I will go to Orneas and tear down its gates as well, and I will not stop until I have crossed the water and toppled the Emperor himself from his white throne!"

A shout went up, and then another, and then the hall was filled with roaring. The warriors pounded their sword and dagger hilts on the table and the chairs. If there were any who dissented, they did not raise a word to stop their companions. Arthras looked at them, seeing he had fired their blood. He walked to where Usiric cowered on the broken floor, and the old man's eyes widened as he saw the glowing crown come closer.

"Warriors do not need kings," Arthras said. "They need war." He caught the king's beard and pulled him close so he could place the burning crown on his gray head, and the air filled with the smell of burning hair, and then the beard burned through and Usiric fell back screaming, clawing at his head as the iron seared through to his flesh, and burned into it.

Arthras drew in a deep breath, drawing down the power inside him, calming so that the heat receded. He cooled, smoke rising from his skin as the color returned to his flesh. He reached down and picked up Usiric's sword where it lay and drew the fine steel blade from the velvet sheath. The king was still wailing and clawing at his head when Arthras lifted the keen blade and hacked down, cutting off his head with one blow and driving the blade through to cut into the stone beneath. A twist and the steel snapped, and he threw aside the broken hilt.

Blood poured across the floor, and Usiric's body twitched, hands reaching for a head that was gone. Arthras picked up the head, the eyes still fluttering, and he threw it onto the ruins of the throne. "Any man who wishes to stay here, can stay. Any man who would go back north, I will not lift a hand to stop him." He turned and looked at the stunned crowd of warriors. "But I am going south to conquer the whole of the empire, and any man who would march with me, marches into legend."

☙

Naked, he went back up the stairs, and Nicaea met him at the door of her room. Her loose hair hung around her face, and he looked beautiful and almost wild. "You speak well, when you are fired," she said.

"And you have courage, when you are pressed to it," he said. He looked away, grunted. "Are you unharmed?"

In answer she opened her robe, revealing herself naked and glorious. "Do you see a wound upon me? Look close."

They came together with a force that lifted her off her feet, and he carried her to the bedchamber, did not reach it, and they went down on the couch together. His hands were all over her, and hers on him. Her mouth was open and wet and she smelled like desire. Her hair was all over, and her skin tasted of honey.

She lifted her leg and opened to him, and he watched her face as he pushed inside her, slowly, so slowly. "Will you come with me?" he grunted. "Come and help me conquer?"

"Will you make me an Empress?" she crooned, legs winding around him, drawing him in. Her hands dug into his arms, her fingers hard and strong. "Will you?"

He leaned down and breathed her breath. "I will."

Chapter Eleven

Princes and Gods

The Stadia was a wide, open space that had once been used for races, before a new, larger one was built to the east of the city. Karana looked at it, seeing the sandy track around the rim now thick with grass, and the truncated pillars that had once added grandeur to races and bouts of wrestling. The stands themselves were like a reef all of stacked stone, some of it white and stained by time, the rest of it of different colors, showing where they had been added to over many years.

"This will be ideal," Thessala said. "Open spaces, plenty of air and room. We can set up tents here in the center, graze animals in the grass, and there are rooms below the stands we can use for shelter from the rain." She glanced at Karana. "If it rains."

Karana looked uncomfortable. That morning she had tried to make it rain a little, managed a drizzle that turned to stifling humidity as the day heated up. Then she had managed a slight sea breeze to cool things off, but after that she swore she would not interfere with the weather unless she had to. It would become far too easy to do more harm than good by fussing with it. It was comforting to be able to think she could undo a drought, but humbling to realize that was probably harder than it sounded.

Thessala held up her arms, indicating the open ground all around them. "And there is controlled access, entrances at one end or the other. It could be defended."

"If we have to defend it." Karana sat down on an old piece of stone, the carvings on it worn away so they were indecipherable. "Surely they will leave us alone."

Thessala shook her head. "I killed some of them, they will come back."

"You said they would come at dawn," Karana said. "But they have not been back for days now." Karana kicked a stone idly. This was the third day, and the various gatherings of the refugees were becoming too difficult to watch for just the two of them. This was Thessala's idea of a solution.

"That worries me more." Thessala drew her hood closer around her face. She was still hesitant about showing her true features. Even some of her charges at the sanctuary were now too afraid to come near her. She tried to be graceful about it, but Karana could tell it still bothered her.

"You think they are planning something larger?" Karana said. The idea of forces moving out of her sight, planning her demise, was unnerving.

"I think between us we managed to convince the Archpriest that ordinary measures would not be sufficient," Thessala said. "He will try again, but it won't just be a handful of soldiers."

"Comforting thought," Karana said. She picked up a small stone and pitched it into the tall grass. Somehow, despite the possibilities, she found the overgrown ruin disheartening. Part of it was simply that she did not really know what to do with herself. Gathering and protecting all the refugees in one place was noble enough a purpose, but she felt that she had not been given this power just for this. It bothered her to have no direction besides reacting to disaster and danger. It felt like a tactical error.

Thessala looked around them. "Do you still want to try it?"

This again. Karana rubbed at her forehead. "It was your suggestion."

"I just meant that I seem more durable, so I would be something you could practice on." She made sure no one was around and cast her hood back, rolled up her sleeves.

Karana laughed. "And you want to try it."

Thessala tried to look serious, but even under her scaled skin, it was obvious she was fighting a smile. Here in the sun her scales looked blue-black, and they shimmered with hints of green and pink when she moved. It was really quite beautiful, and Karana had the sudden urge to see her naked, flushed at the thought.

"Yes," Thessala said. "I want to fly."

Karana stood up, dusted off her backside, still annoyed by the rips in her dress. The best she had managed was to put a few stitches in the biggest of them. At least she had a nice bolt of violet silk for the scarf to cover her hair. "You remember I did not fly, I threw myself into the sky, by accident, and then crashed. That is not the same thing."

"But if you can control the wind, then you *could* fly. You really could." Thessala belted her robe tighter, pulled her skirts tight around her legs and held them with one hand. "Lift me up. Try it."

Karana almost said no, but then she closed her eyes and composed her mind. She breathed slower, and she began to feel what she had that first time, as the wind began to move with her, shifting with her breath. She felt the air move over her, but she felt it around and overhead as well, as though her senses extended far beyond her skin. She began to gather the winds, and she felt her skirts billow, grabbed her robe and held it tighter around herself. "Hold on," she said. "This won't be gentle."

She could feel Thessala, a shape that the air flowed around, and she drew more and more air in, coiled it into a vortex that sucked in more after itself. It fed on itself so rapidly, she feared she would lose control of the reaction. She felt a chill, and then there was too much happening and she had to act. She seized Thessala in a whorl of air and flung her into the sky.

Eyes closed, she could not see her, but she heard her scream as she was vaulted into the air. The backlash knocked Karana down and she landed in the grass, trying to maintain her concentration. She could feel Thessala, and it was like the way a strong wind felt when it pushed against you – like a real thing, solid and with a shape you could never quite define. She held out her hands, tried to guide Thessala, hold her up, control her movement.

She got a grip on her, skated her over the stands, then drew her higher, turned and brought her back, it was so hard to keep her steady, and she wondered if she was managing it. She had to bring her lower so she could land, tried to hold on.

Then a crosswind cut in, stirred by her manipulations, and she lost her grip, could not tell where Thessala was. Afraid, she opened her eyes and saw the other woman tumbling towards her. She didn't have time to try and grab her again, only ducked as she blurred past and slammed hard into the dirt. The impact sounded like a sack of grain dropped from a rooftop, and it kicked up a plume of soil many times taller than a man.

"Oh no!" Karana got to her feet, her scarf gone and her braids loose, and ran toward the impact. She was certain she would find nothing but crushed flesh and broken bone, but instead she heard laughing before she even reached the spot.

There was a divot in the ground big enough to put three people in, and Thessala climbed out, laughing and covered in dirt. Her single long braid was wrapped around her neck, her robe was almost on backwards, and one of her sandals was gone. She smiled, and it looked very white in her scaled face. She came out of the hole and sat down and laughed again, shaking dirt off her arms.

"Attis, are you all right?" Karana went to her, grimacing as she felt the air still shifting and rippling overhead. She had to pause a moment and calm it, smooth away the jagged edges that threatened to turn into weather. "I'm sorry, I told you it was dangerous."

"Dangerous to someone else, perhaps," Thessala said. She got up and started shaking out her clothes. "That was the most exciting ride of my life. So fast! I never went so fast." She wiped at her face and spat out dirt.

"Are you hurt?" Karana said.

"No, no! Not at all. It seems I am much tougher than that, as I said." She smiled, then staggered a bit and caught herself. "I am dizzy, but not hurt."

"I am sorry I dropped you," Karana said. "Controlling the wind is not easy."

"Well," Thessala said. "I suppose that means you should practice."

☙

All through the afternoon, they saw to the relocation of the refugees from their makeshift camps to the grounds of the Stadia. It was not far from Thessala's sanctuary, so it was not difficult for them to keep an eye on things as they managed the movement of people and supplies. Karana saw that food would soon be an issue; with more people closer together, they would quickly run through their supplies. They had pregnant women and growing children who needed food, and soon there would not be any. There already was not enough.

It was shading into evening, and the heat was beginning to break, when there was a commotion at the far end of the Stadia, and Karana hurried to see what it was. She had already been forced to run off a gang of beggars who turned out to be more like robbers, and she hoped they had not come back.

Instead she saw refugees hurrying away from a body of armed men, and just as her belly knotted up at the prospect of more violence, she saw they were not advancing. They took up a formation, and then she saw a cluster of slaves set up a canopy and drape the sides with purple cloth. She watched, bemused, as they unrolled a rug beneath it and then brought forth several chairs and a small table, which they set with a wine jug and some cups.

When that was done, she approached, wondering if this was some kind of joke, or if they perhaps intended to poison her. Instead, a horseman came riding with an escort, and he climbed down with the help of the guards. He did not wear a helmet, and she saw he was an older man, perhaps fifty, with dark hair turning gray and a craggy face with a large nose. He was dressed very well, draped in a red cape stitched with gold and a deep purple tunic, a ring on his finger with a cluster of rubies the size of pomegranate seeds.

He saw she was the only person not drawing away from him, and he came toward her somewhat cautiously. She saw he wore a sword, but it looked more decorative than useful, and while he seemed vigorous, he was not a man who looked like a fighter.

"Good evening," he said. "I am looking for the Storm Girl."

Karana snorted. Storm Girl would never do. "I am she. I am Karana, and that you may call me." She looked at his escort, and his clothes, and she nodded. "You can only be the Autarch."

"I am," he said. "I am Galbos Inarios Desius." He made a slight, almost mock bow. "I am very pleased to meet you."

"I suppose I should be glad you come with a smile and not an army," she said. "What help can I be to such a person as you?"

"It may seem strange to say, but I think we perhaps can help one another," he said. "We do not have the same aims, but they do overlap in places. You are an extraordinary woman, so I am told. Tales of refugees I might be inclined to discount, but I have seen what you did at the Citadel, and I am not such an old fool that I discount the evidence of my eyes because it seems impossible." He gestured to the pavilion. "If you like, I thought perhaps we might sit and talk. You may find that we can do great service for one another."

Karana looked at him, wondering what his game was, then she decided the only way to find out would be to listen to whatever he came to say. She nodded. "All right, but please send your soldiers out of the Stadia, they make our people nervous." She considered. "You may keep two, for the sake of proper forms."

He snorted, amused. "How generous."

"Indeed I am," she said. "Allow me to summon my companion, and we will speak."

☙

Thessala had heard a great deal about Galbos Desius – about his greed, his appetites for women, and his ambition that led him to his high position. She had never expected to meet him in person, much less sit down to discuss politics with him as some kind of equal. Up close he was shorter than she expected, and older, and he had a personal charm and magnetism that made his long career in power make much more sense to her.

She was well-shrouded, a white robe on and her hood drawn up. She kept her hands in her sleeves so he would not see them. Part of her did not want to be seen, especially by a man. Part of her wanted to save her appearance for when it might frighten or unbalance him. Karana was a very smart girl, with strength inside, but she was politically a bit naïve. Thessala was no politician, but her years at the sanctuary, dealing with officials and guards, made her feel like she was a bit more prepared for this.

They sat on the chairs under the canopy. The sun was gone and the sky was lit by the shimmering tail of the star. There were a few clouds, their edges silvered by the light, and there was a pleasant breeze. They sat around a small brazier and Galbos' slaves sprinkled the coals with sweet oils to make for a lovely scent on the air.

"Interesting for you to come and see us, rather than summon us to you," Karana said.

"He doesn't want anyone to hear what he has to say," Thessala said.

Rather than seem offended, Galbos simply nodded, conceding the point. "The most crucial of political discussions do not bear up under scrutiny," he said. He clasped his hands and leaned back. "You know the situation I find myself in. Ilion has fallen. I came in search of more men to reinforce it, but the events overtook me, and now I am here without a power base. I may be Autarch in name, but once the news of my failure reaches the emperor, I may not be for long. My only hope is to retake the city and repel the invasion before that happens."

"You fled Ilion with a great deal of treasure," Karana said. "It did not look good to the people you left there."

"I needed money to raise troops," he said diffidently. "I made a deal with the Almanni, and it went badly."

"You betrayed them," Thessala said.

He scoffed. "I enlisted them to augment my army. They were already being driven from their lands by the Borunai. They had to go somewhere, and with their twenty thousand warriors added to my two cohorts, we had the power to stop them, which we did." He took a drink. "Did I intend them to bear the brunt of the losses in that battle? Yes. I intended to ally them but also weaken them, so that if they became restive, my existing forces could stop them. I had only two reduced cohorts on the northern border. Ten thousand men in theory, in practice less than eight. So I had to stop two barbarian incursions, and together they outnumbered me eight to one. So I turned one on the other."

"You promised them sanctuary inside the empire," Karana said. "I heard about it."

"Yes, I did, and then the emperor denied it, and I was forced to keep them out. I left them behind, promised them food supplies, and left my two cohorts to prevent them crossing the river." He sighed. "The emperor refused the food subsidies, and so the Almanni attacked. They bribed one of my generals – probably with the gold I paid their king – and the other, seeing his situation was hopeless, retreated to Helicon to the west."

"Well," Thessala said. "What is your point? Why are you here with us?"

"Sooner or later – probably sooner – the barbarians will come south. They are not just an army, they are a nation on the move, with women and children to feed. It's early summer, the harvests are not in yet, and they will need to forage. They will want plunder and loot as well, and so they will come this way. They could move to attack Karnathos on the east coast, but the way leads through mountains. No, they will come right for us, here. Orneas will be their next target."

He took another drink. "Think of it. They will pillage their way through the countryside, driving before them streams of refugees. In a few days the first waves fleeing the sack of Ilion will reach us here, and the Archpriest will keep the gates shut against them. As soon as word comes that the Almanni are coming this way, he will round up all those already here, and force them outside the city." He pointed past them at the rising tent settlement.

"What?" Karana didn't stand up, but she looked as if she wanted to. "Why would he do that?"

"Supplies," Thessala said. "He will not want to have to feed refugees, or house them. Only soldiers and rich men will be welcome here."

"She is right," Galbos said, pausing to peer at her, no doubt wondering what was under her hood. "There are two cohorts in the city, but they are not at full strength. I could call in two more from Karnathos. By ship I could get them here quickly. But the Autarch does not want that to happen, and so it will not."

Karana rubbed her forehead. "The Archpriest does not want to defend the city?"

"Of course he does," Thessala said. "He just doesn't want him doing it." She nodded at Galbos.

"Yes. A victory over the invaders would save my reputation, and force back all my enemies who are currently sharpening their knives at the prospect of my downfall. The Archpriest will block all my efforts, then blame me for lack of trying when the barbarians are at the gate. If he defeats them, he will accrue much more influence, and I will probably be executed."

"But he can't stop them," Karana said. "There is the barbarian Arthras. He will bring down the city gates, and the Almanni will take the city. He is like me." She glanced at Thessala. "Like us. No soldiers will stop him."

"But you could," Galbos said. "The Archpriest does not want to believe what he has seen, but I am not so blinkered."

"Also, you are desperate," Thessala said.

He looked annoyed by that, but he said nothing and took another drink. He leaned closer to Karana, and when he spoke again, his voice was pitched lower and more intent. "You want to protect the refugees, I want to defeat the barbarians. Those are not the same goals, but to do the first, I must accomplish the second. The common barrier preventing us is Archpriest Uliamus."

"What do you intend to do about him?" Karana said.

"I am doing it," he said. "I am asking you if you will help me depose him."

ೞ

Karana's head spun at the suggestion. "You wish to dethrone the Archpriest?"

"I do. We can't kill him, it would cause too much outrage." Galbos tapped his chin with a fingertip. "And I do not have the men to force the issue. Not now. Too much of the civic authority is loyal to him and will not be dissuaded, will not act while he is here to control it, despite that my own authority is meant to exceed his."

Karana shook her head, trying to make sense of it. "Then what do you want from me?"

Galbos spoke carefully. "He is already planning a larger attack, to clear out your little nest here." He gestured around them. "When he does, I want you to drive it back, and not restrain yourself. Break the attack, scatter it, and send them running. And then. . . then I want you to attack the Citadel. I need you to terrorize the old man, so that he comes to me and begs my protection." He drank again.

Thessala snorted. "You mean to arrest him."

"Words are unimportant," Galbos said. "What will be important is that once he is under my control, he will be out of my way. I can gather the soldiers I need, and I can still go north and stop the barbarians before they ever reach the city. The refugees will be safe, and I will be a hero." He put his cup down and looked intently at Karana. "We will both get what we want."

Karana shook her head. "But you can't defeat the Almanni, not with the earthshaker among them. Send an army, and he will break it."

"He may have power," Galbos said. "But he does not know battle as I do. I can outmaneuver him. His power cannot feed hungry troops, or protect his women and children. No, he will come here with pride but with weaknesses he does not even appreciate, or recognize. I will meet him and I will throw him back." He leaned closer. "All I need is the freedom to act, while there is still time." He shrugged. "I admit I need your help."

୭

When he was gone, Karana stood looking at where he had been, and Thessala stood by, quiet. The night wind was rising, and Karana found it soothing to feel the motion of the air, undisturbed and smooth. She sighed. "I don't trust him," she said.

"Nor should you. He is a lecher and a killer, with no care for anything save his own ambition." Thessala's voice was hard. "Do not be deceived by his reasonable demeanor."

Karana snorted. "I am not. I lived in Ilion, remember? I have heard all the stories about him there are. I know he is a scorpion." She sighed again. "But I do think he's right."

Thessala made an unhappy sound. "Of course he is, and that's what's worst about all of this. Even if there was not about to be an attack on us, now he will make sure there is. He needs it to set things in motion." She knotted her braid in her hands. "I loathe men like that. They decide what will happen, and then they twist things and lie and betray until it happens." She pushed her hood back, and Karana saw her eyes glitter in the dark. "You know he doesn't care about the refugees at all? You understand that?"

"I know," Karana said. "But he doesn't understand how strong the earthshaker is. Arthras. He thinks he can out-think him, but that won't be enough." She looked at Thessala. "If we want to save this city. We're going to have to fight for it ourselves." She looked up at the sky, at the blazing tail of the star, and she wondered how in the world her life had come to this.

Chapter Twelve

Remnants of War

Nicaea climbed out of the hot water, savoring it because she knew it would be her last proper bath for a while. The comforts of the city were not easily had on the road, and it seemed they would soon be traveling. Her slaves came and draped a towel around her shoulders and gathered up her hair and patted it dry. She would have to make arrangements to bring some essentials with her, so that she might continue to present the proper appearance. Beauty, after all, did not happen by accident.

She dried off, and then lay back so her girls could rub scented oils into her skin. Eyes closed, she began to go over the myriad things that would have to be thought of while traveling. It had been years since she went on a long journey, almost two since she had been to Orneas. A far more cosmopolitan and pleasant city than this border outpost, and she hoped it could be taken without destroying it. It would make a far better seat of power than this place.

She reflected that she had never before traveled with an army, and she had to expect it would move more slowly than a simple retinue. There would be several weeks of marching, and she was frustrated that she was not enough in command of this force yet to really have her hands on the preparations. These were barbarians after all, they could not be expected to be very organized.

Her slaves rubbed her down, and she stood, stretched, and looked herself over in her largest mirror. She was older than she had been when Galbos had taken her to wife, but now she was even more glad she had never borne children. Her belly was still smooth and her thighs still shapely. She did not look like a young woman, but she was still able to wield that power over men that had always brought her what she wanted. Arthras was a more volatile and dangerous man than any she had taken before, but he was young, and that made it easier. If she applied herself, she could make him into an emperor. That was a project worthy of her time.

She sat while her girls combed out her hair, and as it dried they coiled and braided it into a proper coif. She chose a sea-blue gown and draped herself with her most stoutly-built jewelry. She already had all her jewels and gold packed away, to be brought with her. Soon, perhaps, she would add a crown to her collection.

Now she needed to brace Arthras. Last night he had drunk enough wine to kill a pony, with little apparent effect. Like a god, he drank and drank and seemed still sober, though he plainly wished for the freedom wine could bring. Nicaea supposed he was affected by the death of his king, and she understood that to a certain extent – he was young, and had likely never known a king to die at all, much less slain one himself.

She had to get him moving. If he let these men sit and stew for too long, they would start to fight each other, and then the whole thing would devolve into a welter of petty rivalries, and all hope of conquest would be gone. She closed her eyes for a moment and imagined Galbos and that stiff priest Uliamus forced to grovel at her feet while she wore an imperial crown, and the thought was so delicious her mouth actually watered for the want of it.

One of her girls ducked in from the hall. "My lady, there are barbarians on the stairs."

Nicaea nodded and stood up. A delegation perhaps, or more assassins. Well, if there was trouble, she could howl for Arthras, but if not, then she had to start extending her control over this rabble to more than just her pet demigod. She walked with her back straight and her head high, through the door and out into the wide hallway. She took her place there in the arch, like a tomb guardian in a tale. She would ask her riddles and devour if they were not answered.

There were six men coming up the stair, all of them of the same savage type. Tall and pale, with light eyes and that terrible look on their faces. They always looked as though they were about to bite out someone's throat or simply drop dead from fury, and they stared at everything as though it might attack them. Two of them had that strange pale hair, and one of them was red-haired like Arthras. They wore their abominable long beards, and their arms bore dark blue tattoos of serpent shapes. None of them looked as if they had really washed or ever combed their hair in their lives. They had the strong odor of smoke and wine and leather over the musk of men.

"Who are you, and why do you come?" she said, adopting her most imperious tone. She knew with barbarians even a woman must make a show of strength and fearlessness. She was thankful, now, that her father had made her study languages, so she could speak their rude tongue. "Speak."

One of the blonde ones came forward, looking her up and down in that frank way she had learned not to take as an insult. It was just the way they looked at one another. He seemed to hesitate, and then he bowed slightly, that duck of the head that among the Almanni passed for courtesy. "I am called Safrax, lady. I was one of the companions of King Usiric. I come to see Arthras."

"To see him does nothing to declare your intent," she said. "If you intend to try to kill him, I would encourage you not to waste any of his time. If you intend to curse him, then be gone, before I call for him." She let her tone soften. "If you have another intention, pray let me know what it is, so I can judge whether it is worth disturbing him."

The man Safrax seemed amused. "I am come to pledge my spear and my shield to his service. That is not a thing to discuss with a woman, but I will not grudge it, for you are of the empire and know nothing of courtesy." The other warriors smirked at this, and Nicaea had to force herself to show nothing on her face.

"I would say that you and I have different ideas of courtesy," Nicaea said. "And since I am the one who controls your access to the man you seek, I would suggest you curb your tone with me." She saw anger on his face and smiled. "One word, one cry, and he will come and break your bones for daring to raise a hand to me." She smiled wider. "But as you have come to swear faith, I am glad to let you pass." The man stepped closer and she held up a finger. "Wait here, and I shall go and tell him you are here." She met his stare, fearless. "Wait."

☙

The slaves brought Arthras a bowl of water and he washed his hands and his face. He felt terrible because he didn't feel drunk in the slightest. There were three empty wine jugs in the room, and he had drunk all of their contents and then pissed it all out and he felt nothing at all. It brought home to him, more than anything else, how changed he was. Swords did not cut him; he could fall from a great height and not be harmed. Fire did not burn, and the ground shook at his command.

But he could not become drunk, and that seemed strangest of all. Annoyed, he picked up one of the jugs and heaved it against the wall, shattering it. Then the door opened and Nicaea entered, looked at the mess with disapproval. "All right, enough of this," she said. "You're not even dressed."

"I burned off my clothes," he said. "Why put more on?" He wanted to act drunk, but he decided it would be a foolish thing to do. He stood up and looked at her. She was so well-dressed and cleaned she looked like jewelry herself, like something to wear. He took a step towards her and she stopped him with a hand on his chest.

"Not now. I have had more clothes brought, and you will be dressed as befits a king," she said.

He grabbed her wrist, reminded himself to be gentle with her, lest he break her bones. "I am not a king. I killed the king."

"Yes, and it was well done and you spoke well after. The men are primed to follow you, but that means you have to lead them." She caressed his face with one hand. Her skin was so soft. The skin of her hands and her shoulders especially fascinated him.

"I will lead them," he said. In truth the thought unnerved him. He dreaded to give a command, for what if he gave the wrong one? What if they did not obey him?

"Then it is time to start," she said. "A man called Safrax is here with his warriors – he says he is here to pledge his spear and shield to your service. Now you must meet with him, and begin to plan this invasion you have roused them to."

Arthras looked down at himself, at the same time wishing he were dressed like a king, and detesting that he was expected to be. He snorted. "I should overthrow all the thanes and call on the warriors myself. I don't need those proud, gilded bastards."

"Yes, you do," she said. She beckoned the slaves and the girls came with clothes, began to dress him. He grunted and started to shrug them off, and then he stood still and let them do it. She was right. He had to meet this man, and he had to look impressive. As much as he could.

"Those men are not just captains, they are the ruling class of your people," Nicaea said. "They are the ones who know *how* to rule them, and you will need that. If you go to the warriors, you will have warriors. But will you have men who know how to plan a march, or make sure their men are fed and equipped? No. Believe me, these men have experience that you do not even know you do not have."

He grunted, not knowing what to say to that. He did not like being lectured to, or made to feel stupid. He knew she was right, but he didn't like it. In his mind, leading the march of his people would be glorious, warriors gathered behind him, flowing over every enemy, shouting his name, chanting as they thrust their spears in the air. The reality seemed filled with fussy details he didn't understand and didn't care about.

"Well enough," he said. "But I don't like them, and they don't like me."

"You think they cheered the death of Usiric because they liked him?" Nicaea said. "I'll wager you my diamonds that half of them hated him and were just waiting for a chance to see him fall. The tension in groups like that is always the same. Some of them want to take power, but they have too many enemies. They all know each other too well, and they are allied in hostile camps and pacts of mutual defense. If one of them tries to take the throne there would be a bloodbath, so none of them dare to try. Now you have upset the whole cart, and they are all deciding how it will go and what they should do. You have to move quickly and decisively, before they have time to get ideas or start killing one another."

He grunted. "Very well." He beckoned. "Send him in."

Nicaea looked around at the room. The disheveled bed, the broken wine jug and the wine on the floor. "Not in here," she said.

Arthras felt a little glow of anger. "Send him in, woman. I mean what I say."

She looked at him for a moment, and then she nodded, bowed, and went out. He would take her advice on things she knew more of. But he would not let her rule him, or even think she did. The slaves fussed, trying to get the red cloak to sit right on his shoulders, and he shrugged them off, threw the cloak into the corner. Enough.

To pledge spear and shield to a ruler was a solemn, and very serious thing, only done at the death of a king, or at the risk of being hounded as an oathbreaker. The ceremony was ancient and serious, and Arthras had never seen it, had only heard it spoken of in tales. He was not sure what to expect, or what to do or say. He knew for a warrior to come and pledge to him was a great step, and others might turn against the man. It could start blood feuds if he was not careful. There were more than a hundred companions who had served Usiric. If most of them swore to him, then the rest would follow, like a flood, but it had to begin somewhere.

The man came in. Safrax was shorter than he'd expected, and younger. He was not much older than Arthras himself, if at all. His men had a hard look about them, not so gilded and well-dressed. He looked at Arthras, and then he bowed. "You said you would not be a king, so I will not call you one."

Arthras nodded. "I have little respect for kings."

"What about emperors?" he said. Arthras saw the knuckles of his hands were scarred from many cuts. The mark of a knife-fighter.

"To inherit an empire means nothing," Arthras said. "The greatest men are always those who build them. An empire is built on conquest."

"And you plan to conquer," he said, not asking.

"By myself, if I must," Arthras said. "Come with me, and share the spoils."

Safrax looked like he was thinking carefully. "I saw you fall from the sky. I saw you kill Usiric. A king should be a warrior first, and a ruler second. Ruling makes a man forget his strength, and he thinks more and more on comfort and wealth. I wish for neither."

"You were not a thane for very long," Arthras said.

"Before the battle at the Sethion River, the king was desperate for support. He made companions of any man who could pay his weight in gold." Safrx looked disgusted. "My father paid for me and for himself, then died in the battle, pierced by a Borunan arrow. I was a thane, but the king granted me no respect. After we crossed into the empire, you know he demanded gold from all his thanes? No one knows where his money was hidden."

Arthras looked at him narrowly. "You know."

Safrax smiled grimly, then nodded slowly. "I know. His closest companions have gathered it and intend to steal it. There are six of them and their men, and they will try to escape tonight after dark."

Arthras looked at the hard-faced men with him, and nodded. "Then let us go and meet them. Are there others among the thanes who you would rely on?"

"There are some, yes," Safrax said. "There is a great deal of talk. Some men do not believe what they have seen. Some men do not want to believe it. Some want to flee to the north, some want to march south, some want to kill each other."

"And what do you want?" Arthras said.

"I want glory," Safrax said, without hesitation.

"Then bring your men at sunset," Arthras said. "We will begin."

૰

The palace grounds were separated from the rest of the city by several gates, and this was not an imposing one. The pillars that marked it were tall, and there was a decorated arch above, but the portal itself was not barred by any wall or other barrier. It was purely symbolic, and that made no sense to Arthras at all. It seemed like something only made to awe those who were already afraid, not prevent those who were not afraid from coming to take away whatever they wished. Like most of the palace, it seemed wasteful.

He waited in the dark, almost a hundred men at his back. Perhaps twenty of them were thanes that Safrax deemed trustworthy, and the rest were their retainers. All of them had been promised gifts and gold for their war deeds and had been met with refusal by Usiric. All of them were hungry for repayment of what they felt they deserved, and so they hunkered in the shadows outside the gate, swords drawn and helms down over their eyes.

When he joined them, Arthras had half-wondered if they meant to try and kill him, but they made no move, and he relaxed a little. He was not accustomed to anyone being on his side, and it made him nervous, waiting for the betrayal. But he would have to earn the loyalty of these men if he wanted to rule his people. Even the thought gave him a shiver of unreality. *Rule his people.* It filled him with eagerness and also a great deal of worry.

He heard the creak of cart wheels, and he smiled. Safrax had not been wrong. Arthras wore no armor, only a tunic and a pair of breeches that were too big, because he thought it likely he would burn them off. He peered around the corner of the gate and saw two wagons moving slowly toward him, each drawn by heavy dray horses and obviously heavily laden by how low they hung on their straps. Two men steered each one, and a force of some thirty warriors escorted them, hands on their swords.

Arthras knew he did not need to use his power to stop them. He had more men, and they could not stop him regardless. But he knew he needed a demonstration. He gestured, and men moved to ignite bonfires laid to either side, and in a moment fire sprang up. In the glow, the men with the wagons looked stunned, and he saw their white faces, turning to look around them as warriors flowed out onto their flanks.

He stepped out into the center of the arch and called up his power. It came easily, very easily, and the earth shook under their feet. The horses snorted and tossed their heads and backed away, and then Arthras clenched his fist and the ground split open. A crack opened beneath the wagons, the stone heaved up and tipped the lead one over on its side, spilling gold coins and bars and vessels across the marble. The horses shrieked, and the men tumbled off their feet, crying out in terror.

At the head of the convoy was a tall man in a gold-gilded helm, the eyelets making him look blank and inhuman. He saw Arthras and charged, axe in his hand, his polished shield uplifted in the other. He gave a battle howl as he rushed ahead.

Arthras stood, braced and unmoving, and he knew every man watched to see what would happen. The thane rushed on him, and as he smashed his shield forward, Arthras met it with a blow of his fist that crushed the bronze facing and splintered the wooden planks with a crack like thunder. The man staggered, then drew back and brought his axe sweeping in, deadly and fast.

The blow struck Arthras on his temple, and it was like being hit by a thrown rock. It stung, and his head rocked to the side, but the blade bounced off with a sound like an iron ingot dropped on the floor. Arthras looked the man in the eye, and then he reached in under the mail fall of the helm and gripped the man's throat. Futile blows of the axe fell on his head and shoulders as he lifted the thane off his feet, and then squeezed. He felt the flesh crumple under his hand, and the man gagged, spat out blood, and then went limp. The axe fell ringing to the stones.

Deliberately, Arthras threw the body down before him, and he looked at the rest of the men. One by one they lowered their eyes, let their weapons fall to their sides. He sent a last tremor through the earth, and some of them dropped to their knees. The horses stomped and shook, wanting to be free.

He beckoned to Safrax. "I have orders regarding this treasure, and how well you carry them out will decide how high a trust I place in you." He pointed at the wagons. "Take half this treasure and divide it in measures among the companions as you see fit. Half of this I will take as my own." He watched to see if any flicker of resentment passed over Safrax's face, but he saw nothing. "My half I will not keep. I want it divided and distributed among the warriors. Pass the word that any thrall who marches with me shall be freed from his debt and gold will be put into his hands."

Safrax half-smiled. "As you say, it will be done."

Arthras smiled in return. The freedom for thralls had been his idea; the gold was Nicaea's doing. Together, it would fill his army with men hungry to prove themselves and grateful for his generosity.

Safrax gestured to the prisoners. "And them?"

"Kill them," Arthras said, feeling a sick twist in his belly when he said it. It had to be done, but killing in cold blood did not sit right with him. "Put their heads on spears, so all will know what happens when you steal from your brothers."

Then he turned and walked away, back straight. He did not want to see it done. He had already given the orders to begin, and in three days they would be on the march, headed south, toward glory. He clenched his hands and looked up at the star overhead, shining above the clouds. It seemed fainter today, and perhaps it was fading, but his power seemed stronger than before.

☙

It was dawn when they left Ilion, a long line of horsemen and wagons and behind all the women and camp followers and slaves marching in their wake. Arthras rode at the head, working hard to look at ease, even though he was not a very good horseman. He rode a heavy gray pony, and the army did not move quickly, so it was not hard. He wore armor and a sword on his belt, and he saw faces looking at him from windows and around corners as they made their way through the city.

The army had to take the widest roads, and so they followed the coast along the empty harbor. A few derelict ships lay at anchor, abandoned and still. He saw almost no people, only a few cats and stray dogs scurrying across the side streets at the sound of hooves and tramping feet. It was like a city of the dead, empty and scattered with trash. He saw doors that had been broken in, the street strewn with refuse from where houses had been looted. A few bodies lay in the gutters, already gathering flies. The smell was not a good one in the rising heat of morning, and he was ready to be away from this place and out under the sky again.

He looked back to where Nicaea and her slaves rode in a heavy, ornate wagon. He needed her, but he was wary of her. She was too clever, and while she might know a great deal, there were things she did not know. She was a woman after all, not a warrior. She was Carinthian, not Almanni. She did not know how his people lived, or how they died.

Ahead was a wide plaza, and he started when he recognized the place where he had fought the Storm Girl. Her face was still clear in his mind, and he wondered where she was. He knew she was not dead. If he had survived her bolt, then so had she. Perhaps they would meet again. Close to hand was the building she had fought for, half-collapsed, but still filled with papers and scrolls. Some of them had blown out into the street, or been scattered by thieves. He rode to one side and swung down from his horse, looked at the place for a moment, wondering why she would fight so hard for it.

At his feet there was a bound book, red leather on the cover, and a string wrapped around it to hold it closed. He picked it up, and turned it over, examining it. He wanted to open it and know what was in it, but he knew he could not read the words in it, no matter what they said. He almost tossed it back down to the ground, but instead he put it inside his tunic and got back on his horse. It was a long road south to Orneas. He rejoined the column, men making way for him with their heads bowed, and he moved back to the head of the army, leading them to the gates he had broken, and then out to the coast road that led south into legend.

Chapter Thirteen

Night of Knives

Karana came awake in the dark, not knowing where she was for a moment, and then she saw Thessala's face by the light of the lamp. Strange how quickly she had grown accustomed to the sight of the other woman's scaled visage, how little it bothered her, even unexpected, like this. She sat up. "What is it?"

"There's some trouble," Thessala said in her rich voice. "You should get up."

"I'm up," Karana said. She found that these days she slept with difficulty, and not for long. When she woke she was sharp and alert, without the fogginess she remembered. "Is it them?"

For three days now they had lived in a state of anticipation, waiting for the attack Galbos had said would come. They had moved everyone to the Stadia, set up a community of tents and other makeshift shelters. They gathered food and water and tried their best to manage the chaos. They had not really wanted to be in charge of it all, but people came to them. A lot of the refugees were women with their children, and that no doubt played a part.

Thessala shook her head. "No," she said. "Something else."

Karana grunted and got out of her pallet, rolled it up and emerged into the silvery night. The moon was faded to just a sliver, and the light of the star suffused the sky, though it seemed to be less now. She supposed it would pass on eventually, and be gone. She wondered if her powers would go with it. She doubted things would be so easy.

They had dug a firepit in the weed-grown soil of the Stadia, and even this late, a fire smoldered there. Right now it was just low coals, the wood outlined in dull red and simmering flames. She saw a man with wet hair close beside the fire. He was under a blanket and others were helping him warm himself. He looked up when she came close, and she realized just how young he was.

She glanced at Thessala, saw she had veiled herself again, probably hoping not to frighten the boy. She gestured. "He's come from outside the city."

Karana felt a chill, then she went and sat next to him. "Tell us what happened. How did you come here?"

"The guards would not let me through the gate, so I swam around the walls, in the harbor." He shivered, and Karana was glad the night was warm.

The boy glanced at Thessala, then looked back at Karana. "We came from Ilion. We left over a week ago. On the road we stayed together for safety, and we managed to find enough food." He swallowed and looked down. "They attacked us on the road, half a day from here."

Karana felt her belly knot. "Who?"

"Soldiers," he said. They came out of the forest at a bend in the road and attacked. They killed. . ." He choked and covered his mouth. "I heard screaming, and everyone ran, and they kept chasing and killing. I ran. I ran through fields and when I found the road I ran all night. I came to the gates and the guards laughed at me and threw rocks at me. I came here for help." He looked up, his eyes wet and his face red. "I had to find help. Some of us might still be there, my mother and my sisters are there."

"Shhh," Karana said. She put a hand on his arm. "You did the right thing. It will be all right." She stood up, an anger boiling in her guts. She looked and was surprised to see the old woman who made her dress among those tending the boy. She nodded to her. "Make sure he eats," she said. There was not enough food, but this boy had earned it.

She turned to Thessala and motioned with her head for her to follow, led her aside between tents. "Soldiers," she said.

Thessala nodded. "The Archpriest is more afraid of us than I believed. We thought he would strike here, but he has not nerved himself yet."

"He could be waiting for more troops," Karana said. "It seems he has found a way to discourage refugees."

"Indeed," Thessala said. "And he did it away from the city, so we would not hear of it. We would not have, except for this brave boy."

"I am angry," Karana said, and the wind sprang up and swirled around them. "I am tired of being treated like an unwelcome obstacle. I seek only to stand for the safety and aid of those who need it most, and somehow that has made me an enemy of power." She ground her hands into fists.

"You have to go and check on this, see if you can find more survivors," Thessala said.

"This could be another ruse, to try and draw me away," Karana said.

"No, they made an effort to keep us from hearing of it. That does not seem like a trap." Thessala caught her hood and held it against the breeze. "Gentle now."

"I'm sorry," Karana said. "It gets away from me when I am roused." She took a long breath and tried to calm herself. "I mean it, they could send more men while I am away."

"Let them come," Thessala said. "I am not afraid. Let them send an entire cohort." She twisted her braid in her scaled hands. "Like you, I am angry."

"All right then," Kasandra said. She looked up at the sky, realized she would have to try and find the right place in the dark and almost decided to wait until morning, but then she thought of others hiding in the woods or the fields, wounded and afraid. She would have to do all she could. "All right then. Stay here and guard them all. I'll be back."

She went into her tent and changed, pulled on a loose pair of pants and laced her sandal straps over them to keep them in place. She pulled on a shirt that was too big for her and belted it with a piece of rope, and then she knotted her scarf tighter around her hair so it would not come loose. She had only practiced this a few times, never traveled so far.

Out into the dark, and she went to the center of the Stadia where the old stones lay cracked and weed-grown on the ground. There were no tents here, and it was the only place she could do this. She saw people gathering, crowding around to see, and she felt a terrible self-consciousness, as well as concern. They would see this, and they would think of her even more as a goddess or a witch or both. The fact that there was no help for it made no real difference.

She laced her fingers together, bowed her head and closed her eyes. She had to concentrate. The wind began to gather. She had learned that it was actually better to pull than to push. Once she was in the air, she could ride the wind like it was a big, billowing sheet. Getting there was the hardest part. Well, that and landing.

She focused her mind and *pulled*, in that strange way that was becoming familiar to her, and the wind rushed in around her, pressing in on her, and then she released an inner knot and she was hurled into the sky.

For a moment, there was silence, as if there was nothing, and then the sound of the wind roaring against itself reverberated across the sky. She heard shouts from below, an uplifting of many voices, and she looked down, unable to see much of anything save the open space and the dim crowds there. Already it was vanishing behind her, and she was rising higher and higher. The wind did not rush past her, because she was the wind, and it carried her with it. The ground dropped away, and it looked unreal, like it was a painting, or a tiny meadow lit with tiny lights.

She opened her arms and stabilized herself in the air, felt it all around her, as if she were sliding over an invisible sheet of silk as it billowed and rippled. She saw the city slide past below her, and the towers of the Citadel, and then she left that behind and was over the northern wall, the gate a tiny pinched place below her.

From there the road went north, a pale ribbon in the dark fields, and she set herself to following it, otherwise it would be far too easy to become lost out here in the silvery night. Now she was on her way she felt the giddiness and the dizzying fear of flight, and she found herself laughing, unable to help it, and equally unable to tell if she was terrified or exhilarated. She was free of the earth below, and for a while, she was indeed like the gods of old.

ଓ

It seemed as if she ought to get tired, but she didn't. After a while it became almost boring, watching the earth roll past beneath her. The road was easy to see, but she wondered how she would find the site of the attack. There would be bodies, perhaps, but she was not sure she would be able to see them. She dropped lower, flying along well above the tops of the trees, but still quite low. It made her seem to be going faster, and she thought about that. She was traveling much more quickly than anyone on foot. How far was half a day's travel in the sky? She had no idea, not how fast she was going, nor how fast she *could* go.

She saw lights from time to time, the twinkle of lanterns at the crossroads, or at farmhouses. It was impossible to tell from up here. She looked for any large areas of forest, as most of the countryside here was fields and orchards, not woodland. The boy said the soldiers hid in the woods to stage their ambush, so perhaps they would have a camp she could see from the air.

There. She saw a kink in the road as it passed a knot of forest, and the road was dotted with dark shapes. Her heart knotted up in her chest, and she dropped lower, and lower, and then she came in to land. The closer she got to the ground, the faster she seemed to be going, and no matter how she slowed, she was too fast. Unnerved, she lost her concentration and fell the last two body-lengths, hit the grass and flipped over twice, ending in a heap in the weeds.

She grunted and got up, brushed herself off, and headed back to the road. She stumbled a little, feeling odd and slow on the ground after so long in the sir. She seemed to be inching along, and the short walk to the road seemed much longer than she expected. It was an old imperial road and was bounded by low stone walls. This close to Orneas, they were in good condition, white in the glow of the star. Before she even reached them, she smelled death.

There was the ripping sound of many flies, and she drew back, covering her face. Just a glance over the waist-high wall showed her more than twenty corpses spilled on the road, each of them surrounded by pools of blackening blood. The smell was beyond belief, and she shied away from it, wincing. She had only seen dead bodies a few times in her life, and never this many in one place. She hadn't expected it to be this bad. The dead deserved better treatment than this; they should be gathered and decently burned. But she could not do it – she had the living to worry about.

The men who committed this crime would not be far away, and they might have prisoners with them, to be sold as slaves for profit. She felt anger again, cooled during her flight but now filling up again. This would not go unanswered. She would find the men who lurked along the road, sitting around campfires and laughing at their success. She would make them regret what they had chosen to do.

The reasonable thing to do would be to follow the signs of flight through the forest, but Karana did not have the slightest idea how to do that. In daylight she might have tried, but in the dark it would be laughably impossible. Instead she closed her eyes and rose up on the air, riding gentle currents until she was above the treetops. It was easier to do with no one watching her. The pressure of being considered some kind of divinity was unwelcome, but seemingly unavoidable.

She saw the wind stir the branches as she drifted over the woods, the white trunks of poplars standing out from the darker wood of oak and hornbeam. It was still early summer, and everything was thick with greenery, making it hard to see the ground, but she was really looking for fires, and she soon enough saw the wink of lights below.

There was no telling if they were the lights of refugees or marauders, so she found an open space and dropped down as cleanly as she could, not knowing what she would find. It was farther down than she thought, and she misjudged and dropped rather hard, staggered and fell into a bush. She grunted and fought free, found herself face to face with a cluster of anxious-looking people huddled around a small fire, gripping clubs made from branches and a few knives.

They stared at her. "Who are you?" She heard the northern accent and knew these were people from Ilion. She held out her hands in a gesture of peace.

"I. . . my name is Karana," she said. "I came from Ilion as well. I heard of what happened, and I came to help." She looked around, counting maybe two dozen people, mostly women and a few elderly men, children held close to their sides. "The men who attacked you, where are they?"

The women who spoke looked past her, into the dark. "Out there! We ran into the woods, and we hid. They came looking for us, but then something happened." She shivered. "Something came."

"What?" Karana looked into the dark as well, as if she would see some night demon there at her elbow, but there was nothing, only the silent trees. And then as she looked there came a cry, a human scream that rose higher and higher, and then it was cut off and there was a bellow, like no sound she had ever heard. What in Vasa's name?

She moved that way as the people huddled down among the trees, shrouding their few lanterns, trying to hide their meager fire. The wind gusted unpredictably, bringing to her nose the smell of sweat and smoke and fear, and then in the next moment only the clean scent of the woods. She listened, thinking that sure she would hear if anything large moved through the trees.

There were no night sounds, no sounds of insects or small animals. It was deathly silent, and then she heard footsteps, running fast. It sounded like someone running at a desperate pace, stumbling over rocks and roots. Karana beckoned the woman who had spoken, and she crept closer, holding up her small lantern. Karana helped her hold it, shining a feeble light onto the edge of the wood.

She saw motion first, and then it became a man, white-faced and gasping, running through the dark. Karana saw he wore a breastplate and an empty scabbard flapped at his side. One sandal was torn loose and flopped as he ran. She saw the terror on his features.

Then something black came down from the dark and crushed him to the earth. Karana just had time to realize it was a paw – the paw of some immense beast unseen against the dark, and then the man screamed and the claws clenched and crushed him underfoot. The woman behind Karana screamed and fled, dropping her lantern behind her as a terrible roar split the night. The light went out, and Karana was alone in the dark with something huge.

She heard it. Heard branches slide over something, heard heavy footfalls and breath like wind, and then there was a flicker and she saw eyes. They glowed red like embers and stood higher than her head, and then they turned away and the sound of the thing faded as it slipped away into the trees.

Karana caught her breath and picked up the lantern. Some coaxing and the guttered flame came back to life, and she steeled herself and followed, walking gently on the loamy earth. The dead man lay on the soil, broken and blooded, soaking the ground. Close by she found more tracks left by the thing. They looked like the prints of a lion, only they were enormous – wider than the length of her forearm.

She did not know what it was, but it had killed the soldier and left her and the refugees alone. What if it was someone else like Thessala? Someone transformed and trapped in a body not their own? She did not know what else it could be. She had read of monsters in legend, but had never seen one, and she did not believe there were such things, except now perhaps there were.

It was not hard to follow the tracks, even with the thin light of the lantern, because they were so enormous. They wound in among the trees, and she followed them up a long hill and through a grove of olive trees. She smelled the olives budding on the branches, and then she saw that the tracks she followed were smaller.

The trail wove a bit more, and the tracks grew smaller, until they almost vanished, and the last one she could make out looked like the footprint of a man. She felt her heart speed, looking at the evidence on the ground of something she would not have thought to be possible.

She looked up at a motion in the corner of her eye and saw a man there in nothing but dirty pants. He was not tall, and he was built heavily, with thick arms and short legs. As she looked, he pulled a shirt from the crotch of a tree and shrugged it on. He glanced at her. "Braver than the rest," he said.

"I'm not like the rest," she said. She looked at him, trying to see somewhere in him a sign of the thing he could become, but he looked ordinary. The kind of vagabond who would rob an orchard and sleep in the woods. "You are like us."

"Us?" he said. He pulled a waterskin from the tree where he'd hidden it and took a long drink.

"Yes, I... my name is Karana. I was at Ilion when it fell. You might have heard stories of the storm girl." She felt embarrassed saying it.

He swallowed hard and looked at her. "That you?"

She nodded. "It is. In Orneas I met a woman who is, well... she has been changed too. You're not the only one."

He looked dubious. "They said you fought a giant or some nonsense."

"Not a giant, just another one like us. Someone chosen." She thought it sounded much more foolish, saying it aloud. It occurred to her what a very strange conversation this was, with a man who had just casually changed himself back from a monster. He had obviously placed his clothes and a waterskin here in a tree to come back to when he was done.

He snorted. "Chosen by who?"

"I don't know," she said. "Perhaps the gods." She shrugged. It was not a very satisfying explanation.

"Gods have better things to do," he said. He drank again and this time Karana smelled the tang of wine.

"Maybe," she said. "But you can... change when you wish?" It seemed more outlandish than controlling the earth or the sky. To control one's own body.

"So far," he said. "Four times so far."

"Does it... does it hurt?" she said. She could not imagine that it didn't. How could reweaving your entire body not be painful?

"No," he said. He leaned against the tree trunk and looked at her. "You can make storms?"

"So far," she said, with a slight smile.

He snorted at that, and she couldn't tell if he was amused or annoyed. "Why are you out here?"

Karana glanced back the way she came, worried about Thessala. "We've gathered all the refugees in the city together, so we can protect them. We got word there was an attack out here, that the Archpriest sent soldiers to drive off those coming south on the roads. I came to stop it, but you got here first." She looked at him, wondering what kind of man this was. Karana did not consider herself a great judge of character; she was better at books.

He shrugged. "Not right, killing people like that." He took another drink. "You say the Archpriest sent them?"

"More or less," she said. "It's... rather complicated."

"Maybe I need to pay him a visit." He looked at his wineskin, annoyed. She could not tell what, precisely, he was annoyed with it for.

"We know he's going to send troops against us soon, try and drive all the refugees out," she said. "You could come and help us." She imagined a hulking beast would be more intimidating than just she and Thessala alone, no matter what they could do.

He grunted. "You need help?"

She laughed. "Perhaps not. But soon the barbarians are going to come south to attack the city. And then we would need your help." She looked at him. "You're not from Ilion, are you?"

"I'm from all over," he said. He glanced up at the sky. "You think he'll send more men out here?"

She shrugged. "I know as much as you do about that. Less, probably. How many were there?"

"About thirty, I think. Maybe ten got away." He showed his teeth. "I don't think they'll be back though."

"Well, I'm going to find all the refugees I can and shepherd them to the city. Then if the gates guards try and keep them out, I'll have a word with them." She smiled a little at how confident she sounded. "What about you?"

He sniffed, shrugged, and then scratched at his shaggy hair. "I guess I'll come along then."

"Will you tell me your name?" she said.

He snorted then, pulled a bag down from the tree, slung a worn bow over his shoulder. "Lykaon, they call me. You can call me that too." His eyes glittered in the light of her lantern, and she felt in that moment somewhat less alone.

Chapter Fourteen

Beasts of Old

It was afternoon by the time they reached the city gates. Karana was not tired, and that was a blessing, because herding so many frightened people along the road was not an easy task. Many of them were weak, or hungry, or ill, and she could not do anything for them. Her power, whatever it was, did not allow her to heal the sick or the lame. She could not conjure food from nothingness.

In that respect she was glad for the company of Lykaon. He was obviously a man who spent a great deal of time in the wilds. He knew plants and trees, helped them gather mushrooms and roots and berries that were safe to eat. Karana knew more about berries to be found in far kingdoms than the ones all around her, and was somewhat embarrassed by it. He did not say anything to her; indeed, he said very little at all.

More people gathered to join them through the morning, creeping out of the forest and the brush. As they went down the road their numbers grew, until Karana found she was leading over a hundred people, and she felt a little overwhelmed by it. They did not know who she was, and she made no demonstrations of her power. But they listened to her, and she wondered why. Perhaps she had a new authority and confidence in her manner now, or perhaps they were simply afraid and exhausted, glad to have anyone to guide them.

When they came over the hill and in sight of Orneas, it looked strange and lovely, with the Archpriest's citadel looming over it, the towers golden in the afternoon sun, and the blue-gray expanse of the sea off to the right. She had to remind herself that they might very well meet a hostile reception here, as things had not changed, and the powers in the city had no desire to admit the helpless or the fearful. It made her angry, and she hoarded that, knowing she might need it. The sky was clear, but as her mood grew apprehensive, the wind turned restless, shifting from quarter to quarter.

From here the walls looked much more formidable, standing high against the pale afternoon sky, casting a long shadow. As they came closer she saw men moving on the battlements, and she wondered how bad this would be. The main gate was shut, but that was not unusual. Most traffic moved through the smaller gate set in the larger one, tall enough for a man to enter, but not when mounted. To get a horse through a man had to get down and walk it, and a wagon would fit so long as it was not too wide and was handled carefully.

She motioned the people to stay back, and she saw the fear in their eyes. It was hard to look at that – to see little children afraid of what was going to happen. They had fled from an invading army, and now had as much to fear from the people who should have protected them.

Lykaon sauntered up and leaned on his bow, squinting at the city. He made a disgusted noise and spat on the ground. "Ugly place."

"You don't seem like the city sort," she said. She took a breath. "Watch them, would you? I'm going to go and get them to open the gate and let us in."

He poked his tongue in his cheek, looking at the walls. "And if they don't?"

"Then I'll open it myself," she said. "Keep them back, I don't want to hurt anyone accidentally."

"Just on purpose," he said, seeming amused.

She made no answer to that. Tucking her scarf around her hair, she made her way to the wall, the stones worn smooth by many feet. She approached the small gate and it was slammed in her face, she heard the bolts being shot and ground her teeth. After everything, she had just about had enough of this. She went right up to the gate and pounded on it, amazed by how hard she could hit it, how loud the sound was. "Open the gate!" she shouted, getting angrier by the minute.

There was no response, and she pounded on the door again, the wood shaking and creaking as she hit it. She wondered if she could tear the gate open with her hands. Would that be the best thing? No, no she needed more of a demonstration, and she did not want to damage the gates if she could help it, because when the Almanni arrived they would need them.

She heard a sound above her, a scraping noise, and then she was suddenly doused in hot water. There was hissing as it poured down, and she felt the heat, and steam rose off her skin. She realized the water was likely boiling, or near to it, and had been meant to mutilate or kill her, and she lost her temper.

Wind rushed in around her so fast it flattened the grass. The air bellowed, and then Karana shot upwards, vaulted into the air. She rose over the wall and looked down at the top, saw the battlements were crowded with armed men, and as she rose into view some of them ran, while others lifted bows and fired what looked like a few dozen arrows at her. The wind caught the shafts and slapped them aside, and Karana lifted her hand and gathered in her power, and then brought it down.

The wind roared with sudden fury, and it slammed across the top of the wall like an unseen hand. Men were launched from the wall and hurled down into the street below, scattered along the battlements, and smashed against the stone. Swords and arrows and spears lifted in a cloud and rained down on the street, some of them driven into the rock itself by the force she unleashed. A cloud of dust billowed up, and wind ripped the roof off the guardhouses behind the wall, scattered shards of wood into the sky.

Stunned, Karana almost fell, managing to control herself enough that she landed hard on top of the wall. She stared at the damage, saw the men lying still on the street below, and felt a little sick. Yes, they had chosen to try and harm her, but she was not hurt. She remembered the dead bodies back on the road last night and shook it off. These men had chosen to follow murderous commands; she could not go gentle with them.

She lifted herself a little, swung over and dropped down into the street behind the wall. There were more men here, gathered in tight-packed ranks, spears jutting out. They started towards her, shaking, and she swept out her arm and the wind dashed them against the wall, scattering shields and spears across the stone.

The nearest one staggered up, and she caught him by his armor and lifted him up, shoved him against the wall. "I have had quite enough of you, of all of you. I have brought those seeking protection and shelter, and *they will have it*, or by all the gods I will shatter this gate and leave you to pick through the ruins." She let him drop, saw other men getting up, looking at her, trying to decide what to do. She closed her eyes and called, and the sky answered with a peal of thunder that seemed to crack across the sky and echo from the far horizon. The men hunched and flinched from the noise, and she wondered what would happen if she called a stroke of lightning down on the gate.

"Open the gate, and open it now," she said, and not one of them dared meet her eyes.

☙

Once the gate was open, the soldiers scattered and she saw not a sign of them as she led her people in through the arch and into the city. She didn't know how the mechanism worked, but she didn't want to leave the gate open behind them, so she waited until the refugees were all in, trying to ignore their sideways glances and the look of fear on their faces. Now they knew what she could do as well as anyone did. She herself didn't know what she could do if she tried her utmost.

When they were through she called a wind and pushed the gate closed again, hearing the clank of chains inside the gatehouses. She had to hope she wasn't damaging anything. She looked at the street, saw several men lying there still, unmoving. She felt heavy in her belly as she went to the nearest one and knelt down by him. He was sprawled on his face, and she turned him over. The way his head moved told her his neck must be broken. She had not meant, really, to hit them so hard. She did not yet know her own strength.

This was the first man she knew for certain she had killed, and it weighed on her. She wanted to say or do something, but there was nothing to do, and she had living people who needed her guidance and protection. She stood up, then turned and walked away. The streets were largely empty, though she saw faces looking down from windows, quickly ducking out of sight behind curtains.

It made her tense. She made her way through the crowd to where Lykaon walked, and she nudged him. "Be ready," she said. "I think there will be trouble."

"Oh, I know," he said. "I can smell it." He gestured to the right. "Men pacing us a street over, watching for a good spot to strike." He shrugged. "Do you know where we're going? Because I don't know where anything is in this place."

She shook her head. "Of course. We go ahead, to the square, then follow the road that goes left."

"Square will be the spot, then," he said. He shrugged off his bag and bow, handed them to a small boy. "Watch those for me," he said. The boy looked at Karana, and she nodded. When she looked back, Lykaon had shrugged off his shirt, and she averted her eyes as he kicked off his pants, tossed them to her. "I'll scout," he said.

There was some laughter as he jogged ahead, naked and looking faintly ridiculous. Then he seemed to shiver inside his skin, and the laughter stopped as he dropped to all fours and *changed*. It all happened fast enough that her eye had a hard time following it. He seemed to swell bigger, his bones and joints pushing inside his skin, and then he simply flowed too fast into another shape for the separate stages of it to be distinct.

It was the first time Karana had a really good look at what he became. He looked like a black lion, but larger than any lion she could imagine. His shoulder was higher than her head, and his body longer than three horses. He had a heavy black mane and a long tail like something that belonged on a lizard, spiked with spines and slithering side to side. Fur covered his forelegs and shoulders, then faded to black scales on the back of his body. She stared at the impressive display of muscle across his haunches and back as he moved, and she felt a kind of dizziness at the fact that he had just *changed* himself. It seemed so unnatural.

He shook himself, and the crowd of refugees drew back and Karana heard screams. He was huge and looked impossible in full daylight. His weight cracked the stone and she felt the shudder of his footfalls through the ground. There was a smell from him, like hot brass, and the low growl that came from him made her shiver. Lykaon looked back and showed his teeth in what was probably a smile, and then he turned and loped away, moving easily as a black shadow down the empty street, his claws gouging the paving stones.

Karana shook her head. The world was becoming stranger by the day, and she had no answer for it. She looked back at the frightened faces and held her hand up to calm them. "It's all right," she said, beckoning. "It's all right, he is here to protect you, as am I." She looked ahead and squared her shoulders, gathering her will. "As am I."

☙

Thessala heard the thunder and looked up, hoping it meant that Karana was returned from the hinterlands. Despite her professed calm, she was uneasy. What had happened out there? She had expected her to return soon, but then she thought of the refugees, and she knew that if any survived, Karana would not leave them. She would stay and lead them back to the city once she had dealt with any danger.

So she had tried to relax, going among her people, walking through the tents and trying to make sure everyone had enough water and food. It was getting harder, because food at least was not easy to come by. Merchants knew there was a war on, and many of them had already taken ship and left, while the rest were taking the opportunity to raise their prices as high as they could get away with. It was enough to make her fume. They had bread, and she tried to see to it that at least the children were fed enough.

Many of the newcomers did not know what she was and seemed unconcerned, but others who had seen her face made signs to ward off evil and ducked away. Not all of them, but many of them looked at her differently. The story was spreading around, and no doubt some would not believe it. Half of her felt she should cast aside her cowl and go among them as she was, but every fearful glance was like the stab of a knife. They were afraid, and she could not blame them, and yet she did. She had given her life in service to the needy, and now they did not trust her.

She left the cluster of tents and shelters and walked the perimeter, around the outer border of the Stadia. The stands were old and worn, but she climbed them to get a better vantage point, to see around them. To the east the city grew older and more decrepit, in neighborhoods no one chose to live in, close-packed and dirty. North was one of the old boulevards, wide and open and clean. It led from here to the heart of the city where the Citadel loomed over the old capitol hill. That was the way that worried her, as any large force of men would have to come that way – no other road was wide enough.

Another rumble of thunder in the clear sky, and she smiled. That must be Karana, returned at last. No doubt the men at the gates had orders to refuse entry, and she was contesting the issue. That would not slow her very long, and she would bring them here soon. That would make their food problem more acute, and she knew they would have to do something about that today or tomorrow. She knew there were grain storehouses and other places where food was kept by the Archpriest. So far she had refrained from outright theft, hoping to prevent all-out war, but her options were growing thin.

There was movement on the road, and she crouched down and squinted. Her vision was better now than it had been in years, and she saw with a kind of cruel sharpness as soldiers began to pour into the wide boulevard. Twenty, thirty, and then she stopped counting. It was too many. If she let them reach the Stadia, they would get past her and in among the people in her charge. She could not let that happen.

She was about to signal danger when the soldiers blew horns to get their men in formation, and then she no longer had to, as everyone knew what that meant. She saw faces upturned, looking to her, and she waved for them to take cover. There were rooms under the stands where they could hide the children and the weakest, and they would have to form some kind of defense. They had few weapons, and fewer still fit to bear them, but they would do whatever they could to protect themselves.

They would have to only if she could not. Thessala drew in a deep breath and jumped down from the back of the stands, landing easily after a drop many times her height. Her cowl fell back and she cast it off, shrugged off her robe and went to meet them in her long shift only, arms and legs bare. She took her long braid and knotted it around itself at the back, to keep it out of her way. She walked down the long street without hurrying, one woman against what looked like hundreds of soldiers.

They came on like a wave, and she felt an unreality at the sight of them. How could this be happening? How could she be here? She shook her head and tried to gather herself. She resolved to try and back them down. They had heard what she was capable of, she was sure of that, and she had no desire to kill anyone else. She had spent her years in service to healing the sick and the injured. Violence did not please her, no matter the cause.

Except, in some way, it did please her. She felt again that thrum in her muscles, a pressure at the backs of her arms and her legs, a readiness in her gut. Part of her wanted to be free to fight and to kill, and she tasted that bitter flavor in her mouth again, like ruined wine. She ground her teeth and fought to control her suddenly volatile temper.

The front line formed up, shields locked and ready, spearpoints jutting out in a hedge of steel. Thessala stopped in the middle of the street and held up her hands, fingers spread. "I have no desire for trouble," she called; her voice was very loud when she wanted. "This does not have to happen."

There was movement behind the front line, and then she had a moment to puzzle over the strange plucking sound before arrows started to strike her body. They glanced off her arms and her chest, ripped her shift and snagged in her hair. One struck just to the side of her left eye and she flinched back with a curse, covering her face.

She heard rushing feet, and by the time she recovered, the front line of spearmen was almost on her. Thessala bared her teeth and covered her face with her arms as spears rammed against her scaled skin. It felt like being jabbed with sticks, and then they battered at her with their shields and almost knocked her down. She stumbled as they started to close in around her, and then her temper broke.

She heaved against them, knocking men down, splitting their shields. Spears jabbed at her and she grabbed them, broke them off, hurled the pieces into the faces of the soldiers. Then she ground her hands into fists and struck about her all but blindly, knocking them aside like dolls, scattering and splitting the front line as easily as toy soldiers. One man hurled himself at her, dagger in his fist, and he stabbed her in the chest, only to see the tip of the blade snap off.

He tried to drag her down and she lifted him and threw him aside, knocking more men down. They drew swords and hacked at her and she smashed them aside, feeling armor crumple under her hands, helmets crush like paper when she hit them.

She broke them, and they turned and ran. Arrows slashed at her, glancing off her skin, and she hissed, a sound that came from deep in her throat, like nothing she had ever heard before. It was like the sound of meat on hot metal, like boiling. Her mouth was full of something vile and she spat it out, saw her slaver smoke and hiss on the stone. "Get out!" she bellowed, hardly recognizing her own voice. "Get out of here!"

The men drew away, and for a moment she thought they were fleeing, but then she saw the main body part for something, and there was a device there, something low and dark and evil-looking. She saw a flare of fire, and then she recognized the squat shape of a ballista.

It fired, launching a ball of flame at her, and she covered her face and ducked. The heavy bolt, as long as a man, trailed fire behind it as it hurtled toward her. She felt the iron head slam into her shoulder, and then the firepot affixed to the shaft exploded, and flaming oil engulfed her in a sudden inferno.

Chapter Fifteen

Fire and Blood

Thessala screamed, flailing as she was bathed in burning oil. She smelled it, the acrid stench stinging in her nose and her mouth. The heat was all over her, stinging and crackling. Her shift caught fire and burned savagely, falling away in glowing shreds. It blinded her, and that was the worst part, as she suddenly could see nothing at all. She heard shouts over the hissing of the fire, and she slapped at herself, trying to beat the flames away.

There was another sound like a horse kicking a wall, and then another iron-headed bolt smashed into her chest, knocking her down. She thrashed, losing her sense of direction. Her fingers clawed into the stone, and then she heard running feet, and the clatter of spears.

Men closed in around her, and they struck her with their spears, a dozen blows in a breath, all over her body. She kicked and flailed at them, but she couldn't see, and they were no more than sounds and shadows. They hit her again, the points digging into the skin on her belly, on her neck. A blow hit her in the face, almost in the eye, and she panicked, gave a scream that sounded inhuman, and then her throat burned.

She thought it was the burning oil, but it wasn't. Her throat felt thick, and it swelled. She opened her mouth as it flooded with something bitter, and then she spat it forth in a spray that caught the flames and exploded into a cloud of fire. She heard screams, and then she shook the oil from her eyes and clawed to her feet. Around her men were screaming, thrashing their arms, throwing away their spears and their shields. Fire clung to them, and they clawed at their faces, smoke coming from under the metal. Several of them fell and gagged blood onto the stones.

What had she done? She spat on the stone and saw it smolder there, and she realized there was something in it besides bile. There was some kind of venom in her, something that burned.

The flames were dying out as the oil burned away, leaving her blackened and smudged but unharmed. Naked, she faced the enemy, and she saw the ballista cranking back for another shot, the men who crewed it working like demons to get it ready. At her feet lay the last bolt they had shot her with, the iron head blunted and split from striking her.

A man reeled into her and she shoved him away, started to walk toward the line of men, unhurried and deliberate. She brushed soot from her arms, hating the burnt smell. She saw them form the front again, shields close, spears pointing out. She heard the bows again and more arrows lashed at her, snapping and glancing off her armored skin. Thessala was losing her fear. Steel and iron did not cut her, fire did not burn her. Even a siege weapon could do no more than knock her down.

"You will not pass me!" she called to them, making her voice sound jagged and fierce. "You cannot cut me, you cannot burn me!" Arrows rattled on the stone, and she realized their aim was worsening. She came closer, and the lines of soldiers shuffled back, recoiling from her.

The ballista fired again, and she steeled herself, bracing against the street, her heart hammering in sheer terror. She saw the whole mechanism jump like a kicking mule, the arms snap forward, and then the barely-seen bolt lanced out and hit her in the chest. She felt the impact sharply – not pain, quite, but a hard blow. The iron head crumpled and then the haft snapped and flew apart in pieces. She felt the blow thrum through her, like a note too low to hear, and then she shrugged it off.

She heard someone scream an order to attack, and the lines of men moved uncertainly. The ranks were loose and sloppy, no longer looking as straight as they had, as solid. She knew they were afraid, and she wondered if they had one more attack left in them. Enough of this, time to break their will.

The boulevard was ancient, lined with ruined columns so old not one of them still stood complete. They were made in the old way, layers stacked up one atop the other. Now those wheel-like segments of stone were all fallen down, lying dirty and fractured, some of them overgrown by vines. Thessala turned to the side and went to one, bent down and gripped it with her hands.

For a moment she did not believe she could really lift it, but it came up easily, as if it were made of light wood. She hoisted it above her head and balanced for a moment. More arrows glanced off her, and she laughed a little. The situation was absurd, time to end it.

She threw it, a piece of stone that weighed ten times what she did. It flew in a long arc and then smashed down among the soldiers as they scattered. It bounced, slammed through the archers, and then bounced again before it crushed a last man near the back. There were cries of pain and terror, and she tasted venom in her mouth again. Her heart was beating hard, and she felt almost as though she were outside her body. There was that anger again, that hunger to attack and strike – to *hit* things.

There was another block of stone, and she grabbed it and lifted it over her head, and the front lines scattered, men scrambling to get out of her way. She heard men crying orders, trying to get the soldiers back into formation. She saw them moving at the back, the rear ranks she had not yet faced, and she had a sense then of the immense endurance of an army, how they could keep throwing more and more men at her until they broke or she did.

Then she saw the ballista again, turning to point at her. The crew working to load it again, and she shifted her position, taking aim at it with her chunk of marble. One good blow would smash it, and then she would throw more and more until they gave up and ran.

Something roared close by, sounding huge and terrible, a sound that echoed off the walls and the old buildings, rattled her teeth in her skull. She saw a shadow, and then something immense leaped over the ranks of spears and landed on top of the ballista, shattering it with brute force.

She stared. It was a massive animal, like nothing she had ever seen. Black as midnight, it was formed like a lion, only bigger than any lion that ever lived. It had a vast, shaggy mane, and powerful, clawed forelimbs. The lower part of its body was scaled, leading to a long, serpentine tail that lashed behind it.

As she looked, wondering if she should throw her rock at it, it wrenched the remains of the ballista apart with the flex of one claw, and then it turned and looked at her. It had eyes red as fresh coals, set in that leonine face that was so strangely human. It bared saber-like teeth and licked them, and then it winked at her.

Then it turned and hurled itself upon the cowering soldiers, and their last shred of courage broke. It scattered them like toys, bellowing so loudly the sound made chips of stone dance on the street. She saw men drive their spears against it, and they bent and broke like reeds.

Thessala gave a great shout and hurled her stone, sending it smashing through the ranks of men, and then she charged after it. She saw men throw down their spears and their shields, and they ran. It was astonishing how fast they fled, darting into side streets, shoving one another out of the way. They scattered like ants, and the whole force of hundreds seemed to vanish before her like an illusion.

She stopped. She had no desire to hunt down and kill men, no matter how her arms ached for violence. She turned away and bit her tongue, trying to calm the heat within her that cried out for blood. She spat venom onto the street and knotted her fists and breathed deep, getting control of herself. It was like a storm in her chest, or in her mind. Slowly, very slowly, it cooled.

When she looked, she saw the street was scattered with dead men, and the reality of that struck her. She never meant to kill, never wanted to kill, but now she had. She felt a sudden flux of dizziness and stumbled to a fallen column and sat on it. She remembered she was naked and she looked around for something to cover herself with, but there was nothing not being worn by a corpse.

She heard a growl, low and steady, and then she stood up as the beast came back across the battlefield, stepping over the fallen dead. It picked its way with a certain delicacy. Up close, it looked even bigger and more terrible than it had from a distance. She smelled blood on it, and a musky, heavy smell underneath. It was not a lion; it was some monster out of old times. A chimera or a griffon, only not like either of them.

It came closer and she braced herself, wondering if it was about to attack her; instead it stopped, sniffed the air, and then it *changed*. She blinked as its flesh seemed to run, the black fur to retreat and vanish, and then it blurred too fast and she missed the rest of it, found herself looking at a heavily built man who picked himself up off the ground and stood as naked as she was. She glanced down and then made herself avert her gaze, looked at his face.

He scratched at a ragged beard, and then smiled. "You must be Thessala. Heard all about you."

She blinked. "You. . . you came with Karana." It was the only explanation – he was another one like them.

He nodded. "I did."

"I. . . I thank you for your help," she said. "I have not. . ." She looked away. She wanted to say she had not been in a battle before, but that was not true. She wanted to say she had not killed before, but she had.

He shrugged, seemingly unbothered by his own nudity. "You didn't need help," he said. He looked her up and down, as casually as if he were in the bath house, and then he nodded. "Scales," he said, as if it were a secret between them, and then he sauntered off.

Thessala blinked, wondering if she was meant to say something, but then she heard voices and turned to see a crowd coming down the street. She tensed, but then she saw these were not soldiers. They were dirty and weary and carrying whatever they had, and at the head of them was Karana, and Thessala had never been so glad to see anyone in her life.

☙

Karana was so glad to see Thessala she wanted to run to her. There was a smell of smoke in the air, dead soldiers scattered on the street, and as she came closer she saw her friend was sooty and blackened and naked. Karana hurried forward and drew off her outer robe, draped it over Thessala's shoulders. "Are you all right?"

"Yes," Thessala said, then embraced her hard enough to make her grunt as she was squeezed tightly. "There was a little trouble."

Karana looked around, seeing the broken arrows, splintered shields, and even what looked like ballista bolts. "So I see." She saw the blood around the bodies. "This just happened."

"Yes. It seems the Archpriest just gathered his courage," Thessala said.

"Poor timing," Karana said. She looked and saw Lykaon making his way through the crowd, shrugging back into his clothes. "Very poor. I see you have met Lykaon."

"I have," Thessala said somewhat guardedly. "What do you know of him?" she said, looking at him boldly. "He looks ill-favored."

Karana almost laughed, both at what Thessala said, and at how Lykaon seemed unaffected by it. "He was with the refugees, doing what he could to protect them. He is like us."

"Perhaps," Thessala said.

"Lykaon," Karana said. "Would you lead the new people into the Stadia, there? Thessala will help you look after them."

"Where are you going?" Thessala said. Karana realized the older woman was looking to her to lead, and she wondered how that had happened.

Karana sighed. "I am going to go and have a word with the Archpriest," she said. It sounded ludicrous – her, an archivist, speaking of bracing one of the most powerful men in the empire – and yet she had little choice. "He struck against both of us, sent men to kill refugees on the road. He is not done, and he will try again. But I am done." She felt the anger from before, remembered the dead on the road. She held onto her anger, knowing she would need it. "I am done waiting for him to act, over and again. I have had enough." She looked north, over the rooftops, to the Citadel's towers looming high above the city. "A lesson needs to be taught. An example made."

Thessala caught her arm. "You should not kill him." It was almost a question.

"I wish to kill no one," Karana said. And yet I find again and again that I am forced to it. I killed men at the gate, and you have killed men here twice now, and who has suffered? So long as his attempts cost him nothing, he will continue."

"You are doing just what Galbos wants," Thessala said.

"I am, and I will use him as far as I can, to get what I wish." Karana smiled at Thessala. "I know you think I am naïve, and perhaps I am, but I have read so many histories that these political maneuverings seem almost familiar to me. It is only because I do not understand cruelty that I am surprised by it. I am not a fool. It will be useful to have Galbos to take control of the city government and keep the

Archpriest out of our hair." She shrugged. "Do you see another way?"

Thessala let go of her arm, took a heavy breath. "No, curse it."

"Then keep watch, and I will be back soon." Karana squinted at the towers. "Which tower does the Archpriest live in?"

"The one closest to the harbor, so I have heard," Thessala said. "Go and find out."

"I suppose I will." Karana tried to think of a way out of what she had to do, and then she shrugged and called in the winds. She lifted up easily, the grass flattening around her as she rose. She was getting better at this. She took a last glance down at Thessala below, her tall form holding the robe around her as the wind whipped at it. Then she turned away, looked at the towers, and vaulted across the sky.

ᛞ

She hurled herself across the city so fast it made her dizzy, seeing the buildings sweep by underneath her, the shadows so dramatic in the late afternoon. The sun was setting over the sea, and from here she could see it unobstructed and clear, the clouds and the water both seeming to turn into fire, ripples of orange and gold.

From above, the Citadel actually looked taller, and from here the perspective of the towers made them look too tall – like an illusion. They cast long shadows over the tangle of courtyards and lesser buildings within the walls that made up the whole edifice. She realized that no one else had ever seen it quite like this, like a miniature on a tabletop. She saw men on the walls, like ants crawling around, and she felt dizzy, her mind almost paralyzed by how high she was. She wondered what would happen to her if she fell this far. Would that even hurt?

She steeled herself. Now was the time when she had to be merciless, and she felt it like a knot in her stomach. Karana closed her eyes and pictured the dead on the road, the soldiers at the gates pouring boiling water on her. She imagined them doing that to the people, if she had not been there. Boiling water poured on children and mothers and old men. Anger bloomed in her guts, and she looked at the Citadel and remembered the rich rugs and hangings, the cold, wealthy power it embodied, careless of life or mercy.

Cold winds whipped around her as she floated over the towers, and then the sky above her turned black, and the stain spread like ink in water, billowing across the sky, turning the dying sunlight to something twisted and greenish. Clouds gathered and piled up above her, roiling in the sky. She felt the effects of what she did spread out from her, like ripples in a pond. Thunder growled above, and she felt the flick of rain on her face.

She had to terrify the Archpriest, without accidentally killing him, and she already felt the weather she had conjured growing stronger, threatening to get away from her, out of control. If she let it go too long, she would lose her grip.

Karana closed a hand of unseen air around the tower, and she flexed her strength like fingers. The stained glass in every window exploded outwards, and she blinked at the flash of lightning. Thunder called, so close, and she flinched from it. She felt the scars on her skin tingle with remembered fire, and she saw green storm-sparks leaping from the iron points on the battlements below.

She waved her hand, and the wind grew to a scream and tore the tiled roof off the tower, scattering it like a handful of pebbles. She saw the rooms within laid bare, the walls collapsing, hangings and rugs and furniture sucked up and hurled into the building storm. Lightning flashed and thunder shouted, and in the flickering light she saw people moving in the destruction.

She dropped down, down, and landed in the ruin of the upper floor. She realized she had torn through the top floor and exposed the one beneath it, and servants and guards cowered in the rubble. There was a sumptuous bed, the canopy half-ripped away and flapping in the wind like a torn sail. Beside it was a fallen wardrobe and a jumble of books, and she reached in and pulled the human shape from under it, found she was eye to eye with the Archpriest himself.

"You!" he screamed, and he looked far less composed this time. His white hair was loose and disheveled, and his robe was torn. She knotted the heavy, gilded cloth in her hands, drew it tight around his body, and then she lifted back into the sky, dragging him screaming after her.

She rose high, and higher, and then she held there, the wind holding them both up, lightning flashing again and again, the thunder so close it was deafening. It was getting hard to hold herself steady, the air was becoming so turbulent. Rain lashed at them both.

The Archpriest looked down and screamed again, clutching at her. She held him at arm's length so he could not get a grip, and shook him when he would not hold still. He didn't look powerful now, or dignified, or wise. He looked like a terrified old man, and she found it distasteful, seeing him reduced like this.

She wanted to say something, but now she could think of nothing, and the thunder was so loud she doubted he would hear her easily anyway. So she pulled him in close, stared him in the eyes. "Remember this," she said, pitching her voice over the wind, and then she let him go.

He shrieked as he plummeted, and she let him fall a little before she caught him with the wind, slowed his fall, and then kept him slow as he spiraled down, past the tower, past the walls, and she dropped him in a tree in a courtyard down below.

Lightning flashed, and she felt it, looked at her hands and saw blue lightning crawling on her skin like snakes. Right now she had to fight the storm she had called up and keep it from getting out of control. She turned away and flew back over the city, calming and scattering the energy behind her, leaving a trail of thunder howls and tattered clouds in her wake as she sought a way back down to the earth.

Chapter Sixteen

Road of Bones

Arthras stood on the hill and looked up at the star. The trail of it was fainter, now, and it covered less of the sky. He saw colors in it, against the night, that he had not seen before, little shimmers of gold and pink and green. He could not feel the power seeping down from it, and he felt as if he should feel it, the hand of fate that had reached down and made him a power in the world. It was fading, but he was not, and he did not believe the power given him would fade. He felt the strength of the Bear Goddess in his hands, and he would use it.

He looked down and saw the camp spread out along the road. It was strange to travel so far on a well-laid road. It bothered him in a way, to see a path laid by men that had endured for so long that the land seemed to have shaped itself around it. He had heard, all his life, of the famed imperial roads, but he had not really believed in them.

All around them was farmland, the fields worked in regular, square patterns as if made from stitched cloth, the fallow fields dark and the ones bearing this year's harvest burgeoning with green. Orchards in stately rows and vineyards with their wooden frames to grow the vines of heavy grapes. There were houses and barns and mills and a hundred other small things. Such a long-tamed land. Even the knots of forest and the lines of trees that followed the rivers and streams seemed lesser, as though they huddled on the edge of the works of man.

He had been born in a hard land, with wild woods and soaring mountains on all sides. The fields he knew were rough, hewn from the stony soil, the marks of the plow uneven to go around boulders and stumps that could not be moved. The fences for livestock were from split rails and tied with rawhide thongs, and in the winter rabbits ate the rawhide and the beams fell down and cattle escaped. He had never seen anything like these endless, rolling hills and the sun-blessed fields that seemed overgrown with life. Just looking at it gave him a new sense of the size of the empire and made him feel small by comparison, and he didn't like it.

The army was camped all along the road, spread out into the fields and lit by hundreds of campfires. It was warm by day under the sun, but at night the breezes were cool. He saw so many tents, and many more shelters made with makeshift materials – bolts of looted cloth and spear hafts driven into the ground. He heard singing and laughing, and he wondered how long it would last. The marching had been easy, the foraging rich and the weather pleasant. He hoped they did not forget their ferocity when they needed it.

He walked back down the hill, unnoticed and irked by it. He was the center of this army. He should not pass unremarked; he should be followed and spoken of and bowed to, not ignored. There was so much he wanted to do, and he did not know how to do it.

His own tent was a massive thing, all of blue and purple silks hung with tassels and gold. He didn't much like it, but it seemed grand enough for a king, and Nicaea was comfortable in it, or as much as she could be. He had quickly learned that she had a passion for her small comforts and luxuries. He found it annoying.

He burst through the tent flaps, the men guarding the doorway drawing stiff as he approached them. Behind their helmets he could not see their faces, and he wondered if they were afraid. He wanted to see them be afraid. Sometimes he felt like he slept in a field of knives that would stab him if they could. He had dreams of arrows and swords snapping against his skin, when he dreamed at all. He did not sleep very much anymore, and sometimes even his days had a floating quality, as if he were dreaming everything.

The inside of the tent was like a world apart from everything else, with silk curtains walling off parts of it, so it was almost like being inside a real palace. The ground was covered by rugs and cushions, and there was real furniture in here – chairs and couches and braziers all lit by the low-hanging lamps. It smelled like incense and sweet oils in here, so cloying his nose wrinkled.

As soon as he entered, one of the slave girls jumped up and ran to fetch Nicaea, and he grimaced. He was not accustomed to servants or slaves, and it felt strange to him. To eat or sleep or fuck with other people so close, not speaking unless spoken to. Nicaea had always had them, and she simply acted as if they didn't exist unless she needed them to do something, but their presence was awkward and strange to him.

Nicaea came in, dressed in one of her sweeping white gowns and dripping with a hundred jewels. Her hair was gathered and braided in a bewildering knot, and there was dark coloring around her eyes. She smiled when she saw him, and that at least seemed genuine. She made her slight bow, playful but not mocking. "The night air not to your liking?"

He grunted. "I don't know what to do," he said.

She eased herself down on a long couch and beckoned him, but he paced rather than sat. He didn't like sitting, pacing helped him think. She let it pass with that way she had of simply pretending everything was her idea. "What do you want to do?"

"I want to *lead* this army," he said, frustrated. "I just feel like part of it. The men are all gathered with their chiefs and thanes – no one comes to me to say anything. I have guards but I don't need guards." He waved a hand dismissively. "They all chose to come with me, why do they stay away from me?"

Nicaea tapped her finger against her lower lip. "Barbarians are not like civilized men, but soldiers are the same everywhere," she said. "You must go to them, and seem one of them, but better than they are. You must care for them, see that they have what they need, and you must show there is nothing you will ask of them that you cannot do." She sighed. "But you are not like a normal general or king, you are like a god to them. Do you want them to love you, or fear you?"

"They will never love me," he said. He stood close to a lamp and touched it, feeling the heat, knowing it would burn lesser flesh than his. He put his fingers in the flame, feeling it like water slipping around his skin, something more like air, that he could almost touch, but not quite. "Men don't love kings."

"Maybe not, but they do love gods. But I think you are right. Love comes after fear." She toyed with her hair. "For now, remain aloof. It will make you seem less human, and that will make your legend grow. A god is made of legends, after all. And you are better, because you are real, not imagined."

"The gods are real," he said stiffly. "Bora is real, she has chosen me."

"Perhaps," she said. "Or perhaps the gods were once people just like you. Who can say?"

"Stop," he said, feeling angry at her lack of any faith. It was what made him wary of her, even as he needed her. She believed, really, in nothing. He wanted to trust her, and to a degree he did, but he knew she would turn on him if she saw a better path to what she wanted. She had thrown over her husband for a barbarian in a heartbeat. He did not lie to himself about her loyalty.

She shrugged. "When you appear among them, you must behave as though you are always right. You must do what you will and never hesitate or apologize or back down. You must be a force of nature, like the wind or a fire. Do not allow any man to argue or tell you what you may do."

Arthras grunted again. He liked the sound of it, but he also remembered how the men had turned against Usiric so easily. They had watched him kill a king, and none of them had really tried to stop him. Their courage was thin, and their loyalty was thinner. They had feared Usiric and his power. If they had loved him, they would have died for him. Arthras didn't know ho to make them love him. He doubted it was possible. The legends were full of tales of great kings who were adored and followed even to death, but Arthras thought those were probably just stories. All kings were the same, in the end.

He heard shouting outside, not close, and he stopped pacing and looked up, trying to tell what was happening. It was many voices, not a few, and then he heard the sharp sounds of fighting and he growled and stalked to the flap, flung it open. Nicaea said nothing, and he was glad of that.

༄

He went out into the night and climbed a small hill so he could see what was happening. The sky was ablaze with stars and the tail of the great star, and below were a thousand campfires, so he could see easily. He thought perhaps that some bandits had attacked the camp, or some scavengers had been caught. But who would be as stupid as that? He saw men moving in the dark in a knot, and he heard the sounds of swords and axes clashing and heard cries of rage.

Arthras snarled and stormed closer, breathing deep to control his power so he did not burn himself naked again. There was a crowd gathered to see what was going on, and he pushed through them, shoving men to the ground. When he came into the open he saw there was a fight raging across the camp, with perhaps a hundred men locked together tooth and dagger. Already he saw a score of dead or wounded left behind on the grass. Even as he looked he saw more men run to join the fight, clutching hastily-seized weapons.

It was his own men fighting each other, brawling in the camp. He saw a campfire kicked apart and coals scattered, starting to smolder in the grass. They were shouting and shoving and hacking with swords and axes and knives. No one wore armor, so he knew it was just a spontaneous fight, and it made him angry.

His hands clenched into fists and he felt the heat rising. He knew he wanted to stop this quickly, and he wanted it to be a lesson for them all. The men behind him had seen who he was, and they were rapidly backing away. That was well, because this might go poorly for them if they were too close.

He reached down into the earth with his mind, but not too far. He didn't want a huge tremor, just enough of one. He crouched and put his hand on the dirt, because that helped, and then he sent his power ripping along the surface. He saw the ripple like in a shaken blanket, and it threw men off their feet as it passed beneath them, and then the ground opened up.

A jagged tear opened down the center of the battle, and men screamed as they were tossed away from it. Not a one of them could remain on their feet, and the crack in the earth bulged up like a maw, making a barrier across the battlefield.

In a moment the cries of battle had become screams, and some men simply flung down their weapons and ran, but more of them got up and looked around, uncertain, as if they waited to see who would attack first. The sides were not divided from one another, whatever the grievance was that started the fight. They were all mixed in together, and Arthras saw them eyeing one another, gathering to fight again.

He stood and stalked out into the space between them, the earth shivering at every step, and he watched as they backed away, making room for him. He noted who looked away, and who stared back. He remembered what Nicaea said. Do not explain, be a force of nature.

He stood in the center, surrounded by the men, all of them looking at him, some of them sly, some of them defiant. He chose one of the defiant ones. "You, come here." He sent a shudder through the earth and everyone staggered and grabbed for balance. Somewhere he heard the pack horses screaming.

The warrior came toward him slowly, a mixture of fear and mulishness on his face. He was not any older than Arthras, and his black hair was close-cropped on the side, where his braids had been cut away recently. He gripped his axe tight, his shield ready on his left arm. There was a boar painted on the leather in red that had faded with seasons of sun.

"Tell me your name," Arthras said, giving back the other man's stare.

"Rorik," the man said, hefting his axe.

"Hit me with your axe, Rorik," Arthras said.

The warrior blinked, then he glanced back at the crowd, uneasy. Arthras sneered. "Do you need permission to use your axe? Are you a warrior or not?"

"More than you," Rorik said, angry.

"Prove it, and strike me. *Strike me down*!" He stepped closer, snarling, and Rorik drew back his arm and brought his axe down hard against Arthras' neck. The blow was a good one, and it felt like a cane snapped across his skin. He did not even move, and the sound was like an iron bar striking a tree. The blade bounced back, and Rorik dropped the weapon, shaking his hand.

Arthras wanted to put his hand on the spot where the edge touched him, as if to be sure he was not bleeding. That stroke would have killed any other man, and it was still hard for him to entirely believe it did not even hurt. He looked down at the axe, then at Rorik again. "Pick it up," he snarled.

Now he saw the man was afraid, and he made the earth shake under their feet. "Pick. It. Up."

Slowly, with shaking hand, Rorik bent and picked his axe up from the torn earth. Arthras held out his arms, opening himself up. "Again. Hit me again."

Slowly, the man looked at the axe, and then he shook his head. Arthras slapped the weapon out of his hand. He turned and looked around the circle of men, pausing to look each man in the face. He saw far fewer defiant faces. "Why won't you strike me again?" he said, loud. "I'm not armed. I asked you to. Why do you refuse me?"

Rorik made some kind of low sound and turned his face away, and Arthras stepped in and shoved him to the ground. "Because to strike me is futile," he said, keeping his voice raised so they could all hear. "You cannot hurt me, and so it is useless." He turned and looked at the rest of them. "But you strike each other, when that is worse than useless. Here are the brave sons of the Almanni," he said, gesturing mockingly. "Will I come to the gates of Orneas with a dozen men, because the rest were fools who killed one another? Because I will go alone if I have to, and I will break the gates myself."

He turned and reached down, lifted Rorik off the ground and set him on his feet with one hand. "The next man I see who raises a hand to his kin will fight me next, and I will not be merciful. I will tear the heart from his chest with my hand." He wondered if he could really do that, how it would feel. He turned away from them. "Now clean up this mess and get back to your tents. Let me hear no more of this."

Then he just walked away. He wanted to turn back and make sure they were obeying him, but he knew any look back would make him look unsure and weak. He walked away with his back straight, and the guards drew up tight and tall when he went past them and back inside the tent.

Once the flap closed behind him he let out a breath he had not realized he was holding in. He felt like his hands were shaking, but he looked at them and they were steady. That surprised him. He looked up and saw Nicaea there, still dressed and ornamented like the empress she ached to be, and she nodded, a slow smile on her face.

"That was adequately well done," she said. "Though I think you should have killed one or two, to make your point."

The easy way she said it made his jaw tighten, and the ground shuddered under them without him meaning to do it. She wobbled and then he saw a shadow of fear flick over her face.

"Enough of us have died for foolish reasons," he said, keeping his voice steady. "I value the lives of my people."

She recovered, smooth and relaxed again. "I just meant you did well. You have a certain talent for this. I am glad of it, I could not teach the ways of rulership to a clod." She came forward, and he recognized the roll of her hips that was meant to distract him. "I have sent some of my slaves to make sure they obey you, out there. You have to monitor them, yet not be seen to. Let me handle that. I am well-practiced at gathering information quietly. Give me time and I shall have ears all through the army."

"So long as they fight, and I lead them, they will not be stopped. I don't care what they whisper around their fires, so long as they follow," he said.

"You say that," she said, running her fingers over his arm, and he felt himself stir at her touch. "But there will come a time you will be glad of my devious ways. Let me do my work, and it will be there when you need it."

He wanted to brush her off, tell her to not touch him, but he was tired, and he wanted her, even if he almost wished he didn't. "How much longer until we reach the city?" he said.

"Four days, I think," she said, pulling him toward the bedchamber, pushing aside the silken curtains. "One more, one less, what does that matter? You will reach it, and it will not be able to stand before you. Nothing can."

"Nothing," he said, giving in to his desire, taking hold of her. "Nothing."

Chapter Seventeen

Words and Portents

Karana half-expected Galbos to try to kill or capture her, so she arrived by flying over the walls of the Citadel and descending into the chosen courtyard. She saw horses there, and the retinue around the Autarch milled and shied away as she dropped down out of the sky. The grass flattened and the trees thrashed, and then she landed on the soft earth in between the paved pathways. She was glad to have obtained some new clothes, and she felt less like a vagabond. One thing she had not expected was how hard being invulnerable was on her clothing.

Galbos was on a tall horse, a beautiful white animal that was dressed with silk panels and a saddle so elaborately worked it was almost gaudy. He had a company of soldiers with him, also mounted, and then there were attendants and slaves and others Karana could not have guessed the purpose of.

He controlled his horse while his men did the same. Karana carefully adjusted the scarf over her hair. "You wanted to see me, Autarch," she said. She hoped she managed to sound in control, and not like a supplicant. It was not easy. Galbos had such a tremendous magnetism it was difficult to remember it was all affect. She could level the Citadel with an act of will, if she chose to. That was a greater power, even if it did not seem to help with conversation.

"Lady," he said, inclining his head. "I would have come to you, had you asked. But I thought you should know that my scouts have reported the Almanni are close, and will arrive before the gates no later than the day after tomorrow."

She nodded. "Well, we expected no less." The flow of refugees, steady for several days, had begun to slow. That was as clear a sign as any.

"I expect they will be here with as many as fifteen thousand warriors," Galbos said. "I thought that you and I should discuss the defense."

Karana blinked. She glanced around her, wondering where he had the Archpriest locked up. She felt almost bad for the old man, then remembered what he had done and shunted the thought aside. It was a strange sensation for her to be consulted by the powerful. It made her nervous in a way she could not have articulated to anyone.

"So you have your victory," she said. "The Archpriest locked away and the city is yours. All his supporters falling into line." It tasted sour in her mouth, that she had played a part in such a political game.

"Or at least they pretend to," he said. "It will do for now." A page brought another horse, and Galbos gestured. "Ride with me?"

Karana had not been on a horse in almost a decade, but she gave no sign. It was a beautiful horse, and she took a moment to take the reins and stroke its face, feeling the velvet muzzle spiked with whiskers like quills. She managed to mount without embarrassing herself, and she tried to sit easily, knowing she would make the horse uneasy if she were awkward in her seat. So long as they did not go too fast, she would be all right.

It was a beautiful day; the sun was bright and the air felt clean and cool. Galbos rode beside her, his soldiers and retinue following behind. Karana had not seen the grounds of the Citadel like this, and she enjoyed the flowering trees and well-trimmed hedges. Small statues and fountains accentuated the gardens and courtyards, giving them a dreamlike quality as they rode through them. When she glanced up she caught sight of the truncated tower she had destroyed and looked away. It was too easy for her to wreck things, and that bothered her.

They rode out into one of the wide boulevards that led from the Citadel right to the main gates of the city. The way led them through multiple decorative archways etched with bas reliefs and lined by statues. The trees were heavy with summer blossoms, and the air smelled perfumed.

"They are not just an army," Galbos said. "Their weakness is that they travel as a nation on the move – women, children, livestock, all of it. That means they are vulnerable in ways a normal army is not."

Karana did not like the way his thinking led. "I am not interested in harming women and children," she said.

"Nits make lice," he said, shrugging. "Those children you do not wish to harm will grow to become warriors soon enough. And I have spent time among the barbarian peoples. I know their women are often as dangerous as their men. I will tell you that if the women of the Almanni were set loose in this city, you would not think of them as harmless."

"Perhaps." Karana did not like it, but she had to admit to herself that she knew nothing directly of the northern barbarians. If he had direct experience, then she would have to defer to it. "Your plan is to attack their encampment. Will that not expose your men to counterattack? And you cannot stop Arthras. He has power you cannot oppose."

"You have said we cannot stop him, but I think we can, by directing his attention and intent where we want it." Galbos looked up at the walls as they rode closer to them. "You say he can bring down the wall, and having seen what you are capable of, I believe you. So the answer is to not allow him to attack the wall, to keep him distracted."

They rode into a walled compound below the wall, west of the gate. Soldiers drew to attention at the sight of the Autarch. Some of them looked at her a little too long, and she wondered if any of them had been at the gate when she forced her way in. Had she slain their friends? She didn't like that thought at all.

Galbos dismounted and she followed, managing not to embarrass herself, and she followed him up the steps on the inside of the wall. They were old and worn and cracked, but they gave her a sense of solidity. At the top they had a fine view along the walls to the bulk of the gates, and then through the battlements to the fields outside the city. A steady stream of workers flowed along the road, bringing anything they could into the city to prepare for attack. Refugees shuffled along to one side, dusty and weary and slow. There were so many of them that the Stadia was overflowing, and other bare fields and empty places in the city now burgeoned with people.

Galbos gestured. "They will come down the road, there. They will leave their camp beyond the hills, there, most likely. It has a creek nearby for water and they will need that. Then the warriors will gather and come to attack us." He put his hand on the sun-warmed stone. "Do you think he will come against the gates at once?"

"I don't know why he would wait, unless he plans to threaten us first," she said.

"Probably he will send some kind of message to offer terms." He turned to look at her. "I want you to go out and meet with him. You defeated him once before."

Karana made a face. "I fought him, I could not say I defeated him. I survived, and left him with the city." She looked down at her hands. "Neither of us knew what we were doing."

"Still, your presence will give him pause. He will know this is not an easy victory to be had." Galbos pointed east. "I will send my two thousand horsemen on a path around the roads to the east. They will skirt the barbarian army and move to their rear."

"They will surely be seen," Karana said.

Galbos shrugged. "The Almanni are not horsemen – they may see them, but they will not be able to pursue them. Once the army has arrayed itself I will have orders for the horse to raid the camp. Not to slaughter, but only as a show of force. Arthras will understand he cannot press a frontal attack, because he will leave his camp vulnerable, and with you here, he cannot easily force the gates. He will have to negotiate."

"Is that what we want?" she said. "A negotiation?"

"He has to go somewhere," Galbos said. "An army of barbarians will not just disappear. They are not going to meekly turn around and leave, and we lack the force to destroy and enslave them. That leaves us the oldest diplomatic option there is when dealing with uncouth invaders." He smiled a little. "Paying them to leave."

"You think they will accept that?" Karana was not so sure.

"The Archpriest will be able to contribute a great deal of money to the cause," he said wryly. "I will add food, and offer this Arthras some lands on the northern frontier. We will haggle, as always, but he will take it. The other options are far worse."

Karana thought he was wrong, but she did not say it, because she had no good reason to believe it. She had only her own, short impression of Arthras, a feeling. Perhaps she was wrong. She hoped to be wrong.

☙

Thessala was so busy all day, that by afternoon she was willing to steal some time to herself. Over the past three days so many more refugees had crowded into the city that it was becoming worrisome. Keeping them fed and sheltered was straining the city to its utmost, and keeping them from fighting each other was even more work. It was true that all Thessala had to do to quell disagreements was appear with her face uncovered, but she could not be everywhere at once.

But as the day grew hotter there was less to do as people retired to lie in the shade and try to stay cool. She saw to the distribution of water and then quietly slipped away. The Stadia was crowded to the edges, and so she went back to her sanctuary. She had designated it a place for children without families, and the helpers had their hands full. But many of the smaller orphans were napping, and so it was quiet, and the shade of the trees was welcome.

When she entered her small garden, she found it was not unoccupied. The man Lykaon was sitting in the dirt, letting small colorful beetles crawl on his hand, seemingly completely absorbed in this pursuit. He turned to look when she entered the doorway, grunted. "Sorry," he said. "I'll go."

"No," she said. "No, it is all right." She was curious about this man, who said so little. He had been here for days and she barely knew more than his name. She sat down on the bench. "How did you know this was my garden?"

He tapped his nose, didn't say anything else. She waited, wondering if he would elaborate, but he didn't. She shrugged her hood back, breathed the cool air here beside the fountain. "I use it to grow herbs," she said. She groped for something else to say. "I can see better now, than I used to. I can see in the dark. Sometimes I forget it's dark at all."

Lykaon nodded, turning his wrist so the blue and red beetles crawled across the back of his hand. His hands were stocky and scarred, with dirt under his nails and rubbed into the wrinkles in the skin. His clothes didn't fit well, and they were patched and repaired and dirty. It was hard to tell if his shirt had once been white.

"Are your senses stronger, even when you're not. . . ?" She wasn't sure what to call it. She had seen his other shape, and could not think of a word.

"Some," he said. "Not as much." He looked at her, studying her face, and she thought he was going to say something, but he didn't. The beetles flew off his hand and he snorted. "Bugs."

"You've spent a lot of time alone," she said.

He grunted. "Yes." For a long moment she thought he would not say anything else, and she decided to leave him alone, but he went on.

"I'm a hunter," he said. "Live in the wilds mostly. Hunt for food, but sometimes farmers have a boar digging up their crops, or a wolf after their stock, and they hire me." He grimaced. "Hunted beasts, and now I am one."

"Just sometimes," she said, falling into his short pattern of speaking. "Do you have family?"

"No," he said. "Was married once. Didn't work." He plucked up a strand of grass and chewed on it. He looked at her, seemingly embarrassed. "Wishing for a drink."

"There's some wine," she said.

He waved her away. "No, can't feel it now. Drink and drink and nothing." He shrugged. "No peace."

"Wine doesn't bring peace," she said.

"For a while it does," he said. He chewed grass and looked at her. "Family?"

"Somewhere," she said. She sighed. "I was supposed to be married, too. You could say it didn't work."

"Was he a drunk like me?" Lykaon said, laughing a little, though it was bitter.

"No, no I never got to it. My family had some money, made a good match for me. I was the beauty where I grew up, out in the country." She sighed, wondering if she should stop talking. "I fell in love, had an affair. My family found out and forbade me to see him again." The memory hurt, but not as much as it had once, and that bothered her a little. "He was a painter, very talented, but he was emotional. I remember how he would go into his melancholies and. . . well, not long after that he was found in the sea, drowned. Perhaps he fell, and it was just ill fortune, but. . ." She shrugged. "I will never know. I fell climbing out a window to go to his funeral rites, and broke my ankle." She held out her left leg, flexing it, feeling the old twinge, though it was much less now.

A little embarrassed, she tucked her leg back under her robe. "My injury delayed the wedding, and then I decided I didn't want to be married at all. I left home and came here to care for the sick and helpless. I suppose it is a penance of sorts, but it has been a good life."

"Until now," he said. He looked at her, her face and her hands. "Can I... can I touch your skin?"

Hesitant, she put out her hand, and he took it in his. His hands were rough and strong, but he handled her as if she was delicate. He touched the back of her hand, rubbed his thumb along the bones under the scales. "So fine," he said. "Like armor." He rubbed her arm. "You feel that?"

"Yes," she said, and took her hand back. She might have flushed had she still been able. "But no weapon will pierce my skin now."

"None has yet, anyway. Like mine." He smiled wryly. "My other skin."

"Does it hurt, when you change?" she said.

"Little bit," he said. "It's fast."

"Why are you here?" she said. "I mean, why stay and help us? I am not saying you should not, but I want to know what reason you have."

He was quiet for a long time, and then he nodded, as if to himself. "You live like me, you see a lot of bad. People get ground under. Robbed, killed, all of it. Mostly, you can't do much about it. Mostly you do what you can, but not as much as you really could." He looked at her. "You know what I mean. You nibble at the edges."

She nodded. "I know."

"But now." He held out his hands. "Now I can change, and nothing can stop me. Men can't stop me, walls can't stop me, steel can't stop me. What do I do now? Now I can do anything. Now I never have to watch something bad happen and not stop it. Now I can stop it, now I have to." He shrugged. "Like that."

She smiled then. "Yes, like that." She heard the soft step in the hall and turned to see Karana enter. She looked unhappy, but she smiled when she saw them.

"Good I found you two together," she said. "We have a lot to discuss."

"Your meeting with Galbos did not go well?" Thessala said.

"Well enough." Karana sat down heavily on the grass and tucked her legs under her. "He has a plan, but I don't think it will work. He does not understand how strong Arthras is, or how violent the confrontation could become. He thinks he can be bluffed into negotiating and then be paid off."

"And you don't believe that," Thessala said.

Karana shook her head. "Don't think he will be easily bought off. Why would he? He has power like ours – power that does not derive from someone else, or from just the fear or beliefs of others – power to reshape the world. If he is like us, he could have been no one before it happened. I was an archivist, you are a nurse, he is a hunter. None of us were lords or anyone important before this power lifted us up. If he was a king or a ruler, then perhaps he could be bought, but I doubt he was. Again and again we have had to prove what we can do to those who simply do not want to believe it. The barbarians will be no different. If they follow him now, then it is because he has used his power to bend them to his will. If he shows weakness, he could lose control of them."

She leaned back on her hands, looked up at the patch of sky visible above the fountain. "Galbos betrayed the Almanni. He does not see it that way, but they will. A king might be used to the vicissitudes of power and treaty and negotiation, but a simple warrior will not be. If Galbos pushes him, he will push back." She looked back down, at the two of them. "When that happens, it will be up to us to face him."

"You mean kill him," Lykaon said.

Karana puffed air through her cheeks. "I hope not. I don't want to have to kill anyone. Too many people have already died in this... war."

Thessala felt a jolt at the word, then realized it was true. "I suppose we have to call it a war." She looked at her hands. "Is it strange I don't want to have to kill one of... of us?"

"I feel the same way," Karana said. "I feel like we are connected to him in some way, like we all are."

Lykaon chewed a piece of grass and shook his head. "I hunted wolves sometimes. Big ones. Beautiful animals. They just wanted to eat. Nothing evil about a wolf. It hunts, and it eats, and that's all. Wolves have done that since before men existed." He spat out a piece of grass. "So I got paid gold to hunt them, and kill them, because they killed cows or sheep, and I didn't like it."

Karana looked at him, thoughtful. "But you did it."

He smiled with one corner of his mouth. "I have to eat, too. Wolf would understand, if I explained it. When the wolf shows up, you feed it, or you kill it. You have to pick a side."

Karana grunted. "I suppose that's true. Day after tomorrow, perhaps, the Almanni will get here, and Galbos will try his stratagem. And if it works, then we let it. If it doesn't work. . ." She spread her hands.

"Then," Thessala said, "we pick a side."

Chapter Eighteen

CRACK THE EARTH

Karana climbed the stone steps, still chill from the dawn, and stood on top of the wall looking down as the barbarian army flowed across the green fields like a flood. Dust billowed up from their path, hanging in the sky like a haze. She saw them come on as a horde, not ordered like soldiers, just a mass of men, carrying shields on their backs and spears over their shoulders. They did not come close, and they did not fortify anything. They were not here to work a siege. She saw them cut down fences and torch a few small buildings that would break up their assault, but they did not make camp. They did not intend to wait.

She looked to her left as Galbos ascended the wall. He wore a breastplate that gleamed with silver plate and gold inlay, and a vast blue cloak fastened with a pin the size of her hand. The cap he wore was polished and was more like a crown than a helm. She noted that despite his grandiose appearance, he remained behind the battlement where he could not be seen. He knew the sight of him would enrage

Arthras, and yet he could not resist coming in his elaborate war-gear. Karana found it told her much about the man.

"We should be flying a flag for parley," she said. What if Arthras did not wait, and simply attacked? She knotted her hands into fists and then knotted her scarf more closely over her hair. She knew it would come loose, if there was battle. It should not bother her, but it did. She wondered if she should just forget about it, but it was one of the few traditions from her home she still kept. The thought of abandoning it was bitter.

"He will send an emissary first," Galbos said. "We will agree to meet, and then you will go and negotiate face to face with him."

"And if he asks for you?" she said. She was worried this was all going to go badly. Galbos thought he was dealing with a predictable enemy, but Karana thought he was wrong.

"I will not go out there for any reason. He would kill me. You tell him you drove me out, and I fled. He will believe that. He can see the damaged Citadel from here; you can claim to be in control of the city." He twisted his heavy ring around and around his finger, and she realized he was nervous. That should have made her feel better, but it did not. It finally settled on her that Galbos, for all his experience, did not know what was coming any more than she did.

She snorted. She was in control of the city, even if Galbos did not want to admit it. She watched the barbarians as they spread out in a great semicircle, facing the gates. They did not have the men to surround the whole city, and with the port they could not blockade it anyway. With Arthras, they had no reason to try. Karana tried to count them and could not begin. The scouts had said perhaps twelve or fifteen thousand men, and behind them the mass of families and slaves and loot, too far back to be seen clearly. Galbos had expected them to be left over the hill, but they were not. She thought that was likely because Arthras had no intention of standing for a long wait.

None of the warriors came within arrow range, and then she saw one man on a horse break from the lines and ride forward. He wore gilded, iron-scale armor and a red cloak thrown over his shoulders. He carried no shield and no spear, and the rising sun glinted red on his long hair. Karana felt a knot in her belly. It was him.

☙

Arthras rode toward the gate, looking up at the height of the wall. It was taller than the one that guarded Ilion, but that did not intimidate him. He rode slowly, wondering if anyone would be so foolish as to shoot at him. He saw men on the walls, the spearpoints sticking up behind the battlements, the glimpse of helmeted heads as they peered at him. They would have ballistae and catapults and oil and boiling water or hot sand. Any number of unpleasant things to pour down on attackers who reached the gate. None of it would save them. He felt down with his invisible power, sensing the lay of the earth, the way it was loose and stony until he reached down deeper, where it was solid and heavy, where the power slept.

He turned his horse so his left side faced the gate, as warriors did when calling forth a challenge. Nicaea had wanted him to send a messenger to treat with their emissary, and thus to open negotiations. He would not have it. He would ride out before his men and show them he was not afraid, and if the fools behind the wall tried to force the matter, he would smash the gates down like the hand of Bora herself.

"I am Arthras, Lord of the Almanni!" he shouted, trying to be as loud as he could while still keeping his voice steady. "I am the earthshaker, chosen by the gods! Come forth and surrender to me and I will be merciful! Refuse me and I will break your city in half!"

He waited for a moment, wondering if the Autarch was here, watching, and if he would have the courage to come forth himself if he did. He did not know the man Galbos by sight, but he was certain he would not be able to hide himself for long. "Come forth and answer me! And quickly!"

He watched, wondering if they would answer. The silence made him angry, and he clenched his teeth. Then he saw a small form climb up onto the parapet, and then leap off. He felt a moment of shock, and then he felt the wind sweep past him and saw the shape float down to the earth beside the gate. His horse snorted and tossed its head, not liking the feel of the air. Arthras controlled it with brute force, pulling hard on the reins to quiet it. By the time he looked, back the person was walking to meet him, and he saw her face and he knew her, if he had not already. The storm girl, the one who he saw again and again in his mind's eye.

She looked smaller than he remembered, and she came forward on bare feet, wearing simple linen pants and a long shirt that did not fit her well. Her hair was bound and covered by a twisted purple scarf knotted in place. Her hands were marked by fading henna, and on her bare arms he saw peculiar scars, almost like the traceries of lightning.

She stopped outside of arm's reach, and she looked him over, her face hard to read. He thought she looked nervous, but then he felt nervous himself. She nodded, as if to herself. "Arthras," she said.

He blinked. Had he told her his name? He could not remember. "You never told me your name, storm girl."

"Karana," she said. "We did not have the time for conversation, before." She spoke his language well enough, with a strong accent, but her words were quick. She looked past him. "Your circumstances seem rather improved." She touched the place on her own head, just above her ear, and by reflex he touched his own head – the place where his braids had been.

He felt a flush of anger. "And what are you? A princess? No. You are a scribe of some sort."

"I was," she said. "Until you destroyed the archive."

"I did not destroy it," he said. "It still stands." He shook his head. "We are not here to discuss that. We are here to speak of the surrender of the city."

"To you?" she said. "Why do you want it? It is just another city. You took Ilion, was that not enough for you?"

"And they would have left me there? Untroubled?" He scoffed. "No, the Autarch would gather an army and come for me, and the battle would be on my land, and not his, at a place he chose. No." He shook his head again. "I am not a fool, I will not wait for that." He pointed to the wall. "Is that coward Galbos in there? I know he would not dare to face me alone."

Karana sighed. "Yes, he is there. He asked me to come and speak with you, because he knows you mean to kill him."

"And so you protect him and do his bidding? Why?" He gestured to her. "I remember you. I remember what you can do. You do not need to answer to any of them, certainly not him."

215

"You think I obey him? I do not." She looked frustrated. "I am trying to prevent the fall of the city, as is he. His reasons are selfish, but that still makes us allies." She pointed over the wall, and he saw the towers there, one of them smoke-blackened and broken. "I had to impose my will upon the Archpriest, but Galbos has been willing to help me. I do not trust him, but I have used him more, I think, than he has used me."

"And what were you to speak to me of, if not the surrender of the city and everything within it?" he said. He wanted to glance back at his army and did not; he imagined them growing restless, shifting as they waited for him to take the gates. Instead they saw him bandy words with a girl. "Do you think I will be frightened away?"

She took a long breath, as if controlling herself. "I did not come here to fight you. You know as well as I that if Galbos came out you would kill him, and then there would be war. I came to try and prevent war. This city is full of people who have no part in your quarrel, no hope but to be spared violence while they try to rebuild their lives. They came here as refugees and found nothing but scorn and cruelty. I have had to fight to keep them safe, to keep them from being starved or cast out or simply slain. I will not surrender the city for you to rape and plunder it and enslave the people you have already unhomed." Her voice trembled with emotion.

Karana took another breath. "I am here, because the Autarch, on behalf of the emperor, wishes to negotiate a settlement with you. He will pay and offer concessions and lands in return for peace. I want peace, and so I am here to bargain with you, though it is a task that sits uneasy on my shoulders."

Impressed, he thought a moment, considering. "Do you believe he will keep any agreement we make? Do you believe he will honor what you say he will?" The warriors might be eager for battle and plunder, but good lands and gold would feed their families and give them a new homeland. Perhaps that would be the wiser choice. Nicaea had promised that if he negotiated that Galbos would make such offers, but he did not trust them.

Karana sighed heavily. "For his part, I do not believe he means to. I think he would offer anything to gain the time to plot against you. He feels he must retake Ilion and punish you and your people, else the emperor will remove him from power." She stepped closer, and he tensed as she touched his arm. "But I will guarantee his terms. He may not wish to keep his word, but I will make him keep it. He cannot refuse both of us. Like you, my will can no longer be discounted."

He hesitated. "Why would you do that?"

"Because if there is battle, then the lives of those I have sought to protect are in danger. I am not here to safeguard power and wealth. I am here to protect those who cannot protect themselves. If I can do that without violence, then that it better for all of us."

"They are not your people," he said. "You come from the south, from far away."

She looked offended. "They are still *people*," she said. "My birth matters no more than theirs. Or yours," she said, her tone pointed.

He opened his mouth to speak, but then there was a cry, and a warrior on a horse burst from the lines and rode towards them. The man was red-faced and out of breath, drew rein hard. "We are betrayed!" he said. "Cavalry are on our flank, moving toward the camp and the supply train!"

Arthras felt wrath churn in his belly. He turned to Karana and saw no shock on her face, and he knew. "You! You keep me here mouthing useless words while Galbos plots to attack our families!"

"No," she said, not raising her voice. "It is only -"

"I have heard enough!" He was shouting now, and the horses shook their heads and sidled as the earth shuddered underfoot. "I will not be prey to his lies again! Not again!" He turned to the rider. "Take the men and chase down the horsemen, kill them all! I will break the city with my own hands!" He stared at Karana, feeling a kind of betrayal sting him under his heart. "Now I see what you mean to do. Now you will see what I can do!" The heat rose inside him, and his skin began to burn.

ങ

Karana saw him blacken, saw smoke rise from inside his armor, and she knew it was too late. A thousand words clamored behind her teeth, wanting to get out and stop him, persuade him, but she could not wait any longer, she had to fight.

The wind rushed in as she leaped into the air, putting herself beyond his reach. He screamed after her, and she saw the ripples around him as the earth began to shudder. If he turned his force upon the city, people would die, and she had to act quickly to stop it. She did not want to kill him, she only wanted to keep him back.

She flung up her open hand, calling in the power, and the winds roared around her. When she swept her hand down the air obeyed, and the grass flattened and a cloud of dust rose up into the morning sky. Men and horses were flung back, tumbling like dolls, and Arthras was lifted off his mount and hurled into the sky. She tried to keep a grip on him, but she lost it, watched him smash down into the road hard enough to crack it apart.

Furious, angry with him as well as herself, she called in the sky, saw the light darken as the clouds gathered. She would need everything she had to fight off an army and try to defend the city. She thought of the people inside, children hunkering down at the sound of thunder as it rolled across the sky like an empty helm on a stone floor. Curse him, and curse all of them for forcing her into this position.

Lightning flashed and spoke, and she felt the tingle in her scars, the boiling eagerness running through her veins. She wondered what she could do if she tried, if there was a limit to her power, and she feared that question. Already she felt the masses of air shifting and colliding, beginning to grind against one another. It would be easy to build a storm that raged out of control, and how much easier to feed it until it broke out of all bounds.

Thunder crashed and roared, and she began to have to struggle to keep herself steady in the air as the power of the storm began to build, like a slow-spinning wheel that gained force and speed as it turned. She knew the thunder would also signal Thessala and Lykaon that the battle was joined. Arthras might think he was ready for her, but he did not yet dream that she was not alone. She looked down at the broken place on the road like a splintered eye, and she saw him move, saw him rise, smoking like an ember.

ଓ

His clothes burned away, and the scales of his armor fell smoking and red in a cascade at his feet. The stone melted and ran and clung to him, making a coat of black armor that glowed red where it cracked. He lifted chunks of stone and they melted in his hands, poured over him, covered him. He smelled the burning rock and laughed. The fire was his armor, the earth was his sword. He turned and saw his warriors scattering to get away, and he laughed. "Go!" he shouted. "Fight the enemy of flesh and bone! This is a war of gods!"

He turned, moving heavily, his footfalls shaking the ground, the earth blackening under his feet. He looked up and saw her there, the storm girl calling in her power. The sky darkened, the shadow spreading out from her like a stain of blood in clean water. The wind churned and began to roar, and lightning cracked blue across the lowering clouds. The thunder shook him to his teeth and he snarled. Let her stay up there, thinking herself out of his reach; there was much he could do regardless.

He faced the gate, and he raised his hands, feeling the power coil through him, seething in his muscles and his bones. The soil was loose, like sand, beneath it he felt the great slabs of rock, ancient as giants, waiting for his command. He reached out.

A wall of wind roared down and slammed into him, and almost knocked him off his feet, but weighted with molten stone, he was too heavy. As he leaned in and braced himself, the road beneath his feet melted and he sank into it, rooting him against the gale. It screamed as it lashed over him, and strings of melted stone were pulled away and cooled into strange, jagged shapes jutting from his arms and his back. Dust blinded him, and he saw paving stones of the road ripped up and hurled away into the growing storm.

Lightning flashed and clawed at the sky, and then a tree to his left disintegrated in an azure flash and the instant scream of thunder. Another lash of it tore along a stone fence line, shattering it and flinging smoking rock into the air. He looked up, but he could not see her. She was hurling her thunderbolts at him, but she could not see him to strike.

The wind buffeted him and he hunched down, dug his fingers into the road and held on. The stone melted and ran and he found if he willed it, the molten stone flowed up over his arms, protecting him. Pieces of stone and wood flew through the air, driven like arrows by the wind, but they glanced off him and he felt almost nothing. Enough.

He lifted one hand, closed it into a fist, the glowing hot stone squeezing out between his fingers. He called on his power, and brought his fist down the strike the ground with terrible force. He felt the shudder beneath him, and then the earth split open with a hideous sound and the rift tore across the road and smashed into the gate. He saw the walls but dimly through the storm, but he saw well enough as the gateway exploded upward, hurling into the sky as through a great hand had smote it from below.

The walls rippled for a moment like paper, stones fracturing and shooting outward, and then they burst apart with a roar like demons. Stones erupted from the ground as deep-buried giant boulders reached upward at his command, and the road was shattered. Pieces of rubble began to rain down all around, and Arthras bellowed in answer as the earth shook and cried out beneath him.

Chapter Nineteen

Day of Doom

Karana was in the sky, and she saw the wave of destruction burst from Arthras and spread across the ground. She saw the ripple along the white stone of the road, saw the rocks burst apart and the earth roil like waves on the sea. She saw the shock strike the wall, and for a moment it seemed as if nothing happened. Looking down, she saw the men on the wall flung off their feet, and she saw Galbos in the moment of fleeing down the stairs with his cloak flapping behind him.

The walls seemed to billow like sails, and then they simply burst apart. Stones erupted from the masonry and tumbled down, and then the whole of the wall shattered inward, washed away, men tumbling in among the massive pieces of stone. She saw Galbos caught and driven under, and then he was gone. It all went so fast, she barely had time to comprehend it, even as she felt horror at the destruction, it went on.

A wave of destruction spread outward from the gate, and she watched the cracks spread over the streets and then the houses and other structures shake and slide down into heaps of ruin. Unexpectedly, birds erupted from the falling buildings and spread in a cloud over the city, fleeing toward the sea. She could not hear their cries over the bellow of the wind.

The storm she had called was growing out of her control, and she had to fight to stay steady in the air. The temperature dropped, and she felt a chill on her skin. Clouds spread across the sky, growing and coiling on themselves, black as night. Her clothes whipped around her, and her scarf was torn away. Thunder roared, and she steeled herself. She felt the building power of the storm as the lightning gathered itself, and when it struck the ground it was a physical sensation of release that was almost sexual. It was growing so much stronger so much faster than she had ever expected.

The lightning grew, poised behind her eyes and her teeth, like a word she ached to cry out, and she looked down on Arthras and loosed it. There was the flash and the sound in the air like a thousand hissing irons in quenching water. Then a bolt of energy streaked down and caught a tree, blasted it apart and left the trunk like a chimney burning away from within. Karana snarled and tried again, blue traceries of electric power crawling over her arms, seeming to arc behind her eyes.

This bolt was weaker, and it snaked away, touched a part of the broken wall and left a glow there. Thunder roared all around, almost blasting her from the sky. She flinched and cursed as the aftershocks echoed away, light flickering through the low, leaded bellies of the clouds. It was not as simple a matter as she had thought to hurl a bolt of lightning into him. The energy had its own will, and the paths it wished to follow. She would have to get closer.

It was hard to see, the air filled with dust carried on the wind, rising up from the rubble of the collapsed buildings. The clouds blocked out the sun. Karana knew many people had fled the vicinity of the walls, but in her mind she saw the soldiers atop the battlements – the battlements that now lay flattened into an unrecognizable heap of destruction.

Thunder hammered again and now rain began to slash down, and she supposed that was good – it would help prevent fires from raging out of control. She called on it, and the rain intensified. The wind was colder and looking to sea, she saw a wall of clouds rising up where the land ended, towering to a terrifying height, like a wave stilled in time. It was building there, somehow feeding on the energy of the sea itself. It was so strong, she did not know if she could stop it if she tried.

Looking down, she saw the dark shape of Arthras, limned by the molten rock dripping down his body. Like a giant he approached the fallen gate, walking slow and heavy. She felt the power gathering again, and she let it build, and then she clenched her fists, steeled herself, and swooped down to meet him.

ଔ

Arthras fought through the wind, feeling it batter at him, shoving him back like a terrible hand. It picked up pieces of shattered stone and threw them against him, where they melted and clung to him and made him heavier. He could not see well, kept having to claw molten rock from his face. He moved ponderously, feeling slow but powerful. He looked up, trying to see Karana, and then she stooped toward him like a falcon, flickering all over with threads of blue fire.

She dropped so fast he thought she might collide with him. Her braids were loose, coiling and snapping in the air like snakes, and her eyes glowed with an inner fire. The lightning scars on her skin glowed red, as if they were hot iron, and his thought was he had never seen anything so beautiful in his life.

Then she flared brighter and he threw his arms across his face to shield himself. There was a flash so bright it dazzled him through closed lids, and then the impact struck him like a hammer. Half the stone was smashed from his body, and he was hurled backward to crack the earth with his impact. His teeth buzzed in his skull and he felt a humming in his bones.

He pushed up from the crater he had made, scorching stone and soil black with his touch, more lava flowing up his arms and legs to cover him, renewing his armor. He scraped it from his eyes and looked up. He saw nothing above but iron clouds so low it seemed he could touch them, and then rain began to pour down, hissing where it struck him and cooled his surface. Then he looked down and he saw Karana on the ground, picking herself up from her own blackened mark.

She saw him and lifted again into the sky, but he was not going to let her regain that high ground. He swept his hand up, and the earth beneath her exploded, spraying rocks into the air, knocking her aside, and when her concentration wavered she fell hard to the battered ground.

He thundered toward her, the cooling stone splitting into plates, still heated by the fire within him. His footfalls smote the earth as he reached her, and when she rose he reached out and caught her, his touch searing her wet clothes, sending up smoke and steam. He drew back his hand and closed a terrible fist, lava running between his fingers as he squeezed down.

He hesitated, not wanting to really harm her, but then she recovered and put her hands on his face. He saw lightning crawl over her skin and spark between her teeth, and then there was a flash, and a sound so immense it was like his skull had exploded.

ఌ

Karana put everything she had into the stroke. There was a moment of terror, feeling his hands on her, the burning heat of him, and then he dragged her in close and she was disoriented and felt panic rising in her throat. He was not even like anything human, covered in the molten armor. The surface was cooled and fractured into black plates studded with points and coils drawn out by the wind and the white hot glow within wherever he moved. Then she saw his face, the human face with the stone scraped away, and as he drew back his fist, she reached for the one vulnerable thing she could see and loosed all the energy she could summon through her hands.

The bolt flashed bright as the sun and there was a tremendous crack of thunder, and then she was flung back and her burning shirt tore in half and she landed in the mud, rain pouring over her. There was a moment when she could not even see, could not remember what was happening, and then she heard another crash of thunder and she remembered.

She rolled over in the mud, coughing, and wiped rain from her face. Her hands were seared black and tingled as if she had held them to a fire, but she could not tell what was mud and what might be burnt skin. Her teeth and her bones seemed to hum, and she shook her head as she staggered up. She could channel the lightning close up, but she had to endure some of the power feeding back on her.

Arthras rose from the ground, shaking his own head. His armor was damaged, but even as she looked it seemed to flow in and re-form. It seemed like the molten rock shivered as it climbed up his arms and his legs, as though he made it climb with a constant vibration. She felt the ground shake under her, a tremor, and she did not know if he did it deliberately. The thought that perhaps his own power might grow out of control occurred to her, and that was frightening to contemplate.

He came toward her, footfalls like the tread of doom, and she looked side to side, not sure what to do. The destruction was already so great that she feared more would result if she kept fighting him. What else could she do? Flee? Surrender?

She felt the storm careening out of control, the winds growing more and more violent, the rain splattering down like a thousand stones every breath. The air was cold, and now knots of ice began to fall with the rain. She braced herself, channeling the wind around her body to keep the full force from tearing her off her feet. Even that slight alteration was an effort, and it formed a shell of fog around her that flowed away with the wind, covering the ground. It coiled around Arthras and hissed away in the shimmering heat.

The earth beneath her feet thrashed and knocked her down, and he rushed in, hands grasping. She called down lightning and white fire exploded all around them. It struck him, struck the ground, struck her and shot through her body and exploded from her hands and eyes and mouth to hammer into him and send him reeling back. She staggered to her feet, feeling dizzy. A cage of dancing electric fire surrounded them both, and she struggled to maintain her control of it.

"Turn back!" she screamed, feeling as if she might vomit. "Turn back or I won't be able to control it!"

He leaped for her so fast she didn't have time to dodge. One massive, molten fist clubbed against her midsection and all the air was wrenched from her chest. The sky and ground changed places and she realized she was tumbling, and then she hit hard in a heap of fallen stone from the gatehouse.

Everything went black and spinning for a moment, and then she pushed free of the rubble, coughing, holding herself. Then she was sick, vomiting so hard she saw stars behind her eyes. Her braids hung in her face, sticking to her skin. She felt the earth shake and looked up, saw him coming. He was too strong, and she couldn't stop him. He raised one fist, molten stone hissing as it ran down his arm.

Something moved in her peripheral vision, quick and hard, and then she saw Thessala, scales gleaming green in the stormlight, her eyes glowing with fury. She was too close, and Arthras did not see her in time. Karana saw the shock on his face, and then he tried to turn, too late. Thessala's fist slammed into his chest with a sound like splitting rock. His stone armor splintered apart, and the impact lifted him off his feet and hurled him back to gouge the earth where he fell.

☙

Arthras rolled over, coughing, feeling actual pain in his ribs. He staggered to his feet, hands clawing at the soil to renew his defense. The pain made him angry, and that was good; the anger burned inside him like the fire in his skin, made him feel stronger. He had not felt real pain since the fall of Ilion.

He heard a scream of rage and saw the woman coming for him again. She was tall and long-limbed, and she was covered everywhere he could see with scales like finely worked armor. Her eyes glowed in the dim light, like lanterns. Her hands were knotted into fists, and he put a hand to his ribs. He had never been hit like that, never felt such terrible strength.

She closed on him and he clawed at the ground, ripped up a chunk of rock and hurled it at her, smashing her off her feet. She shoved the stone aside and came up, but he leaped on her, hit her with his rock-covered fist, and fragments of stone splintered off and flew away through the screaming wind. He groped for her, but she was faster than he was. She put a foot on his chest and shoved him back, sent him staggering across the torn ground. So much rain slashed down that it was turning the churned earth and stone to mud, and his feet sank into it.

The scaled woman came at him again, fists clenched, eyes gleaming, and when she swung he put up his arm to block her. Her blow crashed against his arm, cracking his armor and driving him sideways, staggering. She was so strong; she was much stronger than he was. She hit him again, and he held his arms close, blocking her blows. He saw quickly that she was no fighter. Her swings were wild and powerful, but not controlled.

She struck again and he evaded her, then struck back and smashed her off her feet. Her strength had frightened him, but she was not a trained warrior. When she tried to rise he set the earth to shaking, knocked her down again, and then he closed in and drove a fist into her skull as she tried to get up. She cried out and covered her head with her arms, kicking blindly at him. He caught her long braid and hit her in the head, driving her down into the mud. He drew back his arm for another blow, and jaws closed on his hand like an iron trap.

He turned, caught by surprise, and saw some kind of monstrous animal, black and massive in the stormlight. Like a lion it clamped jaws on his hand, then braced itself and dragged him off his feet. It dug terrible claws into the ground and shook him, lifting him into the air and snapping him side to side before it threw him away, sent him bouncing and rolling across the earth until he smashed against the stump of a destroyed tree, sending smoking flinders shooting into the air. The wind screamed, and now hail began to pelt down like stones.

༄

Thessala struggled to her feet, hand shielding her face from the wind. It was madness out here. The wind was like a blade, tearing and lashing at everything, driving the rain so hard it was like being pelted with stones. Thunder boomed and cracked overhead, and the flicker of lightning had become almost constant. She saw the black bulk of Lykaon fling Arthras away, and then he followed him, vanishing into the blinding rain. This was utter insanity. They could not fight like this – if they did not stop it the whole city might be leveled.

She had to find Karana. She waded through the storm, glad enough for the mud that her feet dug into, as it gave her some kind of purchase. It was impossible to tell which way she was facing, or which was she was going. She could see almost nothing in this; even the flickers of lightning could not improve the visibility. She reeled through the storm until she fell against tumbled blocks of stone and knew she was close to the wall. Looking through the mist and rain she saw a human form limned with light, and then she saw it was Karana, her body lit by traceries of lightning. She stood dazed in the downpour, swaying with the wind, naked and wet, her muscles rigid as though she were in pain.

Thessala gritted her teeth and took her by the shoulders, jolting as the shock passed through her. She shook Karana until her eyes opened, and she saw they glowed from within. "Karana!" she shouted, howling to be heard over the wind. "You have to stop it!"

Karana seemed dazed, as though storm-drunk, her eyes half-rolled up into her head. Thessala caught her head between her hands and shook her again. "Karana! Wake up!"

"It's so beautiful," Karana said, her voice barely audible over the wind. "I can't. I can't..."

"You have to stop it, it's out of control!" Thessala pressed her back against a broken stone. "You have to stop it!"

She heard the roar then, and turned just as Lykaon and Arthras came hurtling toward them. They turned over and over in the air, clawing and smiting at one another, Lykaon's tail lashing the air. They seemed frozen like that for a moment, like a relief on an ancient tablet – the monster and the underworld god – and then they smashed down and the stones shattered like glass.

☙

Karana was lost in a world that was half shadow – seeing with half her vision the world around her – the rest of her world was consumed by the coruscating, shimmering inner world of the storm, the architecture of it spread out around her, arching overhead like the roof of a basilica, complex and interlocked and moving, shot through with fearsome energy. She felt Thessala touch her, saw her face, but her voice was seemingly muffled, as if she called from a long distance, or buried under the earth. Karana could not hear her, could not reach her. She was alone.

She did not see what happened. There was a sudden impact, and then she was thrown aside, tumbling over and over. She found herself pressed down in the mud, and she fought free, spitting out stones. When she looked up she saw Arthras there, close enough to touch, straining against the massive black form of Lykaon. Lit by the blaze of lightning, they struggled like titans. Lykaon's claws gouged at the hardened stone that armored the barbarian king, and Arthras hammered his fists again and again into the iron-muscled beast that pressed him down and slashed at him with black fangs.

Panicked, Karana clawed to her feet, and then lightning blazed around her and she screamed. The bolt struck so close the thunderclap was not a sound so much as it was a blow that hurled her backward. She saw Arthras caught in it as in a river of fire that erupted from the earth and tore molten stone from his limbs, and then she was thrown aside and she caught at the wind desperately, forced herself into the sky, away from the battle. The sky was consumed with an unseen engine that ground and thundered and kept getting stronger, and she had to find a way to stop it.

༼༽

Thessala was blinded by the lash of lightning, and she saw Lykaon thrown back. She pushed on through the wall of rain and found Arthras half-buried in the mud, steam boiling from his black skin. Furious, she ran in and kicked him, and again, the blows sounding like an axe on oak. He grunted and rolled over, evaded her next kick and drove a mallet-like fist into her belly, knocking her back, gasping for breath. He came to his feet and then Lykaon fell on him from behind and they rolled over in the mud. Thessala squinted through the roaring rain and the storm, pushed through and leaped in on them both. She coiled her arms around Arthras' neck and pulled, squeezing down with all her strength.

He fought them, twisting, pulling, but he was not strong enough to throw them off. Thessala felt his neck begin to give way under her arms, and then he reached out a hand and clawed at the earth, and she felt the earth tremble in answer.

ଓ

Karana could not keep herself in the air. She tumbled, lost control, and then smashed down within the city. In a moment she found herself in a torrent of water, as the rain flooded the streets knee deep, washing along broken tiles, shredded wood, dead rats and dead people. She was swept down the hill and fetched hard against a stone wall, pulled herself out of the flood and then climbed the wall, her fingers gouging the stone.

She dragged herself onto a roof, the wind clawing at her, and she looked over the city, stunned by the destruction. The wall had been breached, the gates destroyed, and the ruin did not stop there. In the crazed light of the storm she saw the streets filled with rushing water, shoals of debris sliding along toward the sea. Tiles and timbers ripped free of the rooftops and spiraled up into the sky. Everywhere she saw people, struggling in the water, clinging to wreckage, looking out of windows and the torn holes in rooftops. She saw the terror in their faces.

She had to stop it. She wanted to hurl herself into the flood and pull the people out with her hands, but that would be useless, a waste of her strength. The storm was out of control, feeding on itself, growing stronger. She didn't even know if she could stop it. In her mind it was like a fantastic panoply of opposing forces, of wheels within wheels turning all above her, lit by lightning, shot through with fire. She was half-drunk with it, feeling the edges of it surge in her veins like a tide. It seemed to call her and wish her to merge into it, to lose herself in the inhuman coursing of it.

Thunder shook her bones, and Karana ground her teeth together, trying to focus past the madness swirling all around her. She braced her feet on the wall and stood, the wind tearing at her, trying to whirl her away, and she lifted her arms up to the sky. She closed her eyes, seeing without seeing, feeling her way to the heart of the boiling storm, and she wrenched at it.

Chapter Twenty

After the Fall

Arthras could not shake them off. The lion-beast raked at him with claws and fangs, and the scaled woman had her arm locked around his neck with terrible strength. She squeezed harder and harder, until he felt the cords of his neck begin to give way under her power. He grabbed at her arm, wrenched and pulled at it, but he could not make her loosen her grip by even the smallest amount. The beast lunged in and those jaws yawned before his face.

Almost panicked, he plunged his hand down into the earth, feeling the energy already coursing through it, roused by his call, still thrumming from the upheavals it had performed. Desperate, he poured more power into the ground, as if he were emptying his blood into the soil, and the earth answered him.

It began as a low thrum, and then grew to a tremble. He put up his other hand to force the demon jaws back from his face, and then the earth leaped beneath them, and again, and again. The ground jolted as though a great fist were beating against it from below, and the force threw the beast off of him. It tossed him and the scaled woman into the air, and when they fell, her grasp loosened. He drove an elbow into her belly and she grunted. Another shock struck and they were bounced apart.

He rolled over in the ground, clawing at the earth, heat burning everything he touched. He saw the beast gathering to leap on him again, and he pulled at the earth with a savagery he had never used on it before.

The ground split open beneath him, and he rose up on a crest of fractured stone. All around him the field of battle was shattered as boulders from deep under the soil thrust up in waves that emanated out from the center. Shockwaves pounded the earth until it rippled like a sheet, and anything on top of it was tossed like ships on a storming sea. The wind shrieked and tore stones from the air and hurled them in sheets like a storm of arrows.

The earth fractured outward from where he stood, and he saw light flash from the cracks, like shimmering red lightning that slashed up from the center of the world. He heard a hissing sound, and the hairs on his neck stood up as lightning began to fall from the sky, shattering the soggy ground wherever it struck. Thunder roared, piercing through the long bellow of the tormented earth.

Arthras stood on the new-formed peak of stone, feeling the vibrations all around him, shuddering up through his legs. The power was feeding on itself, greater than he thought he could control. He saw the sky and the earth scoured with fire and boiling with the energy he had unleashed. The storm screamed and tore at him, and he laughed.

ೞ

Karana was immersed in her inner world, something that was not sight or sensation, but an awareness of the coursing of her storm that went beyond either one. She heard it, felt it, saw it, all with an inner eye and inner mind that shut out the world around her. Dimly, she felt the wind push at her, felt the crawl of electric energy over her skin.

To this sense, the storm was not violent, but an orderly network of spinning, colliding, turning forces that fed one into the other in a predictable pattern. The lightning moved from here to there when the force in one place was too great, and sometimes dumped into the ground when there was nowhere to go. It was such a fantastical, magnificent panoply that she was loath to disrupt it, but she had to.

At the very center was a great pit into which all the forces pulled, and even as she watched, it began to hollow out, the winds spiraling inward so fast they could never quite reach the center. That was the engine that drove the entire storm, and if she could stop it, she would stop the system. But she was not sure how to do it.

She forced herself to think. The air did not vanish; it was being pulled up and out of the storm faster than the winds could drive it, and that was what caused the storm to grow stronger. If she could stop that from happening, then the storm would weaken at the same speed it now increased.

Karana tried to reach it, to reach up and find that current of air and stop it, but she could not find it, could not feel it through the roiling mechanism of the rest of the storm. The whole was too powerful. Feeding more power into it would not fill the void; she had to disrupt the cycle. She had never thought of her power quite like this, controlling the minutiae of how the storms worked. She had simply commanded and the skies obeyed; now she was paying a price for that lack of attention.

If she could not reach what she needed from here, she had to get higher. She would have to fly up, above the storm, until she could see what she was doing. She swallowed, then she snapped back into reality, seeing the storm all around her. It was thinning here, and she realized the force of it was forming a center where the winds did not reach. So the city was becoming calmer, even as water flooded the streets.

Looking around, her heart dropped at the sight of the destruction. So many buildings were ground down, blown over, flooded and crushed. She covered her mouth and choked. This was not what she had wanted, not at all what she had meant to do. Between her power and Arthras', they would destroy the city more thoroughly than a horde of barbarians ever could.

She felt a tremor in the corner of the wall she stood on, and she wavered, trying to gather the winds to carry her up. It was hard; everything had so much force behind it that to turn it even a little required great effort. She ground her teeth and tried for a better grip.

The ground leaped under her, and she tumbled from her place, grabbing the stone for purchase. Another shock and the wall collapsed, the stones separating, sliding down. One struck her full in the face, and then she fell into the rushing water, crumbling stone weighing her down. She gave a cry in a burst of bubbles, and then she was buried in the black flood.

※

Arthras laughed and felt the stone under him soften and melt. It boiled up red and molten as he sank into it, and then, when he was immersed, he burst free and trod the battlefield in his glowing armor. The rain slashed and cooled it, leaving a cloud of steam behind him. The tremors in the earth shaped themselves around him, so that where he stepped, the ground stilled for his passage.

He crossed the broken ground, shattering boulders with casual shrugs of his strength. He passed uprooted, charred trees, tumbled stones that had once been part of the city walls, bodies of soldiers crushed in among them. The soil was almost liquid from the shaking and the rain, and he waded through it, leaving a trail charred and blackened behind him.

He wanted the scaled woman, and he ripped up the broken masonry of the gatehouse and flung it out of his way, hunting for her. Aftershocks ripped through the ground, cracking the great stones apart. He tumbled the debris aside as though it were nothing, and it made him feel a great warmth in his heart. Here was power, here he walked as a god, not simply the chosen one of the divine, but blessed with the power himself.

He saw something move, and he turned, prying molten rock from his eyes so he could see. There she was, tall and naked and glorious in her dark scale armor. She crouched against the shaking earth, hands hooked into claws. He bared his teeth and rushed on her, his footfalls ponderous yet inexorable, like the tread of doom. When he drew back his arm to strike, she opened her mouth and he saw her throat swell, and then she vomited a spray of something bitter into his face.

Arthras heard it *hiss* on the stone, spitting and crackling as the heat flashed it into steam, but it then struck him in the eyes and he was suddenly blinded by a stabbing pain, as though two daggers were driven into his skull. He cried out and clapped a hand over his face, staggering as he lost his balance, and he heard her scream as she attacked.

ଓ

Thessala screamed as she leaped, giving full vent to the wrath that boiled inside her. The more she fought, the more the fury coiled and burned down inside her, and she no longer saw any reason to contain it. Arthras covered his face and staggered as her venom ate at his eyes, and he pounced on him as he reeled off-balance.

Her first blow slammed into his chest, splintering his stone armor, splashing her with lava that burned on her skin, hissing in the torrential rain. The pain only made her more furious, and she hit him again. The stone covering him made him heavy, so her blows did not knock him away, only made him stumble. He put up a hand to try and block her, but blind he could not avoid her. She ducked his arm and hit him in the stomach, then hooked her arm around his leg and pulled him off his feet, dropping him onto the mud.

The ground was so waterlogged she sank into it, but it didn't slow her down. The heat was terrible, but she didn't let it drive her back. Thunder screamed overhead, over and over as the lightning flashed. She crouched on top of him and pounded three hard blows into his chest and gut. He grabbed for her and she caught his arm, twisted and pulled on it, bending it back against the joint, trying to snap it. He screamed and took his hand from his face, grabbed her by the head and shoved her off him.

They fought in the mud, rolling over, clawing at one another. Every blow she landed fractured more of his armor, left more of it spattered and dripping into the mud. But again his superior experience told, and he fended her off, then gripped her arm and wrenched it behind her, shoved her down into the mud face-first.

She fought him, pushing, but the waterlogged soil gave her nothing to push against. She flailed, her mouth filling with mud as she tried to get free. He twisted her arm, pulling it farther up, straining to pull it from the socket, but she was too strong for him. Leverage meant he could hold her, but he could not dislocate the joint. He planted a foot on her back and pried at her, and she screamed, feeling like she would smother.

Then he was gone, dashed away, and she was free. She struggled up out of the mud, spitting and coughing, and she wiped the slime from her eyes and saw him locked in battle with Lykaon, the beast like a shadow lit only by the flashes of lightning gleaming on his eyes and his teeth. He struck with his deadly claws, shattering the stone armor, and when Arthras staggered back he came within Thessala's reach. She caught his arm as he reached for balance, and she tried to remember how he had twisted hers. His skin burned her as she dug her fingers through the molten stone and levered his arm up behind him.

She didn't have it right, and he simply turned, lifted his arm and her with it, and smashed her down against a huge stone that had once been part of the gate towers. Once, twice, again, until she was spitting out rock shards, and then Lykaon struck him and they all went down in a tangle of scales and teeth and burning flesh.

ೀ

Karana was turned over and over in the torrent, though she found it was not as deep as it looked. If she could stand it would perhaps rise to her knees, but the current was so fast it would be impossible to hold against it. She bounced off several walls, rolled over and smashed head first into something that didn't give way. It allowed her to stop and grab for a handhold. She clawed up from the water, dragged herself into the air, and then she spared nothing to get free. The winds blasted in around her, forming a bloom of fog in the air, and then she was torn from the flood and hurled herself into the air.

The winds were coiling in all around in a great spiral, and she was pulled into their wake. The center of the storm was hollowing as the winds were driven faster and faster, and if she did not stop it the entire city would be leveled. She had forged this beast, and she must tame it.

She fought the spiral course of the winds and forced her way up into the sky. Mist bloomed around her, and it was hard to gather very much speed. The wind was pulled away from her, drawn harder and harder into the cycle that fed itself. Winds were drawn in, rose up, and then blew out the top of the storm in a great coiling motion she sensed rather than understood. The air was drawn up and out faster than it could be pulled in, and thus the storm gathered strength.

Karana rose up into the still air, at the center of the winds, feeling the air so cold on her skin the water turned to mist. She looked up and it was like seeing into the deeps of the sky. A great wheel of clouds funneling up to darkness lit with the gleam of stars, and above all, the Omen Star, casting a glimmering shroud over a third part of the sky. She thought hazily that it was her star, and there was a kinship now between them, and that when it departed, she would mourn, and feel forever a part of herself carried away with it.

The winds rushing upward were where the storm weakened, as the forces there that drew them teetered on a fine edge. That was where she must seize it. She closed her eyes and took a breath of thin, cold air, and then she clenched her fists, and, with her inner power, she caught the rising winds, and forced them back.

The strain was enormous, and she felt everything in the storm lurch at once. Lightning cracked and spat all around the edge of the storm, thunder rolling after it like an echo. She made a terrible, guttural sound, the cords in her neck rigid, her muscles tight as steel as she stopped the flow of the winds with sheer will. She could only do it for a moment, but that was all she had to do.

A column of mist formed up the center of the storm, roiling as it rose up around her. Ice formed in the air, and her breath turned to fog. She cried out, losing her grip on the wind, and then there was a terrible rumble, deeper than thunder. She saw the walls of the storm collapsing, turning to clouds without shape or structure, and then they fell inward, rushing into the hollow center, and when they met they made a sound that split the sky.

cs

Arthras was winning, he could feel it. His fire burned so hot it made the air around him shimmer. He learned to send jolts through the earth beneath his feet to keep his opponents stumbling and off-balance. The beast was harder, as his four legs gave him better purchase, so he knocked the scaled woman back, then split the earth apart.

The ground roared as it opened up, revealing a dark rift with mud and soil cascading down into it. The beast leaped on him and he caught the thing by the heavy mane and hurled it into the cleft. A flex of his will and the crevasse slammed shut, trapping the monster half in the earth. It roared and thrashed, clawing at the soil, but there was too much water, and the ground was too soft to give it a grip.

Arthras stepped in and began to slam his heavy fists into the scaled sides of the beast, hammering at it as hard as he could, the blows sounding like an axe chopping at an oak tree. It howled and lashed at him with its one free arm, claws ripping through his molten armor, leaving trails of pain on his flesh. He clubbed his fists across its head, and then he seized it by the jaws and began to twist it back, bending it farther and farther, wondering when it would break.

Then the slim arms of the scaled woman hooked around his neck and ripped him backward. She threw him, and he had a moment to lose sense of up and down before he hit hard and left a crater in the mud. He came up as she sprang on him, and he grimaced as she hammered her fists into him again. It hurt when she hit him, when he had begun to think nothing could really hurt him. He grabbed at her arms, caught on and wrenched her over, pinned her under him. She rammed her knee into his gut and he coughed, reached down and covered her mouth with his free hand. Molten rock poured over her nose and she thrashed, trying to get free of him.

The wind slowed, and he felt his guts flip over as lightning slashed all around him, coursed up through the storm and ripped at the earth, and then the winds reversed, rushed past him, and there was a sudden roaring detonation so loud the backlash knocked him aside and sent him tumbling through the mud.

Coughing, pain in every joint, he got to his feet. He spat on the ground and saw red in it. So. He was not invulnerable. He trod on the broken roadway and it melted. When he pulled the lava flowed up over him, replenishing his armor, protecting him. Lightning flashed again, and he realized the storm was dying, the winds slowing to a standstill, the rain falling slow, almost gently. He looked up, and he saw a glowing shape descend from the sky, wreathed in blue fire, and he felt fear in his chest.

☙

Karana landed harder than she meant to. Everything seemed to waver as she fought to stand up straight. There was a deep ache in her head, down her back. Lightning still crawled on her arms and legs, flicked across her vision. She swallowed hard, determined to stay on her feet as she faced him. Behind her, Thessala was picking herself up spitting out molten metal, and Lykaon was trapped in the earth, struggling to get free.

Arthras looked none the worse for all of it. The molten stone covered him, and so she could not see any wounds, any sign that he was weakened at all. She had not understood how strong he was, how lucky she had been to escape him the first time. She clenched her fists. "Enough," she said. "Be gone."

He came towards her, deliberate, reaching up to clear lava from his eyes. "You can't stop me," he said. He sounded breathless, hoarse, and did he move a bit more slowly, guarded? She couldn't be sure. "Give way," he said. "Give way or I will kill you all."

The air was clearing, the clouds beginning to break up. Karana saw how churned and destroyed the ground was, the fields and orchards flattened and broken. How had she done this? Everything had gone out of her control, and now she had wrought the destruction she had sought to prevent. She caught that last shred of anger, and she held onto it.

"No," she said. "Be gone." She held out her hand, and closed it into a fist.

Pain lanced down her arm and her back as she pushed with her power again, feeling how much harder it was now. Wind came coiling in, filling the air with a sudden mist. She focused all her strength on him, and him only. Skeins of lava flew off him, cooled to black glass in the wind, and then her main force hit him and he was lifted off the ground. He gave a choking cry, clawing at the air, and then with a last convulsion of strength she hurled him up and away, sending him through the sky, away and out of sight beyond the hill.

She lowered her arm and swayed. She heard Thessala coming up behind her, and she tried to turn, but then pain jolted through her head and everything went slow. Karana saw the sky, the clouds opening up to let the sun come through, and she thought it was beautiful, and then she collapsed in the mud, and there was nothing.

Chapter Twenty-One

Dust and Bone

Arthras woke encased in stone, and this time he did not fear it. He moved, found he was fixed in place, and so he simply bent and flexed his back until the shell cracked, and he could break free of the rest. He shook off the shards of black stone, and then he looked up and found he was at the center of a ring of tents, people already gathering at the sound he made when he emerged. It was a hazy evening, the sky low and indefinite, the glow of the star the only light he could see. The air smelled clean, as after a storm.

Warriors knelt and planted their spears in the earth when he looked at them, and then Nicaea emerged from her tent and he saw relief in her face when she saw him. He wondered how long he had been encased, and then he shrugged. It could not be as long as it felt like. He moved experimentally and felt pains where he had been struck, aches like echoes of the battle. He touched his side and pressed in with his fingers, expecting pain and finding it. He felt unsteady, as if he might fall.

"We have been waiting for you, my king," Nicaea said, her voice too loud for her to be only addressing him. She was playing to the crowd. He looked around and it felt as if he had forgotten the army that followed him here. What had happened to them during the battle? He had lost sight of everything but his own struggle, had not even thought of the rest of them. He looked around and saw the land was devastated, trees uprooted, the ground muddy and churned, rocks scattered everywhere. To his right he saw what remained of a cottage, the roof gone, the walls broken down and scorched.

He shook off his reverie. "How long?"

"We found you here at nightfall, made camp and waited. I never doubted you, nor did they." She gestured around her. He recognized some of them as companions – old thanes of Usiric – while others were new to him. He nodded. He tried to remember. Karana, her name was Karana, and she had lifted him up with her winds and threw him. He remembered tumbling in the air; he did not remember coming back to earth. He looked back at the stone and saw it was the side of a hill, the stone bared by the rain. He must have hit and then his heat melted him into it.

"Nightfall," he said, looking up at the sky again. He realized it was not evening, but morning.

"Come inside, my lord," she said. "You should bathe and eat."

He nodded absently, still feeling bemused and as if he were dreaming. He remembered the others – the beast and the scaled woman. Who were they? He followed Nicaea into her tent and let her lead him into one of the curtained chambers where there was a basin. The slave girls filled the copper vessel with hot water and Nicaea bade him step into it. He stood and let them clean him, scrubbing dirt and hardened bits of rock from his skin. It hurt him, but he gritted his teeth and showed no sign. Nicaea washed and rinsed his hair, and then they dried him and he sat on a cushion and she sat behind him and ran her comb through his hair. They brought food, but he was not hungry.

"We all drew back from the battle," she said. "There were horsemen sent from the city – men of the cohorts – but we drove them off easily. There were not very many of them. Then the storm grew worse and we retreated. The earth shook terribly. We have spent a great deal of time finding the horses and cattle who fled." She picked carefully at his hair. "We could not see what was happening."

He grunted. It was not easy to remember things. They came to him, but in jumbled order, as if everything had happened at once. "It was the girl I told you about. The storm girl. She named herself Karana. She said she wished to negotiate a settlement for us to retreat." He scoffed. "It was the hand of that worm, Galbos. Offering gold and lands to keep us from attacking, and he had deceived this girl into standing in his place because he feared to face me."

"Well, with some cause," she said. "He must know you would kill him."

"Yes. Well, if he came before me and knelt and begged for my mercy, I might grant it," he said.

Now it was Nicaea who laughed a little. "He would never do that, he is far too proud."

"Pride will not save him from me," he said. He turned and glanced at her. "Do you want me to kill him?"

She shrugged. "It would make things much easier, if you did," she said. "But we do not know if he survived. I have never seen anything like that battle. We had to move far away for safety. The storm was terrible – the wind was so fierce the trees were torn down and we could not raise the tents, only huddle in whatever shelter we could find. The earth shook so much it was hard to stand, even from so far back. I saw the lightning flash and heard the thunder."

"She was not alone," Arthras said. "There was a woman with her. She was covered in scales, and she was strong. She was very strong." He thought of saying that it hurt him when he struck him, but he decided he did not want to speak of his weaknesses. "And there was a beast. Something like a lion, black and scaled and huge. It seemed to have the mind of a man. It may have been a man. That one I may have slain." He did not want to tell the rest of it. It was not like a battle between gods; it had been confused and frightening and he knew they had nearly overwhelmed him.

"Three of them, and still you emerged victorious," she said. "That is not a small matter."

He grunted. "Victorious? I was flung away from the city, and unconscious for a day."

She swept her hands through his hair, stroked his scalp. "You are alive, and they are not here. We have seen nothing of them. The city lies open to us, and they have not come to warn us away or drive us back." She sighed. "Some of the army fled during the battle," she said.

"How many?" He was not surprised.

"I am not certain yet. Some of them fled, but they are returning, now it is over. We may have lost a third, perhaps less." She leaned her head against his back. "I feared it was all over. That you would not rise."

"You doubted me," he said.

"I am practical," she said. "If you are slain, I must begin to make other plans for myself. But I would rather be with you."

He almost believed her, and he was wary of how much he wanted to. No matter how he told himself she was part of the empire he hated and worked only for her own benefit, he could not entirely believe it. Moments like this made him feel tender toward her, and he distrusted that feeling.

"The city?" he said. He wondered how much damage it had sustained.

"No one has gone within it yet," she said. "I think they are afraid. The walls are damaged terribly, more than that I cannot see from here."

He sighed. "Help me dress. I must go among the men, and gather them, and then we will go into the city we have won. I will see it with my own eyes." He stood up, pain crawling across his body, but he would not show it. He would not let any of them see weakness in him, not now.

༄

Karana woke, and she felt the motion of waves and heard gulls crying. There was sun on her face and she put her hand up, covered her eyes, and she heard Thessala's voice close to her. "Thank Attis, you are alive."

She tried to roll over and she felt a terrible pain in her bones and her limbs, an ache behind her eyes. A shadow fell over her and then hands were on her, and Thessala helped her sit up. Just that much caused a wave of nausea and she lunged sideways, her belly heaving. She tried to vomit but there was nothing to bring up. Thessala held her until it passed.

She looked up at the other woman and saw with a wrench in her belly that Thessala's face was swollen, one eye almost closed. Karana put a hand up and Thessala shied from it. "I am all right," she said, her rich voice sounding rough. "I was afraid you were not."

Karana found she was wrapped in a sail, or a piece of sailcloth, at least. She squinted against the sunlight and saw they were in a small boat, one single mast and an exposed deck. There was a lone slack sail and the forward end of the ship was filled with the black shape of Lykaon. He did not move, but she saw his sides heaving slowly, so she knew he lived.

She put her hands to her head, trying to remember when she had ever felt so awful. There was a universe of pain behind her eyes, pain in every stiff joint. "What happened?"

"He was killing us," Thessala said, with a terrible, flat tone. "Arthras. He was too strong, and we couldn't stop him. He had Lykaon buried in the earth and was beating him to death. I tried to fight him but -" She knotted her hands together. "I am not a warrior. I didn't know how to fight him. I tried. He hit me so much, I couldn't see. I felt like I was broken inside. The earth was shaking so much I couldn't even stand."

She took a long breath, calming herself. Karana scooted into the shade from the sail, glad to get the sun from her eyes. The brightness on the waves stabbed her vision like knives.

"Then you were there," Thessala said. "You picked him up, and threw him away, and then you collapsed. I didn't. . . I didn't know what to do. I didn't know if you would live."

Karana looked north and saw land, like a smudge on the horizon, the faintest hint of green. "The city. . ."

"Destroyed," Thessala said. "I had to drag you through it. The buildings are down, the streets filled with ruins and.

.. and corpses. I saw thousands fleeing south out of the city, and climbing aboard any boat that still held water. I found this." She choked on her words, covered her mouth. "It was floating away, and I swam to it, and pulled it back. I tried to get some other people to join us, but they were afraid. They were afraid of me."

"We have to go back," Karana said. "We have to go back and protect the people."

"The people are dead, or have abandoned the city," Thessala said, openly weeping now. "There is nothing to protect, and we cannot protect anything, or anyone. You have lain for a day and a night and half another day as one dead. I was afraid you would never wake."

"We have to -" Karana tried to get up and cried out, slumped back to the deck. She hurt everywhere, in ways she had never felt. What had she done to herself? "We can't just leave."

"Arthras lives," Thessala said. "You think hurling him away killed him? No. He will come again, and hurt as we are, we cannot stop him. Even the battle would simply destroy whoever we tried to save."

"Stop it!" Karana said, her voice harsher than she meant it to be. She put her hand over her mouth as a wave of nausea washed over her. Her fault, this was her fault. She had been so sure she could persuade Arthras, that he would listen to her, that a battle could be avoided. And then, under it all, she had been sure she could stop him if it came to a fight. She remembered her former confidence and felt sickened by her own arrogance. She had been so sure of herself, and now how many had paid the price?

Slowly, she sat up, leaned back against the gunwale. They were at sea, drifting, and she did not know where they were. If they went back, then she would have to fight again, and she did not think she could do that. The very thought of it filled her with a kind of dread. She wondered if she were just afraid, but then she remembered the city being torn apart around her, and she knew she had to think of something besides herself. She had tried to match force with force, and it had failed. She did not know how to use or control her power as she thought; she was not a warrior, nor a leader.

"I am sorry," she said to Thessala. "It is not your fault. You believed me, and followed me, and it has cost many people their lives. I swore to protect them, as you did, and now we have failed them utterly. I have failed them."

"It was not only you," Thessala said. "We both made our decisions."

"I trusted Galbos, more than I should have, and we both thought ourselves warriors, when we are not." Karana closed her eyes, seeing his end atop the wall, feeling the aches in her body. "We have made mistakes, as would anyone in the position we find ourselves in. But the cost of those mistakes has been dear. We must see that we do not make the same ones again."

Thessala shook her head. "How can we do that?"

"This battle is lost," Karana said. "But we must look to the next one."

☙

Arthras went into the city, and found ruin. The walls were all tumbled down, broken into long piles of rubble and splintered stone. He climbed over the heap of rubble and stood there looking into the city, and what he saw was devastation. The streets were cracked and they had heaved up from the ground, sharp edges of rock jagged in the air.

The buildings had been flattened, drowned, and crushed under by wind and the shaking earth. It was hard to tell them apart, as they were little more than heaps of broken stone and scraps of wood.

Awed, he walked down the street, the water still standing in pools. He saw drowned rats and dogs and men. They lay bloating in the sun or caught in heaps of wreckage; he saw arms and legs jutting from the ruins where the dead lay buried. He doubted even a deliberate destruction of the city could have worked such damage.

He passed down the long road, and his warriors followed behind, quiet and subdued. Some of them had indeed fled, but as the day passed, more and more of them returned. Here and there they found the corpses of soldiers, crushed or drowned in their armor, and the men stopped to loot them, taking their swords and spears and shields. Arthras knew there would still be plunder in the city, they just had to find it.

There was still a good deal of pain in his arms and legs, and he moved slowly. He climbed the first hill, and then he looked down on the seaward side of the city, and here he found the destruction was less. The mass of the hill had kept the worst of the storm from it, and his shaking of the earth lessened with distance. Looking toward the harbor, he saw more buildings still standing, and there, limned against the sky by the sun, was the Citadel. Nicaea had told him to look for it – the seat of the Archpriest.

Once it had possessed four great towers, now only one stood even halfway. As he made his way towards it, he saw the walls were cracked; in many places the stonework had crumpled and slid down into heaps of wreckage. Here, she had said, was kept the wealth of the church, and he would take it for his own.

He began to see people, and they scattered when they saw the army of men coming up the wide boulevard. There were carts piled with the dead, and places where blocks had been cleared from the road. That made it easier to pass through the heart of the city to where the damaged Citadel loomed against the sky. The walls were slumped and cracked apart, but the gate was intact, and armed men stood on the walls above it and looked down on him.

Arthras grimaced. He didn't want to involve himself with this; he didn't want to fight again, or use his power, or anything like that. He was bone-tired and he hurt, and he was dressed again as a king with armor and a sword and he was not ready to burn it all away again because these men were fools. He looked up at them. "Who speaks for this gate?" he said, lifting his voice enough to carry.

"I do," a voice came down to him. "Come no closer."

"Open this gate, and stand aside," Arthras said in answer. "If you do, you will be spared, and I will not command you to be slaughtered. I have an army, and your city is broken open. I could tear your gate apart with my hands if I wished to sully them. Your gate cannot stop us without walls. Open this gate now, and come forth and surrender to me, or I will give the command and every one of you will die." He was tired, and he spoke with a low, steady voice, neither angry nor threatening, only truthful.

There was a long pause, and then he heard the clank of iron and the gate opened. The soldiers came down from the wall and emerged and they bowed their heads and laid down their weapons, and Arthras heard a great shout come from his warriors. He smiled and nodded, and he turned to his men and raised his own voice in answer. "Go within, and take what you will. But let no one who does not raise a hand to you be harmed. If you kill without cause, I will kill you in answer. I have given my word, and you will pay if you break it." He saw his men nod, solemn, and then he stood aside and gestured, and the army of his people flooded into the Citadel.

☙

They came to tell Nicaea in the first light of dawn, and she rose, cold and huddled in her cloak. She did not know where Arthras was, and she sent servants to find out, even as she dressed quickly and followed the soldiers down to the courtyard. The Archpriest's citadel had suffered terribly in the battle, and the stairs were cracked as well as the many beautiful windows. Her slippers trod on broken glass as she made her way down.

The palace guards had tried to clear away some of the wreckage here, but some of the broken stones were too large to move, and Nicaea had to step around them before she could reach the small grassy place where they had laid Galbos on a stretcher made from his own blue cloak. Now the blue was covered in dust, and stained with blood. When she saw him, she relaxed, and her hand clenched on the hem of her gown let go. It was plain he was dying.

It was actually surprising that he was alive. His face was ashen, though she could not be sure if that was just more dust. There was blood on his mouth and more came as she looked. He saw her and turned his head, very slightly. One of his eyes was dark and shot with blood, almost swollen shut, and both his legs were plainly broken.

She wanted to say something. Something cruel and cutting. She had many such lines in her mind, carefully crafted and saved for a moment like this. Now, when it came, she found she was not quite spiteful enough to say any of them. She came and stood over him, looked down. "You have looked better," she said.

"I am not surprised to see you here," he said, swallowed and winced. "You always find your way to the top."

"I do what I must, to secure my own future," she said. "I always have." There was the barb hidden in there – that he had not done so for her, as he should have. "You tried a gambit, and you failed."

"Had to try," he said, and then he coughed hard, grimacing, and more blood came from his mouth. "I am almost done."

She watched him, saw his chest rise and fall, saw his gaze become fixed and still, and then his last breath rattled out and she knew he was gone. She waited a moment, the men who had carried him in standing silent behind her, and then she bent down and closed his eyes, getting a little blood on her hand.

She heard voices, stood and turned as Arthras came close, pushing through the people gathered here. When they saw who he was, they drew back. He came and saw Galbos and his face grew hard and angry. "Well, I am robbed of killing him."

"He was crushed in the collapse of the wall," she said. "I would say you slew him as much as if you had broken his neck in your own hands."

He looked at her sharply. He was barely dressed in a dark tunic, and he looked very young to her then. "What did he say?" he said. "Before he died?"

"Nothing of consequence," she said. She looked at the body. "He was your enemy. You should bury him with honors."

Arthras snorted. "He deserves no honors."

"You should honor fallen foes," she said. "You will become greater, the greater they are said to have been. And when they are defeated, you can afford to be generous, and thus you will be remembered as noble." She took his arm and drew him back. "Liberality is shown with more than gold."

"I wished to see him suffer," Arthras growled.

"He did," she said, drawing him away. "He suffered greatly."

☙

Thessala made her way forward, holding onto the scarred wooden rail, until she reached Lykaon. In the sun his black form seemed even larger, and he started gently when she put her hand on him. His fur was warm from the sun. She was going to ask if he was awake, but he lifted his bestial head and looked at her with one brass-colored eye, then lay back down.

"Do you hurt?" she said softly, and he sighed, nodded his great head slightly. "Is that why you have not changed back? Because you fear pains in this form will be too much for you as a man?"

For a moment he did not answer, but then he nodded again, his long, reptilian tail flicking slightly. Thessala put her hands on him, feeling his breathing. "You can't stay in this form forever, and you should not. You have to try and turn back."

He drew in a long breath, let it out, and then she felt him tense under her hands. His muscles knotted and he made a low, agonized sound, and then his shape began to flow and change. It played tricks on her eyes and so she turned away, kept her hands on him, and then the ship rose under her as the weight was taken away, and she felt naked skin under her fingers.

She looked, and he lay there, breathing slowly, his face flushed. She touched his head, smoothed his hair. "Is it worse?"

"No," he said. "Better." He turned and sat up, draping his hand between his legs to hide himself. She almost smiled at that, his small gesture of modesty. She had another piece of sailcloth and she draped it over his shoulders. He looked at her and nodded. "Thanks."

"That wasn't me," she said.

"In the fight, it was," he said. "Thank you."

She looked away, embarrassed for no reason that made sense. She was naked as he was, but she found that in her scales she never felt unclothed, not really. She drew her knees up and hugged them. "I am glad you are all right."

"Should have killed him," he said, his voice low. He held up his hand, fingers spread. "Claws wouldn't cut him."

"He was too strong for us," Thessala said. "We all did what we could."

"I have to do better," he said, eyes narrowed. "I'll pay him back."

"You'll get the chance," Karana said, coming forward to lean on the mast behind them. She looked haggard and worn, but her color was better than it had been, and she was on her feet.

"We'll face him again," Karana said. "We'll have to."

"You think he'll follow us?" Thessala said.

"Ilion has fallen, Orneas is his. All of Othria is his to control now. The power to resist him now can come only from the emperor. Refugees who can reach the capital will do so, and the response to this invasion must come from the throne. The emperor will need our help and advice, even if he does not yet know that." She closed her eyes to the sun, leaned back against the mast.

"We could not stop him here," Thessala said. "How will this be different?"

Karana smiled. "Archelion is not just the imperial capital – it is on an island. To reach it, Arthras must use ships, and no ship will cross the strait against my will. I can promise that." She looked back to the distant land, and Thessala saw the pain on her face, knew she was feeling the same guilt that stung her. "We have to go to Calliste, and there we will make our stand."

Lykaon grunted, and Thessala knew that was all he would say. She looked at Karana and nodded. "All right, now we just have to get there."

Karana nodded, and then she closed her eyes again. Thessala held her breath, wondering if her friend had the strength for anything at all. But then she felt the wind stir against her face, rippling the waters around them. Slowly, so slowly, the sail billowed out and caught the wind.

Chapter Twenty-Two

CITY OF KINGS

Arthras walked down the long steps, his way lit by two warriors carrying lanterns. It was close down here, not like the vaulted, grand style of the rest of the Citadel. The steps were steep and close together, and they curved left as they went down into the rock beneath the fortress. He saw that the stone walls were cracked here and there, some of the cracks looking fresh, and he knew that was his work. He ran his hands over the stone as he passed it, touching the marks of his power over the earth.

At the bottom, there was a small open space, the floor uneven and worn, the stones smooth from many years, and the roof was so low he wanted to hunker down, though he did not really have to. There were six more men down here, and all of them turned to look as he approached them. He did not really look at them, only at the door that stood behind them.

It was immense, taking up the entire wall of the chamber, and it was heavy, made entirely of iron and bronze, or perhaps wood covered and bound so thoroughly that the wood was hidden beneath layers of metal. The hinges were as thick as a man's waist, massive and glistening with grease, and the great wheel that closed the door was fixed by a lock centered with a keyhole that looked far too small for it.

Arthras nodded. "This must be the vault. Indeed." He crossed the room and put his hand on the heavy door, feeling the cold metal, the solidity of it.

"It was not hard to find," one man said. "And we broke down the door to the stairway, but we do not know where the key to the door can be found. The great priest must have it."

Arthras nodded. "Perhaps he does. But we will not need it." He studied the barrier, wondering if that were true. It was so solid, so constructed to withstand any sort of assault, that he thought perhaps he could not break it down. But he must break it down. Behind that door lay the treasure of the archpriest, and by pouring out that treasure he would weld his army to him, regardless of the destruction that had made pillaging the city all but pointless.

He glanced at them and saw some of them looked pleased, while others were uncertain. He wondered how much argument there had been about his ability to tear the vault open there had been before he arrived. He gripped the spokes of the wheel and tested the strength of it. He was still weak, down in his bones, and he felt the pain incipient in his muscles when he flexed them. He was not recovered yet from the battle, but this would not wait.

The wheel was too big for the small key to open it, so he reasoned that the key opened a smaller lock that allowed the wheel to turn. He would be able to force it. He gripped the bronze wheel and braced himself, leaned in, and twisted as hard as he could. The wheel trembled under his hands for a long moment, and then there was a scream of tearing metal and the wheel shifted. Something snapped and the thing turned in his hands, and then there was a grating sound and it shuddered to a standstill. He strained at it harder, feeling days-old aches crawl up his arms and back, and the spokes bent under his fingers.

He tried again, throwing his strength against the wheel, and it groaned as it deformed in his hands, but it did not turn. He heard muttering behind him, and it stung him. He snarled, baring his teeth, and wrenched at the wheel no matter that it hurt him. A muscle in his neck bunched up and felt like a metal point drilling into his flesh, but he pulled harder in spite of it, and he felt the wheel bend again, and then with a scream it snapped off in his hands.

He staggered aside when the pressure was suddenly released, and he heard what might have been a laugh. He snarled and threw the wheel aside, and the men had to jump out of the way as it gouged the stone wall and clanged to the floor, wobbling like a fallen shield. Arthras felt rage coil up inside him like heat, and his hands began to smolder.

He watched them turn black, and then he pressed them against the iron door and held them there until the metal began to glow red. Heat radiated from the door, forcing the men to step away, nervous and muttering wards against evil.

The metal turned paler, orange, and then almost white, and his hands sank into the molten stuff as it began to run down the door like wax. Smoke coiled up from his clothes, and he smelled the hot, burning reek of scorched metal. He plunged his hands deeper into the door, feeling the masses and shapes of the mechanisms and melting through them. The whole center of the door began to glow, shining a dim red that spread out more and more.

The smell of molten brass was overpowering, and he gagged on it, but then he set his hands and ripped the molten center of the door open, pulling the metal apart until he had made a hole through the entire door. Molten iron gushed out like blood and hissed on the floor, and the warriors drew back with oaths as it spread around his feet. It set Arthras' sandals on fire, and he grunted and kicked them off. He took a long breath and let the heat fade, pulled his hands back and peeled globs of glowing metal from his skin.

He stood there, waiting, breathing the fumes and wanting to throw up, but he would not show weakness. He watched while the metal cooled, the air shimmering with it, the glow darkening from orange to a dull red, until he could barely see it. Then he grabbed the edge of the ragged hole and pulled, and the door came open. He heard metal strain and creak, and then the hinges swung and the door scraped on the stone as it swung out into the chamber. He dragged it back, stepped out from behind it, and shoved it back against the wall.

He beckoned, impatient, and the men crept down from the stairs, carrying their lanterns with them. He took the first one to come within reach and then stepped forward through the heavy portal, holding the light up so he could see.

Arthras expected a small room, perhaps heavy with treasure, but not large. Instead he saw a hallway, and on each side were a series of archways. He moved slowly down the hall, and as he passed each opening he looked in, and was almost blinded by the shimmer and dazzle of gold. The men crept along behind him, and their eyes grew big and they gave whispered oaths. Arthras felt dizzy, as he had never seen so much wealth, had not even really supposed there was so much in the whole world.

He stepped into the next room, looking at bars of gold heaped on one side, a stack of wooden strongboxes on the other. In the center was a pyramid made of copper pots filled with coins. He thrust his hand into one and brought out a fistful, let them run through his fingers and listened to them clatter down.

He turned to the other men, and saw the flush of greed on their faces. He caught the nearest man by his collar and lifted him off his feet. That made sure he had their attention. "No man will take so much as a coin from this place. You men will guard it, and it will be counted, and then given to the army once we know how much... once I know how much is here. Take nothing, or I will melt it down and pour it in your mouth." He let the man fall, watched him stumble back and catch himself. All of them looked fearful enough to him now. It would have to do.

"Now," he said. "Go and bring me the great priest."

ങ

The largest throne hall in the Citadel had survived largely intact, with only a slight twist to the columns and a crack across the elaborately decorated ceiling. Arthras did not like the throne, and so he did not sit on it. The yawning mouths of the bronze lions unnerved him. He paced before it with guards flanking him and Nicaea sitting on a small seat beside it, close but out of sight, where she seemed to wish to be.

He had changed into fresh clothes, new boots, and a cloak that draped over his shoulders and made him feel more like a king. He had no crown, and did not really wish for one. It seemed foolish, but he wondered if one might be found in the treasure storehouse below, where his men were even now counting and weighing to see how much there was. So much wealth would make the warriors rich and pay for whatever else he needed. He had become, in a day, the richest king in the history of the Almanni.

More guards entered, big men he had chosen for this duty. They dragged between them a small shape that for a moment Arthras thought must be a child, but then he saw it was an old man who had seen kinder days. He was dressed in only a shift of white muslin that had yellowed and looked like it did not fit. His hair was white and there was not much of it. The guards let him go and he managed to stand, rather than fall to the floor. His eyes still had a keenness, and so Arthras knew he was not a dotard.

Arthras looked him over. "So you are the man called the arch priest of your god." He shook his head. "Your god has not protected you, it would seem."

"My revenge shall come," the old man said. "I would not expect a barbarian to understand true faith."

"Faith? Is that what swells your coffers below us? Is it faith your followers paid you with?" Arthras sneered. He had always detested the weakling religion of the empire, and now he had the great priest of it in his power, and he would not pass by the opportunity.

The man gave back a cold stare. "They gave freely so that the holy church might prosper."

"And indeed, see how it prospers," Arthras said. "Your city has fallen, and lies in ruins. You were already imprisoned when we found you. Your fellow faithful did not accord you great respect."

"Not any faithful," the old man said. "It was one you have had some experience with for your own part. Galbos. He said he could protect me from the demon girl, but then he betrayed me, and locked me away."

"You were no friend of his before that," Arthras said. "Why would you trust him?"

The priest looked past him, to where Nicaea sat, and he gave her a sneer of his own. "I see you have plied your only talent as eagerly among the savages as you did to snare your other lovers."

"Have a care how you speak," she said, not raising her voice. "Savage or not, my lord will not endure your taunts, or your disrespect."

"Your lord," he sneered. "Whore. You have always been a whore, and now you -" He stopped with a choked cry as Arthras gestured and one of the guards kicked the back of his leg and sent him crashing to the floor. He clutched his leg and groaned.

Arthras stepped closer, until he stood tall over him. "You should mind how you speak. I rule here now, not you, and I rule with a power no man can oppose. The girl you feared has fled from me, and left me as master of all Othria. Call me savage if you wish, but I am your master now."

"I serve no one but my god, Attis of the thunderbolt. It is he who will judge and preserve me, not you." The old man lifted his chin and managed to look defiant, even lying on the floor. "I fear nothing from you, barbarian, nor from your whore." He shot a venomous glance at Nicaea. "Do what you will, and you may claim dominion over this land, but you will never rule it, not truly. You will always be a heathen and an invader."

"And yet your god was slain by a fiery demon," Arthras said. He glanced at Nicaea, then turned back to the old man. "I had thought to use you to bargain with the emperor himself. But Nicaea assures me that he despises you, and would not lift a finger to save your life." He reached out and took a spear from one of the guards. "And then I thought to torture you, and force you to renounce your god, and then execute you for all to see, so no one would doubt my supremacy."

"I will never renounce Attis, the father of the storms!" The old priest struggled to his feet, stood shivering and thin, looking very old and very feeble. His voice was thin and rough, and for all his shouting, Arthras could see he *was* afraid. "I call upon you, all mighty god, to protect me! Strike down this barbarian! Though he may kill me, I pronounce a curse on him! You shall drown in a river of fire! I shall see you cast down!"

Arthras drew back and stabbed the spear through the man's scrawny chest, hearing the punching sound, and feeling the ribs snap as they parted. The priest's harangue ended with a sudden gasp, and his expression became one of surprise so great it was almost funny.

"And then I decided to simply kill you, and to cast your body down to feed hungry dogs in the street, so that there would be no dignity in your death, no grandeur." He ripped the spear out and the thin body crumpled, hands and legs twitching as blood poured out onto the stones. The arch priest coughed once, and again, and blood came from his mouth. He fixed Arthras with his water blue-eyed stare, and then he died.

"Take the body away, and dispose of it," he said. He handed the guard back his spear and walked to the throne, stood looking up at the cracked portico above it, etched with stylized clouds and bolts of lightning. He didn't want to sit underneath it. He heard a little laugh and looked at Nicaea, saw her smiling.

"I always hated him," she said. "A self-important, venal, vindictive man. I am glad to have witnessed his end." She gestured to the throne. "Sit."

"I don't want to sit," he said. He folded his arms and looked up at the roof far overhead, painted and inlaid with ornate designs. There was a storm there as well, waiting.

ఠ

Karana did not push herself, and with a gentle wind they sailed over a day and a night and with the next day they had crossed the Straits of Amytris and come in sight of Calliste, the Imperial Island, and the ancient birthplace of the empire itself. First they saw the mass of Mount Ara, wreathed in white clouds, and then the green hills of the island called "the fairest" came into sight. Karana stood in the prow of their small ship, and looked forward, as she had read a great deal about this place, but she had never seen it.

The day was bright and clear, with clean wind and a sky touched with pure white clouds. The star was fading on the horizon, low and lending the clouds over the sea a shimmer of many colors. The waves were touched with white, and she saw more ships dotted across the sea, all of them converging toward the white cliffs ahead.

They had found some clothes in a small storage compartment under the deck, and she wore a shirt many times too large for her, belted with rope. It was far from dignified, but it was better than a scrap of sailcloth. Lykaon wore short pants that flapped loosely around his short legs, and Thessala had made a robe from a sheet, with a makeshift hood to conceal her face. She held the stay ropes and kept the sail trimmed as they skimmed across the wavetops. The sight of the fair green country before them was almost enough to make Karana feel hopeful.

She shifted as the wind pulled at them, and she winced. There was still pain, though it was much less now.

Whatever hurts she had taken seemed to be healing, though the deepest wounds seemed to be within. She saw the fear that was inside her now when she looked at Thessala, found the answering guilt there, the weight of what they had tried to do, and what their failure had cost. A dozen times she had almost brought them around, sent the ship back to the north, across the strait to Orneas. But she knew she could not accomplish anything there, not now. Another battle like that, and they might not all survive it. And how many innocent people would go down into death in the course of it? No.

Now they came nigh to another city, the heart of the empire, and she wondered if their arrival passed a sentence upon it as well. They drew closer and she eased her grip on the winds, not wishing to cause crosswinds for the other craft on the same course. She had resolved, now, to be much more cautious with her power. She could not afford to wield it carelessly again.

Archelion lay on the gentle slopes of a low shore, the harbor hemmed in by white cliffs that protected it from storms and from invasions. As they came closer she saw the white glint of sun on the marble towers, and when they entered the wide harbor and the whole of it lay before them like a dream, she could not have found words to describe it.

The city rose up and up on successive tiers cut into the hillsides, and everywhere she looked there were great palaces and sprawling structures lined with pillars and set off by towers that loomed over the deep streets below. The harborfront was lined with great statues, and on an islet at the center reared the ancient figure of Attis himself, arm uplifted and a golden bolt of lightning in his grasp, ready to be hurled down upon the unworthy.

"It's so much bigger than I thought," Thessala said. "I thought Orneas was a great city. It would fit in the corner of this."

Lykaon sat against the gunwale and looked up at the city with an unhappy expression. "Huh," he said, and went back to braiding rope.

There were a thousand stone piers, and ships darted back and forth with seemingly no plan or order. Thessala pulled on the lines and tried to steer them in carefully, but they bumped and scraped against a few ships before they found a place to draw in. Karana jumped across to the dock with a rope in hand and tied up. She stood there for a moment before she realized she had set foot on the island of the emperors.

She was not certain what to do. No one seemed to pay them any attention, and the whole waterfront swarmed with so many ships and people that it was like a great blur without feature. Thessala came ashore beside her, holding her hood over her face. Lykaon came behind her. Karana looked at their ship and wondered if they should tell someone they did not need it any longer.

Lykaon tugged her sleeve, and when she looked at him, he pointed. She looked, and she saw a man coming towards them. He was neat, and dark-haired, well-dressed and with pale skin that bespoke a barbarian of some kind. He held in one hand something that glinted, and he held it up, peered at it, and then he looked at her, saw her looking at him.

Karana tensed, and she waited as he approached. The thing in his hand was a small glass sphere, and he held it up as he came closer. When he was very near he moved the thing side to side, up and down, and then he nodded and put it away in a pouch at his belt. He bowed slightly, and smiled. He had one dark eye, one pale green.

"My greetings to the three of you," he said. "I have been waiting for you to arrive."

Chapter Twenty-Three

Ashes of Gods

Karana looked askance at this strange man who looked like a barbarian but dressed like a prince. Up close, there was silver thread stitched into his black doublet and his pants. His tall boots were well-fitted and he wore the small silver loops on the back that were supposed to take the place of spurs among those who did not actually ride. He had a half-cape thrown back over his left shoulder, and he was very clean-shaven in the imperial fashion.

She glanced at Thessala, saw she was drawn back, hands tucked under her makeshift robe. Karana gathered her braids up in her hand and wished she had something to cover them with, as that made her feel more naked than wearing nothing more than a shirt that was too big. "And do I know you?"

"No," he said. "And I do not know you, but I know who you are. Or I know who one of you is." He squinted at Thessala, nodded to himself and turned to face Karana. "You are the Storm Queen, I presume."

She snorted, unable to help it. Every retelling made her sound more grandiose, and that was the last thing she felt like now. "My name is Karana," she said. "And you. . ?"

"I am called Dagon. Not my real name, but it has served me for long enough that it may as well be." He bowed. "I am at your service, as well as the imperial service, as it happens. I am the adviser to His Imperial Majesty on matters esoteric and arcane. I have come seeking you, and I have been waiting for you ever since it became plain you had left Orneas. I hoped you would come here." He gestured. "Welcome to Archelion. I hope it shall serve you better than the last city you called home."

"I hope we serve it better as well," she said dryly. She did not want to talk about what had happened, it still made her stomach twist to think on it. "How could you know who I am from afar?"

He produced the small glass globe from his pouch with a smooth motion of his hand. Karana saw it was filled with some oily liquid, and suspended inside was what looked like a needle; it shimmered as she looked at it, and, oddly, it did not float freely, but pointed right at her.

"This is a small device which I have made to allow me to track your movements," he said. He moved it side to side, and no matter how he oriented it, the needle pointed right at her. "I will be glad to explain its workings, but perhaps this is not the moment for that." He glanced around. "I would like very much to speak to you – to all of you – but I think somewhere more comfortable and less public." He put the orb away and glanced around at the crowd.

"Where did you have in mind?" Despite the strangeness of the situation, Karana did not find herself suspicious of this man. He was well-spoken, but not oily or unctuous.

"My house will do well enough," he said, still looking around them. "Now if I can just find that boy. Where did he go?"

Karana jumped as a youth jogged through the crowd and joined them. He was lean and handsome, and he moved so easily and lightly he looked as if he could not be real. He smiled at them. "I'm here."

"Oh good," Dagon said. He gestured between them. "Karana, this is Diomedes. He is like you. . . like all of you, if I am not mistaken." He looked past her to where Thessala was silent and Lykaon almost lurking in the background.

Karana nodded. "I suppose, yes. Thessala, and that's Lykaon." She did not offer more, wondering if she should be suspicious and not sure what harm this man could possibly do by himself.

"Greetings, greetings!" The boy Diomedes caught her hand and pressed it, then he went to Thessala, took her hand before she could protest, and pressed it between his. He saw her scales and exclaimed, bent down to peer at her fingers. "Attis' bolts, look at that! That's wonderful!"

Dagon cleared his throat and Diomedes looked chastened, allowed Thessala to recover her hand. He took a step toward Lykaon and was met by a growl that made him back up. Thessala put a hand on Lykaon's arm and he subsided.

"I'm sorry," Karana said to the boy. "We have. . . we have been through a lot these past days."

Diomedes shrugged. "It's all right. I forget myself sometimes."

"Yes, so why don't we take all of this somewhere quieter," Dagon said. "I am sure you would all like to wash and eat and. . . dress?"

Karana nodded. "We would."

"Good, because you certainly cannot meet the emperor looking like that," he said without rancor. "Follow me, then." He beckoned, and as they began to move, he fell in beside Karana. "You are Sydonian, are you not? I mark you by your accent."

"I am," she said. She could not place his accent, but if he had been born a barbarian, that was not so strange. "Why do you ask?"

In answer he drew a black sash from under his doublet and held it out to her. "For your hair, if you would wish it."

She blinked, then she took it from his hand and gratefully covered her hair, wrapping her braids and making the familiar knot underneath. "Thank you," she said, and then did not trust herself to speak any more. Such a small thing, but she felt almost overwhelmed.

"It's all right," he said, touching her shoulder lightly. "This has been a difficult time for many people, in many ways." He sighed heavily as he led them off the waterfront and onto a wide, busy street.

Karana heard at least four different languages in as many steps, and smelled fifteen different kinds of food over the heavy smell of so many people so close together. "I suppose it has." She was thinking of refugees, driven from their homes, desperate and afraid.

"And, unfortunately, I do not think it is likely to easily improve," he said.

"How do you mean?" She was becoming aware of just how tired she was. Even if her body was superhuman, her spirit was not.

"I mean," he said, "it is likely that before anything can get better, it is going to get a whole lot worse."

☙

Dagon's home was a small villa halfway up a hill toward the sprawling imperial palace. As they left the tangled heart of the city beside the water, they found more and more open space, and Karana was surprised to see ruined, abandoned houses and open space grown over with grass. The imperial city was not as perfect as it had looked from the sea. They followed a winding road, and then passed through an archway into grounds that were not as well-tended as they might have been. It was early summer, and the gardens were a riot of flowers and climbing vines that had swarmed up the side of the house all the way to the balcony.

"I don't keep servants," he said as he led them into the cool entry hall. "The baths are in back, and you may feel free to avail yourselves as you like. I will find some clothes for you to wear."

"I can do that," Diomedes said. He headed for the stairs and ran up them, seeming to move too quickly. Karana looked after him, then she caught Thessala's eye and nodded.

"You two go get cleaned up. I'll join you," she said. Thessala gave Dagon a significant look, but Karana waved her away, and she went. Lykaon followed, looking back suspiciously as he went.

Karana turned and saw Dagon watching her with his brows raised. "Your friends don't trust me."

"Why should they? We have never before been met with any kind of hospitality, or welcome. Everywhere we have gone, we have been treated like enemies." She looked around, wishing there was someplace to sit. The windows were overgrown with flowering vines, and the sunlight through them dappled on the floor. "I have to wonder what your motives are."

"My motives are complex," he said. "I am a scholar, after all, and some of my intent is simple curiosity. I want to know more about you, more about what you can do, and how you do it." He sighed. "But circumstances must intrude, after all. I know about the battles you had at Ilion, and Orneas, and those did not go well, or you would not be here."

"You seem to know a great deal," she said.

He shrugged. "Archelion is the center of the empire. Even if the political reality is not what it once was, this is still the heart of trade and travel. News may travel fast, but it always travels here first. Ever since I met Diomedes, I have been listening for news of others like him. You did not take long to make yourself known."

"How did you meet him?" she said, looking up the stairs.

"Actually, he came to me," Dagon said. "He knew me to be the imperial expert on such things – if anyone can be an expert on it – and sought me out, wondering what had happened to him. I had already begun researching the star, so I was able to use him to confirm my hypothesis."

"You mean you know what has done this?" she said, not certain whether that possibility was exciting or fearful.

"I know something of it," he said. He looked up, as though he could see the sky through the ceiling. "The star is a wanderer, which means it is not really a star at all. It is an object from the deep aether, something unknown. Its path has brought it here, and as it circles around the sun, the heat ignites its outer layer, and sends it spraying out behind it. That is what creates the tail you see on any such star."

"Yes," she said. "I looked for charts, to see if this star had come before, but I did not find anything."

"Indeed. If it has come before, then it did not come so close." He leaned against the balustrade beside the stairs, running his fingers around the loops of the wrought iron. "But this time it has come very close, and in fact, our world passed through the tail itself. I studied and investigated, and I found something." He looked thoughtful for a moment, then he beckoned her, and without waiting went through the doors deeper into the house.

Curious, Karana followed him and found herself in what had been intended to be a parlor, but instead seemed to be used as a study. There was a desk and some tables against the walls, and the doors onto the back of the house stood open, letting in a cool breeze and the scent of flowers.

Dagon went to a table laden with glass vessels and other ephemera of alchemy. He opened a small box and drew out something small. He held it up, and shook it, and she saw it was a vial with something silvery in it. "What is that?"

He came back to her and handed over the vial. Inside it, she saw a scattering of fine silvery dust. It was so very fine that it almost seemed to disappear when she moved the vessel. She held it close to her face, and peered at it.

"That is a substance not found anywhere on earth," he said. "It seems to be a residue of the tail of the star. It came down through the sky, settled all over the world, most likely. It seems to collect within living things through some mechanism I have not yet discovered. But it does. I believe every person – every living thing in the world – now has some of this inside their bodies."

He leaned closer and tapped the vial, making the dust stir again. "In some people, it seems to cause changes. I don't know why it affects some and not others. I don't know how much is needed... there is a great deal I don't know. But I do know that what has happened to you, to Diomedes, to your other companions and who knows how many others, is a result of it. This -" he took the vial and shook it, "-is the author of all of this."

"I see," she said, and he smiled sympathetically.

"I know. It is an explanation, but it does not really explain, does it? I know what changed you, but not how, or why." He sighed. "I coated a needle with it, and found I could use it as a kind of compass. I believe it means that you have a greater concentration of the star-stuff in your bodies, but I am not certain." He shrugged. "I am certain of very little." He gave her a long look. "Except that I am talking while you have neither washed nor eaten. Go, and clean up, and I will have food and clothes when you emerge." He quirked a smile. "I don't think the world will end while you have a bath."

ങ

Thessala found the baths were outdoors, under a thin roof now overgrown with vines. The water was hot, and she supposed it must be fed by underground hot springs. The pools were old marble, stained by water and cracked, but too hot to grow any kind of scum in the water, so they were clean enough, despite a kind of metallic smell. There were decorative partitions made of wood staves and woven wicker to allow privacy between bathers in the small pools, while the central pool was wide open.

She considered modesty, but then decided there was no longer any reason. She shrugged off her makeshift robe and climbed down into the water, hissing in pleasure at the intense heat. She found one end was much warmer, hot water flowing into it around her feet, and she immersed herself and lay underneath the surface for a long time. She held her breath, and then held it longer and found she had no impulse to breathe. It bothered her mind long before she felt anything in her chest, and when she emerged, she could have stayed under much longer.

When she came up, she startled Lykaon, who was sitting down with his feet in the water. He twitched when she came up, then relaxed when he saw it was her. "Sorry," he said. He moved to get up, but she waved him off.

"No, stay. We were naked together on a boat for two days. I do not grudge you a bath." She found a selection of pumice stones beside the pool and took one, began to scrub herself mercilessly, liking the rough feel of it. There were oils as well, and soaps, but she was fairly sure they would not do her any good. Her skin was like iron armor now; she would be better off polishing it.

"Our host seems an odd man," she said, deliberately not looking as Lykaon stood and took off his pants, then climbed down into the pool. "What do you think of him?"

Lykaon grunted, and she almost laughed, having expected no less from him. She scrubbed at her face and was alarmed to find some of her scales flaking away. She felt the wounds and found the old scales had given way to new ones. They felt smooth and clean and hard. Good. She had worried her new skin would scar more easily.

Her braid was a stiff, dirty mess. She sighed and looked for a comb, found one on the edge made from a shell, with good thick teeth. She resigned herself and set to picking her braid loose. It was a long process, but not as long as putting it back in. She wondered if perhaps she should find some easier kind of knot to tie it in.

She almost jumped out of her skin when something plucked at her hair, and she turned to see Lykaon, up to his chest in the deep end of the pool, calmly helping her unbraid her hair. For a moment she tried to think of something to say, but then she simply took her hands away and let him, and then she passed him the comb when he reached for it. She found herself as near to speechless as she had ever been.

He was very precise, his thick fingers easily prying the braid apart, using the comb sparingly to pick at it when the strands were tangled. "Tough," he said. "Still soft, though." He made a sort of half-smile, and she almost laughed again.

"You saved my life, back there, in Orneas," she said. She felt oddly embarrassed to bring it up. Days on the ship and they had not discussed any of what had happened. It seemed too near and too painful. "I mean, you probably saved my life."

"Probably saved mine too," he said. He met her gaze for a moment, then nodded slightly. "Was a good fight."

"I... I don't know what's good about it. It almost killed us, who knows how many more were killed." She shuddered at the memory. The howling wind, Arthras like a burning demon that kept coming back no matter what they did. She remembered the burning of his molten armor on her skin and looked at her arms, but the burn marks had already flaked away. She could not see them.

"You were brave," he said. "You fought hard. You never were in a fight before." He didn't ask, it was a statement.

"No," she said. "Not like that."

"Can lose a fight, and it's still a good fight. Feels like a *fight*." He snorted. He had worked her braid loose up to her head, and now he ran his fingers through her hair and she stiffened, felt like she would turn red if she still could. No one had touched her like this for many years. No man, at least. She was suddenly very aware that he was close to her, and they were alone and naked together. He ran the comb through her hair, and she shivered.

"Beautiful," he said, and he trailed his fingers very gently down her back, over the scales along her spine. She twitched, unable to help it, and she wanted to turn and face him, even as she was suddenly overwhelmed with shame at how she looked.

She pulled away from him, splashing out of the water, feeling hot and embarrassed. She muttered something, not even sure what she was trying to say, and then she grabbed up her dirty robe and covered herself. Her wet hair clung to her as she hurried away, making for the doubtful shelter of the house. Karana was just emerging from inside, and she started when she saw Thessala walking so quickly.

"Are you all right?" she said.

Thessala knew her embarrassment didn't show on her face now, but she felt as if it were all over her. She shook her head and went past her into the shade of the house. "Fine, I'm fine." She did not feel fine. "I'm fine." She kept walking, and she didn't look back.

Chapter Twenty-Four

LEGENDS AND KINGS

Dressed and clean, Karana did not even know how to feel. It had taken her some time to wash and pick out her dirty braids, stiff with salt water. By the time she was done, there were clean clothes laid on the warm stones beside the baths. The feel of clean muslin and silk was as refreshing as the hot water. She dressed and went inside, and the boy Diomedes showed her to a room. It smelled a bit dusty, but was far finer than her old cell in the archives. The thought of it gave her a pang, and she must have made a face, because Diomedes looked at her.

"Is it all right? It's not a palace, but then I'm not picky, myself." He scratched the back of his neck, looked at her sidelong.

"No, it's not that. Just. . . a lot has happened to me in the past few weeks." She laughed, and it came out more bitter than she intended. "It's fine."

"Can you really call the storms?" he said.

"Yes," she said, remembering the ruin her powers had wrought. "Yes, I can." She shook off her reverie. "What do you do? I have not had the chance to ask."

"Uh, I got faster," he said. Now he looked awkward, looking around the room. "I've always been a runner and a climber. Now when I run I get faster, and stronger the faster I go. I get so fast everyone else seems like they are slow." He looked proud of himself, and embarrassed to be proud. "I don't know how fast I can get yet."

"That's all right," she said. "I don't know the limit of my power yet either."

"They say you fought a giant," he said.

She almost laughed at that. "Arthras is quite bad enough without being a giant, believe me."

"And he shakes the ground?"

She looked at him, trying to judge how old he was. He looked perhaps twenty, but he spoke like a younger man. "Yes. He shakes the earth so savagely you can't even stand. He gives out so much heat it hurts to stand near him. Metal and stone melt when they touch him. He is. . . terrible to face."

"I'm sorry," he said. "I shouldn't ask so many questions."

"I think we all have a lot of questions," she said. "I doubt many of them have good answers." She held out her hand, and he clasped it. "If it comes to another battle, I will be glad to have you with us."

"You think there will be another battle?" he said. He sounded halfway between afraid and excited.

"Your friend Dagon thinks there will be," she said.

"Why do you say that?" he said.

"Because otherwise he would not have brought us here," she said. She touched her hair under the towel, felt it was wet and heavy. She would need to comb it while it dried. "Pardon me."

"Of course," he said, looking embarrassed. "Of course."

☙

She found a mirror at a small vanity table close to the window, and she sat down, liking the feel of the warm wind over her skin, ruffling the skirts of her new dress. It was dyed in a wash of blue and purple, and she had truthfully never had anything as pretty, or not since she was a small child. Those were the days when her father had been more successful, before her mother died. Good years she could only dimly recall, in the very faintest outline and with little detail.

There was an old comb in a drawer of the table, and she unwound her hair and began to pick through it. Her hair was thick, and would tangle up terribly if she let it dry like this without tending it. She started at the ends and worked at it slowly, enjoying the ritual of it.

She was startled by the soft rap at the door, and paused a moment before she answered, coming back from a distant reverie. It was strange, because her body no longer grew tired, but her mind did, and she had not slept very much since the battle. "Yes?"

She expected Thessala, but it was Dagon who opened the door and looked into the room. "Pardon me. I don't want to intrude."

"It's all right," she said. "I am just combing my hair."

"I understand if I am not supposed to see your hair down," he said. "That is the custom on Sydon, isn't it?"

She shrugged. "I am supposed to keep it covered when I am in public. In private, it is up to me to choose who sees it. I have never made a strict observance of it. It is only my habit." She worked the comb up higher. "But when it is not braided, I have to tend it while it dries, or it will form mats that cannot be combed out."

"Unmarried women braid their hair and cover it," he said. "Married women wear it loose. Warriors keep it braided, but do not cover it."

She smiled. "The old ways. I do not think there are many warriors who keep to that. They are also supposed to shave it up off the sides, and cut off a finger if they lose a battle. Some old ways are best left in the past, I think." She looked at him sidelong. "Where are you from? You are not a native of the empire, I think."

"Oh, I'm from far away," he said. "A place called Idria. East of here."

"One of the lost domains?" she said. "I have seen it written as Edria."

"Yes, but no one from that place calls it that," he said.

"How did you come to be here?" she said.

"How did you? Life is a strange road, and it takes us strange places. For me, I am a scholar, and I ended up here, because this was where there was the most to study. There are no archives anywhere in the world to compare with the ones here in the empire." He laughed. "There are more *untranslated* texts in the archives here than all the books in the biggest library in Idria."

"I worked at the archives in Ilion," she said. "I have been a scrivener, and a translator of histories for years." She sighed. "I think it's gone now." She remembered what Arthras had said to her, but did not know what to make of it.

Dagon grimaced. "Wars are not kind to history," he said.

She reached her scalp, dug the comb in and swept it down, pulling the teeth through her wet hair, slow and even, working it with her fingers to dry it. "Is that why you wanted us here?"

"I have been gathering all the news I could," he said. He found a bench and sat on it. "I have rather good sources of information. I had hoped you could hold Orneas, and if you had, I would have come to you. But when I heard it had fallen, I knew you would come here. And yes, now we will need you."

"You think Arthras will come here," she said.

"A barbarian conqueror who can break down walls with his will? Who has an army of vengeful warriors at his back? Oh yes, I think he will. Conquest does not tend to sate such men, it only feeds their desire for more." He toyed with the clasp that held his collar closed. "But it is different here."

"Because of the sea," she said. "I had thought that."

"Indeed. He will need ships, will have to cross water, and on water he will be vulnerable. He will be especially vulnerable to you." He rubbed at his chin. "It will depend on what he does. He could spend time subduing the rest of Othria, settle in and fully consolidate his conquest. You have met him – do you think he will?"

Karana sighed. "It is not easy to say. He seems driven by a need to care for his people, to provide for them. He has a deep sense of grievance against the empire, and an especial hatred for the Autarch, Galbos." She shook her head. "Though I suppose that no longer matters."

"Really? Did Galbos not survive the catastophe?" Dagon seemed almost pleased.

Karana was unable to keep the anger from her face. "He all but caused it, but he did not survive it. I saw him go down into ruin."

"Ah, I see you know the old bastard personally," Dagon said. "Well, I suppose he managed to escape having to face the emperor. He presided over the loss of the whole of Othria, the old imperial heartland. His Majesty is not pleased at all."

"You didn't like him either," she said, not asking.

"I dislike men who would sacrifice their country for their own aggrandizement or gain," he said. "But I disliked Galbos on a personal level, so you are quite right. I was glad enough for him to be exiled to Ilion, away from here. Now he is dead, so I suppose some kind of justice has been done."

Karana looked at her hand. "But the world has changed." Her arm slipped from under her shawl, and her lightning scars were plain on her skin. "Why did it happen?"

"That would seem to be one of the central questions, a crucial question, when in fact it is not," he said.

"No?" She was half annoyed, half amused by his tone.

"No," he said. "Because it is a question we likely cannot answer, and would be meaningless if we could. We cannot undo what has been done, we can only try to control it."

"So what is the crucial question you would ask?" she said.

"I confess some curiosity as to the why, but I would much more like to know one thing: has it happened *before?*" His tone became quite pointed when he said it.

"Before?" she said.

"We worship gods, who are said to have walked the earth long ago. They changed their shapes, they possessed great strength and could not be slain by mortal means."

Dagon looked intently at her. "They commanded the storms."

Karana gripped the comb hard in her hand, felt the edges biting into her skin, and then it snapped apart. She jumped and almost stood up, but got control of herself. "You mean Attis."

"I do," he said. "This is, after all, the holy city of Attis. He fought and defeated the spirit of the fire mountain. Mount Ara is there." He pointed out the window. "Some say he died there, wounded by the beast of fire. Then again, some say he sleeps, and will wake someday and return to us." He snorted. "I doubt he would be pleased by the state of his church if he did."

"You think Attis was someone like me," she said. "That the star came and touched him."

"Not just him," Dagon said. "His paladins as well. I am sure you know the stories as well as anyone, though I know them better than most. He had his warrior companions, each of them with more than human powers."

Karana stood up, went to the window and looked out. The sun was setting, the light cast golden across the slopes of Mount Ara. "You believe this?"

"It makes sense to me," he said. "We have a lot of legends about that time, but few real records. Those were the waning days of the Old Empire, and it was a terrible time. Chaos, and war, and disaster. When they say that Attis ended the drought and brought prosperity back to the land, I think of you. You could do that, if you wished."

"You don't know what I can do," she said, clutching her damp hair in her hands.

"I have an idea," he said. "I have heard the stories from Ilion, and now they are coming from Orneas." He crossed the room, and touched her arm. "I know what makes scars like that."

She felt anger flash in her, and then she lost it and turned away from him. "I don't know what you want. I am not a goddess, and I will not be one."

"It is not up to you," he said. "You should be ready, when the time comes."

"To call myself divine, and fight Arthras?" She clenched her jaw. All of this was making her angry, and she didn't want to be angry. "I don't want to fight him. I never wanted to fight him. I could have made peace at Orneas, if not for Galbos' interference."

Dagon was silent for a moment, then nodded. "Fair enough," he said. "But I am going to take you to meet the emperor, and you will have to decide what you will say to him."

"What do you want me to say to him?" she said.

"I am not going to tell you what to say," Dagon said. "I brought you here because I believe you can save the empire, and I will help you do that. But I will not try to use you for my own gain, and I will not lie to you."

Karana sighed. She still was not certain what she thought about this man. Right now, she was very tired. "I will consider," she said. "Right now, however, I am going to braid my hair."

Dagon inclined his head. "Of course, forgive me," he said. "Come down when you are done, and there will be dinner."

"I will," she said. She watched him go, and then she turned and looked out the window again, peering through the fringe of leaves from the vines running unchecked over the villa. Beyond the city rose the immensity of Mount Ara, the holy mountain of Attis. She looked upward to the top, and saw it was hidden, shrouded in a halo of clouds, or smoke.

☙

Later, after a dinner that was more plentiful than anything else, Karana took herself out into the back gardens. She smelled the faint copper smell of the hot spring, and the heady scent of flowers fully in bloom. It was cool, the wind off the mountain fresh and gentle. From here she could see the palace and the whole swath of finer villas that spread up the mountainside, lights glimmering in the dark. She sat down on the steps and hooked her arms around her knees.

Someone came up behind her, and she turned, wondering if it was Dagon again, but it was Thessala, her white robe spectral in the starlight, shining as the moon came up over the shoulder of Mount Ara. Karana smiled. "Come sit, it is a pleasant evening. We have had few enough of those."

"I don't know what to do," Thessala said, sitting down beside her. "I feel like I should do something."

"So do I, and we will do what must be done. But right now, there is not anything we can do, so we rest, and enjoy the view." She smiled. "I never expected to see the mountain."

"Nor did I," Thessala said. "It is bigger than I expected. It's so big it almost doesn't look like a mountain."

"I know, I expected something more distinct." She looked up at the dark shape. "They say Attis died on that mountain, in battle with a demon of flame."

"Or that he sleeps beneath it," Thessala said.

"You think he was like us?" Karana said, impulsive.

"Like... you mean Attis was one of us? One of the..." Thessala reached for words.

"Chosen," Karana said. She looked east and saw the glow of the star, so much less now. "It chose us somehow. Something made it choose us and not someone else."

"You think this... this has happened before?" Thessala sounded uneasy, and Karana supposed she was too.

"Dagon thinks so; he thinks I am Attis come again. Not literally, but that I... could be. I don't know. But now it has me thinking. I keep thinking of him. Touched by the star, not knowing what was happening." She shook her head, thinking of the stoic, unfeeling face carved on so many statues. "He must have been so afraid."

"I know I am," Thessala said. "And I don't have power like you."

"I thought it was a gift," Karana said. "Now it doesn't feel like one."

"It's like a sword," Thessala said. "It is a tool, or a weapon. It can do good or evil."

"Yes, but it's so strong. A sword can cut or kill one person at a time. I could wipe a city off the earth, and I nearly did." Karana remembered the deep-toned howl of the wind, the lightning scrawling and slashing everywhere. She closed her eyes to shut it away. "It's too much power for one person to have. Far too much."

"Perhaps," Thessala said. "But I would rather you had it than anyone else. You I can trust."

"I..." Karana did not know what to say to that. She sat silent for a moment, then reached out and took Thessala's hand and squeezed it, glad to receive a squeeze in return. "I am glad to have you here."

"This strange journey we are on," Thessala said, laughing a little.

They both felt it, a tremor beneath them, a shiver in the stone. Both of them leaped up, and Karana found her heart was going like a runaway horse. Another shock passed through the ground and she heard Thessala gasp. There was a distant rumble, echoing down the mountainside, rolling slow over the land like thunder from far away.

"What is that?" Thessala said. "Is that. . ."

"The mountain," Dagon said, coming toward them from the house. "People of other lands may forget that Ara is a volcano, but here it never lets us forget." He stopped and looked up at the clouds around the peak, pale in the rising moon. "It is only the mountain stirring in its sleep. Do not fear it too much."

"It's not the tremor I fear," Karana said. "But what follows it." She gathered her shawl around her shoulders. "I have had more than enough of ill omens." The ground shuddered again, and she closed her hands into fists, wishing the world would lie still for at least one night.

Chapter Twenty-Five

Men of War

Arthras did not sleep very much anymore, so he often found himself awake in dark hours, pacing the halls of his new palace. This one had been grander than the one back in Ilion, but it had been badly damaged, and parts of it lay in ruin. All four towers had collapsed, and whole courtyards below, which had once been manicured gardens, were buried in stone and dust. Walls on the lower floors had burst in and let the rubble in to flood them, so many of the halls were impassable.

He climbed up to the battlements, above the salt smell of the lower city, and walked there in the light of the stars and the moon. If he wanted to see the star, he had to look east, far over the horizon, where the shadows of the mountains hid most of it from his view. It was passing, and soon it would be only a memory.

If he looked down on the city, he saw a blanket of sparks, each one a fire. His warriors built their camps in the open squares and plazas, and in each one he saw campfires lit with the broken wood of the ruined city. Even by night he could see the destruction, because there were large patches of it that were dark, when no light shone. Places where wind and the shaking of the earth had blasted the city down to the ground.

It was better at night. He did not like the look of it by day, seeing how much damage had been done. He had not wanted to wreck the city, he had wanted to take it. And now he had it, it did not seem so fine a thing as it might have been. It was like something gaudy and shiny that tempted, but once grasped it fell into pieces. This was not what he wanted, and that gave him to wonder just what he did want, and he had no answer for that.

He remembered the winter after the Borunai drove them south, when there was no food. He remembered days of hunger, of thinking about nothing but food. And then came the days when he did not feel it, and that was frightening, because he knew he was still hungry. He knew by then that when an infant ceased to cry from hunger, it would almost surely die. There were nights of lying awake, wondering if he would die if he slept. Then came the nights hoping he would. He knew some had simply given up, gone out into the snow to die peacefully.

His people had not wanted to invade or conquer; they just wanted a home. That was something he wanted – he wanted to give them that. A safe place, a home where they could build their villages and cut their fields into good soil. Why should his people starve and suffer when there were soft green lands like this? When he remembered what they suffered to be here, he did not feel guilt for all those who had died from simply being in the way.

But that way was false thinking. He was king now because they called him king and he could not prevent it, but his heart was with those who labored much and gained little. He had given all his soldiers their share of gold and silver, but what was gold in a place without markets or merchants? Gold was not food. When they had entered the city they had broken open storehouses, but much of the grain and bread had been soaked in the flooding, and was wasted. This was good land, and there were farms to be taken, but they could not disperse to work the land; they had to be vigilant. The emperor would not long suffer their presence without some answer. This was only a reprieve.

He grunted and went back inside, down the lamplit halls to his chambers, which had not been the archpriest's rooms, for they said those had been in one of the towers, destroyed by Karana. His breath caught when he thought of her: a mixture of anger, fear, and simple frustration. He did not want to fight her, but she would not stand out of his way. She had stood with Galbos, and that made him angry. Had she not seen what a treacherous bastard he was? He supposed she must realize it now, too late.

The memory of Karana goaded him, and he did not know why. She fought him when she should not, when there was no reason for it. She was wrong in her decisions and he could not understand how she did not see it. And the other two, who were they? The scaled woman, strangely beautiful under her armored skin, so strong. And then the beast. Was he a man underneath? Had he been a man? Three of them, and only one among his people. Even the gods played favorite of the empire, it seemed.

He turned away from that thought, angry. Bora was his guardian, and if she had not made only him strong, she had made him stronger than all the others. There were three opposed to him, but he had fought all three and emerged the victor. He was mightier than they, more favored.

The rooms were grandiose, with high ceilings and rich hangings and rugs. Even the chairs were covered in gold and hung with velvets and jewels. Half of him wanted to go out into the city and sleep in an honest tent, or even tear down the rest of the city and make them all sleep in tents. Living in soft places like this would make them all soft, if he let it.

Perhaps he should lead them north, into their old lands, and use his power to drive the Borunai out and retake their homeland. But he could not do that until next year, at least. If they went north now there would be no planting and no harvest, and they would starve in the winter. And they had begun a war with the empire; they could not go back and pretend it had not happened.

Nicaea was here, curled up in the bed, reading by the light of a lamp. He saw it was the book he had taken from the street outside the archive in Ilion, and he felt angry. He stopped where he was and clenched his hands into fists, trying to calm himself down. He did not know if he was angry that she was reading, or that she was reading that book.

She looked up and saw him. "There you are. I woke, and you were gone. I decided to wait."

He came around the bed, walking slow, and he could tell she knew something had upset him. He swallowed and made a small gesture to the book. "What does it say?"

"I. . ." She looked down at the page, then up at him. "Of course, you can't read it, can you?" She was not really asking. She sat up, folded her legs under her, and beckoned him to come sit beside her. He wasn't sure he wanted to, but he did. The silk sheets were so soft, it almost seemed ridiculous to sleep on them.

"This is a book of poems. It's written in Lyrian, but the style is an old imperial one." She flipped pages, touched a line and trailed her finger along it. "*Some say an army of horsemen, some of footsoldiers, some of ships, is the fairest thing on the black earth, but I say it is what one loves.*"

He did not say anything. He didn't know if he was supposed to. She glanced at him. "Where did you get this book?"

"I found it," he said. "I didn't know what it was."

"Well, a king should know how to read. I will see that you learn, once we have the time for it." She closed the book and leaned back against the pillows. She looked at ease in a way he never felt in these surroundings. "Very soon, the emperor will send an emissary to negotiate with you," she said.

"Why should I negotiate? Every negotiation with the empire is just a way for them to stall until they can betray." He felt this was true, did not want to be convinced otherwise.

"Of course it is, and this will be no different. But now you also have reason to stall. And you cannot be betrayed if you know it is coming. You can be prepared, and lay a trap of your own." She turned and put her legs across his lap, smiled at him in that way she had, making her look both sleepy and predatory.

"Tell me what you think," he said.

"The emperor will offer you lands," she said. "As before. Lands and gold to withdraw from Orneas and go away. He might even offer you lordship of Ilion, but that will just be a way to get you to withdraw. He will plan an attack on you as soon as he can, to drive you out and destroy you."

"Karana is with him now," he said. "And the others. He will know a direct attack will not succeed."

"Perhaps, but nothing is lost on his behalf by waiting. He knows you must feed your army, and not just with food.

Now they have tasted conquest, they will hunger for more." She stretched her toes out, sighed. "You have to keep going."

"And I don't have the forces to hold my conquered cities behind me," he said. "I can't defend my possessions; I have to attack and take more and more."

"Yes, and there are few opportunities for that in Othria," she said. "You can cross the mountains to the east and take Karnathos, but I would call that a waste of time. You need to go straight for the heart of the matter."

"Overthrow the emperor," he said, and he felt a strange thrill of unreality when he said it. He had never thought he would even see the island of Calliste; now he was discussing conquering it. "It will not be easy to get to the island," he said. "I will need ships."

"Yes, and that is why I advise you to negotiate," she said. "You need time. Time to rest and refit and prepare your army for the attack. You need ships. Most of all, you need time to find a way to deal with the storm girl and her allies."

"Deal with them?" he said.

"You have to get them out of the way. Frontal assault did not accomplish that, but there are other ways. Persuade them, bribe them, find a way to kill them." She shook her head. "You can't have them standing in your way when you attack the imperial city. You could never cross the strait in the face of that girl. She could sink a fleet of ships." Nicaea sighed. "It might be enough just to find a way to get her away at the right time, so you could be across before she realizes it. You said she tried to defend the city, but I doubt she wanted to damage it so badly. She would not want to risk that again. If you could cross without her knowing, then she would never dare oppose you."

"I will still need ships, and I have none. They were all wrecked when the storm struck the city. And I will need sailors too, as my people are not people of the sea." He took the book and looked at it, at the lines of words he could not read. Then he put it aside and lay back on the bed. All of this was so much more complicated than he had ever wanted it to be.

"Be easy, my lord," she said. "There are people who have both, and who have little love for the empire. As I said. All you will need is time."

ఈ

He went among his people by day, walking unarmed and unguarded into the streets to see the common warriors and their families. It was something he wanted to do. He did not forget that he had been no one, a single step above a slave. That the Goddess Boru had chosen him for special power and a special fate did not make him forget what it was like to sleep hungry and cold.

The people who had remained in the city had been impressed into work gangs, and now they cleaned the bodies from the streets. Arthras was not going to have a plague ravage through his camp, not now. Having them all camped so close in summer was enough trouble, but corpses would make illness bloom in a matter of days. He commanded that the dead be piled in open places far from the encampments, and then burned. The towers of black smoke and the stink of cooked carrion were not pleasant, but they meant his orders were being obeyed.

He carried a sack of coins and baubles with him, and he gave them away to whomever he wished. It felt almost futile, because there was nothing to buy with treasure.

There were no markets, no merchants. His warriors hunted through the abandoned ruins, seeking whatever there was to take. Even with the storehouses opened, there would not be enough food for them to stay here. It might last the summer, and would feel like an easy life because there were no fields to tend, no reaping to bend their backs to. But when winter came they would go hungry. Nicaea spoke of time, but he did not think they had enough.

He came to where the gates of the city had been, looking at the pile of ruin and rubble, the wreckage of the once-mighty walls. It was both satisfying and sad, to see something men had raised brought so low. He wondered if they would ever be rebuilt, or if the city would dwindle and become a forgotten place. He hoped it would be remade, would become great again. He did not want to be only a destroyer. He had imagined being a king would give him the power to make things, but it was not that easy.

What he really wanted was to be a new emperor, as they had been in the old days. He remembered the stories of the grand armadas of warships, the terrible battles that cast down kingdoms and changed the fate of the world. He wanted to carry the flame of his power into every land, and make the old empire anew, greater than it had been for hundreds of years. He would see the standard borne into the east, to reclaim the lost lands there – Edria and Avandar and Alesia. He wanted to unite the world as it had not been.

Only now it seemed that all those stories were fading before him like haze in the distance. Now he wondered how they had ever accomplished those things, without leaving a wreckage behind them of ruined cities and heaps of dead. He tried to imagine what would be needed to mount a fleet of warships to carry his army across the sea, and it made him flinch to think of all the work. They would need sailors and navigators and supplies, and that was for a journey to Calliste. It was said that the island lay only a few days away over the water. A longer voyage seemed impossible; what he wanted seemed equally impossible.

He saw riders on the road, stood and watched to be sure they were his. He was not a fool; he had his own horsemen out along the roads, looking for trouble, watching for the approach of enemies. He did not think there would be anyone with the strength to oppose him, but he had been wrong about that before, and he would not be wrong again.

Arthras stepped out from the shadow of the ruined gatehouse and the three riders drew rein, bowed from their saddles. One of them jumped down. "My lord," he said. The boy was young, even younger than he was. He was red-faced from the sun and sweating. "My lord, there are soldiers on the east road."

೫

They gathered in the throne room, Nicaea behind him, in shadow, while the foremost thanes gathered around the walls. Arthras stood, still uncomfortable with the throne, and beckoned for the riders to make their report. They were breathless and somewhat in awe, but they bowed and then the leader stood up tall and spoke clearly.

"There is a force of riders on the east road – the one that leads to the mountains. We counted almost a thousand men, with spare horses and pack animals. They were well-armed, with spears and shields and armor." The boy glanced around. "They did not move quickly, they did not seem to hurry."

"Did they see you?" Arthras said.

The boy nodded. "Yes, I am sure of it. They showed no hostility. One of them rode out ahead and lifted a spear to us, but we thought we should come and report to you. I cannot speak for the king."

Arthras nodded. "Good," he said, under his breath. "You saw no foot?"

The boy shook his head. "No, my lord. Only riders."

Nicaea reached out and touched Arthras' arm. "May I ask a question?" she said, her voice low. She was sensitive to how she appeared, did not want to seem to take on too much importance before the companions. He nodded.

She lifted her voice. "Did they bear a standard?"

The boy nodded. "Yes. A blue one, with a serpent on it, I think." He shrugged. "There was little wind, the banners were slack."

Nicaea smiled. "Then I know who sent these men. I would expect these are outriders – scouts for a larger force."

Arthras bared his teeth. "They will not find a warm welcome here."

Again she touched his arm. "Easy, my king. The blue banner is the standard of General Emmeus of Sarda. He will have come, hearing of the downfall of Ilion, and now he turns his eye to Orneas. I am sure he expects a battle, but he is confident, because he is a skilled commander, with the finest soldiers in the empire. But I don't think we have anything to fear from him."

All attention was on her, and Arthras felt a momentary discomfort at how easily she had come to dominate the room. She was good at this kind of thing, in a way he was not, at manipulating moments to go they way she wanted them to. There were little moments when he saw clearly the layers of her understanding and guile, and it made him nervous.

305

She leaned back in her chair and smiled at him. "This is, in a way, a gift from the gods. I was not sure we would receive it, but now it is delivered to the doorstep." She looked very pleased. "General Emmeus is my brother, and I am sure he will be very pleased to find me alive, and treated so well." She stood up. "He has come from Sarda, and to come so quickly, he must have come by sea." She touched Arthras on the shoulder. "I believe your fleet has just arrived."

Chapter Twenty-Six

Crossroads of Empire

The day was still as a glass painting, and Karana took pleasure from the motionless air, the smooth and orderly layers of it she sensed overhead. It was warm, but not too much so. She had heard much of the mild climate of the imperial isle, and now she saw it was not a myth. She took her time and dressed herself with care. She drew on a white silk undermantle, and over it she layered a blue robe, then a deep purple one. She tied it all with a sash that hung with tiny beads that clattered when she moved, and a lovely silk shawl wrapped over her hair. It was purple at the top and faded down to a deep sea blue at the trailing edge. It was not every day that she met an emperor.

She had new sandals of blue leather, and they were soft under her feet as she went down the hall of Dagon's house to the courtyard. He had not stinted with procuring them new clothes, least of all with her, as she was the one chosen to go and speak to the emperor. Thessala worried she would frighten anyone who saw her, and Lykaon could barely be induced to say more than three words.

The gold tips pinched onto the ends of her braids clacked as she came down three steps and then out into the unruly lawn that served as the front court of Dagon's house. She had realized by now that the man did not care at all what the exterior of his house looked like, and only engaged in the most rudimentary of care for the lawns and gardens. She could tell that once the shrubs that flanked the entrance had been cut into the shapes of animals, but they had faded so much she could not say what kind.

He was waiting for her in the sunlight, dressed, as was his usual habit, in all black with accents of blue and silver. He always seemed to be dressed too warmly for the weather, but it did not seem to trouble him. Diomedes stood to one side, as usual dressed lightly in a short tunic and loose pants. He was a scruffy boy, and never looked groomed even when he was. Karana found she was starting to like him, even if it was hard to get him to hold still for a conversation.

Dagon bowed in his way that seemed to mock the convention and not her. "I would say that is a suitable look. His majesty would be offended if you did not seem to have gone to an effort to dress up for him."

"Is he a man who values the surface of things?" she said.

"He would say he is not, but all aristocrats are to some degree – they cannot really help it. If you dressed casually, it would be taken as an insult." He smiled and held out a hand to welcome her. She did not take it, as she had learned his gestures were only rarely invitations for contact. He did not seem to like to be touched.

"And Diomedes?" she said, looking at him sidelong.

Dagon shrugged. "He has the look of my servant. They do not even see him, and that seems useful. After all, by becoming your ally, I will inevitably make enemies, and unlike you I am not immune to daggers or rains of poisoned darts."

They walked away from the villa, out through the crumbling pillars that marked the entrance to the court. She looked back at the house, hoping for a last look at Thessala, but she saw no one. The other woman had become more withdrawn since the battle of Orneas, and Karana found it worrisome. This was so hard on all of them; they had to hold to one another.

Outside the gate was a litter, with heavy poles front and back and a dozen slaves kneeling, waiting to carry it. Karana recoiled, and Dagon made an unhappy sound. "I know. I dislike the convention as well, but it is expected for all imperial visitors. Wheeled vehicles are not permitted inside the palace grounds, and walking is considered crude."

"What is crude is riding on the backs of other human beings," she said. "I will not have it." She squinted up at the sky. "I have other ways to travel."

Dagon held up his hands. "I beg you not to, not now. If you flew into the palace there would be a great deal of outcry. It would frighten them."

"They should be frightened," she said.

"Yes, but not yet. Frightened rulers can act rashly, and rarely in anyone's best interests." Dagon made a placating gesture. "This all has to be managed carefully, or we will face another Orneas."

Karana sighed and controlled herself. She looked back at the house again, and then turned to look up the hill at the sprawl of the palace. "I am going to walk," she said.

Dagon laughed a little. "Well then, will you allow me to accompany you?"

"As you wish," she said, unable to help smiling a little. Then she looked at the waiting slaves and the smile died. "Are they yours?"

"No, no. I own no slaves. They were sent from the palace. I will give them leisure here until we return, and then we can send them back later." He shrugged. "I can do no more than that."

"For now," she said. She beckoned him. "Walk with me."

ଓ

Thessala found Lykaon at the very back of the garden, where there was a stone wall built against the side of the hill, grown heavy with ivy and weeds. The vines were heavy with flowers, and the smell was heady and sweet. He was sitting on a patch of grass, plucking up small berries from the tree and eating them thoughtfully.

It felt good to be dressed. Thessala was grateful for the larger robe she had now, the edges worked with fine stitching on the black border. It had heavy, wide sleeves she could conceal her hands inside, and a large hood. Back here, away from anyone who might see, she pushed it back and let the sun shine on her face. It was a beautiful day, and there were clouds of little butterflies and heavy-bodied bees flitting around the wall of flowers on their tiny errands.

She knew he heard her, and she stepped carefully, sat down on the old bench he had characteristically ignored. It shifted under her weight, and for a moment she thought it might collapse, but it held. She smoothed her robe and arranged it around herself with pleasure. Her hair was loose, and she drew it over her shoulder and fidgeted with it.

He would not say anything unless prompted, she knew that, but she was happy just to sit with him. Just that. He was not much for conversation, and she could not think of anything to say. A bee landed on her arm and she watched it, glad she did not have to worry about being stung. It tickled her skin as it walked along, stopped to rub its face with two fuzzy limbs.

"It's hard to believe," she said.

"Hmm?" Lykaon just grunted, but she was learning what his noises meant.

"It wasn't long ago we were in a battle that destroyed a city, and now here we sit. Everything is peaceful, and calm, and warm. I don't know how many people are dead, and I don't have a mark on me." She stopped, her throat feeling tight.

"It's not fair," he said. "Nothing is."

"I wanted it to be. I've spent so long trying to help people no one else would help. Now I failed them. I thought, because I was stronger. . ." She covered her mouth. "I'm sorry. I didn't come here to say these things."

"It's hard," he said. "I'm a hunter, not a fighter. I thought it was the same, but it isn't." He shifted uncomfortably. "I thought killing was killing."

He looked at her, and she saw a kind of the same pain she carried on his face. He reached up and caught her hand, the bee crawling over his thumb before it flew away. He did not grasp her delicately, but there was a gentleness in him. He pulled, and she did not fight as she slid down to sit beside him on the grass. For a moment she sat apart, and then she shifted closer so they were pressed together.

Lykaon put his arm around her and drew her in close, and she held so very still, as if he were a wild thing who might dart away if she moved. But he caught her hand and squeezed it and she leaned against his shoulder, taking comfort in his solidity, his weight and his warmth.

"It's not good to be alone with it," he said. "Sit here with me."

"All right," she said, leaning into him. "I will."

෪

It was not until she was close to it that Karana really appreciated how big the palace was. They climbed up along the winding road, passing a lot of other litters and a solid line of servants and slaves toting burdens on their shoulders as they carried supplies up the hill to the top. The air was warm and the day grew hotter as they passed the noon hour. All the people on the road made for dust, and several times Karana gave in to temptation and conjured a breeze to wash it away. She kept expecting them to reach the palace, as they climbed up and up among huge estates and gorgeous villas with tended grounds, walked under arbors and smelled sweet flowers and ripening fruits.

In the end it seemed they entered the actual palace grounds without a clear line of demarcation. They were among towers and walking on white-paved courtyards, but there was no grand gate, and no walls to defend it. She had to remember that Calliste was an island, and the city of Archelion had not been invaded for over a thousand years. There was no wall because there was no reason to have one, nor a gate either. Rather than a fortress, the palace was the center of activity, a focusing point for power, politics, and money. It was a market, a citadel, and a repository of art and history all in one.

The grounds were a hive of activity, men and women and animals on all sides, and she was amazed at the ornateness of every single thing she saw. The walls were painted and set with elaborate mosaics, the pillars carved and wrapped with flowering vines. There were statues everywhere, set in alcoves, atop plinths and columns, set in the centers of fountains and gardens. She had never seen anything like it. Even in the glory days of the empire, Ilion had never been like this.

Karana tried to control her staring, but it was not easy to do. Dagon took her arm and guided her as they made their way into the maze of buildings and courtyards and fountains and colonnades. Without his help she would have collided with too many people to count.

"It's a sight, isn't it?" he said.

"I've read about it, but I never. . . Books do not do it justice." She blinked and shook her head, trying to regain her equilibrium.

"Archelion has never been sacked, not once," he said. "It has acquired more treasure and wealth and art than any other city ever has." They passed a wall that was cracked from top to bottom, with several broken columns beside it, and Dagon shrugged. "There has been the occasional earth tremor. Price to be paid for living on the slopes of a volcano."

"The last great eruption was over five hundred years ago," she said.

"Yes, and that one was not as bad as all that. The lava flowed down and set the fields afire. Smoke and ash covered the city for a week. There were some ash flows up in the hills that killed some sheep. The mountain grumbled for a decade after that, but it has been quiet ever since. Mostly quiet." Dagon led her around a corner, Diomedes behind them all but unnoticed. "Well," he said. "We are here."

Karana stopped and saw they stood before an actual gate, made of tall blue doors standing open and flanked by guards in silver-gilt armor with long spears hanging with red pennants. They did not move as he led her between them, and she wondered if they were even real, or just statues that stood guard. The floors inside were a dizzying mosaic that flowed up the walls and scattered across the vaulted ceiling. There were servants going to and fro and yet no one seemed to pay them the slightest attention. Dagon noted her expression and smiled. "I am an adviser to his majesty, remember? I am here often, and they know me. The guards might object if I brought Thessala, but no one thinks you could be dangerous. More fool they."

He led her down a side passage, and he paused to speak to another guard in quiet tones. Karana felt a momentary jolt of alarm, as she was here with a man she barely knew, her friends separated from her. This would be an ideal time for them to try to kill her. Perhaps they thought they could. She clenched her fists, then made herself stop. If they attempted something, she would make them regret it, but she resolved to be gentle. She would not want to destroy the palace.

She heard water, and then Dagon led her through a portico and into a room that breathed with the smells of flowers and the feel of humid air. It was a long blue room, with plants hanging in pots that depended from the ceiling or overflowed planters set in the columns and the walls. At the center was a square pool with only a few inches of water in it, and room for more. Above it was an open roof that looked up to the clear summer sky. Behind that was a couch, and on it a man sat, surrounded by courtiers and attended by four more guards. He saw them approach and beckoned, and Dagon touched her arm. "Bow when I do, and be easy."

Karana said nothing as they went around the pool and approached the man she assumed must be the emperor. The light reflecting from the water shimmered on the blue tiled walls. Closer in, she saw Niceros the twentieth was wan and had sallow skin. His hair was thin and colorless, and his eyes were sunken deep in his head. He was not a man who looked well, but he smiled when he saw them.

"Ahh, Dagon. I am pleased to see you. Have you brought me what your missive promised?" He sat on the couch rather than recline, dressed in a white and red robe that might have fit him once. There was a crown of golden leaves on his head, but it did not seem to fit well either. He held out a hand and she could not count all his rings.

Dagon bowed, came close, and bent to take and kiss the proffered hand. The emperor shifted his gaze to Karana. "And this is she? Come closer, child. My eyes are not what they once were."

Karana stepped closer, unsure of proper protocol. She stopped out of arm's reach, as seemed respectful, and bowed as Dagon had. The emperor looked her over, and despite his watery eyes, his glance was keen and measuring. He might be ill, but it seemed his mind was still sharp.

"Are you the girl who calls the storms?" he said. "Are you the one foretold to come? Attis' own child?" She looked sharply at him, wondering if this was some jest, or a mockery, but there was nothing in his face but a thin hope that was almost sad. He held out his hand, and she almost took it, when someone else stepped in closer, through the ring of attendants. She turned, thinking it was a guard come to push her back, but it was a boy.

Not a boy, though he had a youthful aspect. He was no taller than she was, and had blonde hair in tight curls and his own silver crown of leaves. He was probably no more than a year younger than she was, and he was pretty in a way she did not really like. "Father," he said, "we know nothing of this girl save what Dagon has told you." The way he emphasized his words made it clear what he thought, and she did not miss how he said "father". This was the heir, then.

"Forgive me, Highness," Dagon said. "You know I mean no disrespect, but your father asked that I bring her." He gestured to Karana. "This is Karana, as promised."

Karana stepped forward slightly, placing herself at the center of things. "Your Majesty," she said to the emperor. "Highness," she said, inclining her head to Prince Zeneos. "I never thought to stand in your presences, either of you."

The prince ignored her words. "Father, she -"

"Quiet," the emperor said, waving a hand. He stopped and a servant gave him a white cloth, and he coughed into it. Karana could hear the roughness in it, and did her best not to wince at the sound. When he was finished he handed the cloth back and took a slow breath. "I have wished to see you, girl, and now I do I have a great hope, and a great fear. Can you allay either one?"

"I. . . I don't know," she said. "What do you hope, and what do you fear?"

"I have heard of your power," he said. "I am told you have fought to defend my empire, and that you have laid waste to cities. Some fear you are a goddess, and some that you are not. I must know which."

"I am not a goddess," she said, and then she paused to think. She realized she was treading on very dangerous ground. For a moment she resented Dagon for putting her in this position, but then she shrugged it off. He was not responsible for her, she was. She looked the emperor in the eyes. "I am not a goddess, at least not by my measure of the word. I think if I were a goddess, I would be wiser, and would have less sorrow for what I have wrought while trying to do good."

She glanced at the prince, then away. His expression was not welcoming. "But my power is real. That I promise you."

She heard a scoff from the prince, but she did not look at him; she looked at the emperor, and he nodded. "Show me."

Karana turned away from him and walked to the edge of the pool. She closed her eyes and held up one hand, feeling the ordered layers of the sky above. She was loath to disrupt it, but she put her feelings aside and reached out to the sky. She heard muttering of the attendants, and a snide sound from the prince, and she closed her hand and twisted with her power, and thunder echoed across the heavens.

She heard the muttering cease, and a shocked silence descended onto the room. Karana was only barely aware of it, as she carefully altered and nurtured the disturbance she had made in the clouds above. She nudged and changed and drew, and then the sun above the pool darkened, going from pale to gray to a bluish-green. Wind stirred, and Karana extended her closed fist out over the pool, held it there, and then she smiled and opened her hand, and rain began to fall from above, wetting her palm.

When she opened her eyes there was no sound in the room save the patter of rain. She looked back at the emperor and his court, and she saw faces pale and afraid as well as looks of joy and adoration. Dagon looked on, approving, and the prince looked at her with an intensity she could not read.

The emperor stood, and while his slaves fluttered around him, none of them dared prevent him. He came to her slowly, his steps short and wavering. She put out her arm and he took it, leaning on her. He felt so light, as though he were made of paper. Slowly, he put out his hand, and felt the falling rain, and he clutched her shoulder and cried out softly. "It's true," he said. "It is real." He touched his face with his wet hand, and he closed his eyes and smiled at the taste of the rain.

Chapter Twenty-Seven

Ties of Blood

Still uneasy on horseback, Arthras rode with Nicaea and a small escort out of the city and toward the hills to the east. It was a glorious day, flowers blooming on the green hillsides in clusters of red and purple. Once they were well away from Orneas the destruction faded, and there were no more flattened cottages and uprooted trees. Even the road smoothed and showed no more fractures, gave them easy passage as they went to meet the general and his army.

He glanced at Nicaea as they rode, envious of her easy seat on her animal. She was well-dressed, with a silk shawl to protect her from the sun. She had exchanged messages with her brother and arranged this meeting, and though she was at ease, he was not. It seemed suspect to him for a general to bring an army and then not push for a battle, and he would hardly be glad his sister had been abducted into the bed of a barbarian invader. He expected trouble, even if she did not.

She saw his glance and urged her steed a little faster, rode knee to knee with him. "You are not sanguine about this meeting, are you?" She spoke low, so the guards would not hear.

"I am not," he said. "I do not know the general save by his reputation, and nothing I have heard says he will treat with a barbarian. General Emmeus is a scourge upon men like me, and has been for a decade. You say he will be fair-minded, but I do not trust that he will."

She laughed then, but not mockingly. "You trust me so little?"

"I trust you," he said, though he did not, really. "But you are accustomed to your brother's treatment of you, not others. It has long been his place to war upon barbarians."

"And you are no simple barbarian," she said. "That is why I want him to meet you, so he will see what kind of man you are, and understand what your power means for the future of the empire. My brother has long dreamed of a war to reunite the lost territories. He is a fighting man, and so the emperor put him on the frontier, where he would fight many battles and yet have no chance to exercise power in any real way. He worked to make his army the best it could be, and yet Sarda remains a backwater, far from the centers of power. My brother is a sword seeking a war."

She looked at him. "You wonder that he arrived so quickly? I do not doubt he was loading his ships at the first word of the invasion. This is the crisis he has longed for, though it has not come in the manner he expected."

"I slew your archpriest, and have likely killed your husband and taken you as my concubine. You think he will look kindly on that?" Arthras realized he was genuinely nervous and shook it off. This was just a man, like the rest of them.

Nicaea laughed again, a little louder. "You do not know my brother. His antagonism to the church is only matched by his personal dislike of Uliamus. He would have gladly killed the old man himself, if he'd been given the opportunity, Attis be damned. And he never liked Galbos in the slightest. I was arranged to marry him in part to dampen their rivalry." She sighed. "He will be pleased to hear he is dead."

"Not as pleased as I am," Arthras said.

"You never had to spread your legs for him," she said, and he could think of no response for that. She looked at him sidelong, and then laughed again, reached out and put her hand on his knee.

"It will go well, you will see." She spurred her horse and rode ahead a little way, and he watched her, wondering what was happening here that he did not understand. It might be a great benefit to ally with her brother, the famous general. But it might be a trap he could not yet see. He felt himself alone, surrounded by wolves.

☙

General Emmeus was camped at a villa on the hillside, surrounded by the tents of his army spread out in the vale below. Arthras was not practiced at counting armies, but he guessed there had to be almost twenty thousand men. The smoke from their cookfires made a haze in the late morning air, and the smell of it was familiar to him, like a quick stab of memory.

The path up to the villa was paved with white gravel, and lined by carefully-tended trees. He followed Nicaea while the dozen men of the escort fell behind him. He could tell they were nervous, and so was he. On any other day, this would be a trap, and he would be facing a bloody death. But it was not a day such as that. Arthras knew he could kill every man here and destroy the villa so utterly no one would ever believe it had been here, and that gave him some comfort.

Even on the journey south, Arthras had never seen a villa as fine as this one. The courtyard was wide and well-tended, fenced around with a polished wall lined with trees, and the house rose before him like a white mirage, clean and ornate and with the roof tiles a rich red in the sun. The front trellises were home to climbing grapevines and twined flowers that made a cascade of color down from the upper balcony. Before the door was a small, round plaza with a white fountain at the center, water chiming as it sprayed over a sculpture of green copper leaves.

When he saw places like this, he remembered the rude hut where his mother had died and anger churned his belly. Half of him wanted to overtake the empire and live in luxury and ease for the rest of his life, and the other half of him just wanted to destroy the whole of it, and leave the empire in ruins for the survivors to grub in like worms.

There were soldiers in the garden, though not so many as he would have expected, and he saw them all draw to attention as Nicaea entered. He followed behind her, glad for the extra moment to take in his surroundings. He heard barking dogs, and then a man came out of the villa and approached Nicaea with his arms open.

Emmeus was older than Arthras had thought he would be. He was a heavily built man of late middle age, with a seamed face and intelligent eyes. His smile was open and frank as he caught Nicaea up and embraced her. He was not wearing armor, nor a sword. Only the rick red of his cloak and the elaborate stitching marked him as a man of high birth.

Two dogs came running out and sniffed around his feet, jumped up for Nicaea to pet them, and then they turned and ran to Arthras and snuffled at him furiously, tails wagging. Unable to help smiling, Arthras bent down and petted them, snorted when they licked at his face and hands. When he stood up, Emmeus was coming to meet him, and he felt himself being measured with that cool glance.

"So you are the one my sister tells me about, the barbarian?" He looked Arthras over, tongue poking around inside his cheek. "She says you protected her from infamy at the hands of King Usiric."

He shrugged. "Perhaps. She did not need that much protecting." Arthras was not sure what he should say. Nicaea had written to her brother, and she had told him what she sent, but Arthras could not read it.

"She also says you executed that wretch Uliamus with your own hand." Emmeus watched his face closely.

"Your arch priest? Yes. I killed him myself." He wondered if now there would be anger, but instead the general's face split into a grin.

"I have wanted to do that to him since he was twelve, so well struck. Perhaps you and I can be allies after all." He stepped in and clapped Arthras on the shoulder. "Come, let us eat. We have a great deal to discuss."

ଔ

The feast was laid out in the imperial fashion, with couches for them, and slaves to carry trays of food and jugs of wine to refill their goblets. Arthras did not like lying down to eat, so he sat, and as soon as a slave came close with a plate of something he liked he took it and set it down beside him. The meat was lamb, he thought, wrapped in some salty bread and stuffed with honey and nuts. He liberated a jug of wine and drank directly from it, refusing to recline and be fed as Nicaea and her brother did. Emmeus seemed amused by this, and did not comment on it, and Nicaea pretended not to notice.

"When I heard that Ilion had fallen, I came as soon as I could," Emmeus said. "I was worried about you." He spoke to Nicaea, but for Arthras' benefit. "I would have thought for certain Galbos would take you away if the city were in danger."

Nicaea snorted. "I think perhaps he planned to gather reinforcements in Orneas, but we both know how unlikely that was, with the archpriest in opposition." She sipped her wine. "The city fell with... unexpected speed."

"Indeed," Emmeus said, looking at Arthras. "I have your assurances, and yet I find it hard to credit."

"You would believe all of it, if you saw what is left of the walls of Ilion, or the devastation wrought on Orneas," she said. "Or if you could have seen Galbos and Uliamus broken and dead."

"Would that I had," Emmeus said, laughing into his wine.

Arthras was annoyed that they were speaking as if he were not there. He swallowed his wine, then held his cup out to be refilled. Emmeus nodded to the slave, and then a hard blow fell on Arthras' neck, perfectly placed to pierce his veins and down into his chest. He saw the knife glimmer in the lamplight, and then there was a small sound and the tip snapped off the blade. It spun through the air before his face like a tossed coin, and then it landed in his winecup among the dregs with a tiny, brittle sound.

Arthras flung the cup away and rose furiously. The brawny slave was there, staring at him in shock and terror, and he seized the hand that gripped the broken dagger and crushed down, feeling fingerbones snap. The man screamed and went to his knees, his face turning white.

A tremor passed through the room, shivering under the floor, making the lamps sway on their hooks and the platters rattle where they lay. The dogs were up and whining, fur standing up on their backs like the ridges on wild pigs. They slunk low to the floor, mouths open as they shook. A crack snapped across the perfect alabaster floor, appearing between one eyeblink and the next.

Emmeus was on his feet, and Arthras rounded on him, letting the would-be assassin slump to the floor. He snarled but the general held up his hands placatingly. "Forgive me. Forgive me. It was a test, only. I beg you do not kill the man." There was the slightest smile on his face, and Arthras decided he had his fill of not being taken seriously.

"A test? A *test?*" He sent another shudder coursing through the floor and Emmeues stumbled, off-balance. He heard screams from the servants in the house, and the crash of things falling and breaking, the crack of pottery and the chime of glass. The dogs howled, and outside he heard horses wailing.

The heat rose in him, and he fought to control it. His clothes smoldered, and he knew Emmeus felt it, because his eyes widened, and his face turned pale as he fell back, knocked off his feet by the shaking in the ground. Arthras hooked his hand under the edge of the couch and flung it away. It flipped over twice and hit the wall like a missile from a siege weapon, smashing the plaster as it broke into pieces.

"A test? I think you misunderstand who you are dealing with!" He advanced on Emmeus as the ground shuddered, and the general stumbled back, took slight shelter behind a slim pillar. Arthras slapped the delicate column and broke it in half, shrugged off the top half as it fell on him and broke across his back. He trod shards of marble under his feet.

He caught sight of Nicaea, her legs draw up, her face carefully impassive, and he knew she had not known about this. Yet she reminded him that he needed this general, and that he must be controlled, not simply humiliated. Arthras fought down the heat and took a long breath. He must be like a king, not a brute.

Emmeus got to his feet, and Arthras let him, then he caught him by the tunic and lifted him off his feet and dropped him carefully back onto his couch. The dogs cringed away from him, and that seemed to frighten the general more than anything else.

Arthras took another breath and fought to calm himself. He could wipe this place off the face of the world, but he must not. The fate of Orneas had taught him that he must temper his power, must not let it rule him. "It would be a mistake, General, to think of me as simply a barbarian warlord. A very grave mistake."

Emmeus held up his hands, regaining a little of his composure as the earth ceased to shake. "Forgive me for that. I promise my sister knew nothing of it. But I had to know the truth. If you were truly what the stories said, then you would not be harmed. If you were not, then you would be dead, and my position much clearer." He shrugged, refusing to give way. "I had to know."

"Do you?" Arthras said, staring him down.

"I know enough," he said. "Now I know how the gates of Ilion fell, and how Orneas was destroyed. I know why you are king of the Almanni when you are still so young." He held up his hands again. "I felt I needed to know the truth before I decide what my position is."

"That was a very foolish thing to do," Nicaea said, her voice low. "Did you not believe my words? Did you think I was addled that I would tell lies?"

Emmeus held up a hand to her. "Enough. It was an error, I will not compound it." He looked up at Arthras. "Let us not be enemies. I do not believe either of us wants that."

"No," Arthras said. He looked at the damage done to the room and felt a little embarrassed, though he did not show it. The blade had not even scratched his skin; he had been in no danger at all. Yet his heart still beat quick from the shock of it. His mind was not accustomed to what his body was capable of. "You spoke of your position?"

Emmeus sighed. "Yes. I am, after all, a general appointed by the empire. I am in service to it, and have lived my life as such. Despite personal ambitions, I do not lightly contemplate its overthrow. Given opportunity, I might have sought to raise the standard of revolt and attempt to place myself on the throne. This is not the same thing." He folded his hands together. "Yet the time is ripe for it."

"Tell me," Arthras said.

Emmeus glanced at his sister, who still looked displeased. "Emperor Niceros is not old, but his health is poor. He is failing, and already the factions around the throne are sharpening their knives preparing for the rise of his remaining son, Zeneos. When the emperor dies, there will be disorder, and that is always a good time for a revolt." He laughed a little. "And I am not getting any younger. There will never be a better time than this to move. Otherwise I will spend my life in Sarda, if I am lucky."

"What kind of man is the emperor?" Arthras said. He had asked Nicaea, but she had never met him in person, and had not been able to answer.

"Able enough, or he was," Emmeus said. "Since he became ill his mind has been given to religious irrelevancies. It has sapped the vigor of the empire, as it always does when an emperor begins to fail. The heir is. . . well, I have not seen him since he was a boy, but I didn't like him then either. He liked to pull the legs off insects for amusement. I hear he has grown to be vain and arrogant. Too many princes are like that." He laughed a little. "I don't like the thought of him in command of the empire."

Arthras shrugged. "I want to restore the empire. Not just seize the imperial city for my own glory. I intend to sweep through the lost territories and retake them all. I will conquer Vatharia, Sydon, Atagia, Lyria." The names were mostly legend to him, simply words he had heard, places out of legend where once the imperial standard had flown. He held up his hands. "What city can stand against me? What fortress can resist me? And once they know it is useless, they will not even fight. There will be no sieges, no long wars of attrition. It will be done."

He pointed at Emmeus. "I need supplies for my people, and ships to transport them and your army across to Calliste. We will have to be quick, and careful. If we are seen, the girl Karana can summon a storm while we are at sea, and that would be disaster."

Emmeus stroked his chin. "How many do you have?"

"Twelve thousand warriors, perhaps twice as many women and children," Arthras said.

The general winced. "That is going to take a great many ships, more than I have at my disposal. We would have to ferry them across on more than one trip. It sounds like that would be dangerous."

Arthras thought, then shook his head. "No. Once I am ashore, she will not risk it. She would not sink ships full of people unless she knew she could sink me as well."

"You seem certain," Emmeus said.

"I am. She fought nearly to the death to protect the refugees in the city. She will not kill if she does not have to." Arthras nodded. "A strong landing, with enough troops to take the imperial city, and I will announce my presence. Then she will not risk open battle." He nodded. "She will negotiate. She will not risk another Orneas."

"We can circle to the west side of the island, land there unopposed," Emmeus said. "Once ashore, we will be under constraints, for our supply will be limited. And we will need money for more ships before we can even attempt it."

Arthras smiled. "I have looted the vault of the arch priest," he said. "You will have all the gold you need."

A slow smile spread over the general's face. "Well, I wondered about that."

"I will be emperor, and your sister my empress. No man but me shall stand higher than you, and you will lead the armies that will reunite the empire of old." Arthras held out his hand. "My bargain."

Emmeus took a slow, deep breath, and then he stood up and clasped Arthras hand in his own. "Let it be done."

ഗ

After, when the fires were faded, Nicaea found her brother on the terrace, looking out over the dark lands. He heard her and turned and smiled, beckoned her close and put an arm around her. The summer night was cool, the breezes light up here in the hills.

"I am glad to find you here, so well cared-for," he said. "This is a dangerous path you tread now."

She laughed. He was much older than her, the son of their father's first wife. But he looked much older than he had last time she saw him, it bothered her more than she wished it did. "I have been walking dangerous paths since I had feet."

"This is different," he said, glancing back at the villa. "This man is not like any other."

"No, why else would I bother with him?" she said. "He is a barbarian. Rude, illiterate, and backward. Yet he has cunning, and a greater intelligence than he has been given cause to use. If he was an utter brute he would be uncontrollable. But he wants to be a man, and that makes him malleable."

"If we put him on the throne, you had best not lose your grip," he said.

She disengaged from him and went to the balustrade, looked down over the fields below in the moonlight. "He is on his way, and neither you nor I can stop him." She looked at Emmeus. "We can either stand in his way, or march beside him. I have chosen my place."

"As have I, apparently." Emmeus sounded tired. "I might have thrown in with him even without you here. Fool that I am."

"You were never a fool," she said. "You are ambitious. A man with ability and ambition is difficult to stop, save with a dagger." She gestured to the house. "Arthras is a man who cannot be stopped even by that. Imagine an emperor who cannot be slain."

"He cannot be, but we can. If we are close to him we will make ourselves targets," he said.

"We have both been targets since we were seven years old," she scoffed. "This will be no different. If I am to play this game, it will be from a empress' throne. That suits me well."

"It does," he said. "And now Galbos is dead, there is nothing in your way." He sighed. "You should marry this barbarian as soon as the throne is his."

"He will have me, no fear of that," she said.

"You like him," her brother said.

She snorted, turned her face slightly away so he would not see her expression. "Perhaps I should not, but I do. His arrogance reminds me of someone else I once knew." She turned back to Emmeus and he scoffed at her.

"All this time, and now I raise my revolt and I cannot quite believe I am doing it," he said. "I am a little too old for this."

"You'd best not be," she said. "My hour has come round, and I won't have you spoiling it." She looked up at the bright moon. "I will walk to the highest throne in the footsteps of a titan, and may Attis have mercy on any who try to stand in my way."

Chapter Twenty-Eight

Myths and Legends

Karana wandered the palace, alone. The emperor had insisted they stay and dine with him, but that would not be until sunset, and she found herself at loose ends. She was not comfortable in a palace, and in fact she was quickly lost as she meandered through courtyards and enclosed gardens, pausing to look at the ancient statuary and bending down to scrape dirt and vines from faded inscriptions. She did not mind being lost; it meant that no one else knew where she was either.

She had half-expected Dagon to come and find her, but when she encountered a familiar face it was not he, but rather the blonde, beautiful prince she found herself facing. She was walking down a long colonnade between two halves of a wide garden, and she was marveling at the variety of flowers. Calliste was a volcanic island, and the soil was almost supernaturally rich. She saw flowers and plants she had never seen before, and as she was not a student of flora she could not begin to identify them. She paused to drink from a small fountain and when she looked up she was facing Zeneos and his small cluster of guards and attendants.

He looked at her dispassionately, and she saw his eyes were red, as if from weeping, which did not seem to fit with what she could judge of his character. He was handsome but short, with a well-fed look to him and a face that showed little emotion. His chin was carefully shaven and his blonde hair meticulously styled. He wore a white cape over his purple tunic and a heavy golden belt. He wore a sword this time, and she wondered at that – if he was not permitted to be armed in his father's presence.

She dried her hand on her shawl and bowed carefully. "Forgive me, your highness. I did not see you there."

"Oh, you are so cautious, aren't you?" he said affably. "I might almost mistake you for a real person. But I think I know better."

"I am sorry, my lord," she said. "I am not sure I understand what you mean." She felt a prickling hostility from this boy, and she did not know why and was not sure what to do about it.

"My father may believe you to be a god, but I can see the truth," he said, smiling. "A curse is on you, and all who stand near you. You are a plague upon mankind."

Karana felt her stomach tighten. "Perhaps I have been. I do not make excuses for that."

"Oh, yes," he said, his eyes bright. "Yes, so humble. I cannot forget that, nor can anyone." His face almost shone with a kind of benevolent cruelty. "Must be humble, so you are not blamed, so no one suspects you have come to destroy. Just a girl, only doing her best." He tittered, and she saw a slight flinch in his face, a twitch of his cheek as though he had a tic. His eyes lost focus for a moment, and she noted the way his entourage kept their distance.

"Highness," she said carefully. "If I have given you offense, I humbly apologize for it. What happened at

Orneas haunts me, and will for the rest of my life. It was not completely under my control -"

"Always an excuse, always a good reason," Zeneos said, coming closer to her. She noticed his left hand twitch slightly, and he blinked rapidly. She began to think something was wrong with him. He reached out as though to touch her face, and she moved back without thinking about it, not wishing to be so close to him. His expression became hard, his smiled slithering away. "You dare?"

"I am sorry, Highness. You do not seem well. Perhaps you should take your ease." She fought to keep her voice even. She very badly wanted to get away from him. Up close she saw how sweaty he was, and he had a peculiar smell that she could not place, just under the scents of sweet oils and the blooming flowers all around them.

"I am certain you would like that very much, creature," he said, his voice shaking. "But you should know I do not intend to relax my vigilance. I know what you are, and you will be dealt with. I will not allow the same fate to befall this city that befell Orneas, or the other ruins in your wake. Go and climb the mountain, to the place where Attis lies buried. Look on that and see the fate that waits for you. Gods may do many things, but they must not speak, and they should not live." His eyes were bloodshot, and she saw how they flicked around.

She began to wonder if he were mad, and her heart sank as she realized what she had hoped would be a bastion against Arthras was instead on shaky ground. The emperor was sick, and his son and heir seemed to dislike her intensely, and might be losing his mind.

He seemed to get control of himself, and she saw his eyes open and he looked around as if wondering where he was. He blinked and drew out a cloth and mopped at his face. In a moment he seemed more like the man she had seen before.

"Are you well, Highness?" she ventured, not sure if she should speak.

"Well enough," he said, he seemed confused. He looked at her. "How good to see you again. My father thinks highly of you, do not presume too much upon that."

"I will not," she said. "That is not in my nature."

"You may have power beyond that of mortal men, but you are still subject to the will of the empire, and shall be obedient to its laws." He nodded. "All will be, as it should be. That much is certain."

"Of course, my lord," she said, not sure what else she could say. It was as though he no longer remembered what else he had said. The mad intensity was gone from him, and there was no longer the unnatural light in his eyes, as if someone else looked out through them.

He inclined his head, and she bowed, and he went on, his coterie following behind him, not one of them looking at her as they passed. Karana watched them go, and fallen flower petals swirled across the floor in a gentle breeze.

03

Servants came and found her, in her wanderings, and brought her to the emperor. She tried to keep track of the path through all the halls and stairways and mezzanines, but the palace remained a maze she could not solve, and if she ever had to escape it on her own, she would have to take to the sky.

She expected to be led to a dining hall, but instead she was taken to large, airy rooms with billowing blue silk curtains and a terrace that looked out over the city. It was a view that stunned her. On the left was the massive shadow of the mountain, and she could look down over layer upon layer of the city, the villas and mansions cut into the sides of the slope, gardens like jeweled miniatures. Beyond that the haze of distance and smoke made the lower parts of the city look dreamlike as they flowed down to the blue waters of the harbor, and beyond that, the sea. If she looked northward, she almost thought she could see the southern tip of Othria as a shadow on the horizon.

"Almost the whole of my empire, in a single view," the emperor said, emerging from the shadows. Here, in private, he had only a few servants who stayed behind him, and he leaned on a cane as he walked. He approached her, then leaned on the stone parapet and looked out over the vista that shimmered in the evening light. "I like to look at it all, like this. Especially at dawn and sunset, when it is most beautiful."

He smiled at her, sidelong. "Once the empire would have stretched so much farther than the eye could see, but that was gone long before I was born. When I was crowned, the empire consisted of this island, then Othria and Sarda. I have fought all my life to keep them, and I succeeded until now. Now Othria seems lost, and I have little doubt Sarda will go with it."

"Why?" she said. She knew little of the politics of the border regions beyond Ilion. Now she wished she had read about current political events and not just ones from hundreds of years ago.

"The man who administers Sarda is a general named Emmeus. He is my age, yet a vigorous man. I have long suspected he would like to overthrow my house and rule. He is probably the best war commander in the empire, and he dreams of old glories restored. He is close to Othria, and so he must deal with the realities there. If he allies with this Arthras, then I do not doubt he will come for the throne. He has no loyalty to me or mine." He beckoned her, and she followed him away from the window, and he led her to a corner where there were chairs and a couch, seated himself with a grimace.

"Is there pain, Majesty?" she said.

He smiled. "There is always pain, it is not unendurable." He motioned for her to sit, and so she did. The servants were far back, out of earshot, and she realized how unusual it was for her to be effectively alone with the emperor himself.

He held his hands out, and she tentatively reached out and took them. His trembled, but were still strong. "The power of Attis himself," he said. "Yet your hands are so soft."

"I said that I am not a goddess, and I hold to that. I am just a girl of unremarkable origins and life who has been given a power I do not always understand. I certainly have done nothing to deserve it, whether you consider it a blessing or a burden." She closed her mouth, afraid she spoke too freely.

"Attis was born of woman," he said. "His mother was a shepherd, on the slopes of Mount Ara. They say he was fathered by a thunderbolt, but I think it likely that once he was like you, and then something changed."

She looked at him, not sure how she should respond. "I am not a woman of great faith," she said. "I mutter oaths to the gods of my ancestors, but I have never been to a shrine nor lit a candle to ask their favor. I have not given the offerings to Vasa, or to Sesostris. I have never been a believer in Attis, nor paid much attention to his holidays or his mysteries."

"What do you believe then?" he said. "Everyone has a belief, inside them."

She looked away, then turned back to meet his gaze. "I try to believe in humanity. I have been given this power, and so I have tried to use it to help people, to give protection to those who cannot protect themselves. Because I cannot do otherwise and face my own conscience." She shrugged. "I do not believe I am a goddess, because to me that is a thing that means more than power. Power does not move hearts or undo evils. If I were a goddess, I would know what it right, and I find that I often do not. All I can do is try my utmost to choose wisely. If I fail, does that not mean that I am fallible? And a fallible being such as myself cannot be divine."

The emperor smiled as well. "I wonder if Attis said things very like that, in his life. He was a man, and he became a god. Perhaps he did not wish it either."

"Why do you want me to be a goddess?" she said softly. "Do you wish something from me?"

He sighed heavily. "I want to know. Once, when I was young, I thought the gods spoke to me. I imagined that Attis himself had chosen me to be emperor. I dreamed of taking back all the lost territories, driving back the barbarians, rebuilding what once was." He shook his head. "You can only dream of such things when you are young. Now I see that the empire had its time, and that despite the mists of legend, the forging of it was an act of monstrous violence. We read of battles fought and won, we do not dwell on the blood spilled nor the lives trod underfoot. To remake the empire now would mean war on a scale no living man has seen. A war that would last twenty years or more. And a war for what?" He shook his head.

"Do you think I could reforge the empire myself?" she said. "That my power would allow me to overcome armies and kingdoms?"

"Perhaps you could," he said. "But no. I do not desire that. That would make you less a goddess than a scourge."

Karana remembered the words of the prince and almost spoke, but she did not. It seemed unwise to try and sow discord there, if it did not already exist. If it did, she would be wise to keep out of it as much as she could. "What do you desire?" she said.

He clutched her hands tightly. "That you might rebuild the empire in another way. Not with blood and steel, but by giving the people something to believe in. By bringing together so many different people under the blessing and protection of a goddess they can see and hear, who can work miracles and not simply pretend to work them. You could save the empire by giving it a heart again. Without Attis it was a kingdom without a king, and we have tried to stand in his place, but we are all lesser men, only human, only mortal."

He leaned close to her. "Whether you claim to be a goddess or no, what matters is whether the people *believe* that you are."

"I do nothing to encourage that," she said. "It is too dangerous. I have read my histories. It is far too dangerous."

"I am dying," the emperor said. "You feel the tremors in my hands. They began years ago, and now it is worse. I walk like an invalid, and I forget so many things. It is very hard to keep my mind clear. I am only fifty-three, but I will not live much longer, or else I will lose my mind and the effect will be the same, if less dignified. My son will take the throne, and he is not the best choice, but he would do in other times. But now an enemy comes he cannot stop. My last son will perhaps be crowned, but he will not long remain emperor. The days of my house are ending, I can feel it."

"Majest -" she started, but he cut her off.

"You ask what I want from you. What I want is grace, and you may say you cannot grant me that, but listen, listen to me. If you promise me you will protect my realm from the danger that now threatens it, and promise that you will be a light that draws all men to you, here at the center of all things, then that, for me, is grace. You can make a new empire, built not by war but by belief in a better world, which you will embody, and make real. Do that for me. I have been your emperor, and now I ask you this. The only thing I will ever ask you."

"I. . ." Karana had never expected anything like this in her life. She did not have the slightest idea how to reply, but she could not possibly refuse. She had never given the emperor much thought before in her life – he had merely been a distant presence – but the gray-haired man before her had such desperation in his eyes. And in a way he was right. With Arthras on his way, the empire could not stand unless she made it so. "I will do all that I can. I can promise you only that."

He smiled. "Thank you. Thank you so much. I hoped you would not refuse me. And you are one of the very few people who could." He stood up shakily, leaning on her. "Come, I have something to show you."

○3

He took her down the hall and to a smaller room. He leaned on his cane, and his servants hovered close by, but he moved easier, as though a weight had been lifted from him.

He opened a heavy wooden door with a key he carried, and then let her into a high-ceilinged room with elaborate stonework. It had one high, narrow window set with colored glass forming the lightning bolt of Attis, and it cast the shape as a shadow on the floor.

"This was the private chapel of my father, where he took instruction in the faith from the Mysteriarch." He pointed to a lectern with several books upon it. "There is a box under there, bring it to me."

He sat down heavily while she went to the lectern and pulled aside the velvet that covered the space beneath it. There were more books piled there, but only one small box tucked away on the very bottom shelf. It was heavy, the outside festooned with what she realized were uncut gems. It was old, and she knew it was plated in gold because it didn't make her fingers smell when she touched it.

She brought it to Niceros, and he took it from her hands, his own trembling visibly. There was another chair, but rather than move it she sat down on the rug and watched as he opened the tiny latch. "Here," he said. "Here is a thing you will not see anywhere else."

The box opened, and he turned it to show her a lump of silver. It was in a strange shape, as if it had melted and then been cooled suddenly, freezing in place. "What is it?" she said.

He was quiet for a long moment. "Attis died in battle upon the slopes of the mountain. The thing he battled was a creature of fire, and even the oldest texts do not say what it was. I think – I have always thought – that it is so because the battle was distant, surrounded by smoke and flame. No one saw what it was, not really. A name is given it in the secret writings of the ancients. They called it Nergal."

"Nergal?" she said. "That is from an Ahazunai legend – from the people my race descends from. Nergal was a god of death, a demon of the old world who breathed fire and -"

"And shed silver blood," the emperor said. "This was found after the fall of Attis. It looks like silver, but no fire will melt it, and no hammer or chisel can mark it. And men who have touched it, die from it." He closed the lid again. "The church says Attis died that we might live, and I believe that is true. But how much better if he had lived. How much more could he have accomplished?" He smiled. "You must live, and do what he could not. He was your brother, lost long ago. Now he needs you to carry on where he failed."

Karana took a deep breath, her head spinning. "I do not know what my legacy is. I do not believe in fate, or in destiny of any kind." She put a hand on his arm. "I will do all that I can."

"Thank you," he said, and she saw tears glitter in his eyes and she took the box from his shaking hands and put it down, then grasped his fingers and held them close. He bent his head, and his tears fell on her hands, and she felt a purpose in her, growing resolute. This far, and no further. She had been driven back, but she would not draw back another step. Not one.

Chapter Twenty-Nine

Seas of Darkness

Arthras walked on sand, so fine it felt like powder under his bare feet, and made no sound. It was a misty morning, and the farther he tried to look, the less he saw. All around him lay a haze that hid the world from his sight, above him the sun was only a dim glow through layers of fog, and he could not say which way it was, or which way he walked.

He heard a sound, and that was his guide. It was a low, slow rushing, and he thought at first that it sounded like many voices – a great multitude – all of them speaking at once, the rush of sound as when an army cried out in a moment of exultation. He followed it, leaving tracks behind him. There was a scent all around him, something heavy and metallic, and he wondered what it was. He felt no fear, no apprehension. He walked as assured as a god born upon the earth.

The rushing rose, and he decided it was the sound of the sea. He was on a long strand beside the water, and the smell must be the smell of the sea. It bothered him that he could not remember the smell, to be certain of himself. He had lived all his life in the hills and mountains and meadows, far away and in the north. The sea was new to him, and he was not familiar with all the smells and sounds it made. The mist lay heavy before him, and he walked into it, following the sound.

He began to see shapes in the sand, as if something were buried. Then he saw part of a wall, and a statue broken away save for a noble face carved in stone. There was a city beneath him – he knew that – buried in the sand. He could see it in his mind, could picture all the buildings and winding streets. It was under the sand, perhaps buried by a great wave. Was it a city he knew? Had he done this? Now he could not remember. It began to bother him that he could not remember how he came here, or why.

Arthras hesitated, turned to look behind him, but just then the sound swelled up, and he turned back, looked out toward the imagined sea, and there was a small rise, and he knew that on the other side he would see the waters. He strode up the slope, feet digging into the sand, the black sand. He climbed to the top and stood looking out over the panorama thus revealed to him, and the mist rose and burned away, revealing.

He saw an endless expanse, and he thought it was the sea. But then he saw the waves did not move, and the surface did not ripple, and the sound of it came instead from great rushes of smoke that boiled up from under the surface. He saw the waves jagged and motionless, and where the shell was cracked he saw the red glow, and he knew he looked on a great lake of molten rock, the surface hard and cold, while beneath it seethed with heat.

The sand shifted under his feet, and he looked down and saw it was not sand, but was ash instead, black and powdery. The ashes of a city lay buried under him, where some great eruption of the earth had inundated and entombed it, and now he knew that multitudes lay dead and screaming under his feet, choked and burned into statues like fired clay.

Now Arthras was afraid, and he did not know why. He looked out over the sea of lava, and knew it was a sea of death, and then it began to move. The black surface began to heave slowly, up and down, roiling and cracking the hard exterior so the glowing heat within showed through like spreading veins. The smell grew stronger, like the acrid stink of burning stone and metal when he wore it as armor. He tried to back away, but he could not move; his feet seemed to make only small steps that did nothing.

The sea of fire erupted from beneath, and it rose up in a great mountain of black and red, breaking apart, spraying upward in gouts of lava like blood. In the heart of the glowing liquid fire something moved, something huge and dark and alive, and Arthras saw jaws wide as a tower gate, heavy with long teeth. A black shape heaved in the molten sea, and he saw a vast silver eye. He fought to get free of his paralysis, pushing hard against something unseen.

He woke, pulling himself out of his dream and once more to his bed. He gasped and sat up, alone in his room. Nicaea did not often stay the night, and he was usually alone. There was one lamp burning, and he saw the same room, the same hangings and furnishings. The window was covered by a thin silk curtain, and it glowed with silver moonlight.

He stood up from the bed, as if to reassure himself that he could move if he wanted to. He crossed to the window and pulled the curtain back, looked out over Orneas below him, the many fires of his people camped wherever they could find room. He smelled wood smoke and cooked meat and the tang of the sea. The rush of waves was faint so high, but it was clear in the night stillness.

As dreams do, it seemed to hold onto him, pulling him back to the moment when it revealed itself, but he shook it off. It was not the first strange dream he had endured. Since the battle he had often dreamed of fire and violence, sometimes jerking awake with the memory of lightning shaking in his bones. He wondered if all men of war dreamed of violence after it was done. He supposed that they must. It would take more than dreams to turn him aside from his path.

ଔ

Emmeus marched his soldiers into the city at noon, and Arthras watched from the highest point still remaining in the Citadel. On a hill, as it was, the vantage was still quite good. He had to suppress a certain unease as he saw the serried ranks come down the long boulevard from the ruins of the north gate. Horsemen first, pennons snapping in the wind as they rode, behind them the foot soldiers a dark shadow on the road as they came onward.

Arthras had ordered the Almanni to draw back into the vicinity of the Citadel, and now they were encamped in tight quarters with guards at the perimeter and all men standing to arms with swords and shields and spears at the ready. He did not expect treachery from Emmeus, but he was not a fool. These men had been the enemies of his people for generations, and the Sardan troops were more feared than most. He would not trust the individual commanders, and he would not have them see his people unarmed and squatting in a bedraggled city.

His own men were not pleased by the alliance, and he did not trust them either. So he had them gather in their ranks to remind them they were under his command, and he walked among them in the morning to make sure they did not forget. He would shake the Citadel apart to break up a battle, but he did not want to have to.

"My brother has kept his word," Nicaea said, coming into the room behind him. "Now you see my worth to you."

"You have already proved that," he said. "I do not doubt you." He did not trust her either, but he knew so long as her aims were in accord with his own, she was reliable.

"Will you make me your empress?" she said. "Once you have won your war?"

He turned and looked at her, wondering if this were another ploy. It might be, but she would doubt that he would keep her close after the throne was his. He might not need her then. She wore her beauty like armor, never showing what was beneath it. There was the smallest uncertainty in her eyes, and he wondered if any of it were genuine.

Arthras turned back and looked out the window again, watching the army march in, rank upon rank. "Do you know why I chose you, back in the hall in Ilion? It was not because you were pretty. You are, but there were enough pretty girls. I could have any one of them. Anyone I wanted, and no one would dare question it." He glanced back at her. "I chose you because you faced Usiric, naked, and showed no fear. I saw that. I saw how you held your head up and wore your pride, and that was what I wanted. I knew he would humiliate you, because of who your husband was, and I did not want him to. I did not want your courage debased."

"Noble thoughts for a barbarian fresh from battle," she said.

He snorted. "You do not know anything. I know you think you understand me, but you do not. I have seen so much courage and nobility wasted and cast aside. I have seen men throw their lives away in duels they could not win, so the blood price paid would care for their families. I have seen mothers give their children the last of their food and then die in the night. I have seen warriors stand brave in battle, only to be cut down and have their deeds claimed by another who never shed blood."

He turned to match her with a glare. "I came from nothing. My father dead when I was young, my family poor and hungry. I served under men who were lords by the weight of their birth, not because they were worthy men. I saw them abuse and punish men who were better than they, and have the lords and the laws call it just. Justice is a fable, and right is something only claimed by the strong. You were born at a height I would never have reached, had I not been chosen, and you would have looked on me and called me worthless."

She shifted back from his glance, uncomfortable. "And yet you wish to be emperor," she said. "To be the highest of all. Are you certain you don't simply wish to tear it all down?"

"I have already done that," Arthras said. "I have sacked Ilion and Orneas, and now I have allied myself with the most powerful remaining general of the empire. Othria is mine, and I could keep it and call myself done. This would be a home for my people, and I could say it is enough." He leaned back against the stone parapet, feeling the alabaster under his hands. He knew he could crush it if he wanted to.

"Would that be enough for you?" she said.

He snorted. "Do you think I was given this power to conquer one province of the old empire and call that sufficient? That I should take this gift I have been given and use it to become another petty barbarian king while that old man warms the throne of empire with his backside? No, I am not content with that. Not at all. I have been given a grand power, and it must have a grand purpose. What greater purpose than re-forging the empire that once ruled all the world we know? As I told your brother – no wall can stop me, no army stand against me. The bloody stalemates and long wars that have broken the empire apart for centuries are no more. I will unmake all of it, and create a new world. A better world."

"How will it be better?" she said. "It will just be the old world again."

"Oh no, it will not," he said. "I will unmake the old order. I will tear down the ruling castes and aristocracies that have divided the world into smaller and smaller pieces so they can each have their own part. The problem is not that we have an emperor, the problem is now we have multitudes of them, and each of them is determined to rule their own lands, no matter how hard they have to fight for them, or how small their realms may be. The death of the empire was because of too many men like your husband. Men who would sell the future of all for another scrap of power they could call their own."

Arthras smiled, thinking of it. "My conquest will not be a destruction of common soldiers and farmers while their overlords sit back and pay ransoms to have their rights respected. No. I will drag kings and princes and warlords from their palaces and break them with my bare hands. I will carry the skulls of dead sovereigns wherever I go, and those who oppose me will know that if they only fall upon their masters, they will have freedom, and protection. My empire will be different, because there will be no power but me. None. I cannot be assassinated, I cannot be defeated in war, I cannot be threatened or forced back. I have been made inevitable by fate, and I will not stop."

He walked to her, caught her wrist, and pulled her close to him. "I won't stop, until all is united under my hand." He smiled. "And you will be my queen, my empress. Because I will need you. Battle I know, conquest I can accomplish. But you know how to rule, and I do not, and that is what I will need. While I am traveling, going from city to city, breaking walls and taking lands, you will sit on the throne and rule."

He wanted her, suddenly and fiercely, and he caught her up and kissed her, then kissed her again. She was panting, pulling at his clothes, and he dragged her to the side, flung her own on the couch and went down with her, pulling her dress from her body, feeling the heat rising in him, like a sea of fire beneath his surface.

03

The ships rounded the headland in the early morning, and Arthras came when a slave told him they had been sighted. He climbed the steps and found a good vantage to look down at the harbor, which was on the west side of the Citadel, still in shadow as the sun just began to creep up over the eastern hills. It made the sea seem dark, like ink, and he shook off the thread of a half-remembered dream and looked for the white sails.

There was a cold wind coming off the sea, and he watched the sails of the ships bell outward as they rode it into the harbor. There were so many of them, and more as he watched. He had never seen so many ships in one place. They looked like toys from here, sliding into the harbor, moving aside for more as they dropped anchor. He knew there would be too many to all fit within the arms. Emmeus had told him so.

The general had sent back to his homeland, calling for more ships, willing to lay down gold from the Archpriest's treasure to buy almost anything that would float. Even the largest ships could not carry more than three hundred men at the most. To transport their entire army and supply would take more than two hundred ships. It was not a long voyage, but it had to be undertaken swiftly, and in secret. If Karana caught them at sea there would be a massacre.

He watched for a little longer, then he went down from the Citadel to find Emmeus. He was leaving nothing behind. Not the women or children of his people, not treasure, not Nicaea. Everyone was coming with him, and he did not intend to return.

The general was on the lower level, in the room he had taken as his headquarters, and this morning he was surrounded by his officers and messengers, handling the many, many details needed to prepare for a voyage this size. It all had to be done quickly, because with merchants still plying the sea-lanes, it would not take long for word of the armada to reach Archelion. They had to be underway by the time that happened. Arthras knew that once he was ashore, it would be over. Karana might negotiate and try to control him, but if she fought, there would be another cataclysm. He counted on her refusing that, if it came to a choice.

Emmeus smiled when he saw him. "One hundred and sixteen ships. That is enough to send your entire force across, along with the supply. More will be coming in a few more days."

"I will take half my men, half yours, and enough of my camp followers to provide support in the field," Arthras said. He was not fool enough to sail all his warriors away on borrowed ships and leave his women and children behind. "And you will come as well."

"Oh, I would not think to stay behind," Emmeus said. "If we land with fifteen thousand troops, then we will command a force larger than anything on the island. Once Calliste was guarded by a navy, but it has been so long since she was threatened that defense has fallen by the wayside. We will find no opposition to us once we arrive." He looked at Arthras. "None save your storm queen and her brethren."

"I can deal with her. She will not want a fight, not after what happened to this city. She will know if there is a fight, then the city will be destroyed, and in the shadow of Mount Ara, it could be far worse than here. If we promise a peaceful transition, and safety for her precious refugees, then there will be no fight." Arthras remembered the lightning and had to stop himself from flinching. He remembered her fury all too well. The last battle could have been avoided, but she had let Galbos engineer another betrayal. That would not happen this time.

"One quick voyage, and then we negotiate you onto the throne," Emmeus said. "It sounds too easy."

"It will be easy," Arthras said. "Nothing will stop me this time. Nothing."

Chapter Thirty

CITY OF DREAMS

Karana walked on the sea, and it did not seem strange to her. The waves were stilled, as if fixed in a single moment, gleaming and smooth. She could see each curl and spray of foam frozen and motionless, see the colors play through the water as the sun set behind her. She did not see land anywhere, heard no sound but the low moan of winds, and she knew this was a dream.

Barefoot, she walked over gentle swells, the water smooth and cold as glass. There was a mist all around her, and she smelled the salt of the waters. The wind sounded like waves, only far away, like the voices of many people in the distance.

There was a high swell, greater than the others, and yet not so steep she could not climb it. She went careful up the slope, leaning into it, wondering in that moment how thick the surface was. In her mind she saw a thin layer of motionless water over the top of a limitless black sea. The thought disturbed her, and it was as if that disquiet sent a ripple through the world around her, made her wobble on her feet for a moment.

She reached the top, where the high vantage allowed her to see farther than she had before. Ahead of her, the sea dropped away, and then extended out into the distance flat and featureless. The sky was darker, drawing low with clouds, and as she walked down into the plain she felt the wind stir. She knew she should feel her power, should sense the shapes and motion of the air, but she did not, and that reminded her this was a dream, and yet it was unnerving. Already her power had become so much a part of her, of her awareness of the shape of the world.

Karana walked slow over the empty flatland, and slowly the character of the still water changed, so it was less water, and more like glass. Here and there the surface was scored by cracks, and smoke rose from them like ghosts, coiling and making shapes in the air. Thunder growled dimly overhead, and she saw a faint flicker of lightning, red in the darkening sky.

She wanted to call the rain, wanted to loose her strength against this strange, still world, yet she had no power here, and she drew back from that thought. She stopped where she was, knowing she dreamed, knowing she could wake and be free of this place. Yet she hesitated, as if she were poised to act and yet could not quite awaken the impulse. Red lightning scarred the sky, and thunder cracked.

There was a tremor beneath her feet, a shaking that set fear coiling in her belly, and something began to move in the haze, slow and even, like breathing. Another tremor, and the surface beneath her cracked open. A red glow emanated from the fractures, and she felt a terrible heat come radiating from below. In the dark beyond the reach of her sight, something moved.

The mist roiled and billowed, rolling across the broken plain. It was no longer a sea of still water, but a sea of fire held beneath a cold surface. Rain began to fall, and it hissed when it struck the cold ground. Steam rose in columns, and the red cracks spilled molten blood. Karana looked up, feeling small and insignificant in the face of immensity, and something darkened the mist, something vast that stretched out black wings that filled the sky.

She woke with a sudden twitch and she heard thunder, smelled rain on the wind blowing through her windows. She sat up, shaking off the pall of the dream, wondering if she dreamed of Arthras. He was a dark shadow in her mind, coming closer yet unseen, unstoppable.

Thunder cracked and she realized she had been manipulating the weather in her sleep, and the air above her felt chaotic and energized. For a moment there was the simple, sensual relief of feeling the air and the motion of it, of having her power back like a hand freed from binding. Then the flash of lightning focused her mind, and she sat on the bed, closed her eyes, and began to soothe the storm she had called in her dream.

Slow, slow, she calmed the winds, stroking them until they settled. She slowed the cycling of the air, allowing it to settle. The gusts became a gentle breeze, and when a soft rain began to fall, she did not prevent it. It was something she thought on much now – how her own attentions could alter the weather over a large region, and how it might happen almost without her thinking about it, unless she was careful. She might be able to control wind and rain, but she was given no special power to understand the extremely complex system she was mistress of.

Just as the oncoming storm gentled into a midnight rain, there was a distant sound like thunder, but she knew it was not. She waited a moment, wondering if she would hear it again, and then the earth shook under her, making vases rattle on their shelves and making the beams and floors of Dagon's villa creak and groan. Karana clutched at the sheets as if that would avail her, and she felt another tremor. It was not Arthras; this was the mountain stirring again.

It bothered her. She knew the mountain had erupted before, though it had been a long time. But she wondered what effect Arthras' power might have on it were he to loose it here on the island. Might he waken the sleeping giant? She remembered the power he unleashed in Orneas, not so very far away. Could echoes of that reach this far? Was the mountain stirring because of it?

There was no way to know. Despite her worry and the pall cast by the dream, calming the storm had made her sleepy again. She lay back, eyes drowsing, and she fell back into sleep, forgetting even to dream.

ଔ

The thunder woke Thessala, and she rose from bed and wrapped herself in the sheet, went out to the terrace where the violet curtains billowed. Beyond it was a set of steps that led down into the gardens, and Lykaon sat on the top step with his back to her. He was naked, and she knew he had been prowling in his other shape. He did that at night. The wind was gusting and spat warm rain against her face. She wiped it away as greenish lightning flickered over the mountain.

"Does the thunder bother you?" she said. "I can feel things now, I could not before. Do you?"

"Some," he said. "Don't like walls." He scratched his neck. Thunder rumbled and she drew the sheet closer around her. She wanted him to look at her, and she wondered why that was. She liked waking and finding him close, as though he had been watching over her.

The wind began to calm, and then a gentle rain began to fall. Thessala yelped and ducked back inside, saw him still sitting there, heedless of the rain. She thought of all the nights he must have spent alone, in the dark, huddled against other rains. It made her sad.

"Come inside," she said. "I won't leave you out there."

He shrugged, then he stood up slowly. The darkness would have hidden his nakedness against eyes less keen than hers, and so she averted them, though she did not really want to. Lykaon took three steps, stopped and a look of apprehension came over his face, and then there was a distant rumble and the earth shook under their feet. Thessala gasped and felt a coldness course down her back. She had a moment of seeing Arthras before her, a titan covered in molten death, the air around him shimmering and shaking, and the terrible heat baking against her.

She shook it off, and then there came another shake, harder this time. Thessala heard something break in another room, and then it slowed. She held very still, as though she were afraid that the slightest motion could set it off again. She heard a chorus of howling dogs in the night, and she wondered if that meant it was over.

"That woke me," Lykaon said. "Heard it."

"You heard it?" she said. She realized she was standing on her toes, made herself relax. She kept expecting another tremor.

"In here." He tapped his head. "Funny noise." He shrugged. "Gone now."

Suddenly aware of her nakedness, she drew the sheet close around her again. She wanted to say something easy and knowing, but she could not, she felt it would too brazen, too hasty. Instead she backed into her room, dark and still as the rain came down outside.

"Don't," he said.

"Mwha?" She was surprised, thinking for a moment he had read her mind.

He came closer, took a corner of the sheet and tugged at it. "Don't cover up," he said.

She looked down at herself, shook her head. "It's not. . . it's not that. Not only that, anyway."

"Tell me," he said.

She sighed and sat down on the bed. "I told myself I didn't care, when I changed." She drew her braid around and pulled at it nervously. "When I was a young girl, everyone said I was the most beautiful, and I used it to get people to give me what I wanted. When I. . . when I took a lover against my family's wishes, I just remember being so frustrated that they would not let me have what I wanted. I pouted and sulked and wheedled, but it got me nowhere. Nowhere at all. That had never happened to me before."

Thessala felt so very strange, sitting here, telling him these things. She should have been afraid, but she was not. He was just a solid, quiet presence. "In the city, I made it a point of pride to not use what I had always used. I hid my face. I did not adorn myself. I did not flirt or tease or seduce. I abjured that as a false power. Because it had failed me when I most wanted it to work."

She swallowed. "I spent years mourning for Odario, but over time I realized I was mourning more for the idea than the man. He had adored me because I was beautiful, and I loved to be adored. He was handsome and thoughtless and talented and so, so very absorbed in his ideas about the world." She sighed again. "He never knew me, and I never knew him. I was fifteen, I was not even a woman then. I was just a girl used to having her own way."

She bit her lip, feeling the fine scales against her tongue. "And I wonder what he would think if he saw me now, as I have become. And I know he would be repulsed, and I would have been repulsed as well, when I was young and foolish." She laughed a little. "I spent years pretending it no longer mattered how I looked. But then this came, and I found it still had the power to wound me." She ran her hand over her face. "And I am angry with myself all over again, for how small my mind was when I pretended it was limitless." She looked at him. "This all sounds foolish, doesn't it?"

"I don't know," he said. "Maybe. I look back on myself, and I don't like it." He shrugged. "Everyone does that.

"You think that's true?" she said.

He came to her and sat down on the floor beside the bed. He leaned against her legs, hand on her foot. "I was never pretty."

"You had a family," she said, not pressing. He had spoken of it, but not very much.

"Mm," he said, nodding. "I was a drinker. Like my father. I started hunting with him, and he taught me to hunt, and to drink together. I was good at one, bad at the other. I tried to stop. Was an innkeeper for a little. Hated it." He grunted and scratched at his head. "Drank more because I hated it. There was a fire, one night. I was drunk outside, in the woods. Everybody died but me." He was silent for a long time. "Went into the woods and never came out. Hunted, and drank, and drank some more. Now this." He made a gesture of resignation. "Now I can drink all I want and not feel it. No more drink for me." He looked up at her. "I think the gods make jokes of us all."

"Karana thinks maybe the gods were like us," she said. "Just people who had power and used it."

"Would explain why gods are so useless," he said. "Would explain a lot."

"I'm sorry," she said. "For what happened to you. To your family. That is to say, I have sorrow for it."

"So do I," he said. "Doesn't change anything."

"No," she said. "But it matters."

In that moment they were alone. Nothing but the quiet house and the rain outside. She bent down and he rose up and she kissed him, wondering what her finely-scaled lips felt like. She remembered her one other lover, so long ago. What would he think of her now?

Lykaon kissed her again and drove the thought from her mind. He climbed up and onto her, like a beast. She liked that he took her hands and drew them out and to the sides, as if to hold her down when she knew he could not. Their fingers laced together, and she felt the sheet slip away from her and leave nothing between them.

His kisses were hungry, beginning almost softly and then growing harder, as though the beast inside him woke and wanted out. He touched her, exploring her, and she touched in answer. He was strong and heavy and he smelled of wild places. She felt his manhood, pressing hard against her thigh, and she drew her leg up, deciding. "Yes," she moaned against his mouth. "Yes."

ఔ

Karana was up early, feeling both rested and restless. She wanted to do something, to take action. The whole world seemed to be pausing, holding itself ready for something momentous, even though she knew that was only a feeling. She was the one who felt Arthras' imminence as an oppressive thought intruding on her mind. She had to get him before he crossed the straits, or there would be nothing to stop him. They had tried before, all three of them, and even though now they had Diomedes, he was an unknown quantity. A boy who had a power, but had not been tested. She herself had not believed how strong Arthras was, until she saw it. She dreaded facing him again. Even if she cast him down into the sea, would that kill him? He might simply come ashore on his own, walking out of the sea in a plume of steam, like a giant out of old legends.

She went down and prepared some food for herself, munching absently on bread and pieces of fruit. She was not very hungry these days, and it did not take much to satisfy her. Karana had never liked meat very much, but it was hard to feel full without fish or beef. She took the opportunity to eat little but fruits and nuts and bread. It made her feel lighter.

Then she hunted for Dagon, found him in his study on the second floor. He had an array of glass jars laid out before him, each of which seemed to contain the organs of dead animals preserved in some oily fluid. She resolved not to ask what he was doing.

"Is there word today?" she said.

"Nothing new," he said, without looking up. "There was the report of the ships gathering at Karmathos, and the news that General Emmeus was buying or commandeering ships, but nothing to show the progress of an invasion. Not yet." He looked up from his paper and sighed. "It will be harder to catch them than you think."

"The strait is not very large," she said. "Surely they will be seen."

"Yes, but because it is so small, they could be across before we ever had word of it." He leaned back. "Have you considered that even if you sank him in the sea he might survive?"

"I have," she said. "It is not a pleasant thought." She picked a book up from a chair and sat down. "I don't know what else I am to do. I have to stop him."

"It's not your responsibility," he said. "You are not the ruler of the empire, nor a servant of it. There is no reason why he must be prevented."

"Except that he is a barbarian, who would become a despot," she said. "I cannot imagine what he would do."

"Well, we should try," he said. "And the difference between emperors and despots is often just a matter of timing."

"You mean I should prepare to negotiate with him," she said, not really asking.

"I mean you should be prepared for the possibility," he said. "And no, not you. The emperor would negotiate, not you. But he will do so only if you cannot prevent the invasion."

"If I cannot prevent the landing, then my choices will be between surrender or a battle that I may not be able to win, that would destroy the city in any event." She opened the book and flipped through it, saw it was a history of eruptions of the mountain. "And then there is this," she said, gesturing with the tome. "Who can say what Arthras' power would do to the mountain?"

"The thought has crossed my mind," Dagon said. "Often eruptions are presaged by tremors, but not always. The mountain may simply be shifting in its sleep."

"Or Arthras' use of his power at Orneas – so close – may have bestirred it," she said. She put the book down and rubbed at her face. "There is so much we don't know."

"Too much to make any kind of predictions, yes," he said. "It is my job to predict, and right now I cannot do so with any kind of useful certainty. It is frustration."

Karana bit her lip, considering. "What do you think of Prince Zeneos?" she said.

"The heir? He is. . . often arrogant, sometimes thoughtless. I don't think he will make for a very good ruler, but he may grow into it. Worse men than he have done so." Dagon rubbed at his eyes.

"He seems strange to me," Karana said. "I encountered him in the palace, and while I expected him to scoff, he was hostile, and he did not always seem to remember what he had said from one moment to the next." She shook her head. "It disturbed me. A bad emperor is one thing, but one who is wrong in his head could be much worse."

"Well, he's not emperor yet," Dagon said. "One crisis at a time."

Diomedes appeared in that way he had, almost stumbling in through the door, breathing fast. "Oh good, I found you," he said, smiling. He seemed cheerful all the time, even if there was no cause.

"Which one of us were you looking for?" Dagon said.

"Both of you," he said. He looked at Karana and his good humor wavered a little. "The emperor sent for both of you, though I was just sent to get you, not you," he said, pointing first at Dagon and then at Karana. "The emperor is ill. He's in his bed and can't rise, and he sent for you both."

Dagon winced, and Karana felt a sudden jolt in her belly. She stood up and looked down at her simple robe. She was going to have to find something to wear.

"Well," Dagon said. "Go and tell his majesty that I will be along as soon as I can." He sighed. "It seems we shall do two crises at a time after all."

Chapter Thirty-One

Thunder of War

Karana dressed as quickly as she could and hurried downstairs, only to find Diomedes there instead of Dagon. He smiled at her. "He went on ahead, said I should wait and go with you."

"Well, I suppose that is fine," she said. She wondered if Dagon had taken one of the repugnant litters, and decided she didn't want to know. Diomedes fell into step beside her, easy and relaxed. She looked at him sidelong. He was handsome in a boyish way and almost the same height as she was. He looked around at everything as if seeing it for the first time. "I am sorry if I am slowing you down."

"I don't mind," he said. "I don't have to run everywhere." He smiled at her. "I can run fast, but that doesn't make it less work for me."

"I had wondered if you were an athlete," she said. "You have the look."

He laughed. "Of a kind, maybe. I have spent most of my life as a thief."

She was startled by his frank admission. "Indeed?" was all she could think to say.

He laughed again. "I am an orphan, like many. I am called a child of the temples, as it is a common thing for those who cannot care for their infants to abandon them on the street of temples. The sisters there take the children in. There also you will find homes for those young girls who get with child before they are married."

"Is that a common matter here?" Karana said. She glanced up the hill, to where the cluster of towers stood above the temple district. She had not gone, as she meant to, to the shrine of Vasa. Now she regretted it.

"Well, there are plenty of low-class families who don't much care, but among the better class of people, an unwed daughter with a big belly is cause for alarm." He shook his head. "I suppose that makes them not a better class, but I wasn't asked for my thoughts on it. The girls get sent away to have the children, and some of them never get asked to come back. They wet-nurse for the infants."

"And you grew up this way?" she said. It sounded so very strange.

"I did, and a lot of us ended up as thieves. We started stealing because we didn't have anything, and we kept going because we were good at it." He laughed. "I was a runner. No style. Just fast."

"I take it you would escape by running away," she said.

"Just grab it and run. I was too fast, so they could never catch me. Thank Attis I didn't grow too tall, or it would have slowed me down. A good way to avoid getting caught is to run into places too small for whoever is after you." He looked down at the sweep of the city visible below them on the mountainside. "Lots of places like that down there. Not like here."

Karana looked around at the sprawl of villas and mansions the lined the road they were on. In the high season the gates and walls were heavy with vines and climbing flowers, and not all of the walls were in good repair. It was a tangled, confused landscape, and she wondered how much moreso the place he grew up in must have been.

"And then you were gifted with more speed," she said. "I suppose you could have become an unstoppable thief."

"Well, I suppose, but when it first started, it hurt. I couldn't sleep for three days, my arms and legs hurt so much." He held up his hands, flexed them. "I could barely move, and then Dagon found me."

"So quickly?" she said.

"Yes. He took me to his house and gave me things to help the pain, and I was grateful." He smiled. "I thought he might want to get me in bed."

Karana started. "Did he?"

Diomedes laughed. "No, though that would have been fine, I suppose. No, he wanted me to help him. He wanted to study what I could do, learn from me, and have me be his bodyguard." They rounded a bend and started up a new hill. "When your power came, did it hurt?"

She started to say no, then remembered the battle she had joined almost immediately, and wobbled her head a little. "Not like that. Not exactly. It came on quickly, so very quickly. The city was under attack, and I had to learn to use what I could do very fast. And then I faced Arthras for the first time." She blinked, remembering. Even now it made her guts knot to think of it.

"It left marks on me," she said, and she drew back her sleeve so he could see the scars left on her, the dark trails that looked like spreading roots. "My power did not hurt me like yours did. But there has been pain. There has."

"What does it feel like?" he said, then closed his eyes and shook his head. "Not the pain. No. When you command the winds and the lightning. What is it like?"

"I –" Karana was silent for a moment. "I don't know how I would describe it. You know when you are in the dark, and you can reach out with your hand, and you can feel it, even if you cannot see it? It is sometimes like that. Like I have a sense I did not have before. The sky is a part of me, and I can feel it and direct it and shape it." She remembered Orneas and flinched. "I have much to learn of how it works. If I gather too much power, I can lose control of it. A storm has its own momentum and force, and it can build enough that it runs away from me, and it can take a great deal of effort to stop it." She shook her head. "I have only just begun to learn what I can do."

"Sometimes, when I am running," he said. "Everything is going so fast, and I am not sure where my next footstep will land, or if I will keep my footing or if I will fall. If I can concentrate and keep going it is wonderful – so smooth and fast and clean. But if I lose control, I fall." He squinted in the sun as he looked at her. "Like that?"

She nodded. "Yes, I imagine it might be like that."

༜

Karana was glad of Diomedes when they reached the palace, which still presented to her an impossible maze of rooms and towers and walls and corridors she could make no real sense of at all. Diomedes was not the sure guide that Dagon had been, but with his speed he could vanish down one way or another and then return to tell her if it was the right one. The crowds seemed subdued today, many more well-dressed people with anxious faces milling around in the high halls and long stairways, and she received many curious looks from people she assumed did not know who she was.

There were a dozen guards outside the imperial chambers, and Karana wondered at that. The impulse to more heavily protect the emperor from without when he was in ill health, as if his infirmity could be warded off with swords and shields. They knew her, or at least they allowed her in without questioning. The rattle of their spears on the stone floor as they stepped aside and then planted them was unnerving. It made her jump a little.

She had not been in the emperor's private rooms, and she was surprised to find them so dimly lit. The rooms were high and spare, with gauzy curtains billowing in the breeze from outside, casting shadows on the wide, smooth floors. It was very quiet inside, and in this outer room there was almost no one save hurrying servants. She heard voices, and she followed them, Diomedes close behind her.

Through an arch and she was in the emperor's bedchamber. The bed itself was almost the only furnishing in the room. It was big enough for four people, easily, and seemed built into the wall, with long crimson draperies hanging down from the ceiling to shroud it. There were almost twenty people crowded into the room, and some of them Karana vaguely recognized. The heir she knew, standing to one side surrounded by a reduced cohort of his retinue. Men who looked like doctors huddled beside the bed, and Dagon was there with them.

The emperor lay in the bed, and the size of it made him look very small. He was propped up on a pile of cushions, and while she had expected him to look sickly and pale, he did not. He looked like he had when she had seen him last. He wore a blue robe and was covered to his waist by a sheet.

In this room it was too warm, especially with so many people so close. She could see he was sweating.

Annoyed, Karana gestured, and a breeze surged in through the windows, billowing the curtains and making people clutch for hats and papers. She wove through the confusion, and the emperor smiled when he saw her. "I feared you would not come," he said.

"I would not stay away," she said, feeling a sudden warmth for him she did not expect. She liked him, and perhaps he had done that deliberately, but she felt it the same. He beckoned and she came closer, clasped his hand and felt the tremor in it. "How are you?" she said, ignoring the irritated looks from others in the room.

"I am ill," he said. "This morning I found I could not stand. My legs are weak and I lost my balance. Even now, the room seems to tilt and spin around me, especially when I close my eyes." He smiled. "Perhaps I shall be all right, but perhaps not."

"Don't judge too hastily," she said. "This may well pass."

"I do not know," he said. "I can never know. But I feel weak today, very weak. It is in these moments that I understand how much depends on an emperor being healthy. When I am confined to my bed, the empire begins to slip through my hands." He smiled ruefully, and then his expression grew troubled. "I had a terrible dream last night and I cannot remember it, only pieces."

Karana felt a current of unease run through her like a cold draft. "What kind of dream? What can you remember?" She could only remember parts of her own dream, as though it had happened long ago. She remembered the sea, and the sound of the waves crashing, like vast wings.

"I remember a sky that was dark, and I saw a great glow of fire," he said, his voice weak. "I smelled a burning smell, and then I heard a voice that spoke to me in words I did not understand."

"It is death!" Zeneos said, pushing forward, his face tight. "Death to speak of it. Do not give voice to evil dreams." He looked pale and his eyes twitched quickly side to side. Karana thought he looked more than a little mad.

Niceros waved him back. "It was only a dream, my son. I am not a prophet, nor a seer." He looked to Dagon. "Does my adviser believe in prophetic dreams?"

"Perhaps, Majesty," Dagon said, stepping forward in such a way that he subtly nudged Zeneos back. "But I would think that a dream sent by the gods to tell your future would stick in the mind more readily."

"Yes," the emperor said. "Yes, that is quite so." He smiled and closed his eyes. "So, what is the verdict of my doctors?"

Dagon shrugged slightly. "We cannot say, Majesty. You have had such episodes before, perhaps this one will fade as the others have."

"Or perhaps not," Niceros said. He grunted. "It is why I like you, Dagon. You do not mince words with me."

"I never will, Majesty," Dagon said. "I have too much respect for you."

"Well, we all have our failings," the emperor said. His expression faded, and then he blinked, as though he had forgotten what he was going to say. "I had a dream," he said.

"Yes, Majesty," Karana said. "You told me."

He seemed to see Karana for the first time and smiled at her. "I feared you would not come," he said.

She felt a strange doubling-back of time as she took his hand and smiled. "I would not stay away."

"You should rest, now, Majesty," Dagon said. "Rest, we will not go far."

The old man nodded, his face still unfocused, as though he could not quite see them. Karana felt his hand shaking in her own, and it felt soft and weak. She laid it gently on the bed beside him, and he did not seem to notice it,

Dagon guided her to one side, and she turned to him, worried. "How bad is it?"

He shrugged. "I cannot answer that. I doubt anyone can. The ailment is not of his body, but his mind. His doctors want to bleed and purge him, but I have not allowed it, and for now he listens to me. I believe such treatment would surely kill him." He glanced back at Zeneos. "I am sure that would please some of the people here."

"Do you think he was poisoned?" Karana said the word very quietly.

"No, or at least, I know no poison that could do this." Dagon shook his head. "He is just a sick man, and sometimes his sickness is worse. There is nothing to be done about it but wait."

Karana looked back at the bed, the old man surrounded by so many others, and she had a moment of envisioning them as carrion birds waiting at the feast, and she turned away. She clenched her hands, wanting to do something, but this was something her powers could not accomplish. She was given power to destroy, but not to heal, and in that moment it was bitter to her.

Diomedes slipped into the room, and she was glad to see him. He came quick to Dagon's side and handed him a piece of parchment, and Dagon opened it and read. His expression was not pleased. He looked up, then beckoned

Karana and led them outside, past the guards, into the emperor's spare antechamber.

"What is it?" she said, worried by his expression.

"A report that a merchantman spotted a large fleet of ships crossing the strait," he said. "They were tacking westward, and he did not count them, but that must be Arthras' invasion fleet."

Karana felt a jolt go through her. "I have to go, if I can catch him at sea -"

He put a hand on her arm. "This message was written this morning; they saw the ships day before last. On a direct course, they will already be ashore. I do not think you can stop them in time."

"I have to try it," she said.

"It is an entire fleet," Dagon said. "If it is Arthras, he will sail with the women and children of his people, as well as soldiers. Many of the sailors have been pressed into service, no doubt. Would you kill all of them on the chance you might kill him?"

She grimaced and turned away, shook his hand away. "What can I do, then?" she said. "How can I prevent this war from consuming everything? If he is willing to destroy the city in order to take it, and I am not, then he wins."

"Against you, his army does not matter," Dagon said. "They cannot stand against you. It is he, and only he, that we must concern ourselves with. You assume he is willing to crush the city, but perhaps not. If he has allied with Emmeus, then I would guess not. He might be as appalled by what happened to Orneas as you are, if not from moral cause, than simply by the destruction of what he thought to capture." He sighed. "He has outflanked us, but that does not mean he has won the day. Ashore, any sizeable army will need supply, and it will be on board their ships. You could sink them all and then we could starve the army into surrender. Arthras clearly cares for his people, and so that is a weakness that can be exploited." He looked back at the door to the emperor's chambers. "Once we know where he has landed, we can decide what the next move shall be."

Karana scowled. Dagon seemed far too sanguine about the situation, and she wondered if that was because he had not been at Orneas. He had heard, but he had not seen. He did not know, fully, what he was talking about. She stalked to the window and looked out, up at the slope of Mount Ara, like the shape of a sleeping beast, dreaming of ancient days.

☙

Arthras watched as the island drew closer. In the sun it was a glorious riot of green beyond the white shore, and the mountains in the distance shaded into deep violet shadows. He had never seen anything so beautiful, a land so fair and green, in all his life. Compared to this the wild lands he was born in were gray and harsh, and the heartland of Othria was a crisscross of roads and farms and fields. From here, the island of Calliste looked in truth like the paradise of the gods themselves.

He looked back and saw the whole panoply of the fleet behind him, a huge flotilla of hundreds of ships. Some were small, some large, some pulled with oars while most made do with square-rigged sails. He had never been to sea, and had worried he might become sick as some men were said to, but it did not bother him at all. He enjoyed the wide-open water and the sense of freedom. It was heady to look to distant, hazy horizons and know he could go anywhere. The journey was swift and easy, and now they had arrived.

Some of the ships were shallow, old galleys and such, and he watched as the first wave of them simply rode the waves in and beached along the shore. The ship he rode was heavier, and it stood off in the shallows, casting down an anchor. They would lower a small boat, and he would go ashore as he had left it. He decided he would not wait.

He pulled himself up onto the rail of the ship, and then he jumped down into the sea. He sank quickly, as he had suspected he might. He was heavier, now, than he had been. Perhaps he was becoming like stone himself. The water was clear as glass, and he saw a hidden landscape of undulating sand stretching out around him. The ships moved like shadows on the surface, and clouds of fish scattered away from him as he dropped.

It was not deep, and he landed on the bottom, feet sinking ankle-deep in the sand. He paused a moment to pull off his sandals and left them behind as he walked barefooted across the bottom. He felt shells crunch underfoot and wondered if he would have to breathe. He had not considered the fact that he might not be able to swim at all.

Yet he felt no urgency, no need for air. He walked across the bottom of the sea, and then he reached the shallows and breached the surface. The return of light and sound was startling, and he spat out water and waded ashore, heedless of the waves that rushed around his legs. He heard cheering, and looked to see men on ships and shore shaking their hands in the air and shouting at the sight of him emerging from the waves. He had not realized anyone was watching.

He climbed up from the sea onto the pallid beach, sand sticking to his wet feet, and then he bent down and scooped up a handful of it and let it run through his fingers. At last, and in defiance of all things, he had come to conquer the land of the gods.

Chapter Thirty-Two

Footsteps of Gods

Arthras paced the ground before his tent, watching the armies set up their encampment all along the shore. A constant swarm of smaller boats went from the big ships to the shore and back, ferrying supplies. He had ordered it to be done, so that even if the girl Karana raised a storm and destroyed the ships, they would not starve. Once they were unloaded, they would sail away and return to Orneas for the rest of the armies. Here he had five thousand of his own warriors, and all of Emmeus' army ashore. The rest of his men were back in Othria where they could guard the woman and the children and the old ones. If there was another cataclysm here, Emmeus' men would pay most of the price.

The day was waning, and the sunset across the hills and the distant mountains was spectacular. He tried not to gape at the sight of it, but it was beautiful in a way he would never have thought was real. The light, the rich greens of the valleys, and the scattered colors of flowers growing wild on the hillsides. Even the terraced farms cut into the hills were beautiful. It was like a land out of dreams.

The gentle rolling hills near the shore were filling up with tents and paddocks and men. Emmeus had riders out to the east and west along the shore. Eastward lay the city, and that was where any danger would come from, but Emmeus was suspicious and canny, and Arthras did not dispute him. The general's own tent was pitched across the firepit from his own, and he saw the man busy giving orders and taking reports. It annoyed him, made him feel like he was not really in control, and perhaps, just now, he was not.

Nicaea came out of the tent, wrapped in a loose blue robe and barefoot on the grass. She looked beautiful, and it caught at him. He found himself wanting to trust her more than he should, give her more than he should. It was sometimes hard for him to remember that to her he was only a barbarian, and she would dispose of him if she could. Sometimes, it pained him to think of it.

"Come inside, and take ease with me," she said, grasping his arm with her gentle hands. "They will not attack us tonight. In fact, I doubt they will attack at all."

"You think they will negotiate," he said. "They will make me an offer to stave off war."

"A war they cannot win," she said. "Yes. The emperor has no real forces on the island to repel an attack on the city. Archelion is not even fortified properly. If they use the storm girl against you there will be another disaster, as at Orneas. They won't risk it."

"So we talk. Again. Because they have always been trustworthy," he said. He disliked it when he grunted at her, it made him feel petulant.

"Galbos thought he was dealing with a simple barbarian," she said. "He wanted to strike first to establish a position of strength from which to negotiate. He didn't understand what he was dealing with." She drew him toward the tent. "Now this is an emperor negotiating with a living god and the greatest general of our time. This time he will take you seriously."

Arthras squinted at the hills as they fell into shadow. He thought he saw something move there, something fast. He pulled his arm free of Nicaea's grasp and stepped around the fire, put it at his back so the light did not blind him. Something was there. He heard a rushing sound, and saw a plume of dust. It looked like the trail made by a swift horse, but it was moving far too quickly for a horse. Arthras bared his teeth and reached back, pulled a burning branch from the fire and thrust it over his head. He flourished it, wanting to be seen. If someone was coming for him, he wanted to be found.

He heard the strange rushing noise again, and then a boy seemed to appear before him, moving so quickly it fooled his eye. He slid to a stop across the grass, sending earth and stones shooting up behind him as he left a furrow on the earth. Arthras saw his arms and legs all but vibrating as he came to a stop, and there was a glow in his eyes like the sunset. He was not even breathing hard, for all his speed.

The boy looked at him, up and down, then nodded. "You'd be the one they call Arthras. Earthshaker."

"I am he," Arthras said. He looked the boy over. He was small, and dark-haired, with wide eyes and a sharp jaw. Another one. "Who are you?"

"Diomedes is my name," the boy said. "I am sent as a messenger."

Emmeus came forward from his tent. "Messenger from whom?" he said, and Arthras turned and glared at him. He did not want any question who commanded here.

"I come from the emperor, His Majesty Niceros, Twentieth of that name." He held out a rolled parchment sealed and festooned with ribbons. "I have this for you."

Arthras tossed the burning branch away and held out his hand, took the scroll from the boy and immediately handed it to Nicaea behind him. He ignored the expression of annoyance on Emmeus' face, caught in the corner of his eye. Nicaea broke the seal and unrolled the parchment. He waited while she read it, wishing he could do it himself.

"The emperor wants to meet with you, to negotiate terms," she said. "He has chosen a place partway between here and the city, an old temple."

"I know of it," Emmeus said. He glanced at Arthras.

Arthras nodded. "Tell him I will be there."

"Tomorrow, at sunset," Nicaea said. "That is what he suggests."

"Let it be done," Arthras said. He looked at the boy. "Go back to your emperor and tell him. I will be there." He hesitated, wanting to send a message to Karana, but he could not think of what to say. "Go."

The boy Diomedes nodded, and then he turned and jogged away, moving faster, and faster, until he vanished from sight in a cloud of dust. Arthras snorted as he watched him go. A stranger world he could not have imagined.

ೞ

"He said he will be there," Diomedes said. He looked around the room, notable for the absence of an emperor. The old man was still in his bed, not fit to rise or speak. Karana was uncomfortable sitting here with Zeneos acting as sovereign, and the bevy of courtiers gathered at his back did not give her confidence. Dagon alone she felt as though she could trust.

"Well," Zeneos said. "We shall see what demands this barbarian makes." He looked at Dagon. "You will, of course, make these negotiations last as long as possible."

"Me?" Dagon said. "You want me to lead the negotiations?'

"Who else?" Zeneos said. "You are an expert on these. . . people," he said, giving Karana a glance. "And it would be far beneath my station to bandy words with a barbarian. You are a barbarian as well, so you and this Arthras may have much in common with one another."

Karana bristled, but she forced herself to hold her tongue. She already knew there was nothing she could say to change Zeneos' attitudes. Unless she wanted to simply throw him out a window, she had limited power to control the situation. Sycophants and hangers-on were coming and going behind him through shadowed doors at the back of the room, and she didn't know any of them.

Dagon was less than pleased as well. "I doubt I will have much to discuss with an Almanni. And may I remind your Highness that General Emmeus is with him? He will not be handled lightly."

Zeneos did not seem to be listening, only turned his head as some courtier bent down to murmur in his ear. Karana stepped forward. "Your Highness. . ."

Zeneos looked annoyed. "I have not given you leave to speak," he said.

"I do not need it," she said. She started forward and two guards stepped forward with their spears crossed, keeping her back from Zeneos.

"You do, and you would be well to remember it," the heir said. "In my father's infirmity I am ruler here. You are here at my sufferance."

Karana's fists clenched, but then Dagon put a hand on her arm and she forced herself to calm down. What could she accomplish here, save an explosion of violence? She wanted none of that, so she took a deep breath and let Dagon pull her back. She purposely did not look at Zeneos, she knew he would have some kind of smirk on his face and it would make her angry.

Dagon interposed himself between them. "Of course I will do as you ask, Highness," he said. "What commands do you have besides to stall them? That cannot last forever."

"It will do for now," Zeneos said. He took a long breath and sighed, as if at a pleasurable thought. "All else will transpire as it should. For what else could happen here, in the land of the gods?"

"Of... course, Highness," Dagon said.

"I must say I do not like the way you say that," Zeneos said. "As though to remind me." He tugged idly at his golden curls. "You ask why you are sent to the barbarian? It is simple. If he decides to kill you, I will lose nothing vital." He laughed, and gestured. "You may go, and prepare. I expect only the best from such an illustrious scholar."

ఈ

Karana held her tongue until they were out of the presence of the heir, and then she rounded on Dagon. "Stall him? That is all he has to offer? The last time I tried to stall Arthras, it ended badly enough. This could be worse."

Dagon held up his hands, palms toward her. "I know, I know. I do not know what he is thinking of. Perhaps he means to delay them until he can call in forces from the mainland. Mercenaries from Vatharia or some such thing. I would not put it past him, but he is not thinking reasonably. Arthras makes all such military gambits pointless. I am afraid he is planning something foolish."

"Another such foolishness could raze Archelion to the ground," Karana said. "We will have to negotiate with Arthras in good faith, we cannot dissemble."

"No, and General Emmeus is no one to take lightly either." He rubbed at his lip. "I wonder..."

"What?"

"Galbos' wife, Nicaea. I wonder if she has cast in her lot with Arthras. He left her behind in Ilion, and Emmeus is her brother. That might explain their quick alliance. If she is advising Arthras, then he will be even more difficult to handle. I am told she is a very canny woman." Dagon motioned her to follow him. "We are not in an enviable position. I am to stall them, and no doubt any agreement I did make would simply be disavowed by Zeneos. He thinks he is dealing with a normal enemy."

"Yes," she said, bitter. Again and again they had to prove their power was not a ruse, not a trick, not exaggerated. No one wanted to believe, or if they did, they refused to think of the ramifications.

They rounded a corner and he pulled her to the side. "I need you to come with me," he said.

"Yes, of course I will," she said.

"You will? Oh, good." He seemed off-balance. "I was prepared to persuade you."

She almost laughed. "I cannot let you go to deal with him alone. He would never take you seriously." She shook her head. "He will see this – you being sent to him – as an insult."

"Then I shall have to trust you to guard my life from his offense," Dagon said.

Karana nodded. "Should we bring the others?"

He thought for a long moment, then sighed. "No. I want them here to protect the city, if it becomes necessary. I do not discount that he will find some way to slip past us. Emmeus is a clever general, I cannot afford to take him lightly." He scowled. "There is something at work here I do not see."

ෆ

The old temple was fantastic to see. Arthras looked at it, how the white steps went right down into the blue waters of the sea, and the pillared hall stood roofless yet overgrown with wild flowers and plants like none he had ever seen. At the top of the stair two white carved lions stood watch, looking out over the shore, and behind them against a wall now crumbling down stood an ancient statue of Attis. The image towered over them, immense and impassive, his face blank, his bronze lightning bolt faded to green and covered with vines.

Emmeus was ill at ease, looking around them. He had brought more than a hundred of his cavalry with them, and riders were in the low hills around them, keeping watch. Nicaea simply waited under her parasol until the slaves built her small pavilion, and then she sat down in the shade and ate grapes from a small bowl. "Ease yourself," she said to her brother. "He would have chosen a better place for an ambush. This is far too open."

Emmeus grunted. "That would be assuming the emperor is a sensible military mind. I have no such assurance."

"Enough," Arthras growled, and Emmeus subsided, moved away to sit down on a folding stool in the shade of his own canopy. Arthras ignored them both and paced. The sun was setting in the west, turning the sea to fire. The gulls flew low over the waves and cried out, and he closed his eyes, feeling the sun warm on his skin, on his face, glowing through his closed lids. It was so beautiful, and peaceful here. He envied it, even as he stood at the heart of it.

The wind stirred, backing around to the south, bringing the scent of wild flowers, and then it shifted again, restless. Arthras felt an unease at the back of his neck and opened his eyes. He looked up. The wind stirred his hair, rippled the silk canopies of his companions, and the horses snorted and tossed their heads.

Then he saw the dark mote in the sky, coming down, down. It slowed, and he saw it was not just one person. He heard Emmeus swear under his breath, and Nicaea gasp, as Karana dropped down from the sky, carrying another man with her. The wind she commanded blew away the leaves and flower petals, and she landed as easily as any bird. She was dressed in fine silks, with a blue robe over a white mantle, and a deep violet scarf wound over her braided hair. The man with her was dark-haired and pale-skinned, with one strange eye the wrong color. He was well dressed in black with silver accents, and he brushed at himself, tugging his clothes back into place.

Arthras paid no attention to anyone but Karana. She looked rested and composed, and there was a fierce glint in her eyes. She stood straight and looked at him. "Arthras," she said, her tone cool and unafraid and that made him angry, though he tried to control it. He grunted and folded his arms, looking up at the mass of the holy mountain behind her, then back to her face, implacable as any statue.

଼

Karana watched him like a hawk, trying to read his mood. This was only the third time she had been close to him, and she saw things she had not seen before. He looked younger to her eyes, now in better light, and his muscles looked harder and leaner. He wore a purple tunic and dark breeches, but he was barefoot and had not bothered with a cloak or any other decoration. He looked disheveled, and she supposed he probably did not care.

To her left was a heavy, middle-aged man with gray hair and a ruddy face. He rose, looking at the two of them searchingly. "What is this? I am here to speak with imperial emissaries. Who are -"

"Quiet," Arthras said, and the man obeyed. Karana looked at him and nodded.

"You are General Emmeus," she said. "You could be no one else." She squinted past Arthras at the woman under the canopy, surrounded by her servants. "And this is your sister, Lady Nicaea."

"And I am Dagon," Dagon said, stepping forward with a slight bow. "His Majesty has sent me to –"

"Do not speak," Arthras said coldly, stepping forward until he was face to face with Karana. "Twice before you have tried my power against mine. Will this be the third time?"

"I am not the one who seeks battle," she said, controlling herself, keeping her voice neutral. Already she could smell the burnt-iron scent on him and it made her stomach knot.

"And yet you are in my path wherever I turn," he said. "None of this would be needed without your endless opposition."

"I am here to stand between you and those who you would unhome and despoil," she said, getting angry and regretting it. "Do you wish the same fate upon others that you seek to protect your own people from? What difference could there be?"

"My people are mine," he said. "Not these imperial sheep."

"You are not stupid enough to believe that, no matter how much you repeat it to yourself," she said. "There is no need for this war you seem to desire so much."

"It was forced upon me!" he said, voice rising. "We were betrayed by the empire, so I will take it!"

"Even if you must destroy it?" she countered. "You were wronged, but that does not undo the evils you have done, nor excuse them."

He snarled and stepped in closer, but she gave no ground. "Try it," she said as calmly as she could. "Lift a hand to me, because I am not afraid of you like they are." She jerked her head toward the onlookers. "I am not simple flesh and blood. I can contend with you, as I have before, and this time we will see what comes!"

The ground shook, a sudden convulsion of the ancient stone they stood on. Karana reeled, and when she caught her balance she called on her power and the wind grew hard and clouds thickened over the sea. And then she saw Arthras barely keeping his feet, a look of shock on his face. Emmeus fell hard against the post of his canopy, toppling it down on top of him, and Dagon grabbed at a broken pillar for balance. Karana saw the statue of Attis totter, and then the ancient face cracked in half and fell away.

"Stop it!" Nicaea screamed as she fell to the hard ground. "Stop it!"

The earth heaved again, and Arthras staggered aside, fetched against Karana and she braced him up. "It's not me!" he said, shouting over the deep rumble of the earth. "I'm not... I'm not..."

There was a terrible, deep roar from high on the mountain, like thunder, and Karana looked up to see a massive plume of smoke and ash burst from the stone and billow high into the evening sky, growing and growing at an incredible rate. There was another thunderous sound and a plume of red lava burst from the mountainside, high on the slope, and she saw the remaining clouds dashed away from it like ripples in water.

"It's the mountain!" she cried. "The mountain wakes!" She remembered her dream, the distant sounds and the sea of black fire. She looked at Arthras, saw him stunned and afraid for the first time. She caught his wrist and he turned on her with a wild, uncomprehending look.

"I'm not doing it!" he said, almost desperate.

"Can you *stop* it?" she said back, pulling on him for emphasis.

"I don't... I don't know!" He staggered as the ground shook again, and then he closed his eyes and she saw his skin darken. He clenched his hands and a look of terrible concentration consumed his face. He gritted his teeth and snarled. Another awful detonation rolled over them, so loud she felt it in her chest and in her skull.

Arthras made a deep, hard sound and cords stood on his neck, but then he opened his eyes and looked at her. She felt, in that moment, as if he were looking on her as a true human for the first time, as if he were seeing her. "It's too far away," he said. "I can't reach it."

She pulled herself closer to him. "If you were closer, could you stop it?"

He looked up at the mountain, then back at her. He seemed to understand what she meant, and then he nodded. "Maybe."

"Then hold on," she said. She reached around him, took a good grip under his arms, and she called down the winds. Leaves and flower petals swirled around them, and then the others were knocked back as she pulled in a torrent of air, and sent them both vaulting upward into the twilit sky.

Chapter Thirty-Three

Beast of Fire

Arthras clenched his jaw to keep from crying out. They left the ground so quickly it seemed to drop away beneath them, and he felt a twisting in his belly, and a feeling as if his guts had fallen out and been left behind. Karana's arms were locked tight around his chest, and he had to fight the desire to clutch at her as the wind screamed past them.

He looked down and saw the green land fall away, speeding behind them, and then the sky was filled with ashes, and smoke. Another wrenching explosion rent the air, and he felt it thrum through him and buzz his teeth against each other. Ashes swirled in the air like snow, and here and there an ember drifted, glowing red in the sky. He tried to twist and look down, but he could not tell which way was up, felt completely lost, and vertigo made his head spin.

Karana slowed, and then they began to drop. He felt the lift in his belly, but he had no reference, no way to tell how fast they were going, or how far. He had to struggle not to cry out, as he felt himself plummeting out of any control towards the earth. In his mind he saw the dream of ashes, and the sea of fire, and fear coiled in him like a cold snake.

They fell through layers of smoke and ashes, the air tasting bitter and metallic, and then he saw the ground. Beneath them was a river of molten flame coursing slow down the mountainside, and the sun was blotted out by the vast cloud spreading above them. He saw flickers, and red lightning stabbed between the death cloud and the blackened landscape. Fire crawled across the wooded mountainside like the bright edges of burning paper.

They landed on a ridge of earth, the grass on the soil bent down and gray from the weight of ash already laid atop it. The glow and the heat from the lava was like a forge, and even Arthras flinched from it. The whole mountain seemed to be in motion, stones breaking loose and tumbling down, the air filled with swirling embers and falling ashes. The earth shook again and he had to grab for balance, found himself gripping Karana's hand. He looked up and met her stare.

"Can you stop it?" she said again, the air in between them shimmering from the heat. He let go of her and stood on his own. It made him angry, thinking of his new city – the city he chose as the center of his new empire – buried under a layer of ash and molten rock. He would not lose his glory to a troublesome mountain. He closed his eyes and reached down, down with the power he wielded, and came to grips with the unquiet earth.

ଔ

Karana watched him, tense and shaking inside because there was nothing more she could do now but watch. She had to trust him, and the fate of the city might well depend on his power to still the eruption of the mountain. The air tasted like copper, and it smelled like a foundry. The heat baking from the flowing river of lava was intense, and she saw the edges of her robe beginning to blacken and smolder from the fierceness of it. The lava had slowed, the surface darkening with hardened pieces of stone that floated on the top of it.

The mountain shuddered again, and red lightning slashed the sky, arcing from the roiling cloud of smoke down to shatter the earth where it struck. The lush forests that had cloaked the mountainside were burning, and the smell of it, the thick smoke, was almost overwhelming, but she did not dare summon a wind to disperse it for fear of making the fire burn more quickly. She needed rain, but rain would take more time.

Arthras made a guttural sound, and she looked at him, saw his teeth bared in a twisted snarl and his jaws clenched. His fists were tight and his skin was blackening as she looked. More smoke rose from his clothes as they began to burn. He grunted again, grating through his teeth, and his eyes opened again as another tremor shook the mountain.

"I can't get a grip on it," he gasped. "It's so big, and there's something. . . something making it worse." He staggered as the earth shook again. All around them the world had become a sea of fire flowing around their little hillock, and the heat was immense and unending. Lightning flared crimson again, and Karana looked up, feeling a coldness somewhere down inside her. She had been here before.

The sea of lava heaved, and then it heaved again. Arthras turned and followed her gaze, and he saw it too. She saw a look of sudden terror on his face such as she had never thought to see. "In Bora's name," he gasped.

The sea of fire roiled once again, the dark surface cracking and sliding apart, and then something immense burst from the lava and rose screaming into the burning sky. Karana saw jaws as long as a warship filled with dagger teeth, and she felt a roar that was too great a sound to be heard as it hammered against them like a blow. It shook itself, fire slinging from it in waves, and then its surface cracked and fell away in great pieces of hard stone, leaving it black and gleaming beneath, vast and armored with ebon scales.

She saw a great silver eye glare down on them, reflecting light like a baleful moon, and then the long neck lashed out and the great jaws rushed on them, black and endless. She felt its breath like the blast of a forge, and then she seized Arthras by the arm and launched them into the air.

The jaws slammed shut on the hillside where they had been, ripping it apart, pouring fire down on it. The air was turbulent, and in her haste Karana lost her grip. Arthras yelled as he dropped away and fell into the glowing river of lava where it coursed down the mountainside, and Karana cried out, reaching after him uselessly.

The beast roared as it heaved itself from the lava, and she stared at it, the heat waves in the air distorting its shape as it emerged. Molten rock sheeted from a huge body, and then two vast wings ripped free of the fire and spread wide across the dark sky. Purple lightning danced on the wingtips as the monstrous thing shook them free, scattering lava across the sky. It beat them and the hot wind rushed past her, and she covered her mouth as her stunned mind began to work once more.

And then, from those terrible jaws, there came a voice. It was not like any voice she had ever heard, so huge it was deeper than her ears could really make sense of, it was almost more vibration than sound, formed by a throat unlike that of any human. It spoke in a language she understood, an ancient tongue that had been all but dead when the empire was born, and now was written down only on scrolls of unimaginable antiquity. *"Arallu ka ita Kigalla! Na tu Nergal!"*

I am the King of Death. I am Nergal. The name of a dead monster, a dead legend, a dead god. A dragon in awful flesh, it burst free from the lava and stone that imprisoned it, and began to beat its endless wings.

ଔ

Arthras didn't have time to cry out as he fell. He saw Karana reaching after him, eyes wide and afraid, and then he turned over in the air and slammed down hard into the lava. It was not like striking water, the surface was covered with cooled rafts of black obsidian and the molten rock was heavy and thick. Only the force of his fall plunged him into it and left him beneath the surface. There was no pain, only an encompassing heat. He felt a tickling across his body and realized it was his clothes incinerating. His own inner heat rose, and the lava around him became lighter, heated white-hot by his power.

He realized he was flowing downhill, tipped over an edge and fell, twisting, flailing in along the streams of falling fire. He glanced off the hillside, bounced away and then landed hard on a bare outcrop of rock. His fingers sank into it as he grabbed for purchase, and he clawed at his face to clear the stuff from his eyes and ears so he could hear and see. He spat out a glob of melted stone and gasped for breath.

Above him the sky was a tortured thing of falling fire and coursing violet lightning, and in it he saw Karana, glowing from the power that gathered around her, electric sparks trailing over her arms and her face. A shadow fell over him, and he stared.

The beast emerged over the edge of the cliff, covering the sky, wings beating vast and powerful. The clawed forelegs cracked the stone, and the jaws yawned wide as it bellowed. It was true; it was the beast of old that had slain Attis himself. It was all true.

The beast roared into the sky, and he saw lightning play across it. Bright bolts struck down and gathered around Karana, and then they leaped down to crack against its massive head. It screamed, and the sound almost caused physical pain, it was so close and loud. It reared up, wings spreading wide, neck stretching as it reached for her.

Arthras snarled. He reached up with his power, hooked into the basalt cliff that groaned beneath the weight of the dragon, and he *wrenched* it from within. He had a breathless moment thinking he had not done it, and then he saw a ripple rush up the rock face, and when it reached the top the whole cliffside split apart as though at the blow of an axe.

Howling, the dragon plunged down as the cliff collapsed under its weight, molten lava rushing around it in a terrible cascade. Arthras saw it coming and tried to leap away, but a wave of fire slapped into him, and then he was swept down by a thrashing wing and hurled into the collapse, huge pieces of stone raining down as if they had fallen from the sky. One struck him and crushed him under, and then he was buried.

CB

Karana saw the jaws rushing for her, and then the cliff thundered and collapsed under the beast, dropping it down in an immense slide of broken stone and molten rock. She flinched back as the roaring and thrashing flung shards of stone into the air like knives. Lightning was crawling over her hands and arms, and there was so much power in the air she could not control it. Nergal roared up at her and she held up her hand, called in the lightning.

It gathered there, coiling and snapping across her skin, setting her clothes on fire, and then she flung it down in a bolt that struck that enormous black head and illuminated it for a flickering instant. It was so brutish and strange looking, without grace or sleekness. There was nothing serpentine or lizardlike about it. It looked like an accident, or something cursed. Her bolt had no noticeable effect, save the increased fury of the monster himself. Nergal. She did not want to give it a name, for that seemed somehow to empower it. It made her think on the ancient mind that lay behind that savage visage. That something so vast and terrible could have a mind made her flesh crawl.

It reared up from the destruction below and roared again. Those great wings rose up and threshed at the air, and she felt the power of them pushing against her. She watched with narrowed eyes and realized that the wings were a great weakness, as if it gained the air, she could use the winds to bring it down again. She saw a glow deep down in the cavernous throat, and then Nergal vomited death into the air.

She saw a cloud black as night, roiling and expanding and glowing from within. It boiled up and out and then it slammed into her like a hammer, heat blasting her clothes off and making her scream with agony as she was hurled back through the air. Glowing ash invaded her lungs and she gagged it out, spinning, losing control.

Karana slammed into the hillside and broke it open with the force of the impact, the death cloud of the dragon's breath rolling over her, incinerating anything that could burn, setting the exposed rock to glowing red with the terrible heat. When it was done a layer of ashes settled over her and everything else, and she felt it stir off her as the dragon rose up on beating wings, screaming at the sky.

☙

Arthras clawed his way out of the lava, spitting it from his mouth, and then he stood knee deep in the flood of fire and looked up as the dragon breathed out a cloud of destruction than tore Karana from the sky and buried her in a fall of ash and air so hot it glowed. The beast spread its wings and hurled itself into the sky, gripped the stony promontory with its powerful forelegs and thrashed the tail that seemed long enough to lay an army low with one sweep.

Furious, Arthras leaped out of the molten rock and landed on hard stone. He caught up a boulder the size of a man and swung it up over his head. His fingers melted down into the stone, giving him a surer grip as he aimed, and then he let out a war cry and hurled it.

The missile shattered against the dragon's spined, scaled shoulder, scattering pieces. It did not seem to even notice, and he saw it hunting for something on the ground and knew it was Karana. He looked at the sea of lava between him and the beast, and he reached down with his power. He could make stone shake and move to his commands, he would find out if it mattered whether it was hot or cold.

It was heavy, and he could feel it fighting him. He shoved with all the fury in him, and then the mountain shuddered and a wave of lava rose up and rolled like a slow swell across the lake of fire. The dragon saw it and turned, but it was not fast enough, and the heavy, cresting wave crashed against it and shoved it aside.

It reeled, clawing for balance, and then it heaved up its tail, dripping with fire, and struck at him. There was a sound like an oncoming storm, and then stone and sky both seemed to shatter. He felt the blow smash into him, and then he was thrown back into the cliffside and it crumbled down around him.

◈

Karana clawed to her feet and staggered away as the wave of lava thrust the dragon away from her. Her skin hurt, and she ached down in her bones. She was covered in ash, and she spat it from her mouth and clawed it from her eyes as she ran. Nergal bellowed, and she saw him rise up over the smoke and flame, silver-eyed and covered in fire, and it was not stopping him. Nothing she did was doing more than slow him down. He was too strong for her. She felt real fear in her chest, a panic she almost could not control.

She saw those jaws coming for her again, huge and jagged and breathing smoke. Karana called in her power and leaped into the sky, struggling to control the winds. The great heat of the volcano was creating powerful updrafts that made the air coil and move unpredictably. Nergal's teeth crashed together so close she smelled his furnace breath, and then he was beating his wings again, fighting to rise after her.

She screamed and lightning coursed through her like knives. When she loosed it, violet bolts lashed into him, striking his head and his wings, thunder splitting the air. She watched it crawl over him like serpents, but he never slowed. Those wings thrust down with convulsive power, and the lava was sent washing outward from the force of the downblast. Karana struggled to hold her place in the sky in the face of that terrible power. She hurled bolt after bolt of lightning into him, and he shrugged them off as though they had been nothing.

She heard echoing thunder and then saw Arthras burst from the cliffside, shoving the boulders and ruin out of his way, covered in lava and smoldering like a burning star. She looked at the beast coming for her, and her old enemy, and her mind caught hold and began to work again.

Lightning seared her skin, and she spat into the wind and screamed down at the dragon. "Come then! Come and face me! Come!" She sent more lightning searing into him, and then she turned and flew up into the burning sky.

ඃ

Arthras staggered free from the rubble. His left arm seemed paralyzed, and he was consumed by pain. He sent a shiver through the lava that clung to him and it rippled off of him, shaken loose to fall to the ground half-molten and turning dark. He looked down and saw a long gash down his arm and the flesh of his chest laid open and bleeding. It made him afraid because he had not been truly injured since the star touched him, since he changed. Karana had caused him pain, stunned him, exhausted him, but not made him bleed.

He looked up and saw the dragon rising into the sky, the beats of its wings sending a wind raging across the mountainside, uprooting trees and scattering rocks like pebbles. Above it, higher and rising, he saw Karana at the center of a cage of lightning, sending bolts raining down on the beast as it came for her. He felt a moment of strange, hot pride at the sight of her. He knew she would not flee, would not give way. She was brave, and fierce. Let the demon find that out as he had.

The earth shuddered and he leaned against a boulder, breathing hard. This was a new thing, this fear, and it felt like a black shroud over him, as if he had been plunged backward through days and weeks to when he was simply a thrall, without family or honor. This was the thing that had slain a god, and now he knew, from the blood coursing down his numbed arm, that it could kill him as well. If it caught him, it would devour him, and his power, great as it was, could not prevent it.

He looked up, the smoke so thick he could only see Karana by her light. He felt a wild hope that perhaps she might be equal to the task of destroying the beast, but he crushed that hope. This was the godslayer, so long hidden by legend. Now it was born again, and it was foolish to hope they might destroy it where the gods themselves had failed. He bared his teeth, and he swore he would fight until he was slain.

Then he saw Karana fall, plunging downward, her light growing, and he cried out in a moment of despair as the dragon reached for her.

ଔ

She hurtled downward, pushing herself as fast as she could go, flying past the jaws of Nergal as he snapped them closed just behind her. His wings battered the air as he turned, ponderous and vast. Karana skimmed past his flank, like the surface of a desolate landscape, and then she was headed for the ground below, seeing almost nothing but a blasted place of smoke and pools of fire.

The dragon's roar beat down on her as he rounded and followed her. The winds pulled her down at an almost dizzying speed, and she looked for Arthras, remembering where she had seen him last, hoping to be able to spot him through the smoke and poisonous fumes. The smell of burnt metal and sulphur was thick and made her gag as she dove for the earth. The shadow of the beast was over her, immense, the roaring so close she felt it down her back.

She saw Arthras and dove for him, changed direction hard enough to feel as if her bones were going to snap. He saw her coming, and she had a moment to appreciate his look of shock, and then she swept him up in one arm and was climbing again, higher and higher, arcing up into the sky.

One look and Nergal all but filled the sky. He beat his wings trying to follow her, but he was so huge he could not match her. She almost smiled as she held out her free hand and clenched her fist. She pulled at the air savagely, and Nergal's beating wings suddenly found nothing to beat against. Her power sucked the air from beneath his wings even as she sent a massive wave of it crashing down against him. He flailed and bellowed, but he could not stay in the sky.

Like a great hand, her power drove him into the mountainside, and the impact was so tremendous she felt it in her chest. A pillar of dust roared up where he fell, and part of the mountain broke free and slid down over him, dirt and stones cascading over his body.

"Bury him!" she all but screamed in Arthras' ear. She didn't know if he could do it from the air – she didn't have time to ask.

Arthras didn't hesitate, and he thrust out his bloody hand and she saw his power ripple over the mountain. There was a deep-throated explosion, and a piece of Mount Ara big enough to bury a city broke loose and slid down into a huge, falling wall of rock and soil.

Just before it smashed into Nergal where he struggled to right himself, she had a moment to see the silver eye, the terrible jaws, and then he breathed out another black cloud of death, and just as the hammer of the mountain crushed down on him, the boiling wall of black fire slammed into her, sending her spinning away into the burning dark. She held on grimly to Arthras, though she could no longer see him, and then she knew nothing more.

Chapter Thirty-Four

Empire of Death

Thessala hurried through the streets, Lykaon at her heels. Diomedes was leading the way, but she could see he was holding himself back so they were not left behind. He flitted through the crowds, darting easily between people in his way without disturbing them, like a fish among slower fish. Thessala was not able to do the same, and she ran with her face uncovered, the sight of it frightening people from her path. Lykaon came after, moving more steadily and taking advantage of the gap she left in her wake.

The palace loomed over her, and she was surprised to still be awed by it, even as she was consumed with worry and fear. The mountain loomed over everything, and the cloud of smoke that still flowed from it blotted out the sky. She heard the thunder of it as it cracked and boomed, and she tried not to be distracted by the sound. It could erupt like a furious god at any moment and wipe the city away, but she had to trust that it would not.

Diomedes stopped and waited for her under a high-arched gateway, looking around with a worried expression.

Thessala stopped, catching her breath even though she was not really short of it. Habits did not die easy. "Are you lost?" she said.

"No, but the guards are gone," he said. "That is strange." He shook it off. "This way."

Again she had to run to keep pace with him, as he was so effortlessly quick. He raced up a wide stair and Thessala jumped after him, landed hard on the top step and cracked the marble. She heard Lykaon huffing as he ran after them, but by then she was chasing Diomedes down another long hall, under an arch, and then out into a courtyard filled with scattered servants who looked half frightened out of their wits.

At the center of the court was a huge boulder, strangely melted and amorphous-looking, and beside it Dagon waited, his face pale and grave. At the sight of her, the servants and soldiers drew away, afraid, and she paid them no attention. She hurried to Dagon, not reassured at all by his expression. "What is it? What has happened?"

He stepped away from the stone, and she saw a human hand thrust from the side, the rock rippled as though it had formed around it. Her stomach lurched. "Gods, what. . . ?"

"I need your help," he said. "The mountain erupted, and Karana carried Arthras up onto the slopes to try and stop it, and then there was some kind of colossal struggle. This fell into the sea, and we saw the hand. Diomedes helped me, and these men -" he gestured around them. "- they helped me bring it here, because I said I could open it."

Thessala realized some of the soldiers were barbarians, and she wondered what was happening here. The reason she didn't ask was because it was plain that no one was quite sure. "You mean that's. . ."

"Karana, yes. I have tried tools and acids, but I cannot break it open. I need your strength."

Thessala swallowed hard and nodded. She touched the hand, found even it was covered in a thin shell of hardened stone. She squeezed down at it cracked, flaking away and revealing the skin beneath. Suddenly terrified, Thessala drew back her fist and smashed it against the rock, cracking it apart. Fractures raced across the glassy black surface, and then she hit it again. A crack widened, and she dug her fingers into it and *pulled.*

The stone ripped open with a dreadful sound, and she saw an arm, then she hit the rock again, dug at the cracks and pulled, tearing it open. A shoulder, then she found Karana's face, her braids all frozen in the hard obsidian. She was covered in an ashy dust, and she looked like a statue, or an effigy. Thessala wiped at her face, then turned to demolishing the rest of the stone prison.

She stopped when she found another arm, one that did not belong to Karana. She paused to give Dagon a significant look, but then she returned to her work, muscles bunching as she cracked and split and tore the rock apart until Karana lay there with Arthras, both of them dark with soot and ash, both of them naked and unmoving.

Thessala picked up Karana and carried her to the fountain that was close by. She laid her down on the tiled edge and scooped up water, splashed her and used the sleeve of her robe to clean the dirt from her face. Karana made no motion, and Thessala felt real terror as she cupped her hands and used the water to bathe her.

Karana turned over and coughed violently, twitched and then fell into the water. Dirt spread out from her like a stain, and she heaved up just as Thessala reached out and caught her, pulled her back up to the edge. She was wild-eyed and cried out, flailing, and then she seemed to realize where she was. "Nergal! Nergal!" She coughed and clutched at her throat. "Nergal."

☙

Karana clung hard to Thessala, trying to make sense of her thoughts, as the whole world seemed to be spinning around her. She remembered the black sky, and the fire, and the beast. Now she was here and she did not know where she was or how long it had been, or how she came to be here with Thessala. She saw Lykaon as well, and Diomedes, and Dagon. Dagon's pale face looked paler.

"Nergal?" he said.

"It lives," she said. "We saw it. . ." She remembered Arthras, and then she saw him lying blackened and still on the grass and staggered to her feet. "Arthras!"

Thessala tried to stop her, but Karana shrugged her off and reeled across the ground to where he lay, crushing razors of broken glass under her bare feet and not caring. She caught him and lifted him – he was heavy, but not to her – and she carried him quickly to the fountain and laid him in the water. She hoped the cold shock would awaken him, and it did.

His eyes opened, and then he tried to take a breath and coughed violently, spitting out pieces of rock. He rolled over and fought away from her in the water, pushed himself up and crouched there, leaning on his arms, gasping and coughing. He shuddered, and then vomited over the side onto the grass.

"Are you all right?" she said, putting a hand on his back.

He turned and looked back at her, nodded, then wiped at his mouth and struggled to his feet. She got up as well, and they helped one another stand. He looked around them. "Where is this?"

"The palace," Dagon said. "It took us all night to bring you here. It is morning."

"The beast," Arthras said. "Where is it?"

"Nergal," Karana said.

"It can't be," Dagon said. "That was so long ago. . ." his voice trailed off as he realized what he was saying.

"It said its name," Karana said. "It spoke, and it spoke in a dead language. *Arallu ka ita Kigalla. Na tu Nergal.*"

Dagon face showed a flash of fear that was unnerving to see. "It spoke?"

"It rose from the fire, from the mountain, and it spoke," Karana said. "We fought it. We buried it again on the mountainside, but I don't think we killed it."

"I know we didn't," Arthras said. "It was so powerful. Nothing could kill it. Nothing."

"I have seen its blood," Karana said. "If it bleeds, it can die." She lifted her head, hearing noises from the palace around them. "What is happening?"

"What do you hear?" Thessala said, pulling off her outer robe and wrapping it around Karana's shoulders.

Lykaon sniffed the air, grunted. "I hear screams."

There was a commotion, and a slave-girl ran into the courtyard, her simple dress torn on one shoulder, her eyes wide with fear. She saw Thessala and screamed, jumped back, but Diomedes caught her and held her by the shoulders.

"What is it, girl?" Dagon said, striding forward. "What is happening?"

"The emperor!" she gasped, almost sobbing. "The emperor is dead!"

೧೮

They all hurried through the palace, Karana and Diomedes in front, Arthras right behind them in a loincloth he made from Dagon's cape. Dagon hurried behind, with Thessala and Lykaon at the rear. Diomedes knew the way best, and Karana had to let him draw ahead whenever there was a turn and she didn't know the way.

They rounded a corner and ran head-on into a pack of imperial guards, and rather than part and let them pass they closed shoulder to shoulder and leveled their spears. "Kill them!" one of them screamed. "Kill them all!"

Karana did not even slow, and Diomedes suddenly moved much faster – almost faster than she could follow with her eyes. He was among them in a moment, drawing a sword from one of their belts, and then he passed through them like a whirlwind, striking hard at armored arms and legs, denting helmets. His flurry of blows was so fast it sounded like a handful of rocks dropped to the floor.

They were not even done falling when Karana and Arthras crushed into their ranks, dashing them aside with their bare hands, hurling them against the walls and the floor. Spearpoints snapped against Karana's skin as she crushed armor and bone with blows of her fists. She was recovering from being afraid, and now she was beginning to be angry. There was something at work here, some attempt by Zeneos to hasten his grasp for power, and it made her blood hot with anger.

Behind her Thessala dealt with any guards still standing, and behind her Lykaon took on his dark, monstrous form and trampled the fallen. They had gone through twenty guardsmen without even breaking stride, and not one of them had so much as a scratch.

At the end of the hall she saw guards at the emperor's chamber doors, but Diomedes was ahead of her, already moving too fast to see. She heard blows and the guards pitched back, bleeding and groaning. Diomedes smashed open the door just as she reached him, and they all rushed through. The outer room was empty save for what looked like the corpses of the emperor's doctors strewn in pools of blood. Diomedes flinched back with an oath, and so Karana pushed past him and wrenched the inner door from its hinges.

൵

The room was in chaos, the sheets strewn across the floor, blood smeared on the walls and staining the bed. She followed the trail of red with her gaze to the corner, where the emperor lay twisted and dead, his chest covered with blood. A stained dagger still jutted from the left side of his chest, and the expression of agony frozen on his features was hard to look at. She swallowed, feeling a stab of regret and sadness in her breast.

She turned from the body and saw the shadow of someone on the balcony, behind the curtains that blew in the morning wind. She crossed the room and ripped down the hangings, found herself face to face with Zeneos, standing as if waiting for her. His hands were red with blood, his tunic splattered, and there was red smeared across his mouth.

Karana heard the others crowding into the room behind her, heard them gasp and mutter, and then Dagon was there beside her, his hands shaking. She heard his breathing hard and harsh and knew he was angry; he seemed on the edge of flinging himself on Zeneos to hurl him off the balcony, and then the prince looked up at them and she saw his eyes were so shot through with blood they looked red, and his face was pouring with sweat. He smiled at them, baring his teeth, and she put her hand on Dagon's arm to restrain him.

"*Nam kal aku nat tellai u'a*," Zeneos said, and his voice was like a file drawn over broken glass. "It is a good morning, for death."

Dagon hissed slow through his teeth. "Is it. . . is that. . ?"

"Nergal," Karana said. "He's taken his mind."

"I can do this, to the weak, and the hungry. Those who lust for more than they can eat. Desire makes them vulnerable." The voice coming from him was so much more hideous than his own, and she saw his teeth were blackened and splitting apart.

"How long?" Karana said.

"I have been growing in his mind for many years now. Stronger and stronger, like a sting." The thing in Zeneos smiled. "But my poison burns. He will not last."

"So Attis did not kill you," Dagon said. "You have slept all this time."

"I have waited. I have waited for the star to come, and now I am alive again. You are here, and my hour has come round." It grinned with black teeth. "Your bolts cannot harm me, neither fire nor steel can shed my blood. Even now, I wake. I break free as the mountain calls out. You cannot stop me, and you cannot escape me. You will burn." The thing laughed through Zeneos' mouth, and then Arthras pushed past her, black and smoldering, and he slammed one iron fist into the creature's chest.

Bones snapped, and the remnant of Zeneos was hurled back, splintered the stone rail with his body, and plummeted down into the courtyard below. He spat after the body, then turned to face the rest of them with defiance. "I will hear no more of that."

Dagon seemed stunned, but Karana nodded. "He was not going to tell us anything of use. He was only taunting us." She shook her head. "Why?"

"He wants us to fight him," Thessala said. "Why else?"

"Why would he want us to fight him?" Karana said. She looked at Dagon, and his expression was unfocused. She reached over and shook his arm. "Dagon!"

"I. . . I don't know. He wants. . ." He covered his mouth. "He fought Attis, and he slew him. We thought Nergal was slain as well, but he only slept. He said. . ." He looked up at the smoke-covered sky. "The star. He was waiting for the star."

"The star made him?" Arthras said. "Like us?"

"No, not like you," Dagon said. "Nothing like you. Unless. . . unless he is like you."

"What do you mean?" Karana said.

Dagon looked at them all, glancing from face to face to face. "I had wondered if this had happened before, and now I am sure of it. And now I. . . I think that I know why the heroes of legend all die, or vanish into the haze of antiquity. I wondered why, if there were more like you every thousand or two thousand years, the world was not ruled by you, or those descended from you. I don't know if the power you have could be passed on to children, but now I know that it has never mattered." He shook his head. "Nergal has seen to it."

"You mean that whenever people like us are created by the star's passing, he kills them?" Karana said. "He sleeps and wakes and kills, over and over."

"I don't believe he just kills," Dagon said. "I believe he eats them."

411

Karana felt ill, and she saw an expression of horror on Diomedes' face as well as Thessala's. "Eats?"

"Yes. That is why he wants you all here. That is why he taunts you. He wants you to fight him, so he can devour you. Perhaps it sustains him, the star-stuff, the dust that gathers in your flesh and gives you your power. If he has been doing this for a long time, he would be filled with it, but perhaps it fades away, over time." Dagon scratched at his unshaven cheek. "Perhaps he, and his kind, were the first created by the star, or among the first."

"There never was a beast such as that," Karana said.

"The world was not always ruled by men," Dagon said. "In every country they find bones buried in the earth. Bones that match no living animal. On the coast of Thamyra I saw a place where the cliffs had fallen into the sea, and thus was exposed the skeleton of a great animal, preserved in the rock itself. It had a long neck and a long tail, and it walked on legs, but it was much bigger than any animal I have ever heard of, and resembled nothing that lives. Or that lives now."

He pressed a finger to his lips. "We must imagine a primordial age, not thousands of years in the past, but hundreds of thousands, even millions. An age when the world was ruled by gigantic, reptilian beasts. Perhaps they were only dumb animals, without thoughts or speech, or perhaps they had their own kind of intelligence. We cannot know the truth. But what would happen if the star appeared in their sky, and gave to some of them powers such as you possess?"

"The dragons," Karana said. "Like in the oldest legends of the Ahazunai. The dragons they worshipped as gods."

"Hungry gods, by the stories," Dagon said. He squinted up at the sky, choked by the smoke and falling ash of the mountain. "It was said that in the distant past – perhaps ten thousand years ago, perhaps longer – the dragons warred with one another, and one by one they were slain. The beings which no man could destroy were brought low by the only enemy they had to fear – each other."

"But Nergal lived," Karana said.

"And it may be that he has haunted the world ever since. When the star returns it would replenish the star-stuff within his own flesh, but perhaps he can gather more from those he devours, or his belief in his own greatness makes him unwilling to share that power." Dagon shook his head. "But through all of our history, whenever the star exalts some of humanity, Nergal comes, and destroys, and devours, and he does it so thoroughly that even his name barely survives."

Arthras growled in his throat. "He can die."

"Yes," Karana said.

"Perhaps," Dagon said.

"He was a god once, or like a god," Arthras said. "Now he hides, and sleeps. He does not conquer, he does not rule. He sleeps, and he hides. He erases all who see him from the world so none can tell of him." He clenched his fist. "That means he fears something. He fears death."

Dagon frowned. "You may... you may be right."

Karana looked down from the balcony, through the broken rail and down to where a dark smear marked the final remnant of Prince Zeneos. She saw a phalanx of guards march through the courtyard below, at double-time, and she frowned. "What is happening?"

Dagon blinked. "Zeneos set the guards on us, he might have set them on anyone. With the emperor dead and his heir slain, the city will be in chaos."

"And the dragon will come soon," Arthras said.

"One thing at a time," Karana said. "Arthras, we will need your army."

"What?" Arthras said.

"What?" Dagon said.

"What?" Thessala said, followed by a grunt from Lykaon.

"If the guards were controlled by Zeneos, then they can't be trusted. Arthras has the only army on the island, he can maintain order." She looked at him. "If you will."

"What do you mean?" Arthras said.

Karana took a long breath. "The emperor and his heir are dead, the dynasty is done and the throne is empty." She looked at Arthras. "If you will use your army to keep the peace in the city, and help us fight Nergal, then I will help you become the new emperor." She heard gasps and muttering behind her, but she did not look. She put out her hand, open, and Arthras looked at it for a long moment. She was afraid he would not take it, that he would choose anger and violence this last time. But instead he nodded, and clasped her hand in his larger one.

"As you say," he said. "I will do."

Chapter Thirty-Five

Curses of Night

They hurried to the gates of the palace, and Arthras grew more and more suspicious. There were no more guards to be found, no sign of them anywhere. They saw only the dead. What looked like servants or slaves butchered and left bleeding on the stones. All of this was infuriating, and he felt as if every decision he had made that brought him here had been planned by the beast on the mountain. Now it was leading him to make more decisions that he did not want to make. It was distracting them with all of this foolishness while it prepared to strike.

They reached the gates of the palace and looked down the mountainside into the city, and there he saw columns of smoke and he heard distant screams. He ground his teeth, was not finished snarling when Karana caught his arm.

"What is it?" she said.

"The beast. It scatters us and wastes our time. We have to be ready when it attacks." He pointed up at the smoking mountain. "We should not wait and let it choose when to face us."

"I won't let the city dissolve into chaos," she said, and he saw that same hard glint in her eye as he had seen before the gates of Orneas. He knew she would not be turned, and it was at once maddening and admirable. She seemed to fear nothing at all.

He heard a shout and turned, saw the warriors that had come to the city running quickly to join him. They were blooded, and their weapons were ready. Six of them were Emmeus' men, five of them his own Almanni.

"My king!" one of his men shouted, and he recognized Safrax. "The guards are loose on the city – they have orders to kill all they can find."

He looked them over. "How many did you slay?"

"Ten," he said. "Four more ran away to spread tales of what we did to them."

"They will be back," Karana said, and Arthras grunted. He had forgotten she spoke his tongue. He looked at her, thinking of a hundred arguments, but he voiced none of them. Perhaps she was a fool, but when he faced Nergal again, he would need her with him.

"Leave the city," he told his men. "Take horses and go swiftly to the army and call them here. We will kill the guards who oppose us and seize the city whole. I will be emperor when the day is done, or dead. Go."

He watched them go, grunted and turned back to Karana. "It will be as you say. I hope you know what you are doing."

"As do I," she said.

ঔ

Karana turned to Thessala. "The nobles will have guards to defend them, but not the people of the rest of the city. The guards may already be there, doing their work. Take Lykaon and stop them."

Thessala flinched, then nodded. "I can do that."

"I know you do not want to, but you have to. There is no one else." Karana touched her shoulder, and Thessala nodded again. She wanted to tell her she understood, but there was not time for that.

"Very well, but I will not carry a sword." She looked around, then went to a fallen guard and took the round shield from his arm, slid her own through the straps. She hefted it. "I will be a shield for the helpless today."

Karana smiled, feeling a swelling in her heart. "Go, then."

Thessala turned to Lykaon, and, with a slight hesitation, she climbed onto his back, mounting him as if he were a horse. His inhuman face could not show true expressions, but Karana thought he looked amused. Thessala locked her fingers in his mane and nodded to them all, and then Lykaon's haunches gathered and he hurled himself down the hill, leaping from street to wall to rooftop, and then he was away.

"I have to return to my house," Dagon said. "I want to see it is not destroyed, and there are things there I need."

Karana nodded. "Very well. Diomedes, go with him, then come and find us, and help."

Dagon clasped her hand. "Foolish to tell you to take care," he said. "But take care."

"I am more worried for you," she said. She watched as they left, Dagon hurrying while Diomedes held his speed down, pausing to wave back at her. Even on a day like this, he smiled.

She turned back and faced Arthras, and he looked at her, uncertain. He always looked as though he were angry, or was about to become angry. "What do we do?"

She quirked a smile at him. "Either one of us could purge the guards from the city with an act of will, but not without destroying it. There are not more than a few hundred guards. I was right to say the wealthy and powerful will be safer, but not safe." She sighed. "If there is to be peace on this island, in this new empire you would build, then you will need such people on your side. You and I are going to go and save their lives. We will do it with our hands, so they see us do it."

Now it was his turn to smile wryly. "You plan ahead when we might all be dead by the time the sun sets." He laughed. "You are more like Nicaea than I thought."

"Galbos' wife?" she said. "I heard she might be with you."

He spat. "He is dead. She is not his wife."

She nodded "True enough. Come," she beckoned. "It is time to be a hero."

CB

Thessala held on as Lykaon hurled them across the city. She felt the bunching of his muscles as he gathered for each leap, and then his spring carried them farther than she thought they would, every time. It was impossible not to cry out, whooping like a madwoman as they seemed to skip down the mountainside, leaving rooftops and walls cracked and crushed in their wake, for together they were of a considerable weight, and Lykaon's strength was enormous.

They headed for the smoke near the harbor, and Thessala saw crowds of people, then spears flashing in the light and she pointed. "There!" Lykaon either heard her, or saw it himself, and he turned and went that way. Leaping downhill made the height of the drop dizzying, and Thessala screamed in a mix of vertigo and excitement as they plunged down.

Lykaon slammed down on the stone of the plaza, cracking it with the force of the impact. They were between a milling, frightened mob of people and a tight-ranked mass of imperial guardsmen, shoulder to shoulder as they advanced. Already bodies were strewn on the ground between the masses, blood on the stone.

The appearance of a black beast with a scaled woman on his back sent both sides reeling back. Thessala took advantage of that fear, leaped down from Lykaon's back, and charged full into the ranks of the guards with her shield braced in front of her. They tried to be ready for her, but her strength was too much for them. Shields collided with a terrible sound, and she smashed through their lines, knocking them down. Spears and swords lashed at her, and she grunted and shrugged off their blows. She held her shield with both hands and swung it like a blade, smashing men down to the left and right.

They might have held their nerve, but a moment later Lykaon hurtled upon them like a demon, howling a roar that shook them to their bones. His claws and teeth made ruin among them, and his lashing tail battered down any who tried to get around him.

They broke, and Thessala seemed to feel it, like a knot undone and then they gave back and scattered from her, throwing down spears and shields as they ran. She chased down the slow ones and hit them from behind, using her shield to dash them off their feet and leave them groaning at her feet.

She stopped and breathed, tasting the bitter venom at the back of her throat again, the thrumming urge to violence in her arms. It took her a moment to calm it, to gather her wits and not give herself over to the aggression her new self seemed to long for. If it was ordained that she be a warrior, well, she would not be a mindless one.

Lykaon sniffed her, then rubbed his head against her in such an animal gesture that she laughed, rubbed his head through his heavy fur. She climbed on his back again, and then she heard voices lifted up. She looked and saw the crowd they had defended, and the people were shouting, hands over their heads, pointing and. . . and they were cheering.

It took her a moment to realize they were not screaming curses, or in fear. They had been saved from death and they realized it, shouting and cheering at her. On impulse she thrust her battered shield over her head, the thin sunlight glinting from the bronze, and they cheered louder, jumping up and down, lifting children on their shoulders. Thessala was stunned for a moment, and then Lykaon tossed his head, and she laughed. She had helped people all her adult life, but no one had ever cheered for her before.

Reluctant, she turned away, and Lykaon leaped to another rooftop as she held on, searching for another formation of guards to fall upon. She firmed her grip on her shield and set her jaw. Zeneos, or the demon inside him, wanted a bloodbath in the city. He would not have it today.

☙

This was not the city Arthras had imagined. It was beautiful, yes. He had never seen a city like this, never thought one could exist. Even under ash and beneath a sky full of smoke and fire, it was like a dream. An image in his mind of what the imperial city should be, made real. And yet it was nothing like he had imagined. Not here.

He had always envisioned streets filled by rank after rank of soldiers, all of them armed with steel and deathlessly loyal to the emperor. Legions as of old, ready to march and to die at a command. He saw in his mind the lords of the city as more than mortal men. Tall and bearded and wise-eyed, always with their thoughts upon the greatness of the empire itself.

Now he found it was nothing like that at all. Now he made his way through a series of opulent villas surrounded by elegant gardens, and he found the iron lords of empire huddled inside behind pale-faced bodyguards who were little more than boys in fancy armor. The men he had thought to find as the legions of steel were roving bands of killers sent to slaughter in the name of a madman. They killed any they found, and as the wealthy were hidden inside behind their paid guards, they killed mostly helpless slaves. He saw the bodies in the streets.

They landed in a garden, sending up a great cloud of dust, and he did not wait to push his way through toward the sounds of fighting. He knew Karana did not savor violence, while he found otherwise. With the ashes in the air, he could not see the attackers until he was on them. Dusty helms and cloaks seemed to emerge from the gloom as though they were disembodied. He saw the flash of gray light on swords and he smelled blood.

He fell on them like the stroke of a hammer. His fists crashed against armor and crumpled it, sent men screaming to the ground. They turned on him, a blur of faces and shouts, and he shrugged off their feeble blows and smashed them down with his hands, until a dozen men lay bleeding on the stones. The house guards looked at him with their faces pallid with fear, and behind them, huddled like refugees, he saw well fed men and women who could only be the lords of the city.

He looked at them, unmoving. Karana came up beside him, and a gust of wind drew away the ash and left the air clear for a precious few breaths. "You live," he said to the ones watching him. "Remember why."

He turned away. He had nothing else to say to such people as this. Karana followed him, seeming to be amused. "You speak to the lords of empire as though they were children," she said.

"They allowed this to happen, to be made so helpless. Perhaps they deserve death," he said.

"And their slaves, and their wives and children, do they deserve death as well?" she said.

He grunted. She always had something to say, and it always made sense, and it annoyed him. "It's done, let us go on," he said.

"Indeed," she said. "Let us go on."

ଔ

It had been a long day, and because the sky was covered in smoke, and the air filled with falling ash, it was hard to keep a sense of the time. Karana and Arthras had been all across the upper sweep of the city, breaking up small attacks by squads of guards, and she was tired. Though her body could not feel real fatigue, her mind felt it. Rather, it seemed that her mind knew when her body ought to feel it, like a phantom pain.

Dagon's house was mostly dark, with only a few lanterns burning here and there. Karana approached it carefully, wondering if everything was well. Arthras came behind her, quiet. Before she could touch the door, Diomedes flung it open and smiled at her. "Good! I was hoping you would come." He stood aside to let them in, and Karana was glad to get in out of the night, away from the constant fall of ash that covered her hair and her shoulders. Glad to no longer be alone with Arthras, this man she did not know and did not trust.

"Dagon is upstairs," Diomedes said. "He wanted to see you."

"Very well," she said, sounding tired even to herself. She brushed ash from herself as she crossed the front hall, and then she went up the steps. She knew she should say something to Arthras, to Diomedes, but she was too weary in her mind. In that moment she missed physical exhaustion, wishing she had the excuse to go and sleep and forget for a while. She just didn't want to face what was coming, not now.

She went to the room Dagon used for his workshop, knowing she would find him there. He was bent over something in the lamplight, and he looked up with his odd eyes when she entered. He did not look very pleased, and he cast down his pen almost resentfully. "You fight him, and fight him, and now you offer the barbarian the throne?" he said.

"What would you have me do?" she said wearily. "We need his help, his men, his power. I cannot fight both Arthras and Nergal. The emperor is dead, his son is dead. What else is there?"

"I simply. . ." He shook his head, scratched his cheek. "I don't approve."

"Neither do I," she said. "But the empire – if there is to be one – will need stability. If we left it to the noble houses to choose, what would happen? How quickly would assassination and civil war flame up?"

He sighed. "No, no, you are right."

"You think I am glad of it? That after the loss of lives that has led here, that he will still get what he wanted? I am not pleased by that. But if I cannot stop him, then I must do my best to control him. He is not. . . not an evil man. He is just a boy. Uneducated, young, ignorant of the history of the wider world. Perhaps he could even be a good ruler, but he will need guidance. You and I can provide that, or we can leave the empire to his mercies." She leaned on the table. "You of all the people in this city should understand that ruling means compromise – often a compromise you did not want to make."

Dagon's mouth thinned to a line, and then he nodded. "I know it. Now I see how rulers of past ages could have been so willfully blind to it. It is bitter medicine." He looked at her. "You constantly surprise me."

"I have studied enough history to wish to avoid repeating the same errors made by others. And yet I have made more than enough." She scowled, bitter in her mind. "Arthras will make for a ruler who cannot be assassinated or deposed. And even if I wished to keep him from the throne, how could I? We destroyed one city already when I disputed him. I will not destroy another."

"It may be destroyed regardless," he said. "Nergal will come soon, and then you will all have to fight."

"We will," she said. "All of us."

"I have something for you, for that," he said. He stood and drew back the oiled cloth that lay across the table, and there in the lamplight was a long, straight sword. It gleamed darkly, the steel rippled with subtle patterns that coiled and spiraled around themselves.

Karana made a scoffing sound. "I have scarcely even touched a sword in my entire life," she said. "I am not a warrior. Give that to Arthras, or even Thessala, not me."

"This sword," he said, lifting it, "was forged of metals treated with alchemical substances, heated by lightning and tempered to be harder than any sword ever made." He presented it, to her, the light sliding over the blade. "It will not break, not even under the strength of your arms. I give it to you because you are not a warrior."

"That makes almost no sense at all," she said.

"It does," he said. "Warriors fight, that is what they do. They have skill. But skill will not matter so much in this battle. Nergal is not going to duel against you, blade to blade. If this sword will pierce his armor, then you are the one best able to reach him and find out. You can fly." He smiled. "And it is an ordinary day when warriors make war. But when one like you takes up a sword, that is a thing to fear. You will not fight for fun, or for glory, or for a love of battle. You will fight to win." He held the sword out to her, and she looked at it as though it were a serpent that might turn and bite her hand if she touched it. Slowly, she reached out, and took it.

Chapter Thirty-Six

Night Of Ages

It was so dark. The clouds of smoke still lay over the sky, and so there was no starlight, no moon, only the light of lanterns and the dim red glow on the mountainside. Karana looked up from the balcony, straining her eyes, but she saw nothing. If the dragon came now, they would never know until he was on them. "Why do you suppose he waits?" she said.

Dagon moved behind her in the darkness, came out into the night with a lamp in his hand, set it down on the stone parapet carefully. "You said you buried him in the mountainside. Perhaps he has to dig himself free." He paused for a moment. "You could always go and see."

"I should," she said. "We should all go up the mountain and fight him there, away from the city." She knotted the hem of her skirt in her hand. "I suppose I am afraid."

"Only reasonable to be afraid," he said. "I would not be able to face such a thing with equanimity." He peered up into the dark. "Though I confess I am torn, as I would very much like to see him."

"Nergal?" she said.

"Yes. As a lover of antiquities, how could I not be fascinated? A being so old. I think of the things it could tell us, the history is has witnessed. I wish there was a way to speak with it," he said.

"There was. But it did not seem interested in sharing details," she said. She remembered the shaking, bloodshot eyes of the prince and flinched from the thought of it. It did not do to dwell on what the beast had proven capable of. It only made her wonder what other powers it might have that it had not yet revealed.

"Well, that is what I mean. I wish not only that it could speak with us, but that it was willing to. Think what we could learn from a being like that. The last of the dragons." Dagon sighed. "I sound foolish, I know. I was fascinated with them when I was younger. I read every legend I could find about the great ones. Nergal, Anu, Enki, Ereshkigal."

"Dagon," she said.

"Yes, well. I chose the name when I was younger, and the dragon who ruled over knowledge and mysteries seemed appropriate." He snorted. "I never thought I would meet his brother."

Karana leaned against the stone, smelling ash on the night air, feeling it like fine dust on the balustrade. "I wonder if any of us will live to see the sun rise again."

"Attis fought the beast," he said. "He failed, but he was alone. You are not alone. Allies may make all the difference." He put his hand on her arm. "They will all be afraid. You should speak to them. They will need you."

"Me?" she said with a gentle laugh. "I am not their captain, not a queen nor a goddess."

"No," Dagon said. "But you are their friend."

☙

She almost collided with Diomedes on the stairs. It was too dark to see well, and she stepped back as he muttered something. "I'm sorry, I didn't see you," she said.

"It's all right," he said. "Can't see much of anything in all this," he said. "And the air tastes terrible." He moved closer, so they stood to either side of the one lantern, so they could see one another. "It will be a year before the ash is all cleaned away."

"How do you know?" she said.

"Oh it did this before, when I was young. It's actually done this a few times, but none this bad." He fidgeted. "But I remember the bad one when I was perhaps ten years old. There was ash all over, and when it stopped falling, it lay there, everywhere. I saw people sweeping it up, shoveling it away. It's not like wood ash, you can't even use it for anything. It's just a mess. It was a year before it was all gone. I remember when it rained, the streets ran black, and you could smell it."

There was a long quiet, and then he looked at her, almost shy. "You saw him?"

Karana hesitated. "You mean the dragon? Yes. I am not telling stories about that. He is real."

"The same one who fought Attis?" he said. "Truly?"

She nodded. "I think so. Or Dagon thinks so, and I believe he is right."

Slowly, a grin spread across Diomedes' face. "What a fantastic chance," he said, leaning closer, as though they were conspirators. "What a day to be a hero."

Karana almost laughed. "Is that what we are? I would not be so sure of it."

"If we are not gods, then we are certainly heroes," Diomedes said. "No less than that."

"You don't think we're gods?" she said, amused.

"Well, you may be," he said. "But me? I can do things no one else can do, but I don't feel any different inside." He lowered his voice a bit. "I think if I were a god, I would feel different. I think I would know." He hesitated. "Don't you think? I think I would know. Wouldn't I? Do you think we're gods?"

"I am wondering if there have been any gods at all," Karana said. "Perhaps there have only been people like us. People who were given more power than anyone should have, and then everyone decided they had been gods when they were gone."

"Well, that's not so bad," Diomedes said. "People want to call me a god, they can do that. I won't mind. I can be a better god, really, than other gods. I'll tell people who follow me to be good to each other and make more jokes." He grinned. "And on my holy days it will be all right to steal things. You still have to run away and escape, but if you get caught you just have to give it back, you don't get beaten. None of that."

Karana could not help but laugh a little bit. "None of that."

༄

She found Thessala emerging from the bathing pool in the garden. The water was still hot, fed by the underground springs, but by the light of the single lantern the sight of her was far more mysterious and almost menacing. The light of the small flame glinted on her scales as water sluiced off her body, and when she stepped out into the air she heard Karana and turned to look at her. Her eyes caught the light and gave it back yellow and metallic. The eyes of a beast.

"I can't get clean," Thessala said in her flowing, melodious voice. "I wash, and then the ash falls on me again." She looked around. "Has something happened?"

"Not yet," Karana said. "Or, nothing new. Arthras' army has arrived in the city. He is off seeing to it even now. I have to hope they will keep order, and that we have not simply brought them here to die."

"The dragon," Thessala said. She wrapped her robe around herself and sat down on an ancient bench, brushed her heavy braid back from her face. She toyed with it, wringing water from it between her fingers. "How did we come to this? I tended a little garden, in a little sanctuary where I tried to help the poor and those disabled by defect or by illness. I don't even know what happened to any of them." Her voice grew rough. "I promised I would protect them, and then I fled." She looked at Karana with her inhuman eyes. "I will not flee again."

"No," Karana said. Dagon might jest about it, but there could be no retreat from this place, not for her. She wondered if Attis had made the same choice, one ill-fated day long ago. "No, I drew a line here."

"We drew a line before," Thessala said. "We could not stop Arthras, not without destroying the city."

"Arthras is with us now. He will fight with us, not against us," Karana said.

"He nearly killed me," Thessala said. "I will not trust him as you seem to."

"I do not trust him, but I understand him," Karana said. "He is like us. He was given his power and no one told him what he should do with it. No one told him what he was capable of. He did not mean to do what he did at Orneas any more than I did. He didn't know, as I did not. His power got away from him, and so did mine. We proved the futility of fighting one another. We will not do it again."

"I don't like the thought of him on the throne," Thessala said. "It would be better if it were you."

Karana laughed at that. "Me? Well. That is a thought. But there is one thing about Arthras that makes him a better choice."

"What would that be?" Thessala said.

"He wants it," Karana said. "I made a promise to the old emperor, to care for the empire, and help rebuild it without war and bloodshed. That promise I will keep. But I will not warm a cold stone seat with my backside and give myself titles." She sighed and sat down beside Thessala. "Imagine a scribe as an empress."

"Better a scribe than a barbarian," Thessala said.

"No, a scribe might make a decent ruler, but I would never be happy to be that. Let Arthras have his throne and his fine clothes and feasts and concubines. I will have as much power. I will keep the fields green and turn aside the great sea storms. He will listen to me, because he must. He will be an emperor, but I will be more than that." Karana looked up, wishing she could see even a single star.

"You said you were not a goddess," Thessala said, amused.

"I am not," Karana said. "But that is today."

ॐ

Thessala returned to her rooms and found Lykaon there. He was on the bed on his belly, head hanging off the side along with one arm. He was playing with something on the floor. A closer look and she saw it was a beetle. The darkness did not bother her very much; she could see just as well, and she knew he could too. He nudged the small insect this way, then headed it off when it scuttled away.

"Let it go," she said. "It's lucky to even be alive tonight."

"As are we all," he said. He let the beetle crawl up onto his hand, turned his fingers to keep it from running off as it hurried along. "I was just looking at it, thinking about how large we are to it. To a beetle or an ant, we are like that beast out there."

"Larger?" she said. She came and sat down. If he was feeling talkative, she wanted to listen.

"We are like gods to them," he said. "We are vast, and slow, and we live a thousand of their lifetimes. We do things they can't understand. We are like gods."

"Strange they don't worship us," she said, half-joking.

"Proves they have more sense than men," he said. He let the beetle skitter away, rolled onto his back and looked at her. "We'll die tonight," he said.

She wanted to argue with him, but she didn't. "Maybe."

"Why else are we all here, waiting?" he said. "We know we can't win a fight, we can't escape, so we hesitate."

"Maybe," she said again, wishing she had something better.

"We need a moment," he said. "To savor, to regret."

She caught his hand. "I don't regret."

"I do," he said. "I regret a lot of things. If you say you don't, you're a damned liar."

"Well," she said. "Yes, but not you. I don't regret that."

"Maybe you would, if you had time," he said.

"We'll have the time," she said. "I'm not going to die easily."

"No," he said. "Nor will I. Man like me would never get a better death than this." He squeezed her hand. "I hope they remember us."

She wanted to say something. Words that would heal the wound in the world, bridge the gap between now and a tomorrow that seemed unreachable. Instead she only squeezed his hand in turn. "I hope so too."

◌

Arthras returned, not knowing how late it was, nor how near the dawn. Emmeus was in control of the army now, moving them into key places in the city he seemed to know, and Arthras would not be able to help him in any way. Nicaea was ebullient, glad of her future as an empress. He found he did not want to be in her company. In this moment, he wanted the company of the others like him, and so he returned to the villa and he found Karana waiting for him in the front garden, a pair of lamps illuminating her.

She looked weary, and her hair was dusted with fallen ash, so he knew she had been here for some time. He saw her and slowed, somewhat embarrassed to have her see him return, and from the fact that she had obviously expected him to. It annoyed him that she knew him this well. He felt the book he had tucked under his tunic, touched it, then took his hand away.

"I hoped you would return before morning," she said. "I am glad you did."

"You are quick to forgive our former enmity," he said. "We fought to the death twice before."

"And yet we are alive," she said. "I think perhaps neither of us is fated to kill the other."

"Fate," he said. "The will of gods you believe were false."

"I never really believed in gods," she said. "I find that the idea that they were only people like myself, unsure and afraid, struggling to control and master powers they never asked for. . . I find that thought comforting."

He snorted. "What good are gods who do not watch over us? They are there to guide us and judge us and protect us. A dead god is the same as a dead man – useless." He was angry again, groped at the air as if he could catch the words he wanted. "If there are no gods, then prayers are simply cast into the dark, and no one hears them."

Karana stood up, brushing ash from her skirts. "No one yet knows what happens when we die. If we believe that the spirits of the dead still exist, then those of the gods do as well. They watch us, but perhaps they cannot help. Perhaps they only hope we will fulfill what we are given."

"And what good is that?" he said. "I believed that I was chosen."

"We are chosen," she said. "But we do not know by what." She looked up at the mountain, the red glow on the underside of the smoke. "Now we will face one who has devoured so many of us. Now we will be tested, but not by gods."

"If I am emperor, and have the powers of a god, and there are no gods, then there is no one to call on," he said, and the thought left him feeling empty.

"You are not abandoned," she said. "You are free. We all have a freedom so very few have been given. We can remake the world, if we wish. I think of us, striving against one another, accomplishing nothing but destruction, and then I think of what Dagon said of the dragons. They were so powerful that nothing could destroy them, except each other." She looked at him. "We can fight each other, and we will end like him." She pointed up at the mountain. "One of us will survive only to plague the world. Or we can stand together, and then nothing is beyond our grasp."

"I. . ." He opened his mouth and then closed it. He wanted to say so many things but he did not have the words for it. Instead he reached into his tunic and drew out the book. He thrust it at her, as if it were something accursed. "I saved this."

She took it with a startled expression, bent down to squint at it in the dim light. "Is this from the Archive?"

"Yes," he said. "I saved it. I wanted to know why you would fight for books. I still do." He groped for what to say. "Because you are wise, and strong, and you have courage no man could doubt. I thought you were a foolish girl then, but. . . if you were willing to stand and fight and die for books, then they must be worth something."

She opened the book and touched the paper. "I thought the books were all gone. Thank you for this." She looked at him. "You can't read it, can you?"

He shook his head, feeling annoyed. "No."

"Well, if we live through this day, I will teach you," she said. "It will not do to have an emperor who cannot read. I will not have it."

He laughed at that. The way she said things, as if she would brook no argument, and he knew she really would not. "If we survive. You think we can?"

"You are the warrior," she said. "I am only a librarian."

"I was not much of a warrior before I became invincible," he said, looking at his hands. "I had courage, not skill."

"We have all become something we never thought to be," she said.

The ground shuddered, and they both looked up at the mountain, hearing the rumble as it passed over them. Fire blossomed on the high mountainside, a splash of red and yellow, a geyser of molten stone that began to flow like blood through delicate veins.

"He wakes," Arthras said. He felt cold in the pit of his belly. The wounds on his chest were already healed, and his arm was whole again, but he felt the hurts still, a phantom pain.

"Then it's time," Karana said. She went inside, and he followed her.

༄

They gathered in the dark, there in the hall at the foot of the stairs. Karana looked around at them: Thessala's eyes glittering in the lamplight, Lykaon lurking behind her as almost a shadow, Diomedes looking eager and all but bouncing in place. Arthras stood beside her, silent, and Dagon stood on the steps above them, looking down.

The earth shook, and Karana took a lamp from its hook and put it on the floor between them, so she could see all their faces. "Nergal wakes," she said. "He's freed himself, or roused himself. He is coming, and we have to fight. There's no escape, no way to run. If he wins, we die, the city dies, everyone dies. We could have gotten some people out of the city, but Zeneos' coup made sure there was no time for that. Now is what we have, and it is all down to us. We have to fight, because we're the only ones who can."

She looked around at them. Afraid, nervous, excited, grave. She nodded. "Does anyone have anything they want to say?"

No one spoke; they looked at one another, and the house shivered as another tremor passed through the earth under their feet. Karana nodded again. "I am proud to be with you today. Come." She turned and went out the door into the night, and they followed her.

Chapter Thirty-Seven

WAR IN HEAVEN

Karana felt the earth shudder as she walked out into the garden and looked up at the mountainside. Already the lava was flowing, bright against the darkness. She thought it was still night, but it was hard to be sure. The sky was dark regardless of stars or moon, and the wind itself was hot and laden with ashes. There would be no chill at this dawn.

"He is coming, and he will come for us," Karana said. "I do not know if he can sense us, or if he will simply attack to draw us out. Either way, we must meet him. He can fly, and I am the only one of us that can match him, so it will be my task to bring him down to you, where we can meet him as one. We must fight together, or we will surely die."

She turned and Diomedes was there, looking very young and very excited, though underneath she could see he was afraid. He held out the sword Dagon had made for her, and she took it gingerly. It was a long sword, meant for both hands. It was so well balanced it felt alive in her grip, and with her strength it was easy to wield it. She wondered about a sheath for it, but then she shook that thought away.

No clothes, no leather, would survive the fires of Nergal. If they survived this war, they would emerge from it as naked as newborns.

Karana looked up the mountainside. "There, the ridge above the palace. I will try to bring him to ground there – be ready to strike. You will need all your strength, all your power." She looked at Thessala, at Lykaon. "He is stronger than you imagine. No matter how much you imagine, he is worse. Be ready."

The ground shuddered underfoot, and she fought for balance, then knew she was simply delaying what she must do, and she leaped upward. Her winds caught her and bore her up into the sky. Once she was free of the ground, she felt a tension loosen inside her. The shaking of the earth meant nothing to her up here.

She looked down at the city as it passed beneath her, and she saw so few lights. The people of Archelion knew what to do when the ground shook. They were settled in to endure, with candles snuffed so they could not start fires. She imagined them huddled in the dark, listening, not knowing what would happen. She clutched her sword tight, and she swore to herself that she would protect them. Part of her knew she would not be able to protect them all, but she would not give way. If there was to be another Orneas here, she resolved she would not survive it.

A geyser of red erupted on the mountain, and she rose higher, and higher. From the air, the mountain was a landscape from the imaginings of the damned, where rivers of fire coursed between shores of blackened rock, while the air streamed with smoke and poisoned fumes. She heard then the roar of the dragon, and she watched as he rose from the darkness.

The great wings spread wide, shimmering with reflected fire, and then she saw the silver eyes glowing like stars. Nergal roared again, and the vast wings drew up and then stroked down with such terrible power that the sea of lava was flung outward in a wave that lashed over rocks and flew in whorls through the air. He bellowed as he rose into the sky, ponderous and terrible and magnificent. The upstrokes of his wings drew fire coursing up around him, and then he emerged from the pillar of fire, black and gleaming.

He roared again, and Karana screamed out in answer. She thrust her sword up to the sky, and lightning stabbed down from the smoke overhead and danced along the steel, limned her body and set her clothes to aflame. She felt the fire crawl over her skin, saw violet tongues of electric power crack at the ends of her fingers.

Nergal looked up at her, and he roared again, and she felt the heat of it even though he was not close. She pointed her hand at him, and lightning exploded across the dark sky to smash into him. He bellowed again, opened his jaws, and he breathed out another cloud of roiling black death, a flow of superheated destruction that came for her like a storm.

Karana clawed at the air, and she brought a great wave of her power smashing in to meet it. The death cloud struck an invisible barrier, and there was a cry of thunder as the air was heated until it glowed. The cloud spread out, and then arced away, falling toward the earth below, dissipating in the air. Karana laughed and hurled another stroke of lightning, and then Nergal exploded through the smoke and came for her.

She dove, glowing as she hurtled downward through layers of smoke toward the palace below. From so high it was hard to tell exactly where she was, and she fought to see the ridge she had chosen as the place for battle. When she glanced back, expecting to see Nergal fast behind her, she saw he was curving to follow. She had not realized how slow he was to turn. He dropped lower and lower, and then his wings snapped open and he swept in low over the rooftops of the city. The wind of his passage ripped off roof tiles and dragged down walls.

He was low, and then he beat his wings and rose higher as he came for her. When he passed over the palace he smashed through two towers without slowing or seeming to notice, sending cascades of masonry tumbling down to raise pillars of dust. He was closer now, and she saw his mouth open, saw the inferno glowing in his throat.

She flew higher, trying to draw him up, but he was too close. He was faster than she expected, once he was moving. He breathed out a cloud of destruction, and she pulled in the wind to try and shield herself, but she didn't have enough time.

The burning cloud slammed into her, and her power only blunted it, did not stop it. She tumbled through the air and crashed hard into a wall, through it, stone splinters falling all around her, and then she was buried.

ଔ

Arthras felt the dragon come to earth, the shaking of the ground as it came down, the wind lashing with its wings. He ran, leaping over lesser obstacles and crashing through what he could not jump. He let his power loose within him, and his skin turned black as night. He felt the heat inside him, blazing up from whatever source it was born, and it suffused him. He left cracked and blackened footprints on the polished stone as he ran toward the battle.

He saw great towers falling, stone breaking and sliding down into ruin, dust billowing up into pillars that reached to the blackened sky. And then he saw the great tail crash through a wall, scaled and slow and majestic, and he was there. There was fear in him and he shoved it aside. He remembered that he was Almanni, that he was the son of a thousand years of warriors, and from this battle he would not shy.

He leaped to the pile of rubble, and then he plunged into it, the stone melting around him, forming the armor he had come to know. He burst free, wiped molten fire from his eyes, and then the dragon was there, looming before him. He saw the massive head, one claw raised to dig at the ruined tower. He saw the jaws drooling slaver that smoked on the stone, and he saw the silver eye shift to look at him.

Arthras leaped, caught one jutting horn, and smashed his fist into the heavy skull just behind that eye. The hardened lava fractured off him from the impact, and Nergal roared. It tossed its great head, and Arthras found himself flung away. He hit the ground, bounced, and then hit a wall and went through it.

Nergal bellowed, and then a black hell of boiling smoke and fire roared from its jaws and smashed aside walls and stones and split the earth with its heat. Arthras did not feel the fire, but the force of it knocked him down and buried him in stone ruin. It began to melt around him, and he sent vibrations through it, trying to make it shake itself off him, and he had the gleam of an idea.

☙

Thessala clung to Lykaon's back as they raced for the place of the battle. It was easy to see the rising dust and hear the tearing roars and the crushing sound as the palace was destroyed. She set her teeth, every skein of her body eager to be set loose. She envisioned Karana already dead or hurt and she almost spat poison with her need to get there and strike.

There was a blur on her right, and she looked down and saw Diomedes there, moving faster than even Lykaon could. He had a sword and a shield, and he saluted and then raced ahead of them. Thessala bellowed with frustration, and then they were in the cloud of dust, Lykaon moving swift among the fallen stones, and the dragon loomed over them, majestic and terrifying.

Thessala stared at it, her mind almost refusing to believe the sheer size of the beast. It was too big for her to really grasp, too big for her to even see it all at once, especially in this dust and smoke. The air was filled with floating embers and the dragon was like a part of the mountain come to life, black and jagged and glossy as obsidian.

It was so enormous, she did not really know how she was supposed to fight it. Lykaon did not hesitate, and he leaped for the long neck, digging his claws into the scales when he struck. Thessala almost lost her grip, then saw the beast round on them, one silver eye gleaming in the dark, and she pushed off Lykaon's back and leaped for the head. Her strength carried her across and she landed hard on the jagged skull, dug her hands in for purchase.

Nergal bellowed and tossed its immense head, and the motion almost shook her loose, but she clung. She lifted one hand and smashed her fist down on the plated armor, and again. Scales cracked and fell away, and the beast roared again. It bent down and brought up one huge leg to paw at her, claws as long as her body raking over the scales.

Thessala slid out of the way, almost lost her grip, and then she found herself hanging in front of that immense eye.

It was so smooth and gleaming that she saw herself reflected in it, as in the very finest mirror. She heard the demon draw in a heavy breath, and then she did the same, felt the acrid burn in the back of her throat, and she spat out a cloud of her venom straight into that flawless silver sphere.

ೞ

Karana fought her way out of the rubble, shoving the heavy stones aside with brute force. She heard roaring, and she knew the beast was close. In her mind she already felt Nergal's jaws on her flesh. She used her sword as a lever and found the treated steel easily returned to true no matter how she bent it. It was indeed a fit weapon, and she intended to use it.

She burst from the pile of ruin, spitting out rock and ash, and she found herself in the shadow of the monster. Great wings beat, stirring the dust and rubble into a storm that pelted her with stones that would have crushed the skull of an ordinary woman. She looked up, and she saw something black clinging to the dragon's neck, saw it raking with claws and teeth, and she realized it was Lykaon, trying to tear through Nergal's armored hide.

They were on the grounds of the palace, and every motion of the great beast wrought destruction. This was not what she had wanted, but the battle was here, so they had to fight it here. She saw a flicker and blinked, saw it was Diomedes racing in among the dragon's legs, striking with his sword so fast she could barely see it.

Even as she looked, the beast tossed hiss great head and hurled something aside. She saw Thessala slam down into the wreckage, and she saw a cloud of hissing steam boiling from one of Nergal's terrible eyes. The dragon roared loud enough to shake stones into the air, and then he rose up on his back legs, wings beating. He caught Lykaon in one claw and ripped him from his neck, then hurled him down to the earth and bent down, jaws wide.

Thessala raced in, screaming, and she caught those massive jaws as they were ready to close on her lover. She set her hands on the upper and one foot on the lower, and Karana stared as her muscles bunched and writhed, and she held that unimaginable power at bay.

Karana saw her chance to strike. Wind coiled around her, lashing the dust into a spiral, and then she burst into the air on a shockwave of power. Thunder tolled in the sky above as she arrowed for Nergal's neck, and with both hands on her sword she plunged it into his flesh. The steel bowed in her grip like a reed, and for a moment she was certain it would break, but then the keen point bit true and stabbed in, and she drew it out in a gush of silver blood.

It splashed her arms and she cried out, feeling the molten heat. She felt it on her face and it burned. She screamed as Nergal roared, and then he vomited forth a cloud of death that spread like the blow of a hammer.

The impact drove her back, and she lost her grip on her blade, tumbled through the burning dark and hit hard. She heard the beat of wings and could not tell up from down, could not see from her left eye. Her hands burned and she tasted blood.

૩

When Nergal reared back and roared, he threw Thessala from his mouth and hurled her to the ground. The sudden blast of fire and black smoke sent her flying and smashed her into a wall, and she was blinded, unable to see anything. She felt her fury inside like an animal on a rope, tangled and held and restrained, and now it was breaking loose. Ever since her transformation she had felt the chained rage down inside, the terrible urge to violence, and always she had managed to control it, but now she was losing her grip on it.

A great claw slammed down beside her, talons raking, and she caught it, digging her fingers into the scaled plates until they cracked and buckled under her grip. Before Nergal could draw it away, she twisted, lifted, and wrenched the foot in her grip until the bones gave, and the dragon screamed.

It shook her loose and she fell, smashed to earth, but then she was up and her mouth filled with venom. Now her rage would serve her. It beckoned, promising strength beyond strength if only she would give full vent, and so she would. Now she would wield her wrath like a sword against her enemy. She would protect those she loved and called her kindred, and those who cowered in the dark, afraid. Power sang along her arms and legs, the skeins standing up, and when she looked she saw the head of the beast as it hunted through the smoke for her, teeth bared and one silver eye turned dark.

She leaped on it, and she struck at its head with terrible, hammering blows of her fists. She saw the black scales shatter and break under her strength, and when it shook her off she caught one of the long, tusk-like teeth and ripped it loose, fell in a shower of broken pieces and silver blood that smoked upon the earth where it fell.

A clawed foot smashed down on top of her, pinning her to the ground, and one long pointed talon stabbed into her thigh. Blood gushed out and she screamed, filled with a new fury. She put her hands on the palm of that dragon hand and strained upward, trying to force it back. Her fingers tore through the skin, silver blood flowed, and she breathed her venom into the wound.

Nergal drew back its foot, roaring, and Thessala fell with her hands burning from the silver ichor. She saw the beast above her, a shadow of terror in the smoke and ashes, and it came down, jaws wide to devour. She struggled up, but she would not be able to get out of the way. Her wounded leg brought her down, and she howled in defiant terror as the teeth of the dragon came for her.

Then a hand caught her arm and she was ripped off her feet, the world a blur as Nergal snapped its jaws and crushed a mouthful of earth and stone. Thessala fell hard and saw Diomedes there, looking into her face. He started to speak, but then Nergal spat out ruins and howled for blood, and turned their way.

Then there was a tremendous eruption of stone, and one of the heaps of rubble began to move. It shuddered, and roiled, and Thessala saw the glow coming from within it, as if it were red hot inside. It rose, becoming the shape of a man fashioned from melting rock, only it was a giant, many times taller than any human, and she realized it was Arthras.

༺ ༻

Arthras could not see, because he was embedded in a suit of molten armor as tall as a tower, but he could feel the tremors in the earth made by Nergal's massive footfalls, and he would have to do what he could with that to follow. He felt the shudder as the beast turned to face him, and he attacked.

He felt his own footfalls like thunder, felt stone crushing and melting under him, and then he swung out a great hand and struck. Nergal was so immense he could hardly miss, and he grabbed hold and wrestled with the beast, trying to pull it off its feet. He felt it struggle, heard the bellows of rage. Claws tore at his stone body, cracking the surface and letting the molten rock flow like blood.

Arthras held on and struck at the dragon with his fist, again and again, driving it to the ground. Wings battered at him, the tail lashed like a thunderbolt, and he struggled to keep control of his creation. Holding this much stone in place required enormous concentration, and he could do almost nothing else while he maintained it. He struck again and again, felt for the great throat so he could try to crush it.

He felt an exultation inside him, for this was truly a battle of the ages. Here he grappled with a demon from ancient days with an empire as the prize, and he knew that he would never again fight such a battle, never again feel such clarity of purpose, survival and desire melded into a single moment.

Then the huge jaws closed on his middle, and he felt the stone around his body break and flow away as it was crushed. He tried to keep hold of his concentration, but then he felt the teeth, and it broke, the giant collapsing and falling away. He flowed down in a gout of lava and lay gasping on the earth, blinking, trying to wipe the stuff from his face.

Above him, Nergal shook the remnants of the giant from its jaws and turned down to face him, fixed him with one silver eye. Arthras struggled to his feet and loosed his power, shook the earth under him, cracking the stone and bringing more of the palace down around them all, but

Nergal was so immense he could not be knocked down, not by tremors beneath his feet.

He slapped at Arthras with one claw and dashed him to the ground, half-buried in the stone. Arthras struggled free and felt blood running from fresh claw marks. He looked up and saw the beast's jaws coming for him, and he screamed out in fury and rage. A last defiance.

ଓ

Karana struggled up, spitting blood and half blind. She saw the stone giant torn apart, saw Arthras on the ground. The dragon lunged for him, and she was too far away. There was a flash like something half-seen, and then Diomedes was there, knocking Arthras out of the way with a sudden shove. He stumbled on the molten ground, and Karana had a moment to see him there, the widening of his eyes as he realized he was too slow this last time, and then Nergal's jaws closed on him, and blood splashed the stones. She saw one of his legs twitching on the ground, but the rest of him was gone, devoured.

Now she screamed, and everything broke loose inside her, and every concern or doubt or fear was washed away all at once. The sky rippled as though struck by a heavy stone, and thunder began to roar overhead. The wind rose, and it began to howl. Ash and dust rose up into the air, and coursed in a great gyre. Nergal felt it, and he turned then, looked at her with his single bright eye, and she knew he remembered the other storm-caller who had challenged him, and who had made him bleed.

She heard a croaking voice and looked down, saw Lykaon there in his human shape, covered in dirt and dust, one arm hanging twisted and useless, blood on his mouth.

In his one good hand he held her sword, straight and bright, the hilt and leather all burned away, leaving a weapon of only steel.

"Take it," he gasped, and she took it from him. It thrummed in her hand, and she realized the air was alive with storm-power, sparks already dancing on the tip of everything metallic, lightning ghosting along the blade.

She saw Nergal bend to where Arthras lay, and she called in a great fist of wind as wide as a battlefront, and it caught his vast wings and hurled him backward, howling as he rolled over through another part of the palace, burst through the outer walls, and tumbled down the slope, trailing fire and dust. She leaped into the air and followed him, streaked down without the slightest regard for her own flesh, holding back nothing.

Lightning arced down from the dark sky and seared into him, tearing pieces from the hillside as it chased after him. Karana dropped down into the forest of bright bolts and fell upon the flailing monster, and she struck at him with all the power she had. The sword splintered scales and drew more of his deadly blood, and she leaped clear when he rolled over, landed and smote him again.

He caught himself, and his great head came for her, bloody jaws snapping shut just short of her as she rose. "Come then!" she screamed. "Come and face me! You want war? *I will show you a war like no one has ever seen*!" She pounded on him with bolts of lightning, the thunderclaps like hammerblows that broke stone and ripped the sky.

His wings tore at the air, and he rose, and she led him higher. Surrounded by a nimbus of dancing fire, she rose up before him, a star into the black sky. She screamed into the sky, and she called the storm. The sea was close, the air thick with dust and smoke and heat from the mountain. There was so much to work with, she only had to give it the right motion. She whirled as she rose, eyes shut, hand outstretched, and the sky began to move.

Around the city the wind began to whirl, moving slow, then faster. The wind girdled the city all around and rose like wall around it, faster and faster. It ripped up trees, it scoured the earth, it lifted stones big as houses, and it flailed the sea and drew it up into a flood that flowed onto the land. Lightning crowned the sky, and it raced and snapped and danced like a battle of spears made by the gods. And at the center of the whirl of wind, where the city lay, there was nothing, not so much as a breath. In the eye, the city was whole and untouched.

And at the center of that eye, Karana rose in terrible wrath. The dragon followed her, wings beating relentlessly, single silver eye blazing as he came. Silver blood trailed from wounds and hardened in the wind like steel in the quenching.

Karana felt a terrible power in her, a clarity like she had never known, a fierce, bright hold on her power that was new and frightening, and she felt the burns on her arms and the pain on her face where her left eye was blind, and she realized it was the blood. The blood of the dragon. Silver because it was filled with the star-stuff, taken from so many others devoured over the ages. This beast from a prehistoric age had become a demon that devoured gods to feed itself, and now she understood why, if this was the power and the vitality it gave.

He rose toward her, bloody jaws open, an endless hunger, and she saw the forge-fire glow in its throat and waited for her moment to strike. She saw blackness, and then the beast breathed out his cloud of death. Bright in the center under the shroud of ash, it came for her, and she drew down freezing wind and struck with hideous strength. Her blow drove the cloud back upon Nergal, smashing him backward in the air, and he roared, thrashing his wings to keep himself in the sky. They were high now, perhaps high enough.

Karana dove, cleaving through the cloud of flame, and she lifted her lightning-edged sword in two hands and struck as she flashed past Nergal's monstrous head. The blade flashed as it rove through scales and bone, and then it ripped into his one good eye, and then she was past, leaving the gush of silver blood behind her. She flew past his arching neck and she stabbed it in and dragged it along the length, tearing his throat open in a trail of sparks.

Then she almost collided with his wing, and instead of dodge aside, she slashed through the membrane, leaving him struggling with a wounded wing. His deadly blood rained from the sky, and he howled, blinded.

Nergal trailed smoke like a burning ship as he fell away from her, fighting to stay in the sky. He fell into a glide, and without eyes he could not see that he was diving right for the wall of the storm.

Karana flew after him, goading her storm to even greater power as he approached it. By the time he felt it close to him, it was too late to turn. She landed on his back in a fury of lightning strokes, and she drove her sword into the joint of his wing and shoulder. Nergal screamed, and he fell into the storm.

The sound of the wind was a deep-voiced moan, and it caught him with incredible power. His wounded wing folded, and the bones snapped against each other. Karana was ripped from his back and almost thrown down his throat. Instead she clung to the spines of his head and struck him again and again as the storm carried him around in a great arc, from sea to shore, higher and higher, tumbling over and over as he screamed and clawed at her, unable to right himself, or even to see. She heard a different sound in his bellow, the sound she had wanted to draw from him, the sound of fear.

Lightning crawled over him, flaying him alive as he rolled over in the air. He could not see the mountainside coming, but Karana did. She stabbed him one more time, and then she ripped her sword free and vaulted into the howling sky as the full force of her great storm hurled him into the mountain with enough force to crack it open.

Lava gushed out, flowed over him, and then froze black in the deadly wind. He fell, bleeding, sliding down in the ruin of the mountainside, until he finally came to a stop, half-covered in melted rock, bleeding, and done.

Karana drew in a deep breath, feeling herself shaking on the very edge of control. She had fed the life of her storm to make it powerful, and now she ceased, turned it back, and there was a sudden slowing in the wall of wind, a shuddering, and then the storm dissolved with a thunderclap that shook land and sea and sent ripples outward that cleared the smoke from the sky and left her there alone, high above the city, just touched by the first rays of the sun.

Chapter Thirty-Eight

CROWNS AND GRAVES

Karana lay under the water for a long time. The sun was high and it turned the sea a deep, dazzling blue all around her, and the bottom below was white sand layered with shells and haunted by a myriad of colorful fish. Small crabs crept this way and that, and down here the pull of the waves was gentle, barely felt. It was quiet, and it soothed her. She felt no need to take a breath, no desire for air, even if she thought about it.

Slowly, she drifted up, toward the sun, and she let herself go. Arms spread, naked and unfettered, she floated upward, until she broke the surface and lay there in the sun, feeling the warmth and hearing the sounds of the waves and the sea birds. The sky was a depthless blue, touched here and there with white clouds. The mountain lay wreathed in a haze of smoke, but it no longer poured out to cover the whole of the sky.

She put her feet down in the soft sand and stood, waded in to shore, liking the feeling of being uncovered, of having nothing about her that bound her to the world, to life. The shore was white sands, set here and there with lumps of black volcanic rock. Embedded in the nearest one was her sword, driven point-down into the stone. She looked at it, the black sear on the steel, the threads of silver blood cooled and frozen to it here and there. The sight of it made her arms ache and she looked down at them, saw fresh burns etched there, trails of liquid fire on her skin.

The left side of her face was painful, and her eye was still blind on that side. She wondered if it would ever return to what it had been. Perhaps it should not. She stood on the shore and stirred the wind a little so it would dry her more quickly. In the sun, she looked down and saw the trails of lightning scars all down her body. She was scarred as no warrior had ever been. Or perhaps that was not true. She thought of Attis and felt a strange kind of regret. She would never know him, the other one like her. Perhaps they could have been close.

She heard a horse and turned, resisted the urge to cover herself and stood waiting. Dagon rode into view on a black horse, leading a bay behind him. He saw her and averted his eyes slightly, rode closer and drew rein. "Apologies," he said.

She shrugged. "It does not matter to me. Not today."

He coughed and drew out a robe, held it out to her, and she took it and covered herself. She found it made her feel a little more like her old self. A little. "How did you find me?"

Almost sheepishly, he took out his little glass sphere and held it up to the sun. "It's a bit harder now, with the beast lying dead on the mountainside, but I still managed to follow you. I thought you would be close to the sea somewhere."

She squinted into the sun. "Diomedes?"

Dagon said nothing, only gave a small shake of his head. Karana found her eyes stung, and she turned away to get control of herself. "I saw it," she said. "I saw him die, and yet I hoped that somehow, he found a way, or perhaps I was wrong." She covered her mouth. "I wish I had known him better. I think he was the bravest of us."

"The bravest always die first," he said. "He saved Arthras' life, and Thessala's as well."

Karana nodded, swallowed. "How is Thessala?"

"Wounded," he said. "But she is already stronger. Lykaon has broken ribs, and a broken arm, and he will recover. Those touched by the star seem to be unusually resilient in many ways."

"Another aspect of our curse," she said, bitter. She looked at him, wanting to ask about the city, how many had died, how much destruction had they caused – yet it was too much. Instead she only touched her face. "How bad is it?'

"Does it hurt?" he said.

"Some. Is it entirely hideous?" She almost told him not to answer.

"The skin is burned," he said. "But the eye is. . . silver."

She caught her breath and covered the eye with her hand. She felt still the sensation of the blood's touch upon her. It was like light inside her, like wind in her blood. What if it was possible for a human to become like Nergal? What would happen if the feeling faded, and she craved to get it back?

"Come back to the city," he said. "We need you. Everyone needs you."

Karana sighed, and then she looked at him sidelong. Had there been a certain emphasis on the words? She wondered if he only averted his eyes because he wanted to look. Well, time enough for that possibility. Her father had always wanted her to marry well, and now she knew she would never marry. But she did not have to be alone her whole life, however long it was.

She went to the sword driven into the stone, and she pulled it out, the weapon feeling right and easy in her hand, and she was wary of that. She never wanted to be at ease with her power, or with any power. It should be hard to use power such as hers. She went back to Dagon and looked up at him, shading her eyes.

"Very well," she said. She let him hand her the reins to the other horse. They both knew she could fly wherever she wished, but for now, a slow ride back to the city was what she wanted. She was in no hurry now. There was time enough.

◌

Arthras looked on the ruined palace he had fought and killed for. The towers were broken down, walls crushed and shattered, ashes lying across all of it. Perhaps half of it remained, with the glass all broken from the windows, the stones blackened above them where fires had raged in the night. The imperial banners hung in shreds and drifted in the soft breeze. It was beautiful to look at, and he smiled.

Nicaea came to stand beside him, dressed in her red gown, with a gray overmantle to keep the ashes from it. She carried a small parasol to keep the sun off her face, and she sighed as she looked at the wreckage. "You could not have captured the palace intact?"

"I will build you another," he said. "Fitting, that one age should pass. A new palace for a new dynasty." He caught her arm and pulled her close, making her gasp. "I said I would make you an empress. Now you are one."

"I am an empress when I wear silk and gold, and there is a crown upon my head," she said, only half complaining. "Today I am empress of ashes."

"The city stands," he said. "Your brother's army and mine entered as saviors, not destroyers. I have saved the city from the greatest doom it ever faced, and I shall be both king and god to them."

"Not the only god," she said.

"Kings and emperors may rule alone," he said. "A god should not." He laughed a little. "And what now for you?"

"What do you mean?" she brushed ash from her sleeve, annoyed.

"Your ambition has climbed as high as it may go," he said. "You can kill your way onto a throne, but after that there is no glory that can be stolen." He sighed, gestured to the palace. "Now we must do a harder thing. Now we must build."

She made a sound of annoyance. "I thought it would be easier than this."

"I am asking you, right now," he said. "That is a serious question. Will you build with me? I came to this place knowing if I am to rule an empire, that I have to build it." He put an arm around her shoulders. "I know your natural instinct is to scheme, and to plot. But that is not needed now. Now you must turn your powers to other purposes. Can you?"

She was quiet for a moment, then drew a long breath and let it out. "I don't know. I have fought and schemed my whole life. For advancement, for advantage, for spite. I can hardly imagine a life where I do not have to." She looked at him sidelong, arched a brow. "Do you think there will still be people to plot against?'

"I would be surprised if there were not," he said. "It is a new world, but the old one has not been wiped away."

"Not yet," she said. "You still have work ahead of you."

"I do," he said. He took her hand. "Come with me?"

She snorted, then stood up on her toes and kissed him. "Yes."

※

Karana found Thessala by Lykaon's bedside in Dagon's villa. She slipped away from the bed in a way that told Karana he was asleep, and even though Thessala moved with a crutch and a limp, she managed to be almost silent.

She smiled when she saw Karana, and the two of them embraced without a word. They went into the hall and closed the door. Thessala led her down the hall to the back terrace, eased herself down onto a couch.

"How is he?" Karana asked.

"Broken up, but mending." Thessala sighed. "Like me. He is in pain, but he never complains."

"He never says much," Karana said.

"No," Thessala said, and they both laughed a little. Thessala shifted to ease her wounded leg, gestured at Karana. "How is it?"

"The pain fades quickly," Karana said. "But I am still blind in that eye."

"It looks striking," Thessala said. "Have you seen it yet?"

"I have not quite had the nerve," Karana said. It was something she could only tell Thessala.

"I remember when the skin peeled off my face, and I felt the scales beneath. I spent a long night, terrified, waiting to have the courage to look." She smiled. "Go and look."

Slowly, Karana stood and went to the mirror. It stood half in sun from outside, half in shadow. She saw herself in it, but could not see details until she came closer and stood in the sun. She stopped then and was silent. She reached up and touched her face, ran her fingers over the scarred skin that felt as though it had been melted, up to the sightless eye. She touched it, gingerly, and felt almost nothing. It was cool under her finger, and hard, as if it were silver in fact. It was smooth and flawless, like polished metal.

"This battle has left me so scarred," she said. "I never expected that."

"We have all paid, in our ways," Thessala said. "Diomedes paid more than the rest of us."

"He was more ready to pay," Karana said. "He wanted to be a great hero. I will see to it he is remembered."

"Are you still going to give the throne to Arthras, after all of this?" Thessala sounded resigned.

"Someone must be emperor," Karana said. "But he will not be the only god in the city, or the empire. Niceros charged me to build a new empire, one made from bonds, not from blood. If we build a great enough center, the pieces will come to us. Arthras may rule, but he will not be the only power here."

"Do you think there are others like us?" Thessala said. "In other lands?"

"Oh, I think there are," Karana said. "There will be other powers, and we will meet them. Some will be allies, some will be enemies. That's how things work." She looked back at Thessala. "That is why we will need each other, now and always. We will never really be free again."

"A strange way to say it," Thessala said. "We who have so much power."

"Power is a burden," Karana said. "I never wanted it, nor did you. With power comes the need to use it wisely, and the need to strive against those who will not use theirs wisely." She sighed. "We are not gods, but they will call us gods. They will worship us as gods, look up to us and tell stories of us. We cannot stop it. But with that comes the grave responsibility to behave as though we were gods in truth. We must set examples, we must think on all we do, and we must be ready to protect those who depend on us." She looked at Thessala. "You gave your life over to the care of others long ago. Does this feel different?"

"It will be harder," Thessala said. "But I can do so much more. It is different, but I will not curse it."

"Nor will I," Karana said, looking at her scarred face in the mirror again. "Nor will I."

༄

They stood on the mountainside together, looking down at the corpse of a legend in the evening sun, and Karana looked at Arthras and thought he looked older. This had changed all of them. She tried to remember the skinny boy who had faced her in Ilion. It was afternoon, and the sun blazed down, turning the blackened hillside to gold where it touched. The ground was still warm, and the air shimmered over the black stone.

Nergal lay sprawled on the slope, twisted and broken. He was half-buried in the ruin, legs and wings jutting up from the pile, and his head with jaws wide just below them.

She looked down his throat and wondered if Diomedes had died quickly. She hoped so.

"He saved my life," Arthras said, as if he heard her thoughts. "Do you wish he had not?"

"I cannot answer that," she said. "Not now. You have been my enemy, and then my ally. It remains to be revealed if you can become my friend."

He nodded. "Fair words," he said. He looked at her. "That is a thing I do admire in you. You are always fair, and you speak the truth. You would make a good empress."

"No, I wouldn't," she said. "A ruler who is honest and fair? No one can be a king and be like that. No."

"A goddess you will be then," he said. "Already they drape statues of forgotten queens with your colors and lay flowers at their feet. There will be images of you soon enough. The storm queen with the sword of fire." He folded his arms. "I will make images of Diomedes, the hero of us all. Everyone will learn his name."

"Such are legends born," she said. "There will be others, in other lands. We will find them soon, or they will find us. The old emperor, Niceros – he had a vision of a new empire forged not with blood, but by being a light to all, so that they gather and wish to be part of it."

"A good thing to wish," Arthras said. "But some of those people will be led by those like us. New power will make new warlords, new tyrants. There will be war enough to sate any hunger."

"I hope not," Karana said. "But I do not say you are wrong." She looked down at the dragon. "I wonder if he was the only one. If other beasts like him still live somewhere."

"If they do, they will come and find us as well," he said. He gestured to the great corpse. "Do you wish to say anything over the grave of your friend?"

Karana looked away. "No. We will have a funeral for Diomedes away from here. We will raise a sepulcher and an idol over a place we have chosen, not this place of death." She gestured. "But we cannot leave this thing open under the sky. His blood is poison, and will wash down and poison the mountainside pastures and fields if we leave him like this. Bury him."

Arthras nodded, and then he turned and faced down the mountainside. He lifted his hands, and she felt the earth tremble under her feet. The rumble began low, shuddering up through her legs to her spine, making her teeth chatter, and then the earth heaved up, roiled like a wave, and folded over itself. A fissure opened, and the corpse of Nergal fell in and was buried by the cascade of rocks and soil. It slid down in a great torrent, sending up clouds of dust, and then it stilled and settled, and lay quiet again. The dragon was gone, as if he had never been.

"If I had been one alone," Karana said, "he would have slain me."

"Perhaps you would have killed him," Arthras said.

"No, no, he was too much for me. At most I would have been able to bury him under the ground, trap him in the mountain again, wound him so he had to sleep, and wait. Wait for the star to come again." She looked east, as far as she could see, and there was the star, a ghost of itself, all but vanished into the haze of the horizon over the sea. It lay like a shadow, and she wondered how long it would be before it came again, what would the world look like when that day came?

"It has been before," she said. "It will be again. We are only part of the story, and the whole of it may never be known by any man. I will write down my part in it, and hide it away, so that someday, long years from now, another one like me will find it, and know she is not alone."

"You will mark the world without words," he said.

"Yes, whether I will or no," she said. "Just as you will. But I will leave words as well. I will tell the story, I will tell my part in it." She felt the wind gust over her, stirring her braids, and she smiled to herself. "Come," she said. "Let us mark the world."